MARRY ME

ENCHANTED CAROLINA
BOOK ONE

SHANNA M. ROGERS

CONTENT WARNINGS

While Marry Me is a story with love, happiness, laughter (like…a lot of laughter), and several sexually explicit scenes (with mentions of light erotic choking), it is also a story about healing. There are mentions of parental and sibling death off page, mentions of past relationship trauma, and on page confrontation between the main character and the person who caused her pain.

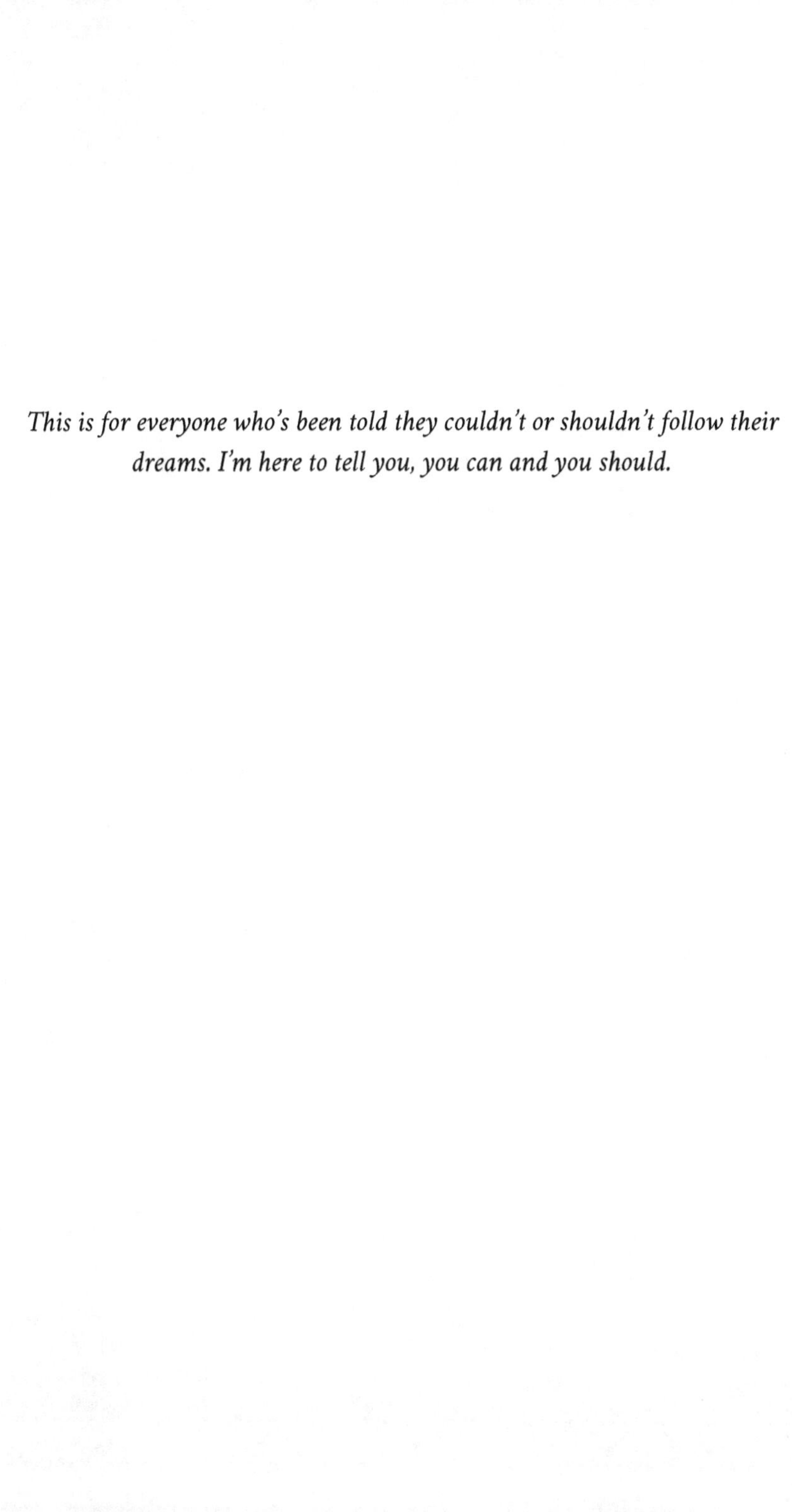

This is for everyone who's been told they couldn't or shouldn't follow their dreams. I'm here to tell you, you can and you should.

LISTEN TO THE PLAYLIST

If you love music as much as I do, then you may enjoy the playlist I put together for Marry Me. It is only on Spotify and features almost exclusively female or non-binary fronted bands that are making dope music in the new age of pop-punk (save for the last chapter, which should be obvious ;)). I hope you enjoy them as much as I do!

Listen on Spotify

Songs and Chapters

- Chapter One: Losing my Head - ColorMeKrazy!
- Chapter Two: sleepwalking - senses
- Chapter Three: Favorite Regret - Finding Georgia
- Chapter Four: novocain - senses
- Chapter Five: Chaos - Stateside
- Chapter Six: Crying in the Club - ColorMeKrazy!
- Chapter Seven: Underscore - Definitely Maybe
- Chapter Eight: I Don't Feel Like Feeling Good - As December Falls
- Chapter Nine: Exit Plan - Lolitslea
- Chapter Ten: Go Away - As December Falls
- Chapter Eleven: Better Off - All There Is
- Chapter Twelve: This Time I Swear - Definitely Maybe, Alone Again - glimmers
- Chapter Thirteen: Life Sentence - High Regard
- Chapter Fifteen: Lost In The Moment - Autumn Fires
- Chapter Sixteen: You + Me - Definitely Maybe
- Chapter Seventeen: fall for you - Jessica Morale
- Chapter Eighteen: Love Feels Like - Yours Truly
- Chapter Nineteen: Risk It All - Haunter
- Chapter Twenty: Full Bloom - Feel Good, Sweet Tooth - Stoned Mary
- Chapter Twenty-one: You're Mine - Dovecage
- Chapter Twenty-two: Touch - As December Falls
- Chapter Twenty-three: Beat Of My Heart - ColorMeKrazy!
- Chapter Twenty-four: Not Good At Goodbyes - glimmers
- Chapter Twenty-five: pieces of me - rosecoloredworld
- Chapter Twenty-six: Love Song - Gold Steps
- Chapter Twenty-seven: Fences - ColorMeKrazy!, Nothing Like You - The Consequences of Our Own Actions, you're not special - Maggie Lindemann

CHAPTER

ONE

THERE'S ONLY ONE THING I KNOW FOR CERTAIN IN THIS LIFE: MY BEST friend, Jae Ryu, doesn't frown. When the universe gives her a dash of humility, she puts a smile on her face through the tears. From the day we met on the bus to school, at the impressionable age of ten, a smile's been exposing the soft dimple on her left cheek. In the two decades since, I can count on two hands how often I've seen her lips curve downward.

That fact makes the way she's scowling at me now all the more penetrating. She's holding out her hand, and the smooth palm is not a suggestion; it's an exceptionally pressing demand. Fast-flicking fingers rush me when I don't move.

"Give me your phone. Right now."

Lavender eyes narrow and crease the warm, beige skin around them. The disapproving sneer I offer the witch on the barstool beside mine does nothing to quell her urgency; purple-painted fingernails beckon me to relinquish the device that's prolonged my pain for far too long. Her head bobs to emphasize the urgency, dark black hair shaking around her jawline.

"Now, Misty Opal Hayes."

Her tone and plunging scowl punctuate the use of my full name. Sighing, I slap my phone down and return my attention to my drink. The lemon rind on the rim is far more interesting than watching my best friend block a number I should've long ago blocked myself. The thought alone makes me queasy—not the copious vodka martinis with twists. They have nothing to do with the apprehension, shame, and sadness coiling in my abdomen. I try to convince myself the nausea is worthwhile, though, as I down the remnants of my drink and train my gaze on the empty glass.

After three months of staring at a single-sided text thread and scrolling through sickening social media feeds until my heart aches, it's time. Blocking Amber completely is for the best. But acknowledging that it needs to happen doesn't mean I want to watch the final unraveling of a dreaded and painful history as it does.

When Jae slides my phone back to me across the metal bar top, I debate throwing it away. Without Amber, I have no use for a phone. I have no family to call about the insignificant moments in life nor a job that will try to contact me after-hours. The handful of people I regularly speak to are in this bar, and I hang out with them often enough there's little reason to call. Instead, I hum a dejected tone of thanks and stuff the empty thing into my pocket.

Maybe Jae can tell how devoid of anything I feel inside because her hand settles on my shoulder in reassurance. "It'll be better. If she can't reach you, she can't hurt you again," she promises.

I nod, trying to convince myself Jae is right. But it doesn't stop the loss from hurting. Nor does it change that I want to send Amber a desperate text asking for one more night of savoring the flawless way she fits in my arms, the laughter between sighs of pleasure, and the cries of each other's names in bliss. Just one more night, regardless of the unimaginable pain it will bring when I wake to a vacant and cold bed.

"Jae's right," comes a voice from the back room.

I can't decide if Rokk Ildra—the owner of this dive bar—agreeing makes me feel better or worse. He appears in the stockroom doorway, and the dim pendant lighting and countless neon signs on the walls highlight the flat expression on his hardened face. To anyone else, it would look like a frown. To me, I know it means he cares.

Rokk is all scowls and cutting glares. The long, thick black hair and the matching beard enhance the rugged appeal. As do the copious tattoos, the intricate horns decorating his head, and the form he chooses halfway between human and Goblin. Owning Big's, the bar I find myself in more often than not, requires a stern exterior to keep patrons in line, no matter the gentle personality inside. It works so well that he seldom has to boot anyone out. After one hundred years since The Exposure, even the dimmest people know crossing magical beings is a faux pas. Especially a Goblin in his own business.

"He's right, too. We're both right. This is for the best," Jae reiterates.

The slightly slurred affirmation still isn't as soothing as she intends, but it should be. Jae seems to be right more often than not, especially relating to Amber. She often correctly predicted how unhinged my ex-girlfriend would react to any news, happy or sad. She even warned me that the signs Amber was about to leave again were there a week before she walked out. I didn't believe her, although based on history, I should have. I should believe her now, too, but something in me still refuses.

"Right," I clip back.

Jae snorts at the derision in my voice. "I'm going to pee." The thump of her feet as she hops off her chair echoes in the empty bar. She spouts something unintelligible while turning toward the restroom, causing Rokk to shake his head. Goblins have far better hearing than wixan and now I'm curious.

"What did she say?"

He just motions to the hours-old sandwich I've yet to convince myself to consume. "Nothing. Now eat, or you're liable to fall down drunk again."

"I'm not that drunk today." Sticking out my tongue doesn't help my story.

The several puffs of laughter he forces out say that much. "Eat." Rokk punctuates the demand by pointing at the sandwich again. "If you pass out on my bar, you can't come back."

"Empty threat."

To some random person, he would've meant the words. To me? Not at all.

It doesn't change the fact he's right. We're all aware I've struggled to eat over the last few months. What my best friends are unaware of, however, is that I've eaten nothing today. Coupled with being a curvy witch barely over the height requirements for most roller coasters, the five—wait, six? Yeah, the six martinis I've devoured in the less-than-handful of hours since I arrived will end up putting me on my ass. Again. This sandwich is a flimsy attempt to gain back my sanity.

Sighing, I pull it into my hands. I intend to take a bite until a notification sound sings through the silence. My eyes drift to where Rokk leans against the bar, smiling down at his phone, and my face starts to tingle. I blame it on the warmth of tart liquor; my eyes are watering from the air conditioner blowing on me when the winter's chill still hasn't moved out, too. Neither of those things are because one of my best friends is finding love after years of the same loneliness I endured, even in a relationship. Not at all...

I'm happy for Rokk for finding someone who brings happiness to his angular face. Jason, a Big's regular, warmed his way in where no other person could. They've yet to go on a formal date, but I know what the smile creasing Rokk's pale purple skin means. It's rare, and I'm thrilled for him that someone can make it appear with just a single text. He deserves to smile like the world isn't oppressively gray. He deserves someone who will support him, someone willing to step behind the bar when it's busy without expecting repayment. Someone who will uplift him when all he can see is the dread of this world. He deserves unconditional love.

All things I never see myself deserving.

Hands grasping my shoulders startle me out of my rumination, making me drop my sandwich back into its wrapper.

"Mike got done with work early!" Jae's grinning as she peers around my shoulder. "I'm going."

"Ughhhhhh." My groan is obnoxious, but the melodramatics hide how I blink away tears. I won't let those emotions overtake me here.

Rokk says, "If you throw up, you're cleaning it."

"She's just being dramatic," Jae replies and readies herself to leave.

I groan again but clear the emotion from my voice enough to say, "And Jae's ditching me again for her boyfriend."

Rokk's snorted laughter floats across the room. "Can you blame her?"

"If Mike's cock's as magical as she says it is? Absolutely not."

Laughter fills the room, and mine echoes above all others. Not unexpected. My laugh is often the loudest. It's also an aspect I love about myself. It's an extension of how intensely I perceive emotions, a skill of which I am incredibly proud. Does the ability leave me sobbing when I witness a joyful moment between two strangers on the street? Yes. It does. Other people's happiness makes me happy.

Unfortunately, delighting in the highs comes with suffering the lows just as fiercely. Overwhelming negative emotions can make me feel downright dreadful. Sometimes I'm so profoundly void it's like drowning in thick, dark water when despair hits. Which has been every waking moment in my recent history. I haven't felt genuine happiness in ages. Right now, I'm so far underwater I can't see the sunlight of elation dancing on the waves above me.

My laughter ends with a sigh and a shrug. "Go on. Get. Leave me here all alone."

"Okay," Jae says as she grabs her things. "Byeeee."

"All alone!" I shout as she slips out the door.

"What am I then?" Rokk asks, mocking disgust.

I wave him off with the flimsy bread when I pull it back into my hands. "You know I love you, but she dragged me out. I just wanted to sleep."

I was just going to rot in bed today, but Jae had other plans. She cornered me when I woke up to pee this morning; if I'd waited two minutes to leave my room, I wouldn't be day-drinking at Big's for the nth time. Alas, I didn't, and although she's the best roommate and friend a girl can want, Jae also has a massive proclivity to choose dick over staying at the drinks she dragged me to. I don't blame her. But it leaves me drunk and alone at one of the divey-est bars in Raleigh on a Wednesday afternoon, clinging to a dry sandwich like a lifeline. Annoyance tries to overtake me, but I shove it down. If I were home, I'd only be wallowing in self-pity alone, crying. At least being with one other person keeps the steady swells of sadness at bay.

"You've done nothing but sleep all day since getting fired," Rokk says.

"Not true. I've gotten drunk here several times." The bark of laughter Rokk lets out is deep and genuine. "And it's not my fault they fired me for being—"

"They didn't fire you because you're a witch." Unmistakable humor loads Rokk's face. I can't help but grin as he corrects, "You called your boss a dumbass in the middle of a meeting."

"Well, he's a fucking dumbass garbage human being," I say. "Always arguing about shit he has zero knowledge of. Someone needed to call him out."

"You're ridiculous." Rokk huffs a single dry laugh before turning his attention to readying the bar for the evening rush.

I'm not being ridiculous, though. That guy was and remains an absolute asshat, which I told him to his face in a rather eviscerating way. In private, I may have received a simple reprimand, but I chose a conference room teeming with people who wanted to say the same thing. I got fired on the spot, but the countless smiles on my trek out the door were more than worth it.

Losing my job is the main reason I've spent so much time at Big's.

Right now, this place feels more like my home than my actual home. After spending several nights a week here for almost a decade, I think it's perfect; I also understand why tourists call the place abhorrent. Big's doesn't suit everyone's tastes. Decades of stumbled footsteps and drunkenly spilled drinks have battered down the diamond carpet patterns—a well-worn relic of the nineties. The liquor shelves, chairs, and chipping dark red paint share the same worn-in look. Everything is sticky. Everything. Especially the bathrooms, which I can confidently say haven't seen the underside of a scrub brush since the day the contractor installed them.

The building is no wider than a semi-truck trailer, and the bar fills most of it, decorated with more band stickers and local flyers than anyone could count. Often, on a busy night, it's impossible to squeeze by people waiting for their drinks. It's worse when bands perform on the small, raised wooden platform masquerading as a stage in the back.

I avoid eating my sandwich and look around, only now realizing the sun's set since Jae and I arrived. Another day in the place I've spent half my life since it fundamentally changed. Not much of a life, if I'm honest with myself. Over the last month, I've been floating in ambiguity. Truthfully, I've been coasting since Amber packed her belongings and left without so much as a goodbye.

The alcohol thrumming through my veins makes those memories bitter: a girlfriend packing her shit and vanishing into the night once again as if she didn't eagerly ride my face hours before. After three years together without incident, I thought we were finally real. I thought we were stable and that she'd never walk out again. I was wrong; so very wrong. I woke up alone for the sixth time just days before the start of Yule, with presents already purchased and wrapped.

The bitterness of those memories makes me take a too-hard bite of sandwich; the bread congeals to the curve in the roof of my mouth. I gag from the dryness and try to peel the literal cement away with my tongue, but the offending nourishment holds strong. The glass of water that appears beside me is more than a suggestion. I snort and push it away when Rokk hovers over me, arms in a loose fold across his chest and half his eyebrow raised.

I despise the taste of water; a fact of which Rokk is hyper-aware. That little tidbit sits near the top of my long list of failures: being a water witch who loathes drinking water. It's not my worst failure of all time, but possibly the most ironic. There are several entries on that list that are far worse. Like never returning to the zoology and magical creatures veterinary program at NC State University and that one time I was arrested in Colorado for fu—

A stool two down from mine scrapes across the grime-covered floor and pulls Rokk's and my attention. Thankfully, because I was too close to ruminating on my long list of failures again. The grating sounds of metal save me from suffering thoughts I've endured far too many times in the last few months. I cling to the relief that floods through me as I inspect this new patron.

"Hey, man, welcome," Rokk says.

The man stays quiet, eyes roaming the shelves for his chosen vice. Although I may have had too much of my own preferred poison, several things are apparent. One: I've never seen the man rising onto the bar stool before. Two: the suit this newcomer is wearing doesn't belong at Big's. And three: he looks disgusted to be here.

"Double of the Macallan. Neat."

I've got zero idea what a 'Macallan' is. Rokk knows, however, and the request surprises him. His single dark eyebrow raises toward his hairline again before he glances up at a bottle that I'm sure I noticed years ago but haven't paid attention to since. No one else has either. Not even Rokk. Spiderwebs with entangled dust branch off the bottle to the surrounding walls. No one has ever ordered whatever it is, and Rokk has never served it.

"Charge whatever you want to open that bottle, if you're willing, and keep it open. If not, I'll take the next best." Then, the stranger pulls out of his wallet the blackest credit card I've ever seen in person. I'm not alone, judging by the wideness of Rokk's almost unrealistically emerald eyes.

"Uh, yeah, sure, of course," Rok stammers. "It'll be…one-seventy a pour?"

At the price, I unintentionally balk into my sandwich, but Mystery Man doesn't even flinch. He nods and flicks the card he holds between two fingers as if waving Rokk off to do his job. The motion makes me snort again because of the nonchalance. He ignores it all.

That doesn't stop me from keeping my hazy gaze on him. Rounded ears poke through his hair, meaning he isn't a fae. Good. Right now, I don't possess the patience or state of mind to chew a damned sandwich without choking. I certainly can't muster enough energy to deal with riddles. There's every possibility he's concealing himself behind spell-work to make me believe he's human. But without proof, I have to take this man for what he's showing: ordinary. Maybe he's in the wrong part of downtown—a human stumbling too far from their intended destination. That's not to say humans don't frequent Big's. These walls welcome all. But it's not typical for humans who drink liquor that would bust my bank account and wear suits that look more expensive than my entire wardrobe to walk through the doors.

Mystery Man continues ignoring me, although my attention lingering on him is his fault. He chose a chair next to one of the lone individuals in a bar with ten times more seats than people. Someone only does that if they want to talk.

So I speak. "You're new."

The alcohol in my veins draws out the words; I muffle them with another bite of my sandwich. He ignores me. Flat out. He doesn't turn or acknowledge that I've spoken. I take Rokk coming back with a tumbler of amber liquor as the reason.

"If you're in here with that card wearing that suit, you must be as miserable as I am."

Huffing a laugh with zero mirth, he draws the fresh liquor to his nose and swirls the tumbler in some pretentious sniffing ritual. The way he downs half without so much as a grimace drowns out the air of obnoxious sophistication.

"Depends on how miserable you are."

"Well, I got fired a month ago, my partner left me again, and to top all that off, my friend bailed on me tonight." I roll my eyes and take the largest swig of water to wash away the lingering sorrow wriggling in my gut. I lift my sandwich to him in a show of mock celebration. "Cheers, right?"

Pulling the drink to his lips again, he downs the rest and holds out the empty tumbler. Without looking up, he says, "Another."

When Rokk fills the glass again and steps away, Mystery Man turns toward me. I almost joke about it taking so long, but the look on his face stops me. I've seen it so often that I don't have to examine it to know what it means. Like countless people before him, he's looking at me like I disgust him at the deepest parts of his soul. He isn't the first to scrutinize me like a stain on the untarnished earth they walk upon—not the last either, I'm sure. Being a witch with such visible markings makes this precise scenario one of the most common occurrences in my life.

Elemental-born wixan markings manifest in various shapes and intensities. Some believe the more prominent the marking, the more influential the wixan. I'm intimately aware that size has little to do with skill. I've grown to love mine as unique and beautiful, but that doesn't change the fact they're odd. Most of us are born with delicate markings resembling jewelry on our hands or small tattoos on our shoulders. Me? The gods and goddesses graced me from head to toe—but only on the left side. Distorted lines of blue wave from my hairline down my chin, over my collarbone, only to slither all the way down my arm and leg to my fingers and toes. Some close to me compare them to rivers flowing down my skin, intersecting and intertwining. Others say they're like a cascading waterfall of deep blue colors.

I say that twenty-nine years of people staring at me like he is now makes the disgust on his face easy to overlook.

"My situation isn't as trivial as yours."

His tone tips the statement over the edge of acceptability into straight asshole territory. Mystery Man could've gotten away with being self-loathing had his tone not sounded like a harsh insult. It could also be the over-a-handful of shots thrumming through me, the months of life hardships, or the loneliness that makes the words sting. Yeah…actually, it's likely all of that which widens my eyes in surprise and flares anger in my veins, but I cannot help it.

"My life falling apart is trivial to you?" Unmistakable heat laces my voice.

"You can find a new job and partner. Your life's not over. I'm sure you weren't a CEO. You can get at least fifteen comparable jobs tomorrow." Dismissive. As if he genuinely thinks he's better than me.

Scoffing, I spit, "What makes you so sure I wasn't a CEO? The blue hair? The markings? Who in their right mind would hire a witch, right?"

His sneer deepens. "Don't be absurd. That's not—"

"Now I'm absurd? My life is trivial, and I'm absurd. Good to know."

"Your life isn't over. You have no reason to be—"

Water always does the trick. No matter who the agitator is, they cease speaking when a jet of water slams into their face. This pompous ass is no different.

Sacrificing the few hair follicles on my arm that it costs for primal magic to surge through me, I flick a finger and douse this pretentious turd with the rest of the water in my glass. Words die in the back of his throat, replaced by a gargled gasp. The searing pain against my arm is worth watching him process every denial stage before settling on angry astonishment.

Wide eyes dart between me, a now damp suit jacket, and Rokk in apparent disbelief, as if he expects the bar owner to do something. Rokk, the lover of mischief that he is, doesn't budge from his spot leaning against the back of the bar with his arms crossed over his chest. His grin grows because he approves of my behavior and won't interfere. He knows I can handle myself with assholes like this, and he already has a card on file for payment.

When Mysterious Asshole turns back to me, I curl my lips up enough to reiterate the condescension in every word I speak. "Whoever the hell you are, it's been one of the greatest displeasures of my life meeting you. You are the absolute antithesis of a delight. And say 'please' next time you order another drink. Dick."

Grabbing my sandwich, I sneer and slide haphazardly off the high barstool, slamming my feet on the floor. I don't care how petulant it looks as I stumble and pivot on the heels of my boots. I pray to several goddesses that he watches me walk across the grime-soaked carpet toward the staircase in the back because the middle finger I hold up the entire way is exclusively for him.

CHAPTER

TWO

The balcony at Big's is always empty no matter the time of day. Rarely do people choose the gloomy loft. Some regulars joke that it's haunted. I know it's just the outdated electrical wiring that causes the dim beer lamp hanging at the center of the pool table to flicker. The ghost stories benefit me, though; they leave this room a silent sanctuary when the chaos below grows overwhelming.

Evenly spaced torn fabric booths line the three walls, all paired with a table and two rickety metal chairs opposite them. Patrons have marked the long-faded maroon paint with drunkenly scrawled sonnets, the initials of lovers who will never visit again, and other random nonsensical drawings. The same amorphous substance covering the carpet below smears the black tile up here.

Again, I think this place is perfect. It's dark and soothing and a peaceful escape from people like the asshole downstairs. No? Nope. Not downstairs. The thudding footfalls ascending the steps moments after I hop onto the pool table can belong to no one but him. The already too-little light seeps into his pitch-black pompous-ass suit when he appears at the summit.

Holding a plastic cup of water and a fresh tumbler of liquor, he moves to lean against the table before me. Confidence fills my gaze, and I sneer, showing him precisely how I feel about his presence.

"That was *not* an invitation."

"I want to apologize." He lifts the water as if it's any consolation.

"Great." Sarcasm drips from my voice. "Well done. Now go—"

"Your life falling apart isn't trivial." He rushes out the words. "I'm sorry that I was a jerk. I've just had—"

"A lot going on?" A quick, effective interjection. It silences him. At least he has the decency to look sheepish. "Yeah, so does everyone else in the world, including me. But I wasn't an ass to you, was I?"

Disbelief replaces his sheepishness. "You threw water in my face."

"After you called me worthless to mine. You deserved it. Apology acknowledged and not accepted. Now go live the wonderful life you're escaping with asininely expensive liquor downstairs, and I'll live my trivial existence up here."

He doesn't move. "I didn't call you worthless, but you're right. My life is shit, too." Sneering, I take a vicious bite of my sandwich to emphasize how little I require his presence, but he still doesn't leave. That same dry laugh from downstairs cuts through the loft's silence as he relaxes further against the table, placing the water cup beside him. With a sigh, he pulls his tumbler up and drinks half before limply pointing it at me. "What's your name?"

"Why would I tell you?"

"Because my undeniable charm is clearly winning you over." Exasperation careens over my face, at which he chuckles, throwing his hands up as if surrendering. "I just want to know so I can apologize appropriately, then I'll leave you alone."

"Or you could just leave me alone."

My words don't settle between us before his phone rings. He looks toward his pocket, then back at me as if seeking permission. An indignant huff passes my lips because I couldn't care less if he answers it. Rolling my eyes back to the last remnants of my sandwich leaves him in my peripheral enough that I see his demeanor shift. Whatever appears on the screen dissolves his placidness. Whoever it is, he doesn't want to speak to them, obvious by how vigorously he declines the call and tosses the device onto the table with a thud.

It immediately starts to ring again, this time vibrating on the table. Disquiet matching the one from downstairs reappears on his face as he grabs the device and turns it off, throwing it down again. That's confirmation enough about his claims about his life. He's dealing with some shit, just like me. The annoyed expression now aimed at his phone, then subsequently at his feet and *not* at me, makes me wonder if he *ever* directed it at me in the first place. Worse: perhaps I was hasty in dousing him with water. That realization stings my pride and makes me flush with embarrassment.

Imagine entering a bar seeking quiet only to have someone bother you with conversation when you don't want to talk. Top that off with getting water thrown in your face because some random witch is taking out their pent up aggression on you? Yikes. If I were him in this situation, I wouldn't have followed me up the stairs to apologize. He did, although there's no real reason for him to. In retrospect, he said nothing too offensive. He just shared an honest reaction to my story. It may have been scathing, but it wasn't wrong. I can secure another job if I tried, I just haven't.

His gaze is steadfast on his foot, tapping against the floor. I'm not sure he realizes he's gone silent, entranced by a steady, anxious rhythm I know well. I do, and I also see how companionable the silence is.

Perhaps solidarity makes me joke, "Who doesn't have their phone on silent?"

He snorts mirthlessly, dragging his gaze back to me. Thick eyebrows bounce mockingly with the toast of his glass before he turns up the contents. The movement makes me recognize the Sahara Desert that the last of my dry sandwich left in my mouth. Thirst flicks my eyes toward the water resting beside his hip. A soft smile curves his lips when my eyes return to his.

Making a show of picking up the cup, he holds it out. "Tell me your name, and it's all yours."

Scowling, I hop off the pool table before throwing my hand into the air and hovering my index finger millimeters above my thumb. "You were this close to being decent for a second."

When I reach for the water cup, he jerks it away and grins when indignation flashes over my face. "A name. Any name. It doesn't even have to be real."

"Misty." The cup lifts between us, and I snatch it, sticking out my tongue. Both of his manicured eyebrows quirk upward with the humor forming on his face. "Yes, I'm well aware of how asinine my name is."

"Wait, that's your *real* name?" Clearly attempting to remain respectful, he stifles laughter, but the mirth encompasses his entire face. My blasé nod doesn't help. "It's—" Another laugh clears from his throat with a cough. "It's very fitting for a water witch. The blue hair, the blue markings, the name—"

"I'm also well aware that my mom had a sick sense of humor and an addiction to puns." I shrug, taking a large swig of water before haplessly indicating myself. "Lean into it, right? Own the esthetic."

Taking the unintentional invitation, he scans me more thoroughly, lingering in several blatant places. I should draw his attention away, but something in me doesn't.

I just thank my past self for choosing to get dressed in real clothing instead of the unwashed pajamas I've lived in for weeks. Often when Jae has two days off in a row and we end up at Big's, we patronize several other places, too. So this morning I got dressed in a comfortable outfit for our day out. Problem is: I've played right into the exact point he's insinuating. A loose blue tee-shirt sits underneath my favorite black leather jacket, a hand-me-down from my mother when she passed. I wear it practically everywhere unless it's the summer; it's seen as much shit as the worn pair of, you guessed it, blue combat boots that cap out my unfairly fitting, freshly washed black jeans I haven't worn in a month.

A slow grin works across his face when he finally decides he's done inspecting me. "It works for you."

"Charming." The words drip with sarcasm that makes his grin spread a little fuller. "You know how to woo a woman, don't you? Call her useless, laugh at her name, and then brazenly hit on her. Well done."

"Want me to throw the water in my own face this time?"

"And deprive me of the pleasure?" I scoff. "I was wrong. You *don't* know how to woo a woman at all."

"I'd only deprive you of pleasure if you asked nicely."

The shock of that statement drops my jaw, at which a smirk turns his lips. With the dim lamp lighting his face, it almost looks lewd. Or maybe the liquor thrumming through me just wants it to. Perhaps it's unintentional, but there's unmistakable heat on his face, and my abdomen coils, an unexpected but pleasant shockwave surging through me.

When did this turn into a conversation that makes me heated around the core, and why does it intensify when he lifts his hand between us?

"Misty. I'm Cade, and I apologize for being such a dick to you downstairs."

Not hesitating, I slide my hand into his, closing a firm grip around it like my grandfather always taught me. *'It's about power.'* I heard those words every time I shook his hand. It's ridiculous how something meant to be a greeting is used to assert dominance, but my grandfather wasn't wrong. The firmer my handshake grew as I aged, the more influence I gleaned around every office in which I worked.

There's nothing different about this moment. This is about power here, too.

Smirking, I add, "It's been *such* a pleasure meeting you, Cade. Now, will you be fucking off or not?" Evidently not. He doesn't loosen his grip, so I don't either.

"I'm sorry you lost your job and your partner."

"It's not like I was a C.E.O. I'll find something else." The curl of his lips upward suggests he appreciates the cheek in my voice while throwing his comment back at him. It takes a moment and several slow scans of his eyes across my face before he releases me. I gesture towards the tumbler in his hand. "If you're staying up here, you have to tell me what sorrows you're drowning."

Pausing, he shifts his gaze towards the liquid, reluctance written all over his face. For a moment, I almost regret asking. He doesn't let the silence linger long, though; he throws back the rest of his liquor with a soft hiss. That perplexed gaze turns back on me, and in the darkened room his face looks somehow sharper, crisper.

"Beat me in a game of pool, and I'll tell you."

A disbelieving puff of air passes between my lips. Part of me wants to tell him to get bent and leave me alone. I don't need his awful presence. But another part of me isn't perturbed about the prospect of having the company Jae promised while dragging me out of the apartment. It may also be nice to have some *new* company. I haven't hung out with anyone other than Jae or Rokk since Amber walked out. I also haven't dated or even thought of someone romantically. Which, staring at this man now makes that feel like a downright shame. And perhaps I'm mistaken, but his expectant expression suggests he's searching for someone to escape his life with, too.

What's one game of pool? A little company, is what.

"You're really bold," I say, turning to walk toward the hanging rack of cue sticks on the wall. "I'm only saying yes because I want so badly to see your face when I kick your ass. I'll rack."

He looks pleased when I glance over my shoulder. With himself or me, I don't know. "I'll break."

"You'll break alright."

Deep laughter echoes through the loft. "Another water?"

"I probably should."

"Water it is, Missy—"

"No!" I bark and startle us both. I take several seconds of silence to process why. Amber always called me Missy, and I always told her I hated it. I still do.

"Sorry." He hesitates, eyes wide. "Do you—"

"Just don't call me Missy. Ever," I interject, trying to calm the abrupt racing of my heart.

Understanding dawns on his face, and he nods. "Then one water it is, *Misty*. I'll be right back."

He taps the table twice with a knuckle and my stomach bottoms out, heart rate flaring for an altogether different reason. He winks and my entire body reacts, tensing in places that a damn flex of the eyelid shouldn't affect. I can't convince my body of that. Thankfully, he doesn't see any of it because he's already heading toward the stairs. I puff out several baffled breaths at myself before turning to settle my part of our deal.

Mystery Man returns as I'm peeling the rack from around the balls. I've not cooled from the unexpected warmth before he makes me hotter. All he does is start readying himself for the game and unknowingly teaches me something. The older I get, the more I learn about myself. That's how life goes, right? But today, I didn't expect to discover how arousing I find someone removing their suit jacket.

It's because of the copious martinis. That's the only plausible explanation why I stand here gawking at a man unbuttoning his cufflinks.

The first roll of his perfectly pressed black button-down draws my eyes to his forearm, and I pray to every deity known to womankind that he can't see my lips parting or hear my soft gasp. It's undeniable now. He's a wizard. Obsidian markings shimmer on the deep tan skin that appears as he rolls up his sleeves. The intricacies momentarily stun me. I can't pinpoint another wixan I've met with as complex or uniquely colored markings as the ones decorating the entire expanse of both of his forearms. And they're absolutely markings, because tattoos don't sparkle like that.

Our markings tell tales of our ancestors, of who we are at our core, of what magic hums in our veins and bends easier to our will than all other magic that flows through the universe. Water wixan markings look like rivers or waterfalls or waves in homage to what gives us our power. Fire wixan markings flow like flames and embers across their skin, often mistaken for freckles before powers manifest in early adolescence. Green wixan have naturalistic vines snaking up their spines, ankles, or wrists, reminiscent of wild plants growing up the sequoias.

Black markings? I'm unsure where to begin with the evidence that he's born from no element yet commands them all with ease. Wixan like him are unheard of in the whole of the United States, let alone North Carolina. What flows through them is old magic, ancient, back from the start of everything; their origins trace back to before the breakup of the continents. Throughout the recorded history of magic, Proteans have always been scarce and cherished. Before The Great Divide, they sat beside kings and held titles in court. They were heroes in battle and leaders in research, psychology, sociology…everything.

And I straight up threw water in one's face.

This stranger could've done anything in response, half of which I wouldn't have seen coming. Instead, he followed me, apologized, and is now preparing himself to play a game of pool with me, someone well below his league.

A chuckle, more like a low rumble, draws my eyes back to his. The smirk on his lips dances crimson across my cheeks because he's most certainly caught me staring with my mouth open like a fool. I roll my eyes again and turn away in a flagrant show of chalking the tip of my cue stick, attempting to hide the blazing heat on my face. The rosiness is from the countless martinis, anyway. Nothing more.

The thunderous crack of the cue against the billiards drowns out his responding laughter. Balls pound the edges of the table and I don't turn around until he says, "That makes me solids."

The moment I turn, the cue ball strikes another ball and plunges it into a far off pocket. He's also moved around the table and if I wanted, I could reach out and touch him. I don't, but I watch him as he bends over the table, eyes locked with mine, and sinks another in the pocket farthest from us.

I wrinkle my nose. "He doesn't take it easy, either."

"Absolutely not." The next shot he takes breaks several balls apart and leaves the table open for me to do with as I please. He seems again impressed with himself as he rests the stick on the floor like it's some scepter and leans against it. "I whoop ass equally, no matter the person."

Oddly, that makes me more impressed and intrigued by this mysterious man. I indicate him with a hand. "You're a wizard," I say, sliding said hand with purpose down the cue and bending over the table.

He watches the entire time while I align my shot. I can't see what he's staring at, but I can feel the heat crawling up my neck under his gaze. It takes a moment, but I shoot and I make none, at which he seems thrilled as he pops his cue stick off the floor and into his hand.

"I am," he admits.

He leans over and effortlessly sinks another ball. When he glances up at me over the smirk of his oncoming crushing victory, I shove away the clenching in my core and say, "And you're an ass, you know that?"

"I've been told a time or two." He leaves the cue ball where I have no shot. My groan seems to spur his lips into a deeper smirk.

"At least you're aware," I say, and I'm not sure if I'm making a show of walking around the table, but he's watching me like I am.

"I've been working on it. For instance, a couple years ago you wouldn't have gotten an apology."

"Well, maybe in another few years you'll be a decent person."

"A decade. Two at most."

I try to catch the snort of laughter behind tight lips, but it bubbles to the surface before I can. The suddenness of the sound makes me whiff my shot, grazing the top of the white ball. I glare at his snickered laughter, but I also feel the same mirth tugging at the corners of my lips.

"Go again."

"No," I say. "No redos. Fair and square."

He appears impressed but shrugs and says, "Fair and square it is, then."

On the opposite side of the table, his slow fingers curl around his cue stick. I catch the motion, mesmerized. Pool shouldn't be so enthralling, but it is. The way he bends, the smooth wood gliding between his index and middle fingers…Goddesses above, I need to stop drinking. The stick splitting through his fingers makes me flush, thinking about something very different.

But then he does the exact thing he said he would—whoops my ass —and it breaks through the mysticism. Sauntering around the table, he scores his final three balls without batting an eye. But when his stick lines up to the cue, in near-perfect alignment to sink the black ball, he meets my gaze again with a fire that has no place at a pool table.

"Center pocket." Smoothly, he drains the eight ball without the white following.

"No—fuck! Come on!" I thrust my hand into the air. "Another game! I refuse to lose that awfully."

Delight lingers on his face as he finds his whiskey to throw back the rest. He flicks the empty glass toward the pool table. "Rack'em up then, beautiful. I'll be right back."

I huff an indignant sound, but my body doesn't share the sentiment. Warmth flares to life deep behind my navel as he winks again and descends into the bar for another refill.

CHAPTER
THREE

Cade reappears with a fresh drink as I'm twirling the plastic rack off the balls. He's holding another water, too, although I've barely touched the second he brought up.

I motion to the table. "Your break, since you won."

"At more than just the game," he says and picks up his stick again as my body heats from the way he scans me. When our eyes meet, I wink. He jerks, just the slightest, but it's enough to show how it affects him and that I'm not alone in the intimacy of our evening. Success sears through me when he shakes his head clear.

This round is more than a straightforward match of pool, and that's clear from the very start. There's no denying his smirk is lewd now, and paired with the crack of the cue splitting apart the balls, my core clenches. We're both dancing to a liquor-fueled warmth, and every movement we make is purposeful, albeit a little clumsy. It's the alcohol that's making me crave his attention so fiercely. Right now, how he tracks my every move is as intoxicating as the martinis, and I can't help but preen at him watching me with rapt attention.

I may not be good at pool, but I'm decidedly good at sensuality, and the longer he purposefully misses shots and stretches out our game, the longer I play it up. So does he. I chalk the tip of my cue stick with deliberate wrist rotations. When he passes me to circle the table, he brushes a few fingers along any part of me he can reach. I push my ass out and arch my back a little further than necessary when bending over the table. He smirks over his hand when our eyes lock as he's shooting his shot—literally and figuratively. It's all maddening.

He still beats me, but this time I score three balls before he puts me out of a misery I would've happily stayed in.

"Two in a row," he says, sliding his stick onto the table.

"I let you win," I say, echoing the movement.

His mirth hums over the commotion of a band sound-checking instruments downstairs. He traces each step I take as I move to stand before where he leans against the table. This close, I can't help but breathe in the scent he bathed me in during our game. It's smooth and woodsy and tropical, and I don't know what it is, but I also don't care. I just savor my body's sensuous reaction. A shiver works down my spine, bathing me in goosebumps, and I want nothing else than to lean in closer to him.

"I guess thanks for not letting me win." In jest, I roll my eyes again. His grin says it reads as playfully as I hoped.

"Never," he says. "Just imagine how good it'll feel when you finally beat me."

I scoff but sway a little further into him and that delicious scent. "We'll never run into each other again after we leave here."

A frown flashes over lips that, this close, I can see are a soft pink and too plump for his own good. "Hmm, no. I don't like that," he murmurs and leans a little closer. "Never say never."

Disbelief knits my brows. "You *just* said never five seconds ago."

"That was different. I was talking about a fact. You were talking about what-ifs."

If I knew him more than as the overdressed mystery man in a bar, I might think he's being genuine and that he truly believes we'll see one another after tonight. But I don't. I don't know who this man is or what he thinks. I'm confident, however, we'll never cross paths again, so I just ignore the words and puff out an exasperated breath.

"I played your game. Now tell me why your life is shit," I say.

"The deal was you beat me, and I'd tell you. You didn't win. Either time."

I jab my finger into his side. A chuckled grunt rumbles in his chest as he bends away, free hand moving to cover the spot as if it actually hurts. "Alright, alright," he acquiesces, but unfortunately, I catch the familiar flash of melancholy on his face again just before he throws back the rest of his liquor. It's gone before the glass lowers. "I'm getting another drink first. You want another water?"

I shake my head. "Rokk knows what I drink."

"Then I'll be right back. Don't leave."

"Maybe I will, maybe I won't."

Amusement overtakes his face before he turns, heading toward the bar. When he's gone, I move to the table by the railing overlooking below. He's simple to find in the sea of people who fill the downstairs awaiting the music. It's almost like the crowd parts for him as he confidently strides toward the bar with perfect posture. The only time I glance away is when Rokk's eyes seek mine in confirmation. My nod brings a too-knowing grin to both of our faces.

Cade glances up and catches my delight. The bastard winks again, and the movement keeps me warm in my core until well after he returns to our quiet loft. I accept the freshly shaken martini he offers and take several sips to relieve the budding dryness in my throat. The liquor's more expensive than I'm accustomed to and it helps, but he quickly makes the attempt pointless. A thigh far thicker than I could've imagined presses so close to mine that no space lives between me and his warmth when he settles in the booth beside me.

For a reason that I staunchly refuse to acknowledge, how he pulls his glass to his lips mesmerizes me. He notices me watching the way he ritualistically brushes the liquid beneath his nose again.

"Want to try it? It's scotch."

Scotch? Absolutely not. The tongue that darts out over his lips to gather a lingering drop after he takes a sip? Maybe. Definitely. But not the drink.

I wrinkle my nose. "Scotch is disgusting."

"It's Macallan's. It's expensive."

"Being expensive doesn't make it any good." I pluck the tumbler from his hands with a huff. His lazy smirk deepens when I pull it to my nose and blanch at the charred scent before dramatically ridding myself of it. "Why in all the hells do people drink that? It's got to taste like licking a campfire."

"It's one of the most popular brands of scotch in the world."

"Is that supposed to impress me?" I ask. "Being expensive and popular doesn't mean it's any good."

"It's won awards. For being the best. In the *world*." My shrug makes him chuckle. "Maybe you have poor taste."

I curl my legs onto the bench beside me, knees brushing him. My smirk rivals his over the edge of my glass when I bring it to my lips. "And here I was, starting to think my taste was you."

"Oh," he murmurs with a velvet baritone. The crooked half-smile on his face snags my gaze. "It's worse than I thought then."

It may be worse, but it's a worse that he likes. All of his body language says he appreciates what type of crazy sits far too close to him in this tattered fabric booth, drunk on a Wednesday night. I can't deny that I like who sits next to me, too.

I nudge his thigh with my knee. "So, why are you here?"

With a deep sigh, he sinks a little further into the booth. His head lolls back, and his eyes flick between several places on the ceiling like he's shuffling through memories. If I were a better person, I'd tell him nevermind and that he didn't need to share with me, a veritable stranger, anything about his life. But I'm not, and I'm curious to a fault.

"I was on my way to my engagement party and ended up here instead."

"What?" The word is louder than I intend, but what the fuck?

His gaze remains steadfast on the ceiling as he rubs a hand down his face. "I guess I was on the way to propose to the woman and then party? I don't know, honestly."

I scoff contemptuously and jerk everything away from him with the sudden simmer of renewed anger that overtakes me. The whiplash leaves me breathless. "What the fuck does that mean?"

Confusion must show on my face when he finally looks at me. Perhaps it's blending with the rage rapidly rising in the racing of my heart, because he seems to realize that I'm not taking his words lightly. Fear flashes over his face and he immediately sits up straighter, fully facing me.

"You should absolutely know if you're engaged or not," I say heatedly. "Are you?"

"No, I'm not." The surety sharpening his face matches the confidence in those words. They still don't relieve any of my rigidness. "I'm not engaged, I promise. I'm just doing what I'm told right now, and my mother said I needed to get married. She set me up with someone on a date, but I didn't realize agreeing meant getting engaged to a woman I literally don't know. I thought tonight was to meet her until right out there," he points to the thin window by the door, "when I found out that I was walking into my own surprise engagement party so graciously hosted by my mother. I hung up on her, and when I looked up, here was this bar. So I came in."

I'm blinking irregularly, eyes wide and mouth agape. I can't help it. This story sounds like some wildly fabricated lie to keep our night flowing. But it also sounds so outrageous that it must be true. Who could concoct such an outlandish story like that at the drop of a hat? No, there's too much emotion in his voice for it to be anything but the truth. The frown that overtakes his face as he watches me process his words is too poignant for this to be a lie.

He puffs out another one of those flat laughs. "Yeah, that's how I feel, too. It sounds unreal, doesn't it?"

"Uh, yeah," I say, bewildered, forcing out an awkward laugh through the muddled annoyance trying to abate inside me. "I'm way more confused now. Your mom...what? Pre-engaged you to a woman you've never met and then wanted you to propose in front of a room full of people at a party you didn't even know about? That's insane."

"I'm well aware," he replies flatly. "That's why I'm here instead. I don't want to marry one of my mom's friend's daughters or nieces or whatever. Especially not without meeting her first."

"Yeah, no shit." I bark a flabbergasted laugh and expect some sort of displeasure at how loud it is right beside him. A smile, rueful as it may be, breaks across his face and eats away a little more of my hesitation. The liquor helps too. "So you really were going through some weird shit, and then I threw water right in your face."

"Yeah, you did."

"I'm not apologizing," I joke. "You were an ass."

"I was," he admits, relaxing a little. "Dealing with water to the face was more than worth it, though."

His lowered lids and the soft yet deep timber in his voice make me clench in a specific place. "Was it now?"

"Absolutely."

Relief seems to flood him when my knees find their way back to rest against his leg. The confidence that the minor interruption stole returns, but not fully. He hesitates when his hand seeks my thigh, but I nudge my knee into him to spur the moment. Warmth filters through my jeans under his touch, a shiver rushing through me when he curls his hand between the ditch of my knee. He squeezes gently and the shiver ripples into goosebumps across my arms, thankfully hidden by my jacket.

His arms, however, are on full display for me this close. The onyx of his markings shimmer in the low light like tiny diamonds on his skin. It's as mesmerizing as the delicate and intricate patterns decorating his forearms. Jagged lines smooth out into geometric shapes with wispy smoke-like tendrils coiling in between. Deep black shades his skin where the symbols don't live. It's stunning how nature painted his tanned skin. I trace my fingers over each masterful line, and I swear electricity seeps off of him and makes my arm hairs stand straight. He tenses, grip around my thigh tightening and flexing his muscles beneath my fingers.

I can't look away or stop the gentle caress of my fingers as I ask, "So you really don't know the woman?"

He shakes his head, lowering it onto the back of the booth again. "I only know her name. I thought tonight was a drink to meet and see if we even liked each other."

"Goddesses above, that would've been so fucking awkward."

"Probably more awkward that I didn't show up."

I chuckle. "It's not too late."

"Oh, it's far too late now," he says, head lolling toward me with renewed heat on his face; the lopsided lift of his lips strikes me with the unique beauty. "There's no way I'm leaving this sketchy ass bar without the beautiful witch I'm with right now."

I clench, unsuccessfully suppressing another shiver. He feels everything, and that lopsided grin turns into a full-blown salacious smile.

"This place isn't sketchy," I say, and for some unidentified reason, his huffed laughter reignites something deep inside me that the last three minutes should have tamped out. It didn't. "I'm probably better than whoever you were gonna meet, anyway. I'm delightful."

"What a coincidence," he says and squeezes my leg again. "I've recently been told I'm the exact opposite. From what I know, opposites attract."

Fuck me, the eye contact with that statement is enchanting. Sparkling hazel ensnares me. I try to tear my gaze away from the spell they put me under, but no matter where I look, I'm drawn further into him. Scanning his face makes me even more enthralled. This close, it's easy to see the fervor fueling his sharp features. Those plump lips look more delectable sitting here with his hand wrapped around my thigh. A short beard with white peppering through it, all the way up into his perfectly coiffed curls, makes me weaker than I ever knew it would.

Paired with his simultaneously cocky yet respectful demeanor, his humor, and his determination? Fuck me, I'm done for. My body tells me that when he squeezes my thigh again, thumb rubbing over the expanse. Excitement ignites my veins and wets my core.

"Hey y'all!" A voice over the speakers tries to cut through and ebb the silent heat between us. "We're Brain Fog and I hate talking so—"

It fails. Soft music ricochets around the loft like a melody meant only for us. The gentle song flares the tension like a wildfire. It pulses through me with every thump of the bass drum.

Trying to dissipate the want budding in my veins, I uncoil myself and stand to look over the railing. The crowd's filled in, but no one's come upstairs, for which I'm oh so thankful when Cade stands to join me. A gentle touch ghosts across my skin, underneath the edges of my jacket. Like he's hesitant that I may push him away. Fair assumption, but I won't. I crave the all-encompassing warmth of his hand settling across my lower back.

I shouldn't stand pressed this close to a man I've never met. I don't know this person, what he wants, what he does for a living, or hell, what his last name even is. Not to mention Amber and I broke up only a few months ago—even if it was the sixth time over the course of our relationship—and he was supposed to be engaged to someone else tonight. I shouldn't be thinking about this man and what it would feel like to have him burying his cock deep inside me. But also…I can really use something to rid myself of the last handful of months, and one passionate night with a stranger I'll never see again may be just the cure.

This might be a mistake, but it's a mistake that all of me wants to make. All of me welcomes his hand snaking further around my waist. Music reverberates around us, and when the drums disappear and an acoustic guitar takes over, his fingers curl into my hip. It takes all my willpower to chance a single glance at him up over my shoulder. My throat tightens seeing molten hazel eyes watching every move I make and every breath I take. Deep crimson blazes over my cheeks, bating my breath. The world disappears as the singer's voice floats through the air in a song that feels like it's meant only for us.

My eyes slip to his lips for a lingering moment. The slow curling upward of the left side into a lazy smirk breathes life into the coiling in my abdomen. Deliberately, I take my time returning my eyes to his. There's an unmistakable question written in the movement and the small parting of my lips. He answers with his free hand skimming along my skin to find a home cupping my neck. A gentle thumb explores the ridge of my jaw as he examines my face again. The burning hazel in his eyes when I tip my chin up toward his is a siege to my resolve. Hopelessly willing, I sink into him.

He leans in and brushes a barely there kiss to the corner of my lips in a patient plea. I grant it, pushing up to slant my lips over his. The kiss is sweet, a swirling of tart lemon with the smokiness of his scotch. Gentle, a mere testing of fit and fullness of our lips as they roll together. A discovery of how our bodies meld in the most insatiable yet satisfying way.

He's smiling when we separate. I don't need to open my eyes to see it; the curve of his lips caresses mine. But I'm so glad that I do. The intensity on his face is palpable.

"Take me home?"

My words are barely above the music, but he catches each one in the lingering notes of the fading song. The growl that rumbles in his chest holds the force of an earthquake then, tumultuous and earth-shattering. I've never heard something so primal before in person. I've read about it in romance books and seen it in the movies. Hell, I've dreamed of it countless times, the sound crawling down my spine in my wildest dreams. But I've never actually heard the sound rumble in someone's chest in real life. It's enthralling.

We don't stay to finish our drinks or to hear the rest of the band's set. We barely make it out the door before I feel the tingle of his magic along my skin.

CHAPTER
FOUR

THERE ARE COUNTLESS NAMES FOR THE MAGIC THAT CRAWLS UP MY SPINE the moment we step outside into the crisp evening air. Fading. Vanishing. Nestao. Sparì. Desapareció. Imigh ó, as I knew it while growing up, thanks to my grandfather's Irish heritage. But no matter who's casting or what they call it, the magic feels the same: shattering down to the atoms in your bones to traverse a liminal space and materialize at your intended destination on the other side.

It's a spell that requires a profound connection with one's own soul and the magic flowing through the world. It also requires one of the greatest sacrifices known to Wixan-kind, which is why most choose not to use it. No one knows the exact number, but researchers speculate the cost being upwards of ten minutes of a magical's life to travel a couple hundred miles. More than that when traveling with someone else. When what we sacrifice in exchange for magic is gone forever, that's an expensive price to pay.

Those facts should make me weary of feeling the tingle in my bones, but I'm just grateful. Mine and Cade's atoms fade into mist, and I still feel his hand in mine while our beings shimmer in the air. It's only a few seconds before our world snaps back into a dark room. It takes only seconds more before the wet heat of his lips is on my skin like a wildfire of want.

Chuckling, I playfully draw away when his lips seek mine. Not far. Just enough that we breathe the same air, yet our lips don't touch. Cade attempts again, but again I tug away. Gruff indignation rumbles in his throat and shoots a titillating tirade of tingles through me. Firm fingers curl possessively into my ass and haul my body flush against his. When he leans in this time, I don't pull away. Soft lips pillow over mine once, twice, and a third time before crushing against them in a bruising kiss that steals any air I can manage.

Hands grab for hems and places to hold as our tongues dance in passionate pleasure. We barely separate to pull shirts over our heads. That marvelous scent bathes me when I tug his off, and it makes my pussy clench as we stumble backwards together, lips locked. We leave our pants behind somewhere. I don't remember taking them off. Don't care, either. All I care about is they're off and I can feel his nails digging into my skin.

This isn't pretty or slow or gentle, but it's what I need. Passionate. Hot. Utterly fucking maddening and mollifying all in one. How his fingers explore parts of me long untouched. The way he kisses me like it's all he's ever needed. The trembling of his body beneath the fingernails I trail over his skin. It's all—goddesses, I can't even think. I don't care what it is. I want it, and I want it now.

A firm hand kneads my breast, and it pillows out between and around his fingers. I groan at every grasp combined with the fervency of our lips together as my calves hit a mattress. Plushness cradles me when I fall back into it; his burly body follows and engulfs me, suffocating me in a blazing heat. I settle into it, trying to draw him impossibly close.

He resists and draws back some, taking a slow moment to scan the lines of my face. "You did mean—"

"Yes," I cut in eagerly. "Yes, I definitely meant."

"Good," he rushes out before slanting his lips over mine in that same searing passion.

I melt into his kiss as a smooth hand slowly explores down every inch of my body. My shoulders, my breasts. The concave of my waist and the curves of my hips. He fervently paints my skin with his touch until his kisses follow. My fingers curl into the longer lengths of his hair and I guide him where I want. He happily goes. My neck, my collarbone. The pebble of both of my nipples that he nibbles tenderly.

"Your markings—" a kiss presses to the blue skin decorating my supple left breast. "Are—" ardent kisses follow the trail of steel blue and press lower on my abdomen. "So beautiful."

He follows the naturally drawn path of my markings directly to the hem of my underwear, making me whimper; I can't help but love them more, writhing needily with every shadow of his lips.

"Like brush strokes of a painting," he whispers against my abdomen, warm breath dusting my skin in goosebumps that his tongue darts out to taste. My stomach tenses painfully, pleasurably. "You're a work of art."

The words flow through me like a deluge of desire, and I buck against his hold. Nimble fingers dust up my thighs as Cade's tongue skims across the waistband of my underwear. I happily oblige in lifting my hips so he can remove the offending fabric. Pools of onyx blown wide with lust, rimmed with fire-fueled hazel, meet my eyes over the curves of my body when he does. Like he's devouring me. Savoring me. My fingers fist in the sheets in sheer anticipation.

Those eyes never break from mine while he bounces his lips between my thighs. A kiss to one that lingers until I'm shivering, and then the searing heat of his tongue drawing a path down the other. The closer he gets to my core, the hotter I burn, the more I squirm and roll to try and force him closer.

He doesn't give in. He laughs against my skin, deep and lustful. "Greedy." Teeth sink into my thigh seconds later, and unadulterated desire spreads through me.

He doesn't let it fade. He parts me, and his tongue finds purpose on my clit. Such good fucking purpose. Firm and unyielding. I arch into the sudden intensity, and a string of unintelligible, blissful babbling tumbles past my lips and makes him laugh. The movement only makes me groan more.

"Fuck, yes," I hiss. "Yes, teeth, use your teeth—"

He doesn't make me ask twice. Fuck what a beautiful quality; when I say what I want, and someone just does it? Stunning. Teeth glide across my clit, and the sting surges like a wave through me. He tests pressure, learning just how I like it from the way I keen. From the way I grip the sheets and cry out. The motions, the sounds only spur him and the way he moves against my clit is inexplicable.

A finger slides inside of my soaked pussy, doubling the pleasure of his tongue that never stops its movement. This man is clearly a giver, and he doesn't hold back. Teeth skim my clit and that deliciously long finger seeks the soft spot inside of me. I squirm. I ache. I beg, "Another," until his responding laughter vibrates against my core.

"Greedy," he murmurs against me.

"Very," I grit out through the tension quickly building behind my navel.

My fingers thread through the tendrils of curls against his forehead, gripping. There's no resistance when I push his face back toward the spot where I crave him. In fact, a wide grin overtakes his mouth moments before it's on me and a second finger slides into me, ripping a moan out of my throat.

I love being finger fucked. But this? It's entirely overwhelming in a way to which I'm unaccustomed. Firm pressure gives way to gentle strokes against that perfect spot inside of me. Pulsing fingers expertly transition to smooth circles of his tongue on my clit. Pleasure pushes my hips out against him but he pushes back, driving me into the mattress as his fingers curl and his tongue flicks and finds a home I hope it never leaves. At that moment, it's impossible for me to imagine any greater bliss than this.

Until he moves up my body, burying himself in the crook of my neck, and asks, "Take one more for me, beautiful?"

I moan out my need, nodding and rolling my hips against his touch. Against my neck, he grins and slowly slides three thick fingers inside me. So slowly. Every centimeter more makes me keen and whimper and writhe. He rides my movements, letting each digit sink a little deeper and spread a little wider until his palm is flat against my clit and my mouth can't stay shut from the bliss building inside me.

"Good girl."

Oh, good fucking gods. Those whispered words drive me crazier than I ever thought two words could. I tense so viciously, but he devours the reaction and guides me through it. I twitch and thrust and pant and grab at whatever I can to hold as he moves all of those diligent fucking digits inside me.

"Already going to come for me, beautiful?" The depth of his voice makes it harder to hang on. A finger disappears and the others drive deeper, frantically flexing and he growls, "Good fucking girl, let go—"

I lose my grip on control. Shattering, shuddering, I twitch as my release careens through me. Waves of wanton pleasure pulse through my body as he furls his fingers inside me until I'm so tense I can't move. He can and does, finger fucking me until that knot of tension snaps and I shout his name like a mantra. Until my pleasure crescendos and coats his hand and me in the warmth of it all.

He's grinning as I slowly relax, legs loosening enough that he's able to pull his hand away. It's glistening in a low light I didn't even realize he turned on. He makes a show of running the moisture over the tip of a gloriously crafted cock. Seriously. The gods must have hand-shaped the thing in their image. I've never been so desperate to wrap my lips around something. Both sets. Repeatedly. Watching his hand coat his cock in my wetness makes me crave it inside me. I ache for it as he watches me watch his every slow stroke.

It's obvious how badly I want him, but he doesn't move to relieve me of my want. Granting me only the smallest bit of reprieve, he kneels between my thighs with dick in hand, stroking base to tip. He presses his length firmly to my clit, and his knuckles brush the sensitive nub in a maddening repetition. He keeps rhythm, massaging just the head of his cock and me repeatedly until I try to force him closer with my heels.

A good man knows not to make a partner ask twice. Cade barely makes me ask once before he aligns his swollen tip at the warmth of my pussy and pushes into me. He lets me savor the feeling of stretching around him for several long, pulsing heartbeats. If it's taking anything in him to move this slowly, he's not giving any of it away. He's teasing me at every turn, and I'm devouring every moment like a woman starved.

I drive my heels against his thighs again because, fuck me, I want to feel all of him so badly. Fire flares over his face, and that lewd smile returns as he oh so slowly starts pushing, thrusting, and teasing both of us with every long inch of his cock, stretching me. Filling me. So fucking well. Bigger than it looks, it doesn't make it all the way in before pressing against the back of my bliss and drawing shared gasps.

Groaning, his head tips back, and the lines of his muscles beneath his bulk show with the tension building inside him. "Fucking magnificent."

He's the one that looks so fucking magnificent. More so when I slowly roll my hips against his, and his entire body tenses more. Neck muscles, abdomen. His fingers wrapped firmly around my hips. The cock buried inside me. They all flex and make me shudder. Make me drive my heels into the backs of his thighs again.

He grins when he finally drops his chin and gazes back down at me. "Does my greedy witch want me to fuck her now?"

"Hard."

That was the right word. I'm sure anything I could've said would have spurred him. But the lust that darkens his face and the sheer pressure of his lips crushing against mine says he craves exactly what I said.

And he gives it to me, thrusting without restraint into my already sensitive pussy.

He rolls his hips against mine, clit brushing the hardness of his pelvis, and I force my hips up against his in a beautiful dance. The rhythmic thrusting leaves me speechless. Thoughtless, boneless. I can't even fathom anything beyond the pleasure and the magnificent heat surging through me. I latch onto the feeling, every part of my body tensing and grasping for something I haven't welcomed in far too long.

His head falls to my shoulder; my arms cage him in and my fingers drag against his back, his scalp. Cries grow soundless, and my legs tremble as I wrap myself around him to hold him close. As if he would move away. Neither of us would dare. Not when we're so precariously close to a shared euphoria.

Quick thrusts turn into slow rolls of his hips. Slow, but there's nothing soft in the way he fucks me. His hips snap into mine and he takes what he needs, giving me what I want, until too suddenly, he stops.

"Fuck—you feel too good—" he groans into the delicate space where my shoulder and collarbone meet.

I whine and roll my hips to meet his, more out of desperation than anything, groaning when his cock sheaths inside me. I'm greeted with a bruising grip on my hip pushing me down into the mattress and the ghost of a laugh across my skin.

"Careful," he mutters. "Or it's gonna be over too quickly."

Salt coats his neck when my tongue brushes up the long column towards his ear. "I want to feel you come in me," I whisper. The demand is purely selfish. I want to feel him inside me when he tumbles over that edge of bliss. I want to experience how unimaginable it is when his thick cock swells and stretches me fuller than it already is.

He groans. "Fuck me—are you on—"

"Yes," I cut in. "Now fill me up, sir. Please."

"Gods above," he growls, and it doesn't take much more than me grabbing his hips and tugging for him to take back over.

It's slow and measured and maddening, and my pussy pulses around him in appreciation. Cade groans and drops his forehead back to my shoulder in a cage I never want to escape, shifts his legs up, and pounds into me. My nails rake down his back with my bliss, and when his teeth sink into my shoulder, I scream and hang on to the last shreds of reality I can.

"Please—" he grunts against my skin. "Please, may I come?"

I groan, fingernails scraping over his back again. "Y-yes—come—for me."

It's orgasmic. He thrusts into me frantically and I fall with him one final time into that dazzling abyss of pleasure. When he swells and twitches, moaning a sound of absolute bliss, I shatter. Ecstasy surges through me, stiffening every place our bodies touch as he fucks me through both of our releases until we're panting.

He looks too satisfied when he eventually rolls off me. I miss the heat when it disappears, but it doesn't move far. He lays beside me, firm chest pressed against my arm, slowly working his hand around my waist to pull me closer with a sated and lazy grin.

"That—" A barely there huffed laugh plays between us. "—was embarrassingly fast. Sorry. I'm blaming the scotch."

My laughter is breathless. "I don't think that's how that works."

"Okay, then it's your fault."

"Oh, yeah?"

"Yeah," he agrees. "I could've lasted longer if you didn't look so fucking beautiful when you come."

A lazy grin that matches his spreads over my face. "Don't worry. I used my time wisely."

"Oh, *you* used your time wisely?" He cups my jaw like he owns it and I happily nuzzle into the warmth. "I didn't have any part in it?"

I shake my head. "None at all. Were you there?"

"Witch," he growls and drowns out the sound by capturing my lips in a kiss that blanks my mind and leaves desire singing in my veins again.

There's an unnameable emotion on his face when we separate. Nothing that makes me uncomfortable as he scans my face, but my stomach does react, fluttering and flipping when he reaches up to my temple and lifts some hair out of my face. The flutters double when a gentle finger traces the mark running down over my eye, my jaw, his eyes following the path.

"W-what?" I whisper.

"Did you know Renoir's muse was a water witch?" I just shake my head, throwing hair back into my face. Again, he moves it away, tucking it behind my ear, fingers brushing down my jaw in retreat. "Some say her beauty and her markings inspired his every painting."

I can't respond through the lump in my throat. I just lean into the hand he uses to cup my face again, sighing when that thumb brushes over my lip. He's so warm and his touch is far more comforting than it should be. But right now, I don't care. It's all I need to anchor me to this moment and the present.

"If she had even a tenth of your beauty, he was an unfairly lucky man."

Jagged breaths shudder through me. Cade doesn't hesitate or stutter. The words are an honest truth if the look on his face and the surety in his voice say anything. The kiss he gives me when I desperately pull him in reiterates every word. I crave the way my body needs him, yearning for the feeling of his words careening through me. He provides, pulling away to sear hot kisses down my markings again.

"I must be the luckiest man to ever live."

I moan unabashedly, and before it fades, his hand is between my thighs again. His lips meet mine and he swallows my groan when two fingers slip back through his mess dripping out of me.

"I want to see you come one more time," he says, pressing hot kisses down my jaw.

I try to respond but it just comes out in shattered praises of his giving nature. I thank him for his fingers, for his movements, for himself, as he adds a third finger and vibrates his hand. Wet sounds fill the space my moans don't, and I grab his arm for something to hold, pushing my hips out to his rhythm. With my clit already so sensitive, it doesn't take long for that knot inside me to tighten.

"P-please, fuck, please—"

"Good girl. Let me see how fucking beautiful you are when you come for me."

I do, eyes slamming shut as my legs do the same around his arm. He doesn't stop until I unravel once again, twitching with the ecstasy surging through me. He rides every wave that wracks my body until I go limp, faint spasms lingering as a sated smile grows over my face.

"Fucking hells," I whisper. "Talk about quick."

Our laughter is nothing more than puffs of air at this point. He captures my lips in another kiss, this one far gentler and a deep departure from the passion that pervaded every kiss before it. Even his voice is softer when he pulls away and asks, "Need some water?"

I draw out an exaggerated hum, lolling my head toward his voice. Relaxation and what I can only amount to pride shape his face when I finally manage to open my eyes again. "Frozen into little cubes and shaken in a martini, maybe."

Another puff of laughter kisses my skin. "Martini with a twist it is. Now go pee."

"Excuse me?" Disbelief breaks a full grin across my face. Partially with his demand, but partially because he remembered my drink order. "Did you just tell me to go pee?"

"Absolutely. I can't have you getting a U.T.I. after the first time we have sex. So be a good girl and go pee, and I'll have your martini ready when you're back."

Then he captures my lips in a slow kiss that's once again loaded with fire before abruptly leaving the bed. A bit in disbelief, I chuckle at myself and shake my head. "I can't believe that just turned me on."

"I can be rather convincing."

I scoff and roll off the bed to make my way toward where he points. "That's not always a good thing."

"I only use my powers for good."

"Somehow, I don't believe you—oh my fucking goddesses!"

Something clatters in the other room. "What happened?! Are you okay?" He's behind me in the bathroom doorway in an instant.

I just turn to him, eyes wide, and flail my hand toward the tub. I've been known to be dramatic. Ask any of my friends what my top five personality traits are, and every single one of them will say being over-dramatic ranks among the top three. But this time, I'm not overplaying my words: the bathtub looks like it was sculpted into the bathroom walls either for or by the gods and goddesses themselves. It's the literal bathtub of my dreams. It's like a personal hot spring. Rocks build up the dark walls like this basin was cut out directly from a cave. The stones are jagged, but the tub itself is polished smooth. It's either real dark marble or an expensive imitation, but either way I'm enchanted. It's honestly too good to be true, but it's also perfect and I've fallen into immense love with it on the spot.

And he's only looking at me like my excitement is better, wearing a too-dazzling smile. "Makes sense a water witch would find my bathtub so—"

"*Your* tub?" The words are loud and out of my mouth before I realize truly what we've both said: this is *his* tub. We're in his house. Surprise slackens my jaw. "This magnificent work of art is *yours*? Bullshit. This is a hotel. It's too nice."

Soft laughter echoes around us. "So surprised. You told me to take you home, so I did. Where'd you think I was getting a martini?"

I flail my hand back toward the tub. "No, you took me to the most magnificent tub I've ever seen."

"Want to see something better?"

"I honestly don't know what could be bet—"

He proves me very wrong very quickly. He flicks two switches beside the door simultaneously and I actually gasp. Soft, warm light filters through the crevices of the rock formation, painting the room in a beautiful sunset hue. Lights in the tub turn on, and if there were water, they would tint it a cerulean blue and give it a moonlit glow. It's unrealistically beautiful. A bathroom should never be this stunning. Never. But soft light flickering around the room and glistening off everything proves me so deliriously wrong. I don't want to blink.

Gentle fingers coil around my waist and pull me back against a firm chest. The curve of Cade's grin against my neck when he leans down flares heat in my veins.

"How can a bathroom be so freaking pretty?" I ask, leaning my head back against his shoulder, opening my neck a little more.

Laughter jumps his chest against me before he brushes a few barely-there kisses over my skin. "Only thing that could make it more beautiful is you relaxing in it."

"You really do try to charm your way right through everything."

"Is it working to charm you into my bath?"

"I wish." I sigh. "I'm honestly heartbroken that I can't."

"Why can't you?" He's smiling when I look back at him, bewildered. "It's only eight-thirty, and I've got nowhere else to be tonight."

I level him with an exasperated lift of my eyebrows, pulling away so I can face him. "Except for your engagement party?"

"They can add me into the photos later," he replies. He picks another bit of hair off my face and watches his hand move it away. "Personally, there's nowhere else I *want* to be, and I really don't want you to leave either." Gentle fingers cup my jaw again. "Run us a bath so I can clean you up before I fuck you into my mattress again until you're sweaty and begging me for another one."

I almost go weak in the knees.

I should leave. I should find my clothes, head home to eat something else to soak up the rest of the liquor, and wait for Jae to get home. He's supposed to be proposing to someone else tonight; granted, he doesn't know her like he doesn't know me, but even the thought of it happening in the future should deter me. It should send me home.

But good goddesses, I don't want to go. I'll do anything he asks if he keeps speaking to me that way and looking at me how he does now. I glance back at the tub, and the excess of it all washes over me. Opulence and luxury aren't things in which I frequently find myself indulging. But right now, I think I deserve it. After the last few months, but especially after the last thirty-some odd days, I deserve to savor this little slice of the heavens. I deserve a night just to relax and not think. And so far, the man staring expectantly at me when I look back at him has been a wonderful distraction.

"How hot do you like it?"

He grins. "Hotter the better. Make it sting, beautiful, and I'll be right back." I preen at the barely there kiss he presses to the tip of my nose before leaving me alone with the most beautiful tub I've ever seen.

CHAPTER

FIVE

"I planned to have the tub removed before I moved in. Glad I didn't."

Cade leans against the door frame, holding a tumbler of amber liquor and my martini when I open my eyes. Hot water soothes my joints, and I stretch out with an unabated groan as he scans me. I let myself do the same of him. He's naked, cock hardening with every drag of his gaze up and down my body, and gods dammit in this lighting, he looks glorious.

Cheekiness morphs my features. "I can't fathom how you even considered something so blatantly wrong."

"And you call *me* the jackass?"

"I never said I wasn't a jackass. I just made sure you knew you were one, too."

It's impossible to look away from the grin that brightens his face. "So, you're saying we have things in common?"

"Barely. We're both jackasses that like sex. Not the most ideal foundation."

"What more do we need?"

I snort and leave the question alone because the answer doesn't matter; nothing will happen between us after tonight. Once I leave, we'll never see each other again. Instead, I say, "All I need is this beautiful bath and that martini."

"You're a very inexpensive date then, beautiful," he replies jovially. "Lift up."

"I feel like that should offend me," I say, doing as I'm told, taking the glass he offers while watching with no shame as he steps into our bath with a soft hiss. Every muscle tenses, but there's only one I'm watching. The stiff sight of his cock right in front of my face makes my mouth water. Thankfully, he sits before some primal urge pushes me to wrap my lips around the tip. The water rises to the emergency stopper and the sound of some escaping breaks through the damn-near catatonic state he put me in.

A strong arm glides through the water and wraps around me, drawing me back. I happily settle between his legs and lean back against his chest. We sip our drinks in unison; his ends in a sigh so similar to that of his release just minutes ago that I clench.

I have to clear my throat in order to ask, "So, what does the ring look like?"

He chokes on a mouthful of liquor. "What?"

"You were proposing tonight, so you have a ring, right?"

"I wasn't proposing." His reply is flat. "I was meeting someone for a drink. That's it."

"But you do have a ring," I say, emphasizing his non-answer and punctuating it with another long drag of my drink.

"I *do* have a ring that was handed down to me several years ago, yes, but it wasn't with me. It's still securely in my nightstand."

"Well, show me."

"You want to see it?" I nod, holding out my free hand, flicking my fingers in beckoning. He chuckles. "Oh, you think you just get to see my family jewels so easily?"

I chortle at the obvious innuendo, turning my gaze over my shoulder. "Look, I know I'm not who Mommy wanted you to marry—"

A squeal rips from my throat and my empty glass drops into the water when firm fingers grip my side and flex. Repeatedly. Cade relentlessly tickles me. I flail and try futilely to escape his clutches, but the arm around my middle anchors me in place. I can't escape. Water sloshes over the edge of the tub and against the stones, and my laughter echoes around the room. Thankfully, I don't have to beg him to stop.

His fingers drip with water when the offending hand moves to cup my jaw again. Before my laughter dies, our lips slant together in a kiss that steals the last remnants of air in my lungs and closes my eyes. This part he's superb at. The pressure of our lips together. The way he sucks my bottom lip as his fingers curl further around my neck. The gentle compassion in the chaste kisses he presses to the corners of my lips when we part. It leaves me a whimpering mess.

He's impressed with himself when my eyes open again. I puff out breathless laughter, and whisper, "Now you definitely have to show me, jackass."

His thumb brushes over my cheek. "Couldn't have asked before I got in the bath, huh?"

"Didn't think about it."

"Alright, then. What do you say?"

I can't help the smugness that threatens my lips. "Off you go—"

A gasp tears from my throat. His hand wrapped around me shifts and presses firmly against my pussy. His laughter then is nothing short of sinful—thicker, smoother, delicious like chocolate with wine. I swear I can taste the sweetness on his thumb as it brushes against my parted lips.

"Off I go into the cold?"

I whine and nod against his hold on my jaw. "Yea-usss-" Pressure intensifies on my pussy and a moan drowns out my words.

Whispering, he says, "Only good girls get to see my jewelry. Say please."

Fuck me, I hate that I like those two words so much. Why and how can a simple phrase shatter every restraint I have? Combined with his hand pressing against my core, I tremble out another moan. The shakiness in my voice when I say, "I refuse," gives away that I don't refuse at all. But I won't give in that easily.

"Such a shame," he murmurs against the shell of my ear, and goosebumps skitter across my skin. "I bet you'd like the ring." His touch vanishes, and on instinct, my hand finds his to push it back toward my pussy. It's pointless; he's far stronger than me and it doesn't move. "Guess we'll never know—"

"Please." The word escapes unhindered, surprising both of us with the swiftness of my acquiescence.

He sighs into my skin, making me vibrate with need. "Good girl."

This time, he lets me push his hand back and grants me the pressure I want, the movement I crave. My head thumps back onto his shoulder and barely audible laughter skates over my neck. Purposeful fingers massage the outside of my pussy, teasing the edges of my lower lips, and I roll my hips forward, seeking more friction.

Instead of pressing harder, however, he moves away completely, using the momentum to push me forward. He's out of the water before I have time to protest, and honestly, any complaint I could've mustered would've died into laughter. Watching Cade bounce tiptoe to tiptoe out of the bathroom is almost impossible not to laugh at.

"Fuck! It's so cold!"

"I've heard that excuse before!"

Laughter fades into the depths of his room; Cade's rushing back through the door and sloshing into the tub just moments later. Water spills out and paints the stone walls. He hauls me back again, nuzzling himself into the crook of my neck once more with shivers wracking his body. His teeth even chatter. It's a show of dramatics that could rival my own, and we both laugh. Which feels…nice. It feels nice to laugh so freely. Even if I'll probably forget this by morning, I'll savor these few moments that my laughter feels genuine for the first time in such a long time.

"Better?" I ask.

He nuzzles a little more. "So warm now."

"Good. Then show me the ring."

I don't often wear jewelry; it's not something I crave, and I don't find myself buying it much. Not on any principle. I'd just rather spend my money on other things. But I don't need to know anything about jewelry to know that the ring in the box he flips open is monumentally expensive, exceptionally old, and *really* fucking beautiful. Two stunning deep blue sapphire stones sit nestled together in an understated setting that reminds me of the ocean. Swirls of silver dance along the edges of the two stones, like waves breaking in the ocean over a sandbar. Depending on the angle I turn my head, I can also make out seashells in the gleaming surroundings. Just like my markings, this ring is abstract. It's open to interpretation, and goddesses above how I want to perceive it.

Through the buzz of all the alcohol from the day, I can no longer see my life without this ring. Somehow, it's everything I never knew I needed and makes this night feel even more surreal.

"Beautiful, huh?" I'm too stunned to speak, so I nod. "It's an heirloom. Been in my family for a millennium."

A soft snort of derision puffs past my lips. "Bullshit."

Again he laughs, low and smooth. "Caught me." His arm curls a little further around me. "Sounded good, though, didn't it?"

"I won't believe anything you say from here on out."

"Believe me when I say I want you to try it on," he replies, motioning the box toward me.

"You're kidding right?" The sincerity on his face is answer enough when I shift to see it. "No way. I'll end up losing it down the drain or smacking it on the rocks. Then the stone will crack so badly no one will be able to repair it. *Then* whoever you're actually supposed to marry will get mad, and I'll end up dead and buried in a forest with my fingers and teeth missing, and no one will ever find me."

The more laughter he lets out, the more I hang on the sound. "That escalated quickly," he says, but he doesn't lower the box. Instead, he bumps it toward me again. "It's been around for a long time. You're not going to be the one that breaks it. Promise. You'll just make it look even better. So will you please show me how good it looks on a beautiful woman's hand? One that I choose? Just once, please?"

"Well, fuck. How can I argue with that?"

"You can't."

He's right. I can't. Well, I can, but I'm not going to. I know he's using his weird life scenario to guilt me into it, but right now, I don't care. Not with how much I want to see it on my finger. Maybe the liquor is what's making me even consider putting the ring on, but I roll with it. Slowly, I pluck the thin silver band from the plush black velvet, holding it out to inspect as if I know what I'm looking for. I don't. I'm just giving myself a minute to take in the awe because I'll never have something so beautiful to call my own.

The metal is cold against my skin, but heat flows through me, warmer than the bathwater when I slide it on. The ring fits perfectly, and that, out of all of this, is what makes this moment and night too good to be true. I try not to cling to the thought that this ring could be mine in the future when I hold my hand up to gawk at its full beauty.

Cade tosses the box away, and gentle fingers dust up my forearm, painting my skin in goosebumps before ghosting across my palm. The thump of my heart against the lump in my throat compounds when they spread mine and find a home between them. Like he's displaying the ring and our future lives in the air in front of us, bathed in the jaw-dropping blue lighting.

"Beautiful."

His words whisper across my skin, and I clench. He's right. It's so fucking beautiful, with my blue markings dancing up my finger to kiss and dip beneath the ring like someone sculpted it for me. It takes everything I have to remind myself it wasn't. This ring is not mine. It belongs to someone else. Someone that a mother would approve of; who's vetted and has a job. Who probably has her own place to live and a trust fund to match the money Cade has.

This ring and the future that comes with it will never be mine. But goddesses, right now, I wish they would.

"She's a lucky woman," I murmur.

"Who?"

A pang runs through me. Unmitigated jealousy invades my veins that I try to keep from my voice because the logic behind it is fallible. "Your future fiancée."

"She doesn't exist anymore," he says. "I'm not marrying anyone that I don't know or choose. I want to meet someone and fall in love."

I cannot suppress the shudder that works through me alongside a tidal wave of relief that I won't acknowledge. I have no reason to believe him, but I cling to the words, giving an odd hope to the thought that the ring circling my finger could one day be mine. The thought is so flawed, but I ignore every hole I could poke into it.

"Don't we all?" I joke, leaning against him again, our hands still in the air in front of us. "Goddesses, it's perfect."

"Only because you make it look so perfect."

I almost whimper when his hand leaves mine. Thankfully, it doesn't move far. His fingers trail over my jaw to turn it once again, like he owns it. I could make him work for it. Maybe make him beg a little or pull away like I did when we landed in his room. I don't. I just savor the feeling of the barely there brush of his lips over mine. Three gentle kisses warm me before I shift and capture his lips in a kiss that's far more passionate than this moment should be for two strangers.

His thumb smoothing over my cheek doubles the swirling emotions in me when we part. "Never take it off."

"I won't," I whisper. "It's mine now."

"So you'll marry me then?" There's humor in his voice.

I huff a playful sound of my own. "You just said you don't want to marry someone you don't know."

"We're getting to know one another right now, aren't we?"

I snort a soft laugh. If he wants to play into the fantasy that I'm his fiancée and we have a future together, I can, too. "Hmm," I hum, wriggling my fingers to let the sapphires catch the light. "It does look really good on my hand."

The hand curled around me tightens on my hip. There's a gruffness in his voice when he asks, "That mean you'll marry me?"

"If this ring is mine. Then yes, absolutely, I'll marry you—"

Smooth lips smother my words and the world around me. A firm grip bites into my hip and the back of my neck, pulling me into a kiss that is nothing short of suffocating. In the best way. There's no way I could escape this moment held against him, but I wouldn't want to. Not with the way he kisses me. Not with the way his fingernails drag across my lower abdomen before four fingers glide down and rest against my pussy.

Whoever says anticipation is worth it is a fucking liar. To label the strangled sound I make as a whimper is an understatement. I whine and push my hips toward his hand, seeking friction, but he moves his hand away every time. I even try again to push his hand harder against my pussy, but it does very little to move his.

"Greedy, greedy." A throaty chuckle rumbles in his chest and skitters out goosebumps like a wave from the place his lips touch my shoulder. "So many demands, and so little begging."

I scoff at that, at which he pulls himself away from every place we touch. Instinct flinches me to wrap my hands around his wrist to push back toward my core, letting out a strangled, "No, please!"

That deep laughter dusts across my skin again and his touch is back on me before the warmth fades. "Please what?"

This time, he gives me a hint of what I want. Tenderly, he moves, smoothing soft circles over my clit like he's explored it thousands of times before. His fingers wave upon me like ripples on a lake, gentle yet full of purpose, urging wide my lower lips. I gasp and spread my legs wider for easier access.

"Tell me what you want."

"Please, Cade. Please finger fuck me."

It's quick, the curling of his fingers inside me as he seizes my pussy like a man possessed. Spine-tingling tides of delight wave up and down my body, crashing against my clit as his palm lays flat and vibrates. He works my body like he knows it. Like he's studied every line with relentless diligence and mastered every curve. Drawing in and out, brushing heavy, enthralling circles on my clit before thrusting deeper back into me. Hooking his long fingers just so, caressing the delightful spot that never fails to open me to rapture.

Fuck, maybe the anticipation is worth it because I'm already so tightly coiled I'm ready to snap.

"Let go. Come for me."

I do. Exactly as he commands, I thump my hips against his movement and unravel. Fractals of indescribable bliss radiate through every part of me. Deep waves of pleasure shatter behind my navel, a soundless scream of his name reverberating in the walls of my brain. My mouth hangs open with a strangled whimper. I clutch at his wrist, his legs, the edges of the bath, anything I can to keep me grounded, but it doesn't work.

When I'm pliant, he turns me. Wide hands grip the backs of my thighs, and we're out of the water in an instant. My heart sinks into my stomach at the swiftness and I lean forward to grasp at him in a pointless frenzy. He only laughs in response, a gruff sound drowning out the noise of him stepping out of the tub with me in his arms like I'm no more than a paperweight. I wrap my arms around his neck regardless, anchoring myself in place.

"Don't worry, Princess. I've got you."

"Princess?" I shiver and clench and my heart soars into my throat while I try to hide it all behind the incredulity in my voice.

His grin says I fail. "She likes that nickname," he whispers. "*My*

Princess." That gruff statement does far more to my body than it should after all we've done up to this point. He's had his tongue inside me and yet it's two words that make me crave more.

"Call me whatever you'd like as long as you fuck me with that beautiful cock again."

Again, that growl of need rumbles in his chest and vibrates against me, as tantric as all the media makes it seem. I shiver at the sinful sound and the lustfulness that careens over Cade's face. "Grab the towel," he demands, nodding toward the hook hanging over his glass shower door.

He watches the smirk form on my face, an eyebrow raising. It only costs a few follicles of hair from my arm to wick the droplets down our bodies into the tub. A few more to make said water spark with electric heat down our skin, tingling desire through my body and his, given the way his grip tightens, biting into my skin.

"I suppose that's easier," he says.

"Never been one to do what I'm told. At least, not without a fight."

"A fight, huh?"

"Just a little one."

His fingers grip more, drawing an involuntary whimper in my throat. "But now I can't dry you off, so what excuse do I have to touch you?"

"Fucking me is a pretty good one."

The gruffness of his laughter flares warmth in my veins. "The best one."

My back hits the mattress before I blink, a sated smile on my face drawing him in. I reach for him as he crawls across his mattress, breathless laughter brushing along my skin as he settles between my open arms like the space is meant for him. Thick heat presses against my middle, but he leans in for a too-passionate kiss that blanks my mind of everything except the silken feel of his lips.

I whimper when he pulls away. Lidded eyes and the adoration on his face speak volumes. Hazel eyes soften with every one of my features he inspects in the soft light spilling in from the bathroom. He takes his time with each one, drinking me in like a man deprived. The weight of his admiration is palpable, and I almost can't stand it.

His chest inflates beyond full. Beyond a breath that says he's hanging on to control.

"I want to feel you stretched around me again, *Princess*."

A whimper involuntarily slips past my lips, and I shiver again, using the moment to push forward and sink my teeth into his bottom lip. He hisses in pleasure, pulling away to sharpen the sting of my bite. Pressure pushes against my pussy and pulses need down my spine.

"Tell me if it's too much."

I nod. "Fuck me, Cade—"

He does.

With an intensity that brings tears to my eyes, Cade pushes into me, smothering my body with his so close that I again can't escape. I wouldn't dream of it. Not with his lips on mine in a bruising kiss and his teeth nipping at my lip. Not when he so purposefully moves inside of me, so tantalizingly slow, letting me savor the way I stretch to take him in. Letting me feel all of him, every slow roll of his hips, until reality is crumbling around us and his forehead presses to mine.

"Fuck, you can't imagine how good your pussy feels."

My nails drag down his back. "As good as your cock feels inside me," I whisper, and dig my heels into the backs of his thighs. "Move. Now."

"Yes, ma'am."

He moves so fucking well. It's like a dance we've practiced for years. My legs wrap around him, his hands find a home gripping my thigh to raise my hips to grant him access to that ineffable spot of bliss.

"Look how perfect you are, stretched around my cock."

Fucking hell, his mouth. The words, his teeth nipping at my skin. The passion he presses to my lips. It leaves me a mess. I don't know what way is green or what color left is. I don't think I can feel my fingers or my toes, but I can feel where our bodies connect and move together in a motion so fluid it's natural. I'm shaking, and he's riding every wave with ease.

"You can do it for me," he groans. "Come for me again, beautiful. Let go—"

I do, cresting and crashing into that pool of pleasure. Twitching and losing myself in how he fucks me. No sound escapes me, but my pussy flutters around him in appreciation. I barely come down from the high before my body is tensing again. Before an aftershock of pleasure waits to rumble through me.

"Good girl. Fuck—One more—" he groans and drops his head into the crook of my neck. Never once stopping. "Give me one mor —fuck—"

His cock is pulsing. He's close. My fingers curl in his hair and tug back so I can moan into his ear, "Come—"

The demand dies with the bliss of his release. He fucks me, cock swelling and stretching in that unimaginable way, right until the point he can no longer resist, and pulls out. The heat of his pleasure spills across my stomach and wracks his body. Gods above, it's so beautiful to watch him come. My pussy pulses with every grunt and groan and involuntary, pleasurable twitch as he strokes himself dry. It's like no other moment in his life compares to the feeling of this ecstasy. It's intoxicating. It's—

The brush of his cock back against my pussy stops my thoughts short with an unhindered moan. He's back inside me, this time not waiting. Firm hips slam against mine as he buries himself to the hilt; my body quivers and heat careens through me again alongside surprise.

A deep grin sears across his face. "I said 'one more,' Princess."

I give it to him, caving in on myself as tears slip down my cheeks from the sheer intensity. It comes so suddenly, the wave of unimaginable pleasure that drags down my spine and ripples through my body, that I'm unprepared. My bliss breaks free, and I'm incapable of holding anything back. The buck of my hips against his, the way I shudder and slam my thighs around his body, the way I claw at him with unmitigated need. He takes it all in stride, never stopping his motions until my body tenses, shatters, and relaxes into a pliant puddle beneath him.

I think I thank him for it. Over and over. Each praise separated by chaste kisses and his smile against my lips.

It takes several seconds? Minutes? Hours? I don't know. I don't really care either. However long it takes, my pleasure settles into a sated smile across my face and I can finally open my eyes. He's grinning down at the mess he's made of me when I do.

"Try not to look so satisfied," he says, breathless still.

"Can't," I mumble with the faintest shake of my head. "Dick's too good."

He falls into his mattress beside me and quiet laughter shakes us and the bed both. I'm grinning watching him enjoy the view until a swirl of his hand indicates the release on my abdomen and he asks, "Another drink? You're good right? You can—"

I try to swat him, but he barrel rolls away and off the bed, popping up from the floor with a broad grin. "You're such a—"

"Shit. A Jackass. A fucker. I know," he finishes for me. For a moment, he stands there and inspects me like a masterpiece of his own painting, like that's all he plans to do. So I tip to the side, his slowly cooling arousal shifting toward the sheets. "Ah—witch!" He jerks, flicking open a drawer of the nightstand beside his bed to retrieve a cloth. "Don't you dare move. You know I'd never actually leave you to clean up on your own."

"Do I?" The question is more than facetious, and I shift again. He's beside me then, grinning as wide as me. The cloth is far more plush than expected. His kiss? Far softer than I imagined while he cleans himself off me.

"You do now," he whispers before pulling away and inspecting his handiwork. When he's satisfied, he cuts a sideways smirk at me and adds, "I make a mess of you from now on, and I get to clean you up. You'll never have to clean yourself up."

"Thought we can't say never?"

"Only when it's a fact." The wink he offers is one of complacency and surety. "Now I'm going to make us another drink."

"You make it sound like you're not done with me yet."

"Oh, I'm not. It's barely ten o'clock, and we've got all night."

He grins, and the way he kisses me then makes me believe that he's not done with me at all. If I have anything to do with it? Neither of us are leaving this way too comfortable bed tonight for anything other than drinks and snacks. And that's pushing it.

CHAPTER

SIX

GOOD GODDESSES ABOVE AND BELOW. WHAT FRESH HELL IS THIS? I'M so comfortable, yet fully fucking miserable. My head is simultaneously floating on a cloud and being pummeled into the solid ground. Worse, I don't know why. Or at least, as I skim my tongue through the desert in my mouth, I cannot recall why such a discomfort plagues me. It's unquestionable, however, that the bed I'm in is not mine. My pillows are nowhere near this comfortable, nor my sheets. But the memories of the night prior that left me in an unknown bed are beyond blurry. Blackness shrouds everything in my mind.

I groan, internally begging myself to remember...Remember...It's futile. Trying to summon any memory of being at Big's after Jae left just makes the persistent throbbing that's wracking my brain worse. Like the goddesses are punishing me for attempting to access my hippocampus. Even the tiniest glimpses are inaccessible, and that makes me more nauseous than I already am.

The sound of a toilet that's most definitely not mine, followed by running water, draws me out of my darkened memories because I'm not the one doing any of it. Which means: wherever I am, I'm not alone. Light sears through the thin slits of my eyes when they crack.

The faint gray of an early dreary morning dusts through a room that isn't mine and highlights furniture I can't afford. But none of that is where my eyes land. Rather, they ache as they try to focus on the figure that appears in a doorway across the room, haloed in a soft orange glow.

The sight unlocks the gate that hinders my memories and they flood in. Mystery Man. Do I even remember his name? Cole? Corey? Camden? Shit, I'm not sure. I just know he's the guy whose face I threw water into, who then followed me upstairs in some conquest of apology. He managed alright judging by the flashes of our bodies grinding together that assail the front of my mind and the ache I now notice in my core. Seems asinine that I could forget him, our night together, and a fuck that made me unsure where I ended and where bliss began. But I can only summon glimpses of the evening that give me nothing.

I lay ramrod straight as he returns to bed, crawling in with a single low grunt. Several more follow as he settles himself underneath the sheets that feel smoother than freshly shaven skin against my naked body. He moves for what feels like a full minute, legs and arms and hips shifting to find the precise amalgamation of limbs for comfort. I'm familiar with the movement because I do the same to fall asleep. Not mimicking him now, I lay unbreathing and beseech every known deity that he doesn't search for me underneath the sheets to hold.

If his head throbs or his stomach churns like mine, it doesn't show. He's back asleep in literal *seconds*. I'd be more envious if I also wasn't so thankful he possesses a skill that makes slipping out of his house undetected easier. Fuck, that's right. This is his house. He brought me *home* when I told him to, to the most amazing bed. I want to move, but my body begs me to sink into the mattress and curl my fingers into the cloud-like pillow I clutch for comfort. A faint fragrance of something citrus and woodsy encompasses me, and the scent begs me to stay, too.

I can't. I don't want to deal with the awkwardness of saying goodbye to a one-night stand. Not because I slept with someone I don't know. This isn't the first time and it won't be the last. It's just everything after we both saw stars that gives me anxiety. Recounting those moments is what I want so desperately to avoid. Knowing what I said to this man in the hazy hours of the night and what we did after my memories fade isn't something I want. I'm sure they're full of embarrassment, just like every other time I've found myself on the ass-end of a bottle of liquor.

Past embarrassment layers itself on the rapid unease overwhelming me now. I loathe this feeling, the crawling anxiety that shreds through my gut and leaves me raw. Embarrassment to me tastes and feels like a hangover. I always try to convince myself that it doesn't matter. I'll never see this man again, so even if I showed my ass, I'll be a memory that fades away until he's ninety and looking back on his life. Maybe by then he'll remember our night fondly if he remembers our time together at all.

I repeat that to myself, but the mantra doesn't stop my stomach from sinking into its own depths as I shift from his bed. It's a sore mistake when I stand. I'm not yet all the way hungover; I'm still partially drunk. The room spins so viciously that I clench my eyes shut. I have to concentrate to not yammy on the plush carpet beneath my toes. I almost lose the battle twice, and I curse myself and swear I'll never drink again. It's a lie.

After several long silent moments, the nausea subsides enough that movement feels possible. Only then do my eyes flutter open, adjusting to the dawn light streaming through curtainless windows. The sunrise is peeking out from the clouds, and it highlights my boots and my clothes folded neatly on the bedside table. My jacket lays across them both. Relief loosens my shoulders for several reasons. One: losing my security blanket in a hazy night of drunkenness would be another layer of shame added to the last three months. And two: I don't have to tiptoe over the far too plush carpet to find my things while attempting not to reawaken Mystery Man. Someone already gathered them. I'd thank myself for that, but it was likely the man sleeping unbothered behind me.

I should thank him, but I'm not going to. I just reach for my belongings. My heart sinks further when my phone, buried between my jacket and clothes, plummets to the ground with a loud thud. My entire body stiffens, as if that would help me hide in plain sight, and I beg of the deities again to keep him asleep. He grunts, and I snap my eyes closed as if that will make me invisible. The sound of sheets rustling shoots worry through me, and I have to focus again on not throwing up from the anxiety.

Maybe the deities listened, or maybe it wasn't as loud as it sounded to me, because he doesn't wake. He only resettles himself and evens out his breathing once more. I wait another minute to open my eyes, making sure it's real. I almost snort aloud when I do, looking over my shoulder for confirmation. The sun has split the clouds and a ray beams through the window, illuminating the side of the bed I vacated. Yeah right. Nothing could convince me to crawl back into that bed right now, not even the goddesses.

At least the light also shed on another saving grace: the small cutout in the glass of his window. His Fading access point. Fading might be a handy way for wixan to travel, but it can't penetrate through walls or glass. Most people just leave their windows cracked so their particles can float through the thin slit. Rich magical families? They cut holes in their windows for added security. For that, I am very thankful.

I may not have the life to sacrifice, but the smartest thing I can do right now is Fade the hell out of here. I don't know where I am, even though this lavish room could be nowhere other than downtown. Which means I could walk home, but judging by the scene outside, I'm in a very tall building. More than likely, I'll have to walk through a lobby full of people all watching me from over their cups of tea as I hurry out the front door while looking like a mess. Then I'll have to gather my barrings in the brisk March air on a sidewalk that's teeming with early-birds meeting friends for coffee before work because it's a fucking Thursday.

No thanks. Not a single part of that sounds appealing to the pounding in my head and the tidal wave of nausea in my gut. Perhaps it'll cost me more life than I have to give, but I'm willing at this moment so that I can touch down right in my room.

When I close my eyes this time, it's with intention. All magic is about intent. If someone doesn't possess the Incant cortex in their brains, like natural-born magical beings, they can still access the magic teeming throughout the world if they have enough intent. Non-magical beings might not possess the ability to Fade, but they can manifest things into their life with enough prolonged effort. They can produce rain by dancing in offering and cleanse their homes with the right herbs. They can even make things vanish with only thinking about them, only to turn around and ask where the missing sock went when it's not in the dryer. But only magical creatures blessed with the Incant cortex can call upon the magic long ago gifted to the world. It's stronger when we have ritual offerings of herbs or hair or blood or, with Fading, life-force. But at its core, magic is about intent.

Inhaling a lung-full of air, I envision my king-sized bed that takes up too much of my little room. My pillows that overrun said bed and the plush comforter I found years ago, discounted at some store that's no longer open. My bedside table I found discarded along the sidewalk and refurbished to fit with the dresser I've had since childhood. The small mirror that sits on said dresser, surrounded by clothes I've yet to put away in hopes they'll put themselves up. The unicorn stuffed animal Jae gave me after my mom returned to the waters. My cat.

With every minor element of home I paint in my mind, I feel myself more drawn to it. My navel pulls forward in that all too obvious draw through time and space. With a deep exhale, I step into it and welcome the dissolution of my being into small particles. In an instant, I snap back into comfort. The familiar, lingering scent of Jae's burned lavender incense welcomes me home and washes away a small layer of my anxiety.

Home. Where I needn't crack my eyes to move around the room, but only to see where I land. After almost a decade in this apartment, I know where everything is with no need to see it. Instinct pulls me toward the bathroom. I drop my clothes on my way and snatch the shirt I stole many years ago from a partner I only dated a handful of weeks that's laying on the edge of my bed. I'm not sure my eyes are open as I move through the motions. S.S.S. Except skip the shower and the shave and everything other than the first because the bed is calling me so ferociously I can't stop my body from dragging me toward it after I flush. I collapse into it, burying my arms underneath my pillows to draw my face into the familiar comfort.

Merowwww.

Surprised yellow eyes and pointed ears pop up from the small mound of fur masquerading as a pillow. They're the only thing I can see of the handsome boy I call my familiar in the rising sun when I crack open my eyes. Charlie. My precious, fluffy black and orange and white calico prince. In reality, he's a street cat I found playing beside a dumpster that waddled right up to me, far too young to be away from his mother. So I became his mother, and he's my best little garbage boy. I can't resist reaching out with my right hand to pull him closer. He chirps as I do so.

"Good morning, handsome."

Meroooow.

"Fine. Too early."

He yawns, and a familiar purr revs and washes more of my anxiety away. He agrees. It's far too early for any sort of movement other than the slow process of finding the perfect leg angles. The thought brings me back to just minutes before, when Mystery Man did the same thing. Tasting that embarrassment again, I quickly find my spot and sigh into it until I'm settled yet stiff.

"It doesn't matter," I say. "You'll never see him again. Go back to sleep."

Go back to sleep.

Go back to sleep.

I repeat that phrase slower and slower in my mind to clear away the nagging thoughts creeping in. Like if I say it so many times, I'll convince myself and my body it should sleep off the lingering alcohol thrumming through my veins. Falling asleep may not take hours like it does most nights, but it drags out long enough for me to miss the bed I woke up in this morning. And the sheets that don't feel scratchy because they're eight years old. And, if I'm honest with myself, the warmth of Mystery Man's presence.

CHAPTER

SEVEN

"Misty Opal Hayes!"

A heavy thud slams against the thin wood of my bedroom door and jolts me awake. There's a split second for me to recognize the voice before the door flies inward. Charlie dashes from the pillow beside mine in the same swift panic that fills me as a haze of purple barges into my room. Until this very moment, that purple blur was my best friend of more years than countable on fingers and toes. Now, the reawakened throbbing in my head makes me want to cut Jae out completely.

"What the fuck, Mis!"

Groaning, I grab for my comforter to curl further into, shielding myself from the light and her caterwauling. "Go away."

Jae rips the comforter from my barely functioning fingers; light and cool air bathe me. I try to pull one of the several pillows littering my bed over my head, but Jae is there to snatch it away too and throw it across the room. She does the same with the second pillow I reach for. That's enough to make me open my eyes and snarl up at her hovering over my bed. Through my bleary, narrowed gaze, I can make out that she's not mad; she's bewildered, wearing an expression halfway between excitement and wild abandon.

"It's two in the afternoon!" Jae shouts. "Wake up and tell me what the hell you did last night!"

"*What* are you even talking about?"

"This!"

She thrusts her phone into my face. More aptly, she shoves my face into my face. The side of it, at least. I have to blink several times to make sure I'm seeing what my brain is processing through the last remnants of sleep clouding my vision. When the image doesn't disappear like the dream that I'm desperately hoping it is, the panic in my body explodes into full hysteria.

There's no way I'm seeing what I'm seeing. No fucking way.

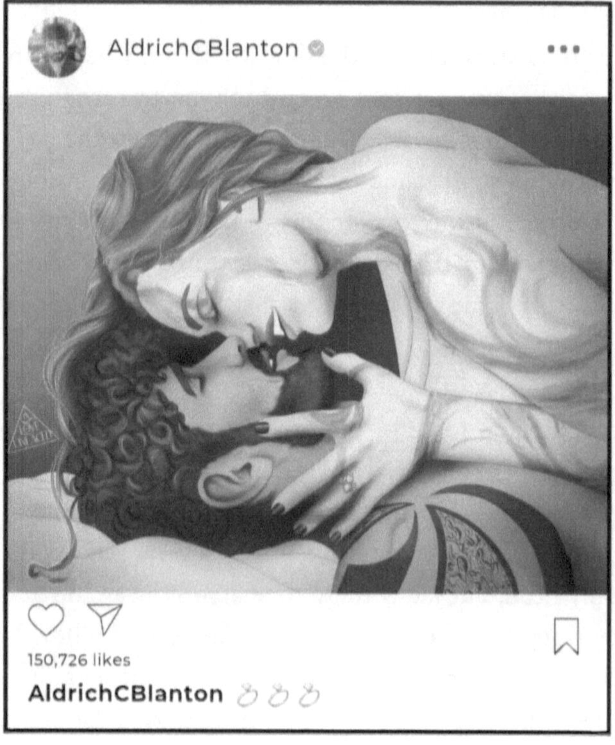

But it's right there. *I'm* right there on her phone screen. It's me and Mr. Last Night, lip-locked as the headline photo of an article on a trashy witch gossip column that Jae loves to read. There's zero mistaking me for anyone else. My markings are on full display. As is the rest of my body, naked and barely shielded by the too-comfortable sheets I slept in last night. My tits are almost completely revealed to the entire world. And I'm *smiling* about it.

So is Mr. Last Night, underneath me with his lips centimeters from mine while he's taking this fucking picture.

"So??" Jae squawks. "You weren't going to tell me you're fucking a *Councilor?*" Confusion shakes my head, unable to tear my gaze away from the phone. Jae shakes the device like I'm not staring at it hard enough. "So this isn't you in the picture naked and sucking face with him?"

"I-I mean, I fucked him last night, yeah, but—" I fumble for words because there's no denying it's me or that I spent the night with this man. I just stare at the picture she's still holding out that I have no memory of taking. Why would I have agreed to this? I don't know him, so why did we document such a non-momentous occasion for the entire world to see?

I notice something then, dead center on the dark image of two strangers kissing in an unfamiliar bed, and my stomach drops further. My hand rests on his cheek like it's rested there for years and not just a handful of hours. And on my finger is that beautiful sapphire engagement ring I'm now remembering he showed me in his bathtub. Memories of us together in sunset orange and cerulean blue saturate my mind and make my heart hammer so abruptly it almost chokes me.

Sitting, I reach for Jae's phone.

"Fuck me!" She shouts when my left hand springs free from under the one pillow she left me.

No, fuck *me*. Fuck me all the way to the underworld and back. Time stands still, and shock forces all the air from my lungs. I can't breathe for several seconds. Actually, I think I momentarily die with how abruptly my heart stops beating, flaring back to life when it plummets on an unrestrained freefall into the new, insurmountable pit in my stomach. I can't move, but Jae can and she throws her phone down before grabbing my hand to haul to her face.

"The article said you were engaged, but I thought it was bullshit!"

It *is* bullshit. Because there's no way what I'm seeing is real. Except Jae's seeing it too, so it must be. The deep blue sapphire ring in that picture is *still on my fucking finger*. I swear the ring gleams in the light as a shrill squeal breaks out of Jae's throat.

Engaged? I'm engaged? No! I'm not!

Unblinking as I watch Jae inspect my finger, I try to remember what Mystery Man and I did last night. It's a mistake. I took the ring home by accident. I just forgot to take it off after we got out of the bath and then overlooked it while I collected my things and rushed out this morning.

Seriously? I didn't feel it at all? I must've been drunker than I thought when I left. That's the only excuse that explains why I have this ring. It's an honest mistake and easily remedied.

But what it doesn't explain is my picture on the front page of a trashy witch tabloid sucking Mystery Man's face and happily announcing our *engagement*.

"I'm not engaged," I mutter back, but it sounds like I don't believe myself.

"Then why do you have this?" Jae asks, flailing my hand in hers. The movement breaks my gaze, and I blink. And breathe? Slowly my faculties fire as Jae damn near drags the ring into her eye. "This thing looks like it cost more than my car, my entire checking and savings accounts combined, the business's bank accounts, your accounts—"

"What the fuck is happening?" I cut in.

Jae drags her gaze away from the ring, giving me an incredulous look. "You're asking me like I know? I left you at Big's and somehow you end up engaged and lip-locked with a Blanton all over the internet? Details! Now!"

"A who?"

Eyes somehow widening further, Jae's gaze darts from the ring to my face several times. My expression must make it clear my question is genuine.

"You're being serious right now, aren't you?"

"Yes." Finally, I pull my hand away, and my expression morphs into a soft sneer. "He only told me his name was…Fuck, what was it? Corey? Cam? Cade?"

"Yes, Aldrich *Cade* Blanton!" Jae looks like I confessed I don't know the entire alphabet or how to add one plus one. "Do you really not know who he is?" The look on my face is again enough because Jae's jaw slackens in surprise. Her hands flail. "He's on practically every news outlet right now! He's months away from taking over his grandfather's seat on The Council. You seriously didn't know?!"

"No! I just thought he was some pampered asshole!"

Jae barks back in disbelief, "How could you not have known?"

"Well, he didn't say anything either!" I retort lamely, as if that's an excuse. "He could've introduced himself properly and not been all 'Hey, I'm mysterious and an asshole but like, I'm kinda hot in the dark so—'"

"Drop your panties and marry me?"

"No!" I shout. "He came into Big's and acted like an ass, so I threw water in his face—"

"What?!" Jae shrieks, and horror runs across her face.

I make an exaggerated show of throwing my hand between us and wriggling my ring finger. "Don't worry, *clearly* the story turns out fine!"

Jae follows on my heels when I vault up and make for the bathroom. "But how the hell did you end up *engaged*?"

"I didn't!" I reaffirm with a final exasperated glare before closing the bathroom door between us. "We just played pool and drank and ended up going home together. I woke up this morning and Faded out."

I can see the shock on Jae's face through the door based on the noise of absolute disgust she makes. "You assaulted, slept with, and then *walked out* on a Blanton?!"

"I didn't know who he was! Nor do I care!" Reaching for the toilet paper makes me sneer because all I see is the sapphires glistening in the overhead light, mocking me the entire way. As if they have a mind of their own and they're choosing to make me cringe. "This is your fault!" I shout. "If you stayed, none of this would've happened!"

The maniacal laughter that fills the apartment says Jae doesn't agree in the slightest. At least one of us can laugh. I lose the ability to do anything when I wrap my fingers around the ring to take it off because it doesn't move. Momentarily motionless with shock, I forget to breathe again. But when a panicked realization cascades down my spine, it jolts me back into motion, and I tug as hard as I can.

The cold metal doesn't move a single millimeter.

I almost throw up from the swell of nausea that overtakes me, worse than anything I've felt all day. Panic is an ever present plague for me today, it seems. My heart rate flares again and heat overtakes my body as I inspect the ring *adhered* to my finger. I pull and pull and pull, but the thing doesn't budge. It's like I'm tugging on a boulder that water erosion has embedded into the earth for over a millennium. The force of my tug doesn't even move my hand; I can't even feel the pressure on my finger.

Which only means one thing: this ring is enchanted.

There's not much further my heart can sink without falling out of my ass at this point. Panic dusts my tongue in a fresh layer of sour as I stare at my hand, hearing nothing more than static.

Fuck. Fuck, fuck, fuck. What can I do? It's not too tight because I can't feel it on my skin. Maybe I can find something to stick down between it and my finger to get better leverage because no way someone enchanted this ring. I refuse to believe that much bad luck can happen in a single night.

Sudden adrenaline drowns out the pain in my head and dread in my chest; I thrash through the bathroom to find something, anything—*yes*! A bobby pin! Triumph sears through me as I unceremoniously hold up my treasured find, as if there's someone around to see it. It just as quickly fades to resentment when the bobby pen doesn't slide beneath the metal band, even though there's enough room. It just bounces off some unseen shield every time I try desperately to force it underneath.

Say goodbye to my heart because it's never coming back from the all-encompassing pit of dread in my stomach. It's down at the bottom, not beating. I've died, and the only thing keeping me afloat right now is the lick of dismay and taste of utter embarrassment.

No. No, no, no! I refuse to believe some ancient magic is adhering this metal to my finger. It's just *stuck*. Super fucking stuck. Good goddesses above. All I can hope is that it's not a 'need to be cut off' kind of stuck.

I need something slick. That will do it. That will get it off. I rip open the second door in the bathroom that links my room to the living room, and I'm through it just as quickly, charging toward the kitchen.

"What's happening right now?" Jae's voice calls behind me as I tear open a cabinet door.

"It won't come off!" I shout, and I'm at the sink, dousing my hand in olive oil before Jae can catch up.

"Mis, what the—"

But her words stop short when she makes it to the island counter that overlooks our living room because she sees the same thing I've been seeing for the last two minutes. I almost vomit into the sink because that means I'm not making this up. I'm living an actual nightmare. Even with olive oil seeping over every part of my hand except beneath the ring, the damn thing won't budge. Panic constricts my throat. I push it, pull it. I smack it on the washcloth over the middle of the sink and try with all my might to drag the ring off.

It doesn't move.

"Stop—Stop, Mis!" Jae's hands are on my forearms then, tugging them apart.

"No!" I try to pull my arms away. "I have to get this off! It's enchanted, it's—"

"*Cursed!*" Jae shouts back. "It could be cursed, so stop! It hasn't killed you, but keep tugging on it like that and it might!"

That word slaps me in the face with logic like a glass of ice cold water. A curse. Of course. Someone could have tainted this ring with dark magic meant to harm the person who removes it. Darker magic is malignant. It festers and feeds off negativity and worry, and I could make it even more powerful just by freaking out. I doubt that Mystery Man would've done it himself based on the very hazy recollection I have of him, but that doesn't mean that someone in his family didn't place a curse on this ring throughout its lifetime.

Jae's right, yet again, and her words slacken my entire body; with a little prying, she's able to drag my hands apart, setting both in different sections of our sink. "You need to calm down. Do you hear me?" There's a quietude in her voice that she's trying to impress upon me.

"It won't come off…"

"I know," she affirms, letting go now that she can trust I won't inadvertently hurt myself. She turns the sink's taps all the way hot, just the way I like it, and picks up the bottle of soap we keep beside the faucet to douse my hands. "Wash that off, then sit down. Okay?"

"Jae, I need to figure out how to—"

"You're not going to figure out anything while freaking out like this, are you?" Jae motions toward my hands, which still haven't moved.

"Right…" I try to cling to the calm that's attempting to battle away the panic.

"Okay, then what you're going to do is wash that off—"

"Sit down," we say in unison.

"And relax. Exactly," Jae finishes. "I'm going to go to the store to restock some herbs and things we're out of. When I get back, we'll see what we can do. Okay?"

Although slight, Jae's words make the churning in my stomach lessen. I internally praise her ability to stay calm under pressure. If I were alone, I most certainly wouldn't be washing my hands clean of this oil just to *sit*. But she's right. Right now, that's the only legitimate option I have until my body no longer shakes from uncertainty.

"Okay." I force out a deep exhale that pushes out some of the panic. Warm water on my oily hands helps, too.

Jae turns and disappears into her room as I wash the remnants of my panic off of myself, and the counter and sink that suffered the same fate. Embarrassment coats my tongue as I wash the slimy yellow liquid down the drain, noting I'll have to replace the bottle because it's now empty.

Goddesses fucking dammit. Add this moment and all of last night to my increasingly long list of failures. I never should've gone home with Mystery Man. This must be the goddesses punishment for me trying to move on from Amber when it was my fault she walked out. I should've gone home to deal with the emotions inside me rather than pushing them away in favor of a night to help forget them. I knew better. I don't make good decisions when I'm drunk. And yet again, it's landed me somewhere unimaginable.

My heart pounds against my chest as I dry my hands and the counter, disregarding the deep breaths I try to take. The ashamed adrenaline surging through me makes me pace into the living room; I debate sitting, but there's no way I can right now. My feet wander back and forth, wearing a hole in our carpet, while I struggle to avoid looking at my hand.

I swear the ring gleams in the daylight with every sway of my arms just to taunt me. It wins. Looking at my hand makes it hard to breathe again, and I sink onto the sofa, foot shaking against the floor. I reach—specifically with my right hand—to pick up the television remote to find some sort of distraction. Beverly Hills Kitchen Witch is on, as it always is, so I turn it up louder than necessary. Although it's mine and

Jae's comfort show, right now it only eases the tension in me the smallest fraction.

"Okay," Jae's voice comes before she reappears dressed and staring at her phone. "I'm leaving. While I'm gone, you message him and get—"

"Message him?! Absolutely not!"

Jae's head snaps up, and she glares at me. "Time to put your big witch panties on Misty Hayes." The look on my face must show exactly how disgusted the thought of messaging Mr. Last Night makes me, because she barks a laugh and turns toward the door. "You need to figure out how to get that ring off before we end up killing you by doing something wrong. So message your *fiancé*."

Again, her logic is sound and soothing. All I can reply with is, "He's not my fiancé." It sounds as lame out loud as in my head.

Jae snorts, slipping on her shoes beside the door with an exasperated roll of her eyes. "Message him. It's probably not cursed, but we should be sure. We can look for counter-enchantments when I get back, but it'd be even easier if we found out the exact enchantment that was placed on it. Which the ring's actual owner should know. So message your *not*-fiancé."

My phone buzzes before I can think of the next lame excuse why I don't want to message Mystery Man; it's Jae sending me the article that started all of my panic.

"Oh, and you're coming back to work at The Toasted Oak," Jae adds. "You clearly need someone to watch you so you don't make awful decisions, and I need a barista."

She's out the door before I can complain about how deeply I loath coffee, as if that would do any good. It wouldn't. I'm just left alone with my phone and a keen awareness that it's just my embarrassment that doesn't want me to reach out to Cade.

How could I not have known he's a future member of The Council?

The Council is a big deal. Wixan-kind have a lot to thank them for, even though there's bad, too. When humans wrought an unthinkable brutality upon us over eight hundred years ago, they gathered all magical beings and put us all into hiding. We survived for centuries in the shadows, but when technology advanced so far that magical creatures could no longer roam the forest without pictures being taken and shared in newspapers all over the world, they brought us back into the light through The Exposure. Both moves saved thousands of lives because magic use is finite.

When The Great Divide happened, Wixan-kind agreed to use our powers as the shield between worlds. Over the centuries, we lost countless lives to burn out trying to protect the secrets in this world. Our numbers dwindled so low that extinction was a real possibility. So The Council integrated with human governments as they once had centuries before, and when the time was right, made magical creatures known again. Thanks to The Exposure, everyone knows The Council and what they can do.

Except me, apparently, because last night I fucked a future member and hadn't known him from Adam. Every other wixan would've known who he was while they stared him in the face, naked and sweating. But not me. In my defense, I didn't get a good look at him. Okay. That's a lie. I got several deliciously good looks at him last night. I just hadn't a clue who he was because I never cared to pay attention to The Council. They did nothing for me other than make my life more difficult by saying what magicks I can and cannot use, so I didn't care about who they were or what they did.

Until now. Until a future member became my fucking fiancé.

Embarrassment floods me again as I click the link and it opens to the picture I haven't been able to scrub from my mind underneath the headline "Councilor Heir Finds Unexpected Love!"

"My ass," I bite out bitterly to no one but myself and the image that's staring back at me.

The words taste of vermouth and disappointment that only grows as I scroll the page down to see the full image again. My stomach tightens. My hand on this man's face is far more delicate than it should be. So is our half-kiss. The way our lips are brushing through our smiles is much too loving for strangers who met hours before. We look like a proper couple that's been together for five years and not five hours, and I look *proud* of it. I'm *flaunting* the ring that still encircles my left finger, laying in a bed that I laid in once and never intended to lie in again.

In a picture I don't even remember taking that I realize was posted to his social media account as I inspect the image more thoroughly. His username is in the screenshot the author of this article took. Why this photo exists in the world makes more and even less sense now.

Rarely do I ever open my social media apps, but I do now. I type in the username, but I'm greeted by someone more unknown than the man from last night. Whoever owns this profile, presumably managed by some public relations team, is different. This is the future Councilor Aldrich Cade Blanton, next in line for a pretentious ass job. This is an Oxford button down and blue suit wearing man who would never dare to roll his sleeves in public wearing a sterile, placid smile in every photo. He looks like he'd shake your hand in greeting and then forget you when he turned around to the next person in line.

This can't be the same person, but it is. The eyebrows, the nose. The salt-and-pepper curls trying their damnedest to be free from their confines. The genuinely beautiful hazel eyes that shine through the placidity of this profile. They could only belong to the man I met last night. Everything else? Nothing matches the jovial person who pounded whiskeys and then me after we played pool in a dive bar on a Wednesday night. There are no wide smiles or barks of laughter in these staged photos. There's no evidence of happiness behind his blank stares as he poses shaking hands with other placid people.

Most importantly, there's no evidence of me.

Someone wiped any thought that this man would ever be engaged to a witch like me from this feed in the brief hours between when he posted the photo and the article releasing. All evidence of me is gone.

But deleting a photo doesn't change that something happened. It doesn't delete the kisses and the desperation. It certainly doesn't change the fact that I still have his ring around my finger and it won't come off. If whatever plan Jae has doesn't work, there is only one other person on the planet who might help get this ring off. He's also the person who likely wants said ring back the most so he can give it to his actual future fiancée.

So I click the button on his profile to send him a direct message.

I have your ring. Should we meet?

CHAPTER
EIGHT

I HADN'T A CLUE I COULD HATE AN INANIMATE OBJECT THE WAY I DESPISE this ring. I've disliked my fair share of chairs and picture frames and houses. Shit, I even thoroughly dislike coffee in every form. But I've never *loathed* something so passionately that I'd rather cut off my finger than look at it.

I wish never to see another sapphire in my life. Especially not the two still encircling my ring finger, mocking me every time I glance at my hand. As a barista at The Toasted Oak, Jae's pride and joy and highly successful coffee and tea cafe in the heart of downtown Raleigh, that's practically my entire job. I almost signed up this morning to clean the bathrooms because I'd have to wear gloves. Alex, Jae's assistant manager, volunteered instead. But I would have just for a break from the incessant sight of this damned ring, even though I abhor cleaning bathrooms.

It doesn't help that it's stunning, making every time it gleams in the overhead fluorescent lighting more taunting.

If only Jae and I had found a counter-enchantment to release the ring's death grip the night after that article was written. We didn't, but we did stay up much later than my post-hangover head would've liked attempting the scant few rituals we found in the grimoires we had on hand. One burned right ring finger, now sporting a colorful bandage, and a charred coffee table later, we called it quits. That was all we could do in the absence of any response from Cade—which even now, four days later, still hasn't come.

Maybe Aldrich Cade Blanton, heir to a bank account that's likely bigger than several countries' treasuries, doesn't care about retrieving his ring. What's one ring when you can afford a million, right? But I care. Deeply. I don't want this damn thing permanently adhered to me, and I most certainly don't want to be known as his fiancée. Perhaps that's the biggest aggravation of it all: I didn't choose any of this, and yet, I'm suffering the consequences alone.

Added to the shitshow my life already was? It's difficult to keep myself from breaking down in the middle of the shop. How the hell did I end up engaged to a random man, who's famous enough that I should've known to stay away from him, just months after being walked out on? I'm in the papers and tabloids and social media posts of countless random people, and part of me wonders if Amber has seen them. Or if she has, does she even care? The other part of me loathes that I'm wondering about that at all. Her opinion doesn't matter. The only person's opinion that does right now is mine. But frankly, that opinion is lower than how I feel about this ring.

Annoyance surges through me with that thought as I pull the lever to steam some almond milk. The sapphires catch the light again and glint like they're winking at me after telling me some haughty joke I don't understand. I want to rip the ring off and chuck it across the room, but there's no escaping it. With every frothy drink I make, I hear the ring spewing everything I'm sure its owner will say whenever he finally responds.

"As if I'd ever be on your finger."

"You're certainly not good enough for me."

"You'll ruin me like you ruined my real engagement."

Okay. That one's not nice, but it's true. I've narrowly snagged the thing on the counter countless times because I'm not accustomed to the extra height hanging off my finger. I almost do it again when I slap a lid on a plain black coffee with a little room for cream—No. No fucking way. My stomach bottoms out as I look at the name printed on the ticket. I beg the goddesses that it isn't the same man.

It is. A pair of sparkling hazel eyes and a soft smile are staring back at me when I look up from the frother. Cade. As if my thoughts summoned him here. Static over-saturates the sound in my ears and I stand motionless, gawking at this man under lights far brighter than shabby pool table chandeliers and makeshift candlelight.

Today, he isn't Aldrich, the future Councilor. Today, he's just Cade, and he may look even more like Cade than he did the night we met. Reconciling him with the man on that sterile profile that I sent a message to several days back is hard. A thin cotton hoodie hugs and emphasizes the curves of his arms and chest, drawing my eyes down to where he's rolled the sleeves up to display his shimmering onyx markings. Memories threaten to heat my body, but I won't let them. I snap my gaze back up, but perhaps that's worse than allowing the memories to overtake me. The backwards baseball hat, with the faintest tuft of his curls sticking out over the small strap, almost makes my knees weak. Thankfully, they don't buckle, but only because another cup slides down in front of me and startles me out of whatever trance his appearance put me in.

"It's more polite to greet customers than gawk at them." Frivolity permeates his voice.

I sneer. The sticker on his cup says 'Cade', but I bite out, "Jackass," and push the cup across the counter a little harder than necessary.

He laughs and steps to the far side of the circular counter marked 'Pick Up.' I refuse to look his way on principle when he says, "Thank you."

"You're welcome," slips out on instinct, even though I don't mean it. I quickly add, "It's also more polite to respond to someone's messages instead of showing up at their job."

"I did respond," he asserts, seriousness replacing levity so suddenly that it makes me peer over my shoulder to watch his expression shift from complacency to dismay.

"Rebecca," I call to the room at large before frowning deeply. "I definitely didn't get a message."

"You did," he reaffirms, and the surety of his voice almost makes me doubt myself. "You messaged my public profile, and one of the media managers saw it and told me. I responded from my personal account."

At least a million people have seen us lip-locked in a photo in an online tabloid, but one person close to him reading the message I sent makes me more embarrassed? How can that be possible? My cheeks heat. "What an awkward conversation that must've been," I say and slap another label on a cup.

"That's the least uncomfortable conversation I've had in the last four days, I assure you," he replies. "Nothing is more embarrassing than my *fiancée* not even reading my messages."

The emphasis he puts on that word hangs me up and I jerk, fumbling the next cup I reach to grab. I recover, but there's no way he didn't see it. "I'm not your fiancée," I say plainly. "And I never saw a message."

"I assumed. When you didn't read them, I thought showing up here was my only option to get the ring back."

I scoff and pull the lever to steam milk instead of responding. Perhaps I shouldn't feel as perturbed as I do that he only came to retrieve his ring and not see me, but I am. I won't reveal that, though. He was just a one-night stand. Nothing more. A fact of which I'll be sure of once I get this ring off.

I put a lid on a latte and say, "Lee." I turn to Cade with a sneer. "How did you know where 'here' was?"

Lee walks up between us and stands, adjusting his single blonde roast to his liking. Cade peaks his head around him, saying confusedly, "Because you sent me a message?"

"My profile doesn't have any of my information."

"But it does have a few pictures with a friend."

"Jeanne," I call before shooting him another annoyed glare. "So you stalked me through my friend's account?"

Jeanne steps up and asks, "Can I get a stopper?" At the same moment that Cade says, "It wasn't stalking." I nearly snort at the aversion that overtakes Jeanne's smile. She shoots Cade a sneer when she plugs her drink, just as unaware of who he is as I was on that fateful night a few days ago. That makes me feel marginally better because I can see her green wixan's markings on her arm. I'd feel worse if she wasn't magical.

Sheepishness sweeps over Cade's face at her response, and he politely nods Jeanne off before turning back to me. "Her account has this business's page tagged all over it, and the first picture this morning was of you standing in the same spot you are now. Made it pretty simple to find you."

Jae's eyes are wide when my narrowed glare turns to where she stands at the registers at the back of the room, taking orders. She either heard him over the noise of the shop or his thoughts were just as loud as his voice. Either way, she's grinning and there's not a hint of remorse on her face. It hits me then: she knew he arrived before I did and didn't give me any sort of warning. She gleefully helped Cade find me and then allowed him to sneak up on me when he did finally show up. Okay, that's probably an exaggeration. Jae couldn't have left her spot, even if she wanted. If I stepped out of my thoughts for a single moment in the last half hour, I probably would've seen him waiting for his drink or in line to order. The shop's not that big, and he had to walk past me twice to get to where he stands now.

But that doesn't stop me from mouthing, "*I hate you*," down the bar. Jae knows I don't, so she winks at me and turns her attention back to the last person remaining in the now vacant line, only ordering a muffin. Which is just perfect because that means there's no drinks that I can focus on rather than him. So I narrow my sneer a little more before turning back to Cade.

"Whatever. Is there some special way to get the damned thing off? Because I can't."

That's clearly the wrong thing to say. His eyes widen almost comically, and his lips pull into a thin line that says more than his silence. A familiar worry careens through me. He doesn't help by asking in a voice far less jovial, "You can't take the ring off?"

"I just said that, didn't I?" Displaying, I raise both hands and tug as hard as I can on the ring. Wide hazel eyes remain glued to my hand until I stop and shrug. "Proof enough? I'd love to give it back, but I can't. The only thing I can think of is to have it cut off."

"That won't work," he breathes.

I barely hear the words over the noise of the shop, but I do, and the tangle of worry inside me knots a little further. I don't want to believe him in the slightest, but the sincerity in his gaze meeting mine doesn't make that easy. He seems confident in his words. Very fucking confident. And worried.

"W-why? Why won't it work?"

"You accepted my proposal."

"No." That word comes out a lot louder than intended. A few people from the crop of tables behind him glance up. Recognition dawns on several of their faces and makes me feel even more like a fool. They know who he is, and they just saw me yell at him, no matter how accidental. Shaking my head, I lean over the counter and say quieter but much firmer, "No, I didn't. And you didn't propose."

"Yes, I did. In the bath. And you said yes."

I stare at him, mouth agape, unable to respond. Mostly because he's right. That happened judging by the hazy recollections of our night that returned to me over the last four days while obsessing over what I couldn't remember. I claimed this ring and him as my own while in his bathtub. The cloudy memories walk to the front of my mind now along with a budding horror inside me.

No. My head shakes. It couldn't have been real. It can't be real. We didn't mean it.

The ring patently stuck to my ring finger says otherwise.

"T-that was obviously a joke. We don't know one another."

As if realizing himself and where he stands, Cade's spine straightens and his gaze darts around the room for something it seems he doesn't find. He turns back to me and quietly says, "Can we take this somewhere more private? I'd prefer not to end up on the front of another tabloid fighting with my new fiancée in public, days after we announced our engagement."

"I'm not your fiancée," I hiss reflexively.

"I'm well aware," Cade replies, voice low. "But every person turning to look at us right now doesn't. I don't want to end up on the front of another magazine. Do you?" Clearly, the two seconds of silence I offer in response is answer enough. "So, can you take a break now?"

The retort, 'No, because I'm working to make money to pay my rent. Do you know that word?' poises on the tip of my tongue, but firm hands wrap around my biceps and stop me. Jae slathers on a wide yet weary grin and says, "Yes, she can absolutely go on break right now," before I can do anything to stop her.

Cade takes that as gospel. "Outside?"

"Perfect," Jae says, nodding while Cade turns toward the door.

"What the hell," I snap as Jae unlaces my apron, pushing me out of my spot on the cushioned standing pad. She has the good sense to look sheepish when I cut a glare at her. "You posted me on the business's pages?"

"I thought posting you might bring in some business. I didn't expect him to show up here, but it worked out. You two need to talk." Sheepishness is completely erased as a wide grin stretches across her face, and I notice the deep violet tint to her eyes—a telltale sign that she's recently heard more thoughts than her own. Most times, she can control when it happens, but some people make reading their minds so incredibly easy that they slip through her shields. "Though, I could've done without all those thoughts he was *screaming* about you—"

"Stay out of his mind!" I scold. "You know better!"

"It's not my fault he was shouting them at me like an open book!" She grins and slaps her hands on my back, pushing me toward the split in the counter. Just before we make it, she leans in and whispers to me, "Honestly, I'm so fucking horny right now. The things he thought—"

"Ugh! I don't want to know!"

Only because I don't want to hear what Jae has to say do I relent and throw off my smock to meet Cade outside. Jae pushes his coffee into my hand that he must've forgotten in the same panic that plagues me again as I round the counter. Recognition grows on the faces of some of the people in the dining room; they know who just walked out moments before me, and they're realizing now where they've seen me before. The headlines write themselves along the walls with every person I pass. I stare forward, shoulders tighter than they've been for the last several days, but I don't quicken my steps. Not in my own workplace. This is my space, and he will not ruin it for me, even if the mounting dread and chasm of discomfort in my stomach says differently.

CHAPTER

NINE

Cade leans against an inconspicuous black sedan parallel parked right in front of The Toasted Oak. It's ordinary, and not what I envision from an individual in his tax bracket or position. It blends into the crowd of everyday passersby. But in this light and regular clothing, maybe Cade himself does, too.

Various lightings make this man appear completely different. There's 'dimly lit bar' Cade, 'fluorescent coffee shop' Cade, and 'ring-lit sterile' Aldrich. Then there's whoever this man is, leaning against his car with his hands in his pockets and his face upturned toward any sunrays that break through the overcast above. He almost looks whimsical. Ordinary, with his sleeves rolled down to cover the markings I know are there, but still somehow magical.

A frigid breeze whooshes down the block then, bathing my arms in goosebumps, and I understand why his sleeves are down. He's not hiding from people; he's sheltering from the weather that I ignored in my haste to escape the increasing interest inside the shop. Today isn't one of those wonderful early-March days where summer temperatures warm the height of the day and sweater weather cools the evening. Yesterday was. It was a beautiful seventy degree day that brought everyone out to the park across from the shop and into our ordering queue. Today, not so much. It's one of those weirdly gray days between a beautiful one and an arctic draft where the sun can't quite break all the way through the clouds.

All that to say: I need my jacket. But it's too late to turn back now, even for warmth. Cade's already dropped his chin to look at me. Expectantly.

I shuffle toward him, close enough to hear but not touch. He acts like we both haven't been watching one another and takes me in from head to toe before smoothly saying, "I'd ask if you wanted to grab a cup of coffee but—" he flails a limp hand toward mine then the shop.

I remember the cup in my hand then and hold it out to him. "It's the one you ordered. I hate coffee."

His expression curls into one of disbelief as he takes the cup, but he puffs out what I assume is an attempt at a laugh that brings a crooked smile back to his face. "We're learning things about one another. That's good."

I choose to ignore whatever conversation he's struggling to start with that comment and glance toward the park over his shoulder. On those beautiful spring days, people overfill the small copse of trees and the pathways that wind between them. There's never a bench free for long. People rotate in and out, reading or chatting with friends, inspecting the enchanted, perpetually blooming flowers, or drinking their freshly brewed coffees. Today's cloudy sky leaves it mostly empty other than the people seeking a hint of green during their monotonous daily life.

I point toward the empty pathways. "We can take a walk to talk."

He peers over his shoulder, brows furrowed when he looks back. Another breeze cuts through the trees and my bones at that moment, and I cannot suppress a shiver. "You're cold. Let's just sit in my car," he says, pushing off of it. With the same skepticism he offered the park, I glance at the passenger side door. I've never been good at concealing my emotions; they play all over my face through most situations. Now is no different, apparently, because he adds, "Or not. Got another idea close by that's inside?"

I almost say yes in reflex, knowing mine and Jae's apartment is behind me inside, up an elevator, but thankfully another breeze gusts and whirls my hair into my face and stops me short. I sneer at the cockiness that flirts with his expression. "Fine, but the doors stay unlocked the entire time."

Digging into his pocket, he pulls out and dangles a single key from his finger. "You can hold this."

Unlocking the doors, he hands his car key out in a show of earnestness. I eye it, but snag it as he opens the passenger side door and moves aside. Part of me is getting annoyed with how expectant he seems to be for me to follow along with his movements. I've never been one to do things the way other people expect me to; especially not a man I don't know. I've always been this way, headstrong and obstinate. It's helped me in the past, but it's also one of my biggest character flaws. I know.

I won't start solving that issue now, though; I just scoff and bury my arms together across my chest for warmth while shuffling around his car. The driver's side has a lot of extra leg room when I sink into it, showing exactly how different we are in height, as if it wasn't already obvious. There's mystification on his face when it appears in the passenger side door opening. Bewilderment shakes his head, and he's smiling softly when he finally slips into the car and closes the door.

Clearly, that was unexpected; as is me stretching as far as I can to push my foot down on the brake. Lights all across the dashboard flare to life when I turn on his car, although I can't hear the engine actually start. Cars so new that they still smell of the formaldehyde used in the manufacturing process have the luxury of silence. My fifteen-year-old beater doesn't share the same. Nor does it share the fancy display screens, electronic gauges, or chrome finishes decorating the dashboard. His car may look ordinary on the outside, but it screams luxury on the inside; maybe that's the perfect allegory for him, too.

I almost say something about that, but music blares to life and takes us both by surprise before I can make some crude joke. Apparently, the Cade who drove here was in a different mood than the man who stood in the coffee shop moments ago. He quickly fumbles to turn down the music before I can make out exactly what the rhythm is, but it sounds familiar. Like something I've heard countless times but I just can't place it.

I sit a bit stunned as he turns up the heat and the seat warmers and says, "Sorry about that."

"Well then," I say, and it nearly sounds like a joke with the way I scoff out a laugh.

He chuckles too. "*Well then*, it's good to see you again."

"Oh, have we met before?" I ask with a sudden incredulity. "I'm not sure we have, Mr. Councilor."

He clearly doesn't take that as a joke, and I'm not sure I even meant it as one. A budding calm drops off his face. "Would it have mattered if I told you?"

I open my mouth to respond, but something seizes the words in my throat. Honestly, I don't know if it would have. Does it even matter now? He's just a man with what I can only assume is a shitty job. Actually, he's an ass with a shitty job.

I almost laugh at that thought, but externally, I shrug. "I just would've known why you were a jackass."

I'm not sure if the way his eyebrows raise is because of intrigue or offense. "And why's that? Because you're over-generalizing me into a group of people you think I fit into based on cherry picked information?" His tone definitely indicates the latter, and guilt builds inside me.

He's right. That's precisely what I did, even though I blame people for doing that same thing to me based on my markings. I took one aspect of him and made a sweeping generalization about his entire being without considering anything else I know about him, which is admittedly very little. Although I didn't mean to, I won't admit that's what I did. I just answer with a sneer and that cockiness shows again on his face, telling me he knows he's right.

"How do I get this ring off?" I bite out to move this moment along.

"Would you mind if I—" He motions toward my hand.

"Think I'm incapable of removing a ring?"

"No. I just like to confirm things for myself."

"A micromanager," I say. "You're right, we are learning things about each other."

He arches a brow, barely moving his head to slant his gaze up at me. The action slides a coy smile across my face as I hold my hand out to him, wiggling my ring finger, knowing he won't be successful in doing anything but tugging on something that won't move. The action makes us both pause; I wonder if he's also reliving a very similar moment in his bathtub when our every touch was like lightning cracking across a mid-summer storm.

There are no sparks this time when his fingers brush my palm, though. My abdomen, however, coils tighter, albeit in a drastically different way than the last time he touched me. My nerves are a wreck, and it's not because of how close he is or how wonderful I now realize he smells in this confined space or the faint music playing in the background. It's because he's inspecting my finger and his expression is slowly souring as he turns my hand over repeatedly.

For a moment, when he slots his fingers around the ring, I let myself hope that perhaps if someone from his bloodline tries to take it off, it will work. It very well could. Old magic is fickle, and based on how antique he made this ring sound, there's no telling how ancient the magic lacing the metal is. Maybe his magical signature will loosen whatever enchantment plagues me and we can be on our merry ways, back to our separate lives.

My hope is pointless, however. I deflate when he wraps his fingers around the ring and tugs. It doesn't move, just like I knew it wouldn't. Brows furrowing, he tugs again. And again. And then he cuts his eyes to mine and back to the ring a few times as if asking for permission for something. I only nod. Nothing he tries will work, but I'll let him get out whatever he needs to in order to soothe his distress, just like I still do every morning when I wake up and every night before bed.

Long fingers that could easily encircle my wrist twice wrap around me, and I ignore the warmth they bring as he maneuvers us until he's got our hands where he wants them. With a deep exhale, his grip tightens to hold my hand in place as he pulls as hard as he can. The only place I feel anything is my wrist. Just like every time I try to remove this accursed ring, I can't feel anything on my finger and it doesn't move a single inch.

He keeps tugging until I wince from the grip around my wrist, at which he seems to realize himself. "Sorry," he rushes out and releases me.

I just nod into the uncomfortable silence his apology leaves. We sit speechless, and the longer it drags, the more anxiety claws up my spine. The vacant look in his eyes as he watches my hand while gazing into nothing, screams louder than any words.

"So?" I ask, trying not to sound desperate, although I am. "How do I get it off?"

"You can't." Those words plummet my heart into my stomach again. The look on his face only sinks it further into the pit that's perpetually lingered there since Thursday morning.

"Funny." I laugh mirthlessly. "Very funny joke."

But his face remains stoic, and he doesn't say a word. He doesn't do a damn thing other than sigh while sinking back into the bucket of the passenger seat. The glassiness that works over his eyes when he draws into his own thoughts, gazing out the windshield at the traffic light changing from yellow to red, makes me sick. I feel like I'm going to yammy all over this shiny car.

"I need you to laugh, please. Right now," I beg, unable to keep the desperation from my voice.

His face pinches inward like that statement pains him. It absolutely pains me. Still, he doesn't speak or laugh or say a single thing to reassure me. Maybe it's because he knows there's nothing he can say.

"Good goddesses," I force out through lips that barely move, frozen in disbelief. "This can't be real."

"It's as real as we are." His voice is flat. "You accepted my proposal wholeheartedly. It won't come off until one of us dies."

That makes it impossible to breathe. "It-It can't possibly be real!" I don't intend for my voice to raise, but it does.

He finally looks at me, face still furrowed inward in a way that makes him look like he's thinking too hard about something too perplexing. "We wield magic and a magic ring is unbelievable to you?"

I hiss a disgruntled sound. "That's not what I meant. I mean that we can't be engaged!"

"Why not?"

I'm not sure why the flippancy of that question throws me off. My eyes widen, and I feel my head shaking. "Because we don't know one another?" I scoff. "Because my ex just fucking walked out on me? Because we met in a bar and had a one night stand? That's it. That's fucking it. We absolutely are not engaged. I can't be engaged to someone that I don't even know how old they are or their favorite color! I barely remembered your name the next morning!" Dramatically, I throw my left hand up between us. "If this didn't get stuck, we never would've seen each other again. So we're not engaged. End of story."

He doesn't say a word. Instead, he shifts a little in his seat, sighs, and glances out the windshield at nothing again. He's silent for a painfully long moment; so silent that I can hear my own labored breaths nearly drowning out the lowered music. The unnerving calmness on his face makes the anxiety in me boil into hysteria. Indignation sears through me at just how calm he is. I open my mouth to say whatever string of words choose to come out, but he beats me to it.

"Thirty-six."

Shock jerks my head back and my brows together. "What?"

He cuts his eyes toward me, but his head barely turns my way. "You said you don't know how old I am. I'm thirty-six."

This time, shock blows my expression wide. My mouth hangs open as I shake my head to process how that could possibly be the only answer he came up with after everything I just said.

"That's *all* you heard?"

"No," he says flatly. "My favorite color is purple."

"Oh, fuck off!" I screech. "You know what I meant!"

"Yes, I do. But those were the only things that I can do anything about. Now you know your fiancé's age and favorite color because there's nothing we can do to get that ring off."

"The hell we can't!" My voice is probably too loud. I don't care. "You didn't ask me to marry you and I didn't accept. It was a joke. We don't know one another and we're not engaged. End of story."

He says nothing to stop me from throwing open the door. The car screams because I still have the key clenched tightly in my hand. If I were a better person, maybe I would've politely handed it back to him. I'm not. I haphazardly toss it toward the back of the driver's seat. He's staring at it when I lean back in for good measure and say, "I'm getting this ring sawed off even if I have to lose my finger. I'll mail it back."

He snorts. "You can keep the finger—"

I slam the door, probably too hard. I don't care.

When I charge back into the shop, Jae looks like she's going to say something, but she reads the look on my face. Or maybe whatever thoughts are actually coherent in my mind are loud enough for her to hear. Whatever it is, she decides to tell me later and doesn't stop me from stomping through the store to the stockroom in the back. Kicking several bags of coffee beans doesn't do a single thing other than make my toes hurt. Maybe my pride, too. Nothing's going to help the ever present anxiety or nausea inside me other than removing this accursed ring. But right now…I can't muster the hope that it will ever come off.

CHAPTER

TEN

Tuesdays at The Toasted Oak are typically a respite from the weekend and Monday slog, allowing us to refresh and prepare for the rest of the week. Jae and I don't know why, but it's been this way since she first opened the doors over eight years ago. Today? Based on the number of iced coffees with almond milk I've made, this may end up being her best sales day ever. It's been non-stop business from open to well past closing for four days straight, all because Aldrich Cade Blanton won't leave me the hell alone.

Okay, well…the droves of people that flock here during the day are only partly his fault. He could work anywhere else in the world other than the small table in the corner taking up as little space as possible. But everyone else could also stop posting about him being here on every social media account they have, Jae included. She's capitalizing on the buzz of Cade's presence by staying open late and posting sneaky photos of me and him working around the store. Several of which gossip tabloids picked up for articles alongside random photos of us in his car last week that look intimate and not like we were arguing. Accompanying headlines are instructing people to come here for face time with their future Councilor, and it seems every wixan in the Triangle area is doing as they're told.

There was even a small line at the front door when Jae and I walked down from the apartment to open the shop just before six this morning. It's getting asinine now. I've seen at least seven—no, no, there's Frank, so I've seen eight people here every day for the last four days. Most of whom don't even approach him. They just weirdly point and stare or awkwardly take a not so hidden picture of him while whispering to their friends. Or, hell, attempt to steal him away from me if the snide remarks and cutting glares I've endured are any sign. As if there's anything to actually steal.

Part of me wants to scream, "He's just an annoying man who doesn't know when to quit!" until they shrink away and find someone else to stalk. Or at least stand outside to watch him like he's an animal behind glass at a zoo. The other part of me knows it won't make a difference. Even if to me he's just some man I slept with once, to everyone else, Cade is a future Councilor and, apparently, a rather big fucking deal.

That makes him the easiest person to pin my unpleasant mood and aching feet on. If he didn't visit every day from just after opening to just before closing to work, sip coffee, eat lunch, and enjoy tea, these crowds wouldn't be here either. More importantly, I wouldn't have to work so hard.

Yes, I know that in the grand scheme of things, he can't leave me alone. I have his ring. I also know his presence is more helpful than harmful. Jae might make enough money to pay off a few loans if business stays this booming. All because I slept with the wrong—or right—man. That doesn't stop me from wanting him to leave.

His name is on the last ticket that slides my way and my eyes instinctively travel to his corner. "Visitor" number seven before noon is still talking at Cade with her hands, but Cade is nodding along and making it appear like the woman has his full attention. She doesn't. Ever the chameleon, Cade holds himself differently depending on who approaches him. When a lobbyist finds their way into his space, his spine is ramrod straight, shoulders pulled back, and face fully placid as he tells them to fuck off in far more eloquent words. His broad shoulders sit a little looser when salespeople work up the courage to approach him, but he's still aristocratic.

It's when he finds a visitor truly intriguing that he settles into his chair with loose shoulders, an inviting smile, direct eye contact, and complete attentiveness. More often than not, the people who bring this Cade out are the ones that other Councilors would label as a nobody. His real constituents. One's with gripes about the latest magical laws enacted or ideas on how to shape the future of our society. Even a small child who spoke her truth about the impacts of deforestation on dragon habitats, with her mother standing proudly behind her.

Not that I've specifically noticed or anything…All of that would be obvious to anyone who sat through four days of these conversations. Anyone could tell which visitors Cade would efficiently avoid and which he'd hear out.

Based on the stiffness in his face now, Visitor Seven is nearing the end of her time limit. With the slowness in the rush, I take it upon myself to stretch my legs and take Cade his coffee. Maybe that'll make Visitor Seven leave and force one more person out the doors to slow this day down. Before I turn, I pick up a stir stick and drop it in the cup beside the frother, where I've been counting the visitors in case I need to win a bet with Jae later. By the time I look up, the woman is walking away with a mixture of happiness yet befuddlement on her face.

Visitor Eight beats me to Cade, however, and the sudden and undeniable stiffness in his posture can only mean that this man won't last long. Good. Another one quickly out the door, and hopefully my interruption will move it along quicker. A disgust deeper than I've seen in the last several days morphs Cade's face by the time I make it to him. It doesn't fade when I wedge around Visitor Eight to stand between them. The man scoffs and his exaggerated breath blows through my hair.

I ignore him and say to Cade, "Your coffee."

Cade, however, isn't ignoring Visitor Eight at all. Disgust shifts to something downright repulsive in the several seconds it takes for me to look at the table and set his coffee down. "Leave," he says, and he didn't intend the explicit command for me.

Visitor Eight attempts to hide his annoyance with another puff of air. "Mr. Blanton, if I could—"

"You may not. And if you ever look at my fiancée like you just did again, I'll make sure you can't look at anything else. Leave."

In the second it takes for his gaze to slip to mine, a demureness reshapes the displeasure on his face. Hazel eyes shine up at me, and for the first time I think I might understand the phrase "their eyes sparkle." In combination with his words, something in me flips; I'm able to hide the shudder behind the tightening in my abdomen, but it doesn't stop me from inhaling deeply. I shouldn't react this way, considering I'm not actually his fiancée, but...I like the way he so freely claims our fake relationship and the defensiveness he shows of me.

"Thank you, beautiful," he says, and his voice is far softer than I expect.

Nodding a bit dumbly, I counter with, "A-anything else I can get?"

"A glass of water, please?"

"Of course," I reply without hesitation.

Visitor Eight sputters dramatically in what I can only assume is an effort to seek our attention. Neither Cade nor I give it to him. I simply ask, "You want ice?"

"Not today."

I can actually hear Visitor Eight's blood pressure rising behind me. He still hasn't walked away, so I keep this conversation going by asking, "What size?"

I almost grin when the man huffs and spins on his heels. The wind he creates swishes my hair as he disappears into the crowd of people. Or I assume he does because Cade's posture fully relaxes.

"Thanks for that." He motions toward his cup.

"You can thank me by leaving with him," I say, leveling him with the smirk that I wanted to give Visitor Eight. He barks a sudden and full laugh and brings a lot of curious and envious eyes upon us. They're a reminder that I'm annoyed with him. Sneering at the lady beside me, mirroring the looks she's giving me, I hiss, "Will you be quiet?"

"No," he says through the remnants of his laughter.

As it fades, he shifts in his chair. This posture? It's one I haven't yet seen in his time here. He's facing me, opening himself fully, and I'm momentarily caught off guard by the look on his face and how he leans toward me. He's interested. And not in any way he's been interested before.

I lace my arms across my chest to hide how I want to squirm. "Whatever. I'll get your water—"

"Always so feisty," he interjects, eyes not leaving their steadfast hold on mine. "I don't want the water."

"Then what do you want?" My subconscious throws that question out. I hear it the same time he does; he instantly has an answer on the tip of his tongue. I squash whatever annoyingly charming statement it is by continuing, "I mean, why do you even come here to work if you just have to deal with that?"

"It gets me out of the office," he says and closes his laptop like he intends for me to stay and chat. "It's just a bonus that I get to see my fiancée and support her best friend's business."

"You know we're not—"

"Do I?" He finally breaks my gaze to look toward where my left hand's still buried deep in the opposite elbow.

Okay, yes, I do currently still possess his ring that costs a small fortune. That doesn't mean we're engaged. Whatever gargled sound of annoyance I make seems to amuse him more.

"Can you just find some other business to darken with your presence? We can barely keep up on a normal day, but Alex is on vacation so we're short staffed."

"And miss out on seeing your chipper face every day?"

I don't respond verbally, but my body does. I suppress the reaction again by forcing out a deep exhale. "Just ugh—all these people sitting around hoping you'll notice them are making my days awful."

"Noted." His grin grows and it's absolutely not the response I'm wanting at all, but I can't help but watch. "All of the customers bother you, but seeing me doesn't."

Goddesses above, help me. I almost smile. I can't help the flutter that walks across my skin, but I am able to purse my lips to hide any reaction. I hope it comes off more as a derisive pout than clearly hiding mirth behind tight lips. The way his eyes flash to it and brighten says differently.

"I promise that's not what I meant," I say to throw him off. "You're at the top of my shit list right now." Which is a feat, frankly, with Amber having held that position for so long. But I don't loathe this man like I do her. I'm just really annoyed with everything that comes along with his presence.

"Think so highly of me? Top of your list feels like an honor." He laughs and it makes me roll my eyes. Of everyone I know, he's the most able to make me do so this often.

"Nothing would be more honorable than you leaving."

Another huff leaves his lips, and with it goes his jovial expression. Seriousness replaces it. "It took longer than I expected, honestly."

"What did?"

"You kicking me out. I figured I'd last a few hours tops," he says. "But if I'm truly impacting your life that badly, I'll leave. I promise."

"Okay, well…Good." My words end up sounding like a confused question.

Cade notices something around me that brings his smile back. "Right after I finish my lunch and tell you what I've found regarding our situation."

Timing is always everything. Jae makes his timing perfect by sliding by me with a smile and a plate of our best selling sandwich in her hand. "Here you go."

"Exceptional service," Cade says with a smile. "And the coffee's delicious too."

"Flattery will get you everywhere," Jae replies with a wink before she turns to me and bounces her eyebrows.

I just shoo her off without a second thought. The only thought I'm clinging to is his last statement. "You found something?"

"Hmm?" His attention is now on his sandwich.

"You said you found something. And you're just now telling me? What is it?"

"You may want to get back. I hear you're short staffed. I'll tell you on your break." I narrow my eyes on him. He only smiles and says, "Oh, and don't forget."

"Forget what?"

"To add another stirrer to your cup for that guy. Don't want you to lose count."

I can't suppress the jerk of my head, but I play it off by rolling it into a shake. "No clue what you mean."

He hums and winks at me before taking a bite of his sandwich. I wonder how many times he winks in a day. It seems to be his favorite hobby, like eye rolling is mine. I respond in kind before turning to stomp back to my station. I do add the stirrer to the cup, but I turn my back toward him so he can't see me do it.

The line of drink tickets waiting for me is completely my fault for stepping away for two minutes. Huffing and rolling the tension from my shoulders, I scan the tickets for what will be the quickest—one large ice water, no ice. Perfect. I pull out a large cup and fill it while scanning the next several tickets. Two identical lattes so those will go easy together. I snag those two tickets as I reach for a lid for the water.

"Chloe," I say and push the cup over the pickup counter, immediately turning to pull milk out of the refrigerator at my knees.

I need to learn to look up. Maybe that will help me catch some of the surprising things that happen to me in this building before they happen or save me the embarrassment of ending up on another trashy witch gossip column. Or maybe, I need to cut the problem off at the root and find some time magic that can send me back a week, maybe even two. That way, I can prevent myself from visiting Big's that Wednesday. That would resolve all of my most pressing and most annoying problems. If only it wasn't so illegal.

If it wasn't, maybe when I straighten, a full cup of ice water, no ice wouldn't slam against my face.

It takes a moment for me to realize what happened and why the entire room gasped and went silent. When I do, my heart sinks into my stomach and rage constricts my throat. It only doubles when I look down and see all of my clothing darkened with water as droplets drip off my face. It's a small consolation that the woman still holding the empty cup pointing at me is trembling when I finally bring my wide eyes up from my now soaked attire.

Anger contorts her beautiful face, too. Resentment, maybe? They look and feel the same. Trust me, I know at this moment because I'm feeling them both, too, directed at this woman. Problem is: I have no idea why she has these strong feelings toward me.

I've never once in my life seen her. Not that she blends in. She's tall, proper, and has long blonde hair with a lived in style that's clearly maintained on a regular basis. A form fitting dress that looks more expensive than my entire closet hugs her stunning body, making me in my worn jeans and faded tee-shirt feel a little subpar. Diamonds dazzle in her ears, matching the necklace around her neck. From head to toe, I have zero familiarity of who this person is, other than knowing there's simmering rage in her, too.

She sneers and shakily sets the cup down on the counter, looks me dead in the face, and says, "Next time, don't steal someone's life."

Ah. So it's karmic retribution that made this unfairly adorable woman open the lid of her drink and douse me with it. If her words weren't confirmation enough of who she is, Cade appearing at the scene of this crime of passion with a look of absolute horror on his face is.

Chloe is the woman who Cade was on his way to propose to when he ran head-first into Big's and me. The ring held firmly on my hand should be adorning her thin, long ring finger. Not mine. This woman was supposed to be the next Mrs. Blanton, and to her, I stole that right. Without even knowing it.

What she doesn't know is that I didn't want any of it. I don't want any of it. I don't want every single pair of eyes on me when I'm in the room, which is yet again happening. I don't want the man that came with the ring or the life he lives. I don't want the ring on my finger. And I most certainly don't want to be the reason someone thinks I've stolen a life they were promised. But I'm getting all of that regardless.

The entire dining area is watching and whispering and there are several people with their phones out recording the silent seconds where I try to figure out how to respond. I most certainly will not cause a scene because I don't want any further excuse to be on the front page of news outlets. Though, judging by the number of articles that were written of Cade and me just sitting in a car, I doubt I'll escape them no matter how much I don't want the klout. I'm not lying. I don't want this.

Cade speaks before I can figure out what to say. "Chloe, what—"

"Shut up," I hiss as my brain finally filters through and processes the moment. Running a hand quickly down my face, I flick the water away and make sure the annoyance is obvious when I turn to Cade and say, "I don't need or want you to defend me. I don't need or want anything from you."

Chloe's eyes are wide when I turn to her and her resentment is gone. She's confused now, and I think that's fair. Clearly Cade hasn't explained the situation to her at all, and while part of me understands why, he basically never broke up with this woman and showed up in the news engaged to someone else.

So I try to take that into account and smile, leaning over the counter to say so only she and Cade can hear, "From one woman who doesn't know him to another, I didn't and still don't want the life he promised you. I had no intention of stealing it. When I get this ring off, you can happily have it and the jackass that comes with it."

Shock is clearly making her unable to do anything but blink; I don't wait for her to fully process the statement before turning on my heels and making for the stockroom for a moment of reprieve from the attention I loathe. I don't care about her response. Not in the slightest.

But one thing does stop me short to turn back to her with. "And water? Seriously?"

Sheepishness overtakes shock but flashes away just as quickly. "I-I didn't want to be too wasteful."

Godsdammit I didn't expect that. Cheapness maybe. But not that. Scoffing, I say, "Well, I guess that's actually pretty thoughtful," and turn to storm as lamely as I possibly can into the stockroom so the videos and pictures aren't interesting. I won't give anyone the satisfaction of seeing me running off scorned and embarrassed even if I am.

ELEVEN

A WAVE OF THICK TENSION TRAVELS UP MY ENTIRE BODY FROM THE TIPS of my toes the moment the stockroom door flaps shut. I haphazardly punch the air in lieu of making any noise that customers back in the dining area could hear. Thankfully, because the door opens and shuts again before I'm done flailing.

Part of me doesn't need the confirmation I seek when glancing over my shoulder because I know who just walked in. The indignation that courses through me when I do is palpable. All I wanted was one moment alone to let out a few frustrated and embarrassed tears. A few quiet minutes to shed some steam and clear the water from my clothes before reemerging into a room full of people who just witnessed one of the most embarrassing moments of my life.

Cade doesn't give me that luxury.

"You're kidding, right?" I snarl. "What is it with you following people? What makes you think I want to see you right now?"

"Nothing," he admits.

"At least you're self aware." A flick of my hand whisks away the water from my clothes, and I barely register the sting of whatever I've given away in exchange for the magic. The anger in me is simmering so vehemently that it drowns out every other feeling. It burns in the back of my throat and in the corners of my eyes. I attempt to blink it away. I won't cry in front of him. "You're not even supposed to be in here. Just go away."

Sheepishly, he motions over his shoulder with his thumb. "Jae said I could come make sure you're okay—"

"Of course she did," I cut in, voice low and unmistakably annoyed. "Am I okay? After being assaulted at my own job? Yeah, I'm peachy fucking keen. Thanks for asking."

"At least it was just water—"

"Just wat—" The strangled bark of disbelief that leaves my lips echoes in the room, and red momentarily flashes across my vision. "Of course it's just water and I can just dry it," I snarl, enunciating every word. "But it's the principle of what just happened that's the issue. You understand that, right? I didn't ask for this obligation." My ring finger bolts up between us like I'm holding up the one beside it.

Guilt riddles his face. "I know. I'm—"

"Then you know I definitely didn't ask to be followed by reporters or assaulted by a jealous whatever-she-is. Yet, here I am, standing in the stockroom of my own fucking job, covered in water waiting for yet another article to come out online about me and how much of a mess I am. How much of a mess my life and relationship are. So sure, I'll just wick all the water away."

There's a momentary silence after my words, and they linger heavily between us. Okay…it's a lot longer than a moment and in the time my words settle, several emotions flit openly over his face. He's clearly choosing not to conceal any of them because I know he can after watching his interactions for the past four days. Annoyance melts into understanding, and understanding bleeds into apprehension and apology. He shifts under the weight of my gaze, which I haven't managed before. It leaves him…

Actually, I don't know this expression or posture. I've never seen him nearly slump in on himself, shoulders hung low and his eyes cast down at the ground. Manicured eyebrows knit together, and he shifts from foot to foot. Not even in his car did he show such remorse. It's enough to hit me with a dash of humility, but not enough to cool the heat of rage on my cheeks. Humoring himself doesn't erase what happened.

"You're right. I'm sorry," he murmurs, looking up at me through his lashes and kicking his toes against the ground. "I didn't expect Chloe to show up, and I'm sorry about that. I'm sorry about all of this. If I knew the ring was enchanted, I never would've let you try it on. But I didn't, and I'm sorry."

The sincerity in his voice washes down more of the residual anger in the back of my throat, like the glass of lukewarm water that was just thrown in my face. I actually flinch at the words, and I wonder if my visceral response is because there's a part of me that's surprised to hear them at all. A genuine apology. Not some off-handed placation to sate me for a few days or more while nothing changed, while behavior stayed the same. There wasn't a moment where he blamed me and said I was at fault. There wasn't an underlying tone of disgust in the words. There wasn't a hint of the way Amber 'apologized' on the rare occasion that she did instead of me constantly apologizing for things that went wrong.

There was none of that. He openly took accountability for how I've been hurt, apologized, and meant it. His demeanor is enough to tell me he does genuinely mean the words, even if there's a part of me that doesn't want to believe it. But I try to believe that he's sorry for everything that's happened since the night we spent wrapped in his sheets and our lives became entangled in this weird, hopefully brief story.

"Thanks." My arms cross over my chest as a shield from the vulnerability. "But an apology doesn't make my pride hurt any less after being on the ass end of a large non-ice-water."

He huffs an astonished laugh, but it's rueful and a far departure from any I've heard in our short past. "No, but you handled it beautifully, so the media won't latch on to it. I'll make sure of that. I've already texted my team."

The snort of derision I let out is instinctual. "Great to know."

My words fade in the most awkward silence we've encountered together. Neither of us say anything. Cade pushes his hands into his pockets and keeps staring down at his foot. I lean back against the shelves, trying to cross my arms further to keep myself from shaking. The sounds of the shop fill the space that we don't, and the muffled murmuring only adds to the awkwardness. Just as I'm approaching the point where I can no longer stand it, he clears his throat.

"Anyway…Before I go, I want to tell you what we've found."

Oh…Wait. That's right. Being served my own method of punishment made me completely forget that he insinuated he found a potential solution to our problem. Something akin to hope buds in me again, but I try to beat it down, nodding my head for him to continue.

"Right…Well, my mother has had people scouring everywhere she can think of to find the documentation for the ring, but we're not having luck. She's also had some people researching up at The Annex in D.C. and they found something that might work."

The Annex. Archives founded long before libraries were a staple to non-magical communities. Through The Great Divide, it operated hidden but otherwise unhindered. Branches span the world over from Tokyo to London to Rio de Janeiro to Sydney and beyond. Surprisingly, The Council chose Raleigh as the home of their American Southern branch after The Exposure. Though not as large as its main counterpart in Washington, D.C. or the original location in Cairo, it still holds several floors worth of grimoires and spell books and research documents from centuries of wixan-kind. Among the stacks are thousands of years of our history alongside records of other magical beings.

I've been waiting for days for my application for re-admittance to be approved so I can reenter the stacks to research a way out of this situation because they've yet to digitize anything. I understand why all the knowledge that's held in their walls is only in their walls, though. On top of a majority of the books being infested with destructive magicks, the stacks are plentiful. It would take decades to scan them all into a secure platform for access to everyone around the world.

It does, however, make searching for a solution to my problem very cumbersome. Of course, though, someone on The Council would have no issue gaining access to the archives. The favoritism would make me more annoyed if, in this case, it didn't also help me.

"So?" I ask when he doesn't immediately continue.

"I know you said you'd cut your finger off to get rid of me, but I assumed you didn't actually want to maim yourself, which took out a surprisingly large majority of spells." I snort a vaguely humorful sound. The corner of his lips twitch like he's trying to suppress a laugh while digging his phone out of his pocket to hand to me. "An unbinding ritual. It's old, so it's—"

"Dangerous." I do everything in my power to not touch him as I take the phone.

The picture on his screen is of a book that looks older than the city of Raleigh, and possibly the entire country of America. Finding some ritual in a book that's over three centuries old doesn't give me much hope. But there is the slightest bit building in me at the prospect of *anything*. Especially if I can keep my finger. It's dashed just as quickly as every ounce of hope has been over the last week. Someone has already translated the instructions from the faded ink and the scraggly written language I don't know, and the first line squashes my optimism.

The apprehension must flash across my face because he says, "Yes, it's blood magic."

Hearing the words confirmed aloud drops my stomach. Blood magic. Ancient, as innate to this world as the shifting of tectonic plates, and just as dangerous. That magic is so powerful on a large scale that during The Exposure, The Council outlawed it; too many individuals throughout wixan history used it to topple empires and fight wars and gruesomely grow their way to the top of business, politics, and celebrity. When The Council wrote The Articles of Reincorporation, blood magic was at the top of the list of forbidden practices. It didn't stop anyone. Those taboo practices are still around on small scales, but those who use them tempt fate.

The blood spilled in spellwork is gone forever, just like all other sacrifices we make. It's not for the faint of heart. It takes commitment and dedication, and the largest toll a wixan can pay. If a spell doesn't work, the costs for repeating can grow exponentially.

All of which is why I'm astonished that a future member of The Council is suggesting we use such a spell. Though, I suppose using a little blood magic is better than cutting off my finger…And if a Councilor is participating with me, there's no way I can get reprimanded without shedding a lot of light on a lot of hidden things. Plus, it's only enough blood to coat my finger and the ring, so it isn't a huge toll to pay for a single attempt.

"If you're not busy tonight," Cade says when I've been silent for too long. "We can try—"

"No." I shake myself from the shock and stagnation and force out his phone between us. "We're not going to do anything. I'll do it and you can have your ring and be off to your future wife out there in no time. Just send me a picture or copy—"

"You're stubborn in all the wrong ways. Do you know that?"

Indignation draws another scoff past my far too tight lips. "Piss off. I am not."

A scowl works over his face, and he takes his phone. Instead of putting it away, he points it at my left hand. "Oh? Then I'm sure you know that having both parties involved in that original enchantment would make this unbinding ritual more potent."

Bristling, I say, "Of course I do."

"So then you're just being stubborn and refusing my help?" He pauses and actually expects a response. His eyebrows raise in question, and in reflex, mine furrow in distaste. He takes that as an answer, huffing and stuffing his phone back into his pocket. "Fine. I'll have someone bring copies of what you'll need tomorrow. Goodbye, Misty."

Not waiting for my response, he turns. I think that's a play right out of my own book, and it works fabulously because I hear myself saying, "Okay," to stop him from leaving, although I really don't want to.

He indeed stops just before the door, growing what seems like several inches when he turns back to me. It's the cocky grin that tells me I've stepped right into wherever he wanted to lead me.

"I'll help. On the condition you go on a single date with me if it fails."

Shock loosens my jaw, and I bark a grim laugh before the words fully process in my mind. Because there's no way he's being serious. Wheezing out my disbelief, I shake my head. "You're joking, right?"

"No."

A single word in a tone so sure it can only be true. He's not kidding. He's genuinely serious. I scoff in disbelief. "You goad me, then give me an ultimatum? How are you seriously asking me on a date right now?"

There wasn't much space between us to begin with in the small stockroom, but he closes the short distance with two leisurely steps. It forces me to have to look up at him to maintain eye contact. Far up. Again, it's like he's grown several inches more to tower over me with earnestness on his face and eyes cast downward over the ridge of his nose. This is another angle of his I haven't completely learned. Looking down at me from this close with intensity that I can almost taste.

"Unlike you, who evidently had the worst night of her life, the night we spent together was one of, if not the best, I've had in a long time," Cade admits. "I wasn't lying when I said I want to meet someone and fall in love. It turns out I met that someone a week ago and I can't stop thinking about her even when I try to focus on anything but her. And I don't know about you, but that's something I don't want to walk away from."

I don't know if he's looking for a response, but I'm confident that I don't have one. If I did, the words couldn't possibly make it through the sudden thickness in my throat.

Thankfully, or unthankfully, he continues before I can muster up any sort of response. "But if this ritual works, I will. I'll walk away just like you want, take my ring, and go marry some boring person I don't know and you'll only ever see me again in articles or magazines." There's another pause and I'm sure he's trying to gauge my reaction to the words. I try my hardest to stop the sudden and unexpected disappointment from careening over my face. He just sighs. "If it doesn't work, we're stuck together until the ring comes off, right?"

He actually waits for a response this time. The expectant look on his face says as much. I huff because he's not wrong. I'm not just going to keep this ring if this doesn't work, and he's not just going to walk away and let me keep it, either. It's a family heirloom and, more importantly, it's already promised to the woman who just threw water in my face. No matter how I feel about her, or about him, this ring is not mine. I have to give it back.

I begrudgingly bite out, "Yes."

"Yes?"

The quiet, questioning inflection hangs between us. He wants to know what I'm saying yes to. I'd also like to know, but I don't amend the statement. I just inhale to inflate myself, a thinly veiled attempt to make myself grander and more assertive here, trying and failing to ignore the way it seems to make his face alight. Like he likes my defiance.

"I need a day to recover," I say. "Be here Thursday when Alex is back, an hour after closing. We'll get the ring off and we can be done with this little obligation."

"I'll be here," he says without hesitation, and the surety in his voice hasn't changed at all. If anything, it's deeper. Somehow, he's also gotten closer. So close I can smell his cologne and the memory of it bathes my forearms in goosebumps. I don't look away to give him that power, but the eye contact makes his next words more bewildering. "But just so you know, I don't want to be done with this 'little obligation.' I haven't stopped thinking about you. And when we don't get that ring off, I'll prove that to you."

"That's only because I'm all over the news."

"I'm sure that's it." Laughter fills his voice now. "You looked me up yet?"

I scoff. "I'm getting more than enough of you during the day. The last thing I want to do when I get home is see more of you."

He smiles. And it's one of those smiles that lights your face from hairline to chin. No muscle goes untouched. Certainly not the response I expected for such a scathing statement, even if the lilt in my voice held a hint of playfulness. I also don't hate it, nearly smiling myself. I hide the emotion behind pursed lips.

"Good. Keep it that way."

"Telling me what to do now?" The question is facetious. I know exactly what he's saying. What I don't know is why I'm playfully lifting my brows at him.

"I've told you what to do before." That smile morphs into something far more salacious in a matter of seven words. He shifts closer again, but this time I think it's unconscious. I don't completely mind the closeness, and I'm fairly certain I contribute to the lack of space between us even if I play it off as swaying on my feet. "Don't look me up," he reiterates. "Let me be the one to tell you about myself and show you the person I really am. Not that fuck-all figurehead. Deal?"

"Promise. I won't spend a moment more of my time thinking about you."

Again he chuckles. "Then I'll get our supplies and see you Thursday, Princess."

He winks when those words wash over me, throttling my lungs. Not with annoyance, but with a fervor I probably wouldn't feel if I didn't know the feeling of his lips on mine and his cock buried inside me while he whispered them against my skin. I thank the goddesses that he turns and paces out the door without looking back to see me shiver from my toes to the crown of my head. Giving him that ammunition would put even more of a damper on any of the power I have in this odd relationship.

The Toasted Oak has deflated none when I step back out into the light of day. Some people are watching Cade pack his things, others are whispering between themselves while staring and pointing at me. In order to avoid ending up on the front of some trashy, barely famous tabloid flicking off customers, I don't raise my single finger at them. I only make my way back to my station and try to ignore the shop's buzzing.

The chimes above the door sings someone's departure. I can immediately tell it's Cade because the room seems to breathe an odd sigh of relief. I try not to glance out the window, but something inside me overpowers my logical side. Maybe his gaze calls to mine because he's watching me, one arm resting on the hood of his car. It's nonchalant, but it's obvious. He's not looking at any of the people sitting around, hoping to make a lasting impression. He's looking directly at me.

My heart staccatos in my chest, and no matter how much I deny it, I like it when he winks one last time before waiting for my response. I roll my eyes, but I also smile. That seems like more than the response he's expecting because one last grin stretches across his face before he sinks into his car and disappears.

During the rest of my shift, I catch myself smiling when I glance down at the ring more than once. I try to stop myself, but even when I'm in bed that night, I stare at the ring clouded in Charlie's fur as I pet him while falling asleep. I think I may even see the ring in my dreams. I know I see his smile.

CHAPTER

TWELVE

BEING A METEOROLOGIST IN THE SOUTH HAS TO BE SIMULTANEOUSLY ONE of the easiest and most challenging jobs in the entire region. In the winter, the rain can turn to snow in the blink of an eye when previously predicted to bypass the area entirely. In comparison, in the Spring, all one has to do is put 'sunny with a chance of rain in the afternoon' on every day's forecast for a guaranteed eighty-five percent accuracy. The only thing consistent in the forecast is that it's almost never right.

Today's forecast called for sun and seventy-five degrees. The black clouds shielding all sunrays have other plans. Sheets of rain pour down in an unrelenting deluge, making this day all the more gray by washing away the layer of green pollen that blanketed the entire state overnight. Between the storms keeping people in their office buildings to the increasing number of social media posts indicating a lack of Cade's presence, foot traffic is slower than it's been in days. Not even our usual customers came in today to work their afternoons away from their desks.

On any other day, I wouldn't complain. But today, the breaks in time were unbearable. Impatience is often my middle name. Waiting is the worst, and all I've done since waking with Jae's phone in my face is wait. The lack of customers made sitting behind the counter waiting for The Toasted Oak to close agonizing. The bountiful time I had to contemplate my life and what happens after Cade is gone for good wreaked havoc on my nerves, aided in no small part by the ring on my finger.

Silver glitters in the overhead lighting when I glance at my hand. A taunt, but it's one of the most beautiful taunts I've encountered. After over two weeks of trying to reject my feelings, I can no longer deny my fondness. I love this ring. The way some of my lighter markings end just perfectly under the band is endearing. It's like somehow my magic, through those lines I've lived with my whole life, fuels the sapphires' gleams.

But its beauty has just been a distraction from the downward spiral my life was on before that fateful night two weeks back. Everything since that night—the cameras, the photos, the articles, and the countless people whispering and pointing—were all just distractions. Cade was just a distraction.

With all the fuss and worry and endless nausea, I hadn't thought about being fired or dumped. A small blessing in disguise, but only just. Now, as I move toward this mistake's closure, I have to deal with the shit hand of cards I've dealt myself. I have to face my life, little that there is, as it teeters on a very precarious precipice that I'm not sure I can climb. I have to figure out where I'll land if I do indeed fall as I take the next steps to rebuild myself and my life.

Today's hours of near-silence brought all of that to the front of my mind, nestling right alongside the thoughts of no longer seeing this ring and the man who unwittingly bestowed it upon me—a belated realization that made my stomach hollower than expected. Never seeing Cade again was supposed to be a good thing. Him taking the ring and leaving without a second thought was the first step in renewing my life. Yet, for some reason, my every second, third, and fourth thought today has been about him and how the ring coming off means he'll actually be gone. Only a portion of which gave me any sort of relief. Every single thought about Cade leaving my life should make it easier to breathe. Hardly any of them did.

Sighing, I glance back out at the empty sidewalk. Still nothing other than the rivers of swirling rainwater and pollen make their way down.

The stockroom door flaps open and Jae barks a sound that's full of condescension. "I told you to stop staring at the door."

"I'm not," I reply with a petulant scoff. "I'm looking outside."

"For him," Jae says, and I snort a derisive sound that doesn't throw her off one bit. "You were the one who asked him not to come back until after closing."

"Well, it's after closing. He should be here."

"He'll be here. You've got—" she draws the word out until she's leaning back against the counter facing me. Her hand lifts, and she looks at her wrist with a far too eager grin as if she's actually wearing a watch. "Fifteen minutes until you told him to be here. So he's not late."

"I don't even know why I said he could come."

"Because as much as you hate him, you know he's right: having him will help."

"I don't hate him." Those words are out before I think them through, because I don't have to. I don't dislike Cade. Jae doesn't believe me. I add, "He's just annoyingly present. But once the ring is off, he'll be gone and I can focus on…anything else."

"I don't understand why you won't give him a chance." A regurgitated statement she's said every day for the last two weeks. The look of annoyance I give her doesn't perturb her at all. "Has he said that he doesn't want to be with you?"

No. The exact opposite, actually. But I won't give her that ammunition. She doesn't need more encouragement to turn me into her next romance novel. "It doesn't matter, anyway. He's got Little Miss Water-Thrower waiting in the wings. There's nothing to keep him here once this is all done."

"Oh, please stop the self-loathing bull," Jae demands flatly. "You know that you're way more interesting than Aquawoman Jr."

"Am I Aquawoman?" Jae's sudden and mischievous grin makes me snort a laugh that I don't intend. She's not wrong. I often flick water in people's faces, just like I did to Cade. Trying to hold back my smile is pointless, even though I'm brooding. Brooding and laughter don't go together unless you're best friends with Jae. The two don't stay mutually exclusive for long. I puff out the levity to gather back some semblance of indignation. "I'm not more interesting to him. They have more in common than we do."

"Because they're both rich?" There's exasperation in Jae's voice that not even I can overlook. "You said they didn't know one another. And as he himself told you, all you know about him is that he's thirty-six, rich, uber good looking, and he fucks like a—"

"Okay, I get it. I don't know him."

"So then you don't know that they're more similar than you and him, either. If he does stay around—which he absolutely will, and I'll bet a month's pay on that—will you give him a chance?"

I didn't tell Jae about his "one date to show you who I really am" stipulation if the ring doesn't come off. She's already far too invested in the idea of Cade and me together. She'd be insufferable if she knew. Plus, there's no actual guarantee that he even meant the words, other than it sounding like he did. Not that he's given me any indication he didn't. If anything, he's given me no reason at all to disbelieve he keeps his word; he's done everything he said he would since the day we met.

Nonetheless, all of me refuses to believe him. I can't stand the thought of trusting someone again, only to be let down when they inevitably walk away. There's no reason to get my hopes up about a future with this man.

"No," I say with a hollow authority. "He doesn't just get me by default. I'm not going to bow down and marry him because we got drunk and fucked."

"And I'm not telling you to do that," Jae replies. "Even though you clearly liked him and his dick enough to agree to marry him after one night."

I bark a laugh, but I make the sound as rueful as possible. "You're ridiculous."

"And you're lucky."

"How so?"

"You skipped the awkward parts of meeting someone. Now you don't have to spend six awkward dates deciding if you enjoy someone's company enough to fuck them. You don't have to worry about if they're good in bed or a decent kisser or if they have a job or will support themselves." She sneers like she's remembering some of the past men she's dated; some of whom we do not even mention by names other than fuckwad and dipshit. "That all fucking sucks. Trust me. And you got to skip all of it. With a Blanton. If nothing else, at least fuck him one more time before he's gone."

"For someone who reads all of those romance books, that's a really unromantic view of the world."

Jae shrugs, and another grin splits her features. "Take it from someone who does read all of those romance books—the protagonist almost always gets their billionaire no matter how hard they fight it."

"Well, not this protagonist, and not that billionaire," I reply confidently. "We don't know one another. We haven't even made it to that awkward period yet, and we won't. The ring is coming off tonight, and then this nightmare will be done. We can go back to our mostly boring lives of watching Beverly Hills Kitchen Witch on the couch too high to do anything else, and he can marry Chloe and never think about me again."

"Lame. Why are you so against him?"

"I'm not. It's just that…"

Silence slips between us as I glance back out to where the rain has lightened to a drizzle. I spend too long trying to come up with a reason. Partly because I don't have any excuses ready to go and partly because I don't really want to admit why I'm so against it. I truthfully haven't thought it through that far myself. But as the silence stretches, the reason becomes more and more obvious to the both of us: Amber, and her impact on everything I am and everything I think, feel, and do.

I can see the growing displeasure on Jae's face in my peripheral, and shame builds inside me so thick it tightens in my chest. "Please tell me it's not because of her." I remain silent, and she knows I can't. "Seriously?"

"We just broke up," I murmur. "We could—"

"What? Get back together so she can leave you high and dry without a fucking word and break your heart again?"

"Ouch." It's the only word I can manage because she's right. Again.

Firm hands settle on my arms, pulling me back into our conversation and out of the painful memories I see shifting through the hazy rain. Gentle thumbs put pressure into my biceps, keeping me here and not in my mind. Jae's expression softens and opens itself up to comforting me. Again. "Look, babe, I'm sorry, but this was the sixth time. Sixth. In the span of what, five years? That's more than once a year. At this point, there's no excuse not to see it. She's a completely useless person, and even if she does try to weasel her way back into your life, you have to move on. You have to—"

"It was my fault." I mutter the admission I've been holding onto for months. "I can't just move on. Not when it was my fault."

It takes a moment for me to realize that Jae's silence, wide eyes, and parted lips are because she's appalled. She's processing my words at the same time I am. Unavoidable shame and remorse constrict my throat, threatening tears to slip down my cheeks. Her gaze hardens, and she frowns; my chagrin only doubles at the movement.

I attempt looking away but she moves into my line of sight. "You don't really think it's your fault that Amber kept walking out, do you?"

The unmistakable concern in her voice makes the distress on her face harder to ignore. My throat tightens further, burning with the insurmountable heat of humiliation. "It...doesn't matter."

Jae's grip tightens on my biceps, and while it's intended to be reassuring, right now it doesn't work. It feels more like she's caging me into her inescapable and unwavering gaze. I can't make myself smile to convince her I'm okay. Not this time. I can barely look at her through the haze of moisture in my eyes.

She squeezes tighter. "It absolutely does matter, Misty. Please tell me you don't think her being a completely manipulative trash person is your fault."

Eyes averting to the space beside Jae's head, I blink rapidly to keep in tears. My silence is answer enough. Shock crosses Jae's face, and her grip tightens on me in an unconscious stiffening.

Over the last few months, I haven't been able to hide how I feel about Amber and I's split behind the false bravado of sass like I once had. But it seems I did hide the reasons it ate away at me so badly. Jae hasn't known I've blamed myself.

Deep in my core, I know I'm the reason Amber walked out. I was inconsiderate; I always agreed to things before running it by her or checking if she was free. I always made her look like the bad guy when it turned out we couldn't go because she didn't want to. I was indecisive and constantly changed my mind after it was made up. I debated if I'd made the right decisions after I made them, and burdened her with the worry that plagued me. I was loud and dramatic and rarely did I ever suffer my emotions alone. I was forgetful and sporadic. All of that's just the top of the list of things that are still wrong with me to this day. So…it's no surprise that my partner walked out time and time again.

Loving me can't be easy.

I'm sure something in my childhood made me the way I am. Maybe my father leaving before I was born or every shitty thing that happened with my grandmother after my mother passed away. Maybe, maybe, maybe. But those are excuses. They all just mean Amber was right: I'm a shitty person, and I need to do better.

A glassy sheen coats glittering violet eyes and unmitigated rage outlines every one of Jae's delicate features when I drag my gaze back to hers. In any other circumstance, I'd be mad that she listened in on the thoughts swirling in my mind. Not right now. I'm relieved I don't have to admit any of that out loud. She heard everything, and I can feel her shaking against where she holds me.

Air passes her lips in scoffs and huffs and puffs, head shaking, eyes blinking rapidly, before she finally manages to say, "I want to punch Amber right in her filthy, manipulative, dirty, skanky fucking mou—"

The chimes above the door ring out and drag both Jae and I's attention toward a mostly wet Cade standing in the doorway with wide eyes. He doesn't step in; he just takes in the obviously tense scene between us and I wonder how much of what Jae said he heard.

In a smooth move, Jae releases my shoulders, and her face turns up into a polite smile. "Hey! Come on in."

Cade wavers, but takes a single step into the doorway. I turn away, discreetly wiping my eyes from any offending moisture that escaped, but I can still feel a very heavy gaze on me as Jae moves to greet him.

"Sorry about being a few minutes early," Cade says, hesitancy and concern filling his voice. I ignore it and attempt to make myself look busy with finalizing our closing routine. He's not concerned for me, I tell myself. He's concerned about the ring on my finger. That's it.

"Nonsense! You're right on time," Jae replies and the two front door locks click into place.

"Locking us in?"

"We live upstairs, so we'll leave through the lobby entrance to the elevators," Jae says. "Let me just flip the lights off and we can head up."

With that, Jae disappears into the back, leaving behind silence as the lights turn off set by set. But when the last set turns off and Jae doesn't reappear, I can't push out greeting him any longer. He's been standing beside the split in the counter waiting for me to address him. I turn and nod stiffly.

"Hey, Misty."

I offer some sort of lip movement that's supposed to resemble a smile. "Hey."

"Everything alright?" The concern in his voice is playing all over his expression. I don't want to look at it nor acknowledge the reason he so freely shows his emotions to me and no one else.

Clearly, the grief from the moment he witnessed must be lingering. I flex my muscles to calm it, but it's pointless. The unease doesn't disappear from his face. So I push the hand with his ring on it up between us and say, "Yeah. Just ready to get this off," to throw him off my scent.

He considers me for a moment. The concern doesn't fade. "Well, I hope it works."

"Do you?"

"I do. I don't like seeing people miserable. Especially not my fiancée."

I huff, but it's weak. "Thanks, I guess."

"'Thanks, I guess?' Now I know something's wrong. No sassy little comment about how we're not engaged?"

"I'm just tired."

"Surely you can do better than that," he says. I just roll my eyes and lean back against a table, arms crossing over my chest to hold myself and my emotions in. He's standing in front of me before I can tell him not to, even though I probably wouldn't have, expression unreadable and his hands in his pockets. "I get it. I'm a stranger. But if you do want to talk—"

"Don't you have a security team or something that needs to sweep my apartment for booby traps?"

"There she is." The left side of his lips turn up into a smirk. "And no."

"No? I'm genuinely shocked."

"I'll be fine between my enchantments, warded jewelry, my own power—"

"I get it," I say. "You exploit magicals for your own gain."

He snorts. "Nothing I have or own was exploited in any way. Everything was a consensual agreement and paid for."

"Because paying someone for their life-force is consensual."

"It's their jobs," he rebuts mildly. "Don't act like you haven't used your magic to make a dollar."

I have a retort on my tongue that I'd never, but…memories of dousing male patrons in bars with water before slapping them and taking a shot float to the front of my mind. I could easily make a couple hundred dollars a weekend while I was moonlighting as a bartender just offering off-the-menu hurricane shots. It was one of my biggest moneymakers, and I have a large spot on my leg that's hairless because of them.

Cade knows he's right, but doesn't belabor the point this time. Instead, he says, "I was serious. If you need to talk, I'm here."

"I think I'll save the trauma for another day."

There's a response on the tip of his tongue, but I can tell he bites it back and laughter fills its place instead. "Another day then." When he says it, it sounds way too much like a promise, but he pulls out a card from a small black bag I realize he's been holding and redirects my thoughts before they delve too deeply into why. "This is from Chloe."

That name stabs me through the heart in a way I never could've expected. In my state, my throat tightens again and the corners of my eyes heat. "Oh?" Is all I can manage, glancing between the card and him.

"I talked to her about everything," he says. "When I told her what happened, she was absolutely mortified about what she did."

I take the letter, inspecting my name in a delicate handwriting across the front. "You told her?"

"I didn't have much of a choice," he says, and a look I remember vividly from our night together floats over his face. The same one he wore when talking about his false engagement. "To no one's surprise, she'd heard some…things from my mother that weren't true. That's why she ended up here."

"Ah." A quiet stretches between us where he again looks at his feet. I hold up the envelope to draw him back and ask, "This my invitation to the wedding as a consolation prize then?"

His laughter doesn't sound mirthful. "No. The wedding is definitely off, considering I introduced her to someone else. It's an apology."

"You introduced her to someone else?"

"Yes. It wasn't her fault she didn't get proposed to. Just like it wasn't your fault that any of this happened. So I'm trying to fix my mistakes."

Ah…So he's on a quest just like I am, only slightly different destinations. He's being selfless in all of this, taking a brunt of the anger and humiliation in stride and finding two different women's happiness even if it means the detriment of his own. That stings my heart again, both because I hear that I'm a mistake he made and because he's willingly putting himself second, even if it hurts.

"Didn't she just throw water in my face over you?" I ask to lighten the mood.

"She's part of a Council family," he says. "They'll probably be married in a month."

"That's insane."

"Yeah, well, it's how a lot of those families live. I didn't think I did, too, but—" he nods toward my left hand and chuckles. "—I guess I do. Only took me a couple hours to propose."

Thankfully Jae reappears so that I don't have to think too much about any of that or acknowledge how knowing his wedding to Chloe is formally off the table makes me feel. Jae pulls Cade into polite conversation as we head toward the elevators inside the high-rise that The Toasted Oak sits in the bottom of. He holds the door open for us, offers to carry her things so she can easily lock the doors, and waits until we both walk into the elevator to follow us.

Under any other circumstance, it would be sweet of my significant other to do those things out of just the goodness of their heart. But this man isn't my significant other, even though the world thinks we're engaged. We're barely even acquaintances, and by the end of the night, we'll again be strangers.

Today is the last day that I'll see my fiancé, Aldrich Cade Blanton.

And then I can focus on myself for a while. For real. I can do the things I always tell Jae I'm doing after every time Amber leaves. I can… heal. That thought threatens tears again, but I blink them away, latching onto the small hope that builds as the elevator closes. I know I shouldn't let the feeling break through anything yet, but I can't help it.

The next leg of my life all starts with getting this ring off.

CHAPTER

THIRTEEN

Jae wasted one of her days off yesterday meticulously cleaning the apartment. I didn't complain, nor do I ever. I benefit from her neurotic need to make the apartment look like no one lives here when someone visits. A member of The Council coming to our little two bedroom, two baths in a high-rise that we shouldn't be able to afford? I ended up getting my closet organized last night regardless that Cade won't see it. I think she even scrubbed off some of the porcelain from the toilet in the bathroom I share with our visitors in her ever-obsessive quest for cleanliness.

As Cade stands curiously inspecting our living room, I'm overjoyed for Jae's quirk. For some unfathomable reason I refuse to identify, I find myself caring what he thinks. I watch, star-struck, like the people who visited The Toasted Oak to see him, as he scans our living room. Jae nor I ask him to remove his shoes; he simply follows our practiced motions, respecting her heritage, and exposes bright teal socks.

"Up to code?" Jae jokes.

Cade's laughter sings differently in our apartment. Deeper. Perhaps a little warmer? The lower ceilings have something to do with the sound being richer, no doubt. It's definitely not because I'm remembering it rumbling in my ear while he fucked me or how much I liked it.

"Far beyond. I wasn't expecting it to be so cozy."

"Mis does all the decor." Jae nods toward me, obvious and eager. "I'm going to change, and then we can get started."

Just like that, with a wink telling me it's on purpose, she leaves Cade and me alone in the living room that feels too small when her door closes. She's gone before I can muster a wide-eyed plea for her to stay.

"It's very homey. I like it," Cade says into the stifling silence that apparently only I feel.

"Yeah," I reply, as if that's an answer.

He chuckles in response and steps further into the room; the abrupt nausea annoys me as I remain motionless in the doorway. There's no reason that him thoroughly inspecting the intricacies of the decor he passes should make me sweat. But I do. It's an intimate immersion into my life, and he spends his time wisely, dutifully. I don't stop him; I remain rooted to the doormat as he takes in each picture he passes on the walls for a handful of seconds, doing the same with the art throughout the room. He peers over the island counter into the kitchen, nodding as if he's impressed. A movement that continues around the room while he wanders to the writing desk Jae's grandmother handed down to her, then the small reading nook Jae and I share in the corner under the window with plants that hang in front of it.

His attention snags on the bookcase on the far wall next to my bedroom door. Florals line every shelf and span off in all directions, weaving through grimoires and romance novels. Glass and plastic and painted clay unicorns decorate the spaces books don't fill, and he inspects every one like he actually cares, smiling to himself at some of Jae's books like he knows what saucy content lives inside. Perhaps he does because there's a wolfishness in the way he glances back and scans me that reminds me of that ill-fated, completely tantric night we spent together. I try to overlook the way my stomach flips, but it's impossible.

"I've always wondered what apartments in this building look like inside," he says.

"Fancy as fuck, is what." He chuckles and it almost makes me smile. "Jae got a really good deal when she signed the commercial space downstairs. I don't know how she managed to negotiate this lease, but we definitely wouldn't be able to afford it otherwise."

"No shit. I can't even afford it."

That makes me puff out something akin to a laugh, but it's far more condescending than intended. "Okay. Sure. Says the future Councilor with his own media team."

"Well, I can afford it, yes." That brash grin again spans his face. "But I wouldn't. There's no reason these apartments should be this expensive."

Instead of a reply, I just huff another half-laugh half-scoff as he looks toward the old wooden coffee table, littered with the scars of past castings and melted candle wax and the burn from our attempt to remove the ring. Jae and I have already arranged the simple casting circle we'll use tonight. There were a few patterns between the center and the circle itself, but nothing too difficult that we couldn't draw them last night with the chalk we use for all our castings.

Four candles sit at the quarter points around the bowl, outlined in diamond shapes, waiting to be lit. One of Jae's large black scrying bowls sits at the center with herbs to be burned at the bottom: basil, mugwort, patchouli, and wormwood. One of our smaller paring knives rests in the middle, both because I didn't want Charlie to knock it off and hurt himself and because it was also the most reasonable resting spot after we cleansed it. It felt right to reset the energy before Cade and I use it to cut ourselves open. Thinking of the imminence of our bloodletting makes another layer of nausea saturate my stomach.

The circle may be ready, but I'm not.

"Didn't have any trouble?" he asks, moving like he's been here before to settle onto the couch.

"No," I reply, unsure if he's even able to hear the words. I clear my throat and ask louder, "You have trouble with the rest?"

He shakes his head and pulls up the bag he's been holding into his lap, unloading the items he promised to bring and meticulously slotting them into spots around the circle. Moonstone, labradorite, and citrine stones bathed in the moon, petals from daffodils, lilies, and daisies, and a lock of his hair to nestle next to mine in the bowl. Watching him work shows another layer of personality that I haven't seen. He's thorough. The precision he uses while aligning all the last parts of our ritual feels like an aspect of him I *should* know based on the few hours we spent alone together. Including that fateful night.

But in my home on the couch that Jae and I bought recently, where we spend most of our time eating and watching Beverly Hills Kitchen Witch and just existing? I'm having trouble processing the mass mixture of emotions coursing through at the intimacy of it all.

Thank the goddesses Jae reemerges from her room with a flamboyant show of opening her door. "Alright!" she sings through the silence. "Let's get this ring off, shall we?"

"Yes!" I say too quickly.

Cade looks torn between laughing and frowning, but he nods his agreement. "Let's do it." I can tell Jae wants to spout some immature joke at that, but she refrains. He pulls out one last box as Jae takes up residence in her preferred spot on the love seat and sets it before her. "Phosphate. Just in case—"

"The spell burns my finger off." I'm not sure if my voice is soft, loud, annoyed, or bewildered. All, probably.

Cade nods again. "It shouldn't. The spell's just intended to cancel out other enchantments, but it is blood magic, so there's a slim chance that it could—"

"Burn my finger off."

This time, his expression drops, and manicured eyebrows furrow up at me. "If you don't want to—"

"No." I shake my head to emphasize the word. "We're doing it. Just..." Jae's already watching me with those worried eyes that never fail to cut straight through me when I glance at her. She doesn't need to say she's here for me; her eyes scream every word. "Just be ready."

Jae nods and encourages me by patting the cushion on the couch beside Cade. Slightly embarrassed that I still haven't moved away from the front door, I scurry forward and sink into it. The nerves tarrying in my gut flutter throughout my entire body, but I won't admit them aloud. Rarely have I practiced blood magic because I refuse to give that much of myself away. I want to outlive my mother, who returned to the waters far too young. I'd even love to outlive my grandfather, too. Giving away my blood too many times is a way to ensure neither of those things happen.

I also can't overlook the fact that part of my unease stems from not knowing what happens in my life if the ring doesn't come off. And also, what the future of my life looks like if it *does*. I'm nervous about it all, but there's nothing else for us to do. So I inhale deeply and force the unease out through my nose as Jae picks up the knife from the bowl and holds it out to me.

"Alright, Mis. You first. Just a little in the bowl and then coat your finger around the ring and the ring itself."

The blade is heavy in my hand, and I tremble as I glance between the tip and my index finger. Jae's watching me when I look at her again and gives me a small reassuring nod that eases some of my hesitancy. She's been there for me through all the major hurt and joy and happiness and pain in my life. She's my best friend. She held me when my mother died, planned my grandfather's funeral when I couldn't bear it. She happily burned the things my exes left around the apartment when I needed it; she took me to Korea to visit her whole family when we graduated high school because I'd never be able to go alone. And here she sits for me now, helping me through yet another one of my mistakes. I don't deserve a friend so wonderful.

She nods again and eases more of my anxiety, but I still hesitate a moment more because I know it's going to hurt.

"Fuck," I hiss as the blade sinks into my forefinger.

Blood pools when I pull the blade away, handing it handle first toward Jae. I don't look at anyone else; I just watch the blood drip from my finger into the dish, droplets splashing onto the dried herbs and slowly absorbing. The blood is warm on the cool metal when I coat the ring, warmer when I run my finger against my skin.

Nausea swims through me when I do because my blood seeps under the ring—the first thing since I woke up with it enchanted to my finger to penetrate whatever magic embeds itself in the metal. I'm not the only one who notices. Jae gasps, and she's wearing a bewildered smile when I glance her way. Cade, however, has his brows furrowed, eyes adhered to my finger. The furrow is gone before I can process what it means.

The blood on the tip of his finger is like warm silk against my skin when he cuts it. I try to ignore the heat that trails his touch as he slowly lines the other side of the ring. He's much more thorough and precise with the movement than I was, ensuring he doesn't miss a single spot. None of us miss how his blood, too, soaks beneath the ring.

I know I shouldn't get excited; I should keep a level head. But the notion makes a sudden excitement flare inside me.

"Okay, good. That's good. Next," Jae says before pulling out our well-used lighter to light the candles and the bowl of herbs. Fragrant smoke fills the air and wafts around my hand held above the bowl. The flames are warm against my palm, and I welcome the heat with optimism. With hope. With firm intention that this will work.

"We have to chant—" Jae checks the printed instructions, and reads, "Err… I don't know this language. Is it—"

"Irish Gaelic. It's *Bain draíocht*," Cade says.

"Remove magic," I translate with a snort. "So literal."

"I didn't say it was a sophisticated ritual," he replies with soft laughter. "You know Gaelic?"

"My grandfather taught me some. How do you?"

"The same," he replies. "My great-grandparents on my mother's side, the one who passed down the ring actually, were from Ireland. My dad's family is Polynesian."

"Two very different magics."

"It's an interesting mix," he says. "I got more of the Polynesian mana."

"Explains your markings," I say.

"And being a Protean," he adds. "A lot of Proteans have Poly in their blood. We say it's the salt in the air."

"Hmm, interesting," I say, looking back at my hand, which is still hovering over the bowl.

"So." Jae draws out the word into the renewed silence. "*Bain draíocht?*" Her lips pull in like she's trying and failing to suppress a smile.

"Bain draíocht," Cade replies, slightly correcting her again, and I can see the same realization on his face. We both momentarily forgot that we're bleeding and have coated my finger for the ritual. A new heat paints my cheeks.

"Got it. So we're ready?" She looks at us both with that barely hidden smile. I nod, and Cade does the same. "Then you first, Mis."

"Okay."

Sighing, I focus on my hand before closing my eyes and sinking into this moment. Into the intention. I center myself, focusing on what I want: removing this ring. Most magic isn't fan fair like the stories from before The Exposure made it seem. There aren't enormous cracks of lightning or thunderous explosions. There aren't huge flashes of light. There's just intent, focus, fortitude, and consistency. And a little heat.

Intent seeps through me and forces out another deeper sigh.

"Three, two, one," I count quietly before saying, "*Bain draíocht.*"

Cade and Jae's voices join mine for the second time. "*Bain draíocht.*"

The sounds from the outside world fade away.

Bain draíocht.

My muscles tighten.

Bain draíocht.

Heat breaks out across my body.

Bain draíocht.

My fingers tingle; I can taste the magic on my tongue, sweet like powdered sugar, with a hint of copper lingering in the aftertaste.

Bain draíocht.

It burns. Immediately, the blood on my skin feels like it's on fire. I try to hold back the pain and let it work, let it seer this magic right off of me. But seconds turn the heat to blinding agony and I can't keep my eyes closed anymore. They fly open as I squeal, "Ow! Fuck, fuck—"

Like asked, Jae is ready. I don't screech a third 'fuck' before white powder covers my hand, my forearm, my lap, *my everything*. Immediately, I slam my hand against the largest pile of it on my body to coat the underneath of my finger. I don't know if the phosphate can get under the enchantment, but the burn stops, though not quickly. It simmers for as long as it takes for me to process what happened.

For a drawn out moment, I can hear the world outside as if I'm standing in it. It's so quiet in the living room that I hear the cars driving on the wet roads below. The racing of my heart slowly drowns it all out as I pull my hand away from my chest. It shakes, white powder falling onto my lap like the ashes of my hope. I doubt it will work, but I inhale as shakily as I can and try to tug the ring off.

It doesn't move.

My stomach bottoms out. Heat worse than the fire that my finger suffered seers through me, stinging the corners of my eyes and choking me. I try to hold it all in, oscillating between anger and raw, unmitigated disappointment, but it's impossible.

I built this up. I got excited and let myself hope. Once again, it was all for naught. I didn't realize how much I'd hung on this until it all crashed down around me.

Jae and Cade are both looking at me with equal unease when I fall back into reality.

I can't keep the disappointment from my voice when I vault from the sofa. "T-thanks… for… trying, I guess," I say before rushing to my room without waiting for any response. All I want to do is cry, and I won't do that in front of Cade. But my room immediately feels too small when the door closes behind me. Every wall caves and crowds out any light that tries to seep in. I feel tears slide hot down my cheeks before my breath catches, bouncing my chest.

There's a gentle knock that makes me blink away more droplets that try to escape. In my distress, I expect Jae on the other side when I pull it open, waiting with wide arms and complete concern on her face. It's not. The broad chest I look into makes me nearly start crying.

Worried hazel eyes meet mine instead of liquid lavender when I finally work up the nerve to glance far enough up to see Cade's face. "What?" I hiss unintentionally, voice watery. "Come to claim your date?"

"No. I know when to joke and when not to. I just wanted to say that I'm sorry."

"For what?" Anger replaces the heat of sadness, and I know I shouldn't take it out on him, but I can't help it. "Do you know what you're sorry for, or are you just saying that because you think I want to hear it? Do you even know why I'm upset?"

"I know exactly why I'm apologizing, and I at least think I know why you're upset." There's surety in his voice. "You didn't ask for any of the publicity or getting water thrown in your face or for your picture to be on every tabloid known to fucking man. But beyond all of that… I know how badly you wanted this to work, and I'm sorry it didn't. I'm sorry for all of it. I'll keep searching for anything that'll help us get rid of this…*little obligation*."

That phrase. It clearly scorned him yesterday. Hearing it said back in the low tone that his voice dropped into for those words? I see how it did. The words roll off his tongue like a curse, and not the same kind that left two willing and able people magically engaged. I wonder if this is how he felt when I said the words. It sort of sucks. I just nod because I can't do much else.

A barely there puff of laughter leaves a teasing glint on his features. "You may even still be the tiniest bit mad about how badly I beat you at pool."

I snort and throw my arms across my chest, again protecting myself from the oncoming emotionality. "Not in the slightest," I retort on principle, letting the words linger as his soft laughter fills the space and then fades into a reluctant smile.

"I'm going to head out, but I'll need your number," he says.

"Why?"

"To let you know if my family can find anything else at The Annex."

"I'm just going to go and research myself."

"You're a member?" There's a hint of surprise in the question.

"I was," I reply flatly. "I reapplied for a month." Even just the thought of shelling out that much money makes me and my jobless wallet wince. He doesn't miss it.

"Council members and family get free entry. You can use my free guest pass and save the money."

I roll my eyes. "Of course you get free entry."

"One of the very few perks," he replies. "But that means I'll have to join you."

I'm silent for a long moment, just watching him. He's doing the same of me, but it's like he's watching a wild animal he stumbled across in the woods, waiting to see if I'll bolt away. I just cross my arms a little further. "Fine."

"Fine?"

"Yes, fine, okay. Whatever."

His lips twitch again. "I'll still need your number so we can schedule—"

"Tomorrow?" I cut in. "I want to get this done."

He hesitates for a moment, brows furrowing. He rarely looks

away from me when we talk, but he does now, glancing down into nothing. His eyes flick back and forth, and I can tell he's mentally rearranging his schedule in his head before he nods. "I can make tomorrow work."

"Okay, then I'll meet you there. One?"

"One is perfect. I'll see you then." He dips his head like he's bowing. "Good night, Misty."

He nods and says a pleasant goodbye to Jae as he grabs his bag on his way out. I watch him walk away until the door closes, remaining motionless for several seconds just watching the door. Jae is giddy when I finally glance at her on the loveseat, lips rolled together and quivering lightly. She looks like she's about to combust.

"Oh, fuck off," I groan.

She squeals. It isn't a quiet sound either. I'm almost certain if Cade hasn't moved too far away from our apartment door, he may hear it. "Sorry, it's like watching a romance novel play out."

"You read too much!"

"I read the perfect amount, and I've read this story at least three times this week."

"It's my real life," I say as flatly as I can. "Not some smutty book."

"Well, it's feeling pretty smut booky to me!"

"You're ridiculous." I sigh, and lean my head back, eyes closing to hold on to the tears threatening to fall. "I just…I want this to be over."

Hands curling around my arms draw my eyes open and directly into soft lavender. "I know." Concern laces Jae's words. "It will be okay. He's right. We'll figure this out and get the ring off, okay? I promise."

"I know…It's just…really hard to see that right now."

She nods. "Go put PJs on and we'll watch a movie." I open my mouth to decline, but Jae is already shaking her head. "Nope. No saying no. You need a night to wallow properly and not by drowning yourself in martinis at Big's. We're going to watch movies, eat snacks, smoke a few fat bowls and if you want to cry, we'll cry. But you haven't truly mourned any of this. So we're gonna mourn the fuck out of it tonight and tomorrow you're going to call a therapist and find the spell to get that thing off. Okay?"

Tears burn the corners of my eyes, and I nod. "Make popcorn."

"I'll make every bag we have for you, babe."

Jae's already cleaned everything up by the time I emerge in my pajamas. We end up making two bags of popcorn for the duration of our couch sitting. We haven't spent time like this together in ages, vegging out, eating snacks and smoking joints until we can't anymore. It makes me love Jae even more.

Before I head for bed, I do something I've been debating for months. Years, if I'm honest with myself, since the last time I stopped going. I search the internet for a therapist. I can't heal on my own, and as much as I love my friends for their support, I can't rely on them solely either. It's time.

CHAPTER

FOURTEEN

"So you're going on a study date. How nerdy college romance of you."

The disgruntled gargle I force out echoes over the sound of the milk steamer Jae is cackling in front of, standing in my usual spot on the cushioned floor mat. "Why did I even come down here?"

I've been asking myself that for the last five minutes, standing on the customer's side of the counter in The Toasted Oak. It's better than sitting alone upstairs waiting to head for The Annex, I suppose, but only by a thin margin. The noise of the shop brimming with people drowns out the sounds of shame echoing in my brain at getting myself stuck in such a precarious situation. Being with Jae and Rokk helps, too, I suppose. Only slightly, though, when they both gang up on me like this.

"Because you love us," Rokk replies, shooting an uncharacteristic wink at Jae.

"It's borderline hate at this point."

Rokk snorts into his coffee.

"Bull," Jae says. "Just like how your little Annex trip isn't a date."

"We're just going to research. That's it," I reaffirm. "They've only found the one option, and I just don't trust he's looking hard enough—"

"Oh, he's looking hard enough, alright," Rokk says.

"At Mis." Jae adds, and both my best friends laugh.

"Oh, my goddesses!" I groan.

Cheekiness shapes both of their faces, reminding me of those plump lips turning upward and those hazel eyes sparkling with delight at me. It's like somehow they're both taking on Cade's personality traits without even knowing him. Or maybe...I'm just attributing every flash of his mannerisms to him alone. Jae's always smirked at me when she's giddy about something. But every time I see it now, all I can think of is Cade.

I sneer at them both. "How would you even know, Rokk?"

"I came to get coffee when he was here," Rokk says. "Everyone could see that he gawked at you every five seconds."

He looks at Jae for confirmation and she nods eagerly as she pushes a cup across the counter to the sole waiting customer. "I caught you both staring all the time. I wish you'd just admit you like him."

"I don't even know him!" I say. "He could be a terrible person for all we know. He's basically a stalker as it is!"

"Off the bat, he's way better than that bitch was." Nonchalance shrugs Rokk's shoulders.

"Anyone is better than her," Jae adds. "A piece of gum stuck to the bottom of the bleachers in the nastiest stadium in the world is better than that narcissist. She's awful." She looks at Rokk. "Didn't she insult your mom the last time you saw her?"

Rokk nods. "And my sister, too, in one fell swoop. Then played that victim bullshit she always did."

Bullshit that I fell for repeatedly. The same behavior that I still accept fault for, even though everyone around me reassures me it has nothing to do with me. The same behavior that made me feel helpless, out of control, and like I needed to repair whatever was broken, no matter my part in breaking it.

Although it shouldn't, shame builds in me. I catalog the feeling for the appointment I've scheduled to restart my therapeutic journey in a few weeks. Amber isn't the only person in my life to make me feel this way. I've dated several men and women who all leaned toward the same behaviors. Not that I haven't had positive relationships in the past; my high school girlfriend for one. But after we parted because she got into some fancy college across the country and my mother got sick, I've stayed in a spiral of relationships that landed me where I am now. What I want to know is why. Why do I lean toward these people and veer away from those that show me kindness? What makes me believe this toxicity is all I deserve?

I won't solve that here, but I will solve it soon. I will find some semblance of an answer to relinquish that pool of people and redis-cover myself and who I am. Discover what I want out of life and the person I choose to spend it with.

"Okay," I say. "I'm leaving now so you guys can reminisce about my pain."

"We love you, you know that," Jae says resolutely.

Rokk nods and adds, "We're just saying, don't let her ruin this like she ruined everything else. Which she did. Not you."

'Only because I made her', is the first thought that pops into my mind. I catalog that, too, but respond, "We're just researching. That's it. Now I'm leaving."

Rokk huffs a laugh, picking up the second cup from his order waiting on the counter. "I'll walk you out. I've got to get back, anyway. Jason will be there soon."

"Tell them both I said hi," Jae replies, referring to what in her mind is probably both of our boyfriends, before hurrying to the register to take an order.

"So it's going well between you two?" I ask as Rokk and I turn toward the door.

That atypical smile floats over his face again as we step outside. Crisp sunrays punctuate the look, bathing me in a warmth of happiness for my friend. "Jason is…" He slips into some not so distant memory that makes his smile a little wider. "Well, he's damn near perfect."

That makes my shoulders loosen. Joy flits through the nerves inside me. "I'm happy for you."

"And I'm happy for you," he replies, seeing the retort on my tongue and continuing before it can form into a full rebuttal. "I know. You don't like him, but I'm not talking about him. I'm talking about you. I know what it's been like for you over the last few months, and if anything, this is helping you get out of your head and find yourself again. Even if you end up hating this guy, you're on the right path. The path back to you. We all know that spunky Mis is still in there, and she's coming back a little more every day. Just don't let *her* voice in the back of your head convince you that you're not worthy of finding yourself again. Okay?"

I blink back tears, furrowing my brows in nothing short of a pout. He accepts my nod with gentle laughter and throws an arm around my shoulders for an even rarer-than-a-smile hug. We part ways, and I hold myself together all the way to my car, which feels like more of an accomplishment than it is as I back out of my spot and head for The Annex.

I HAVEN'T STOOD in the shadows of this building since I was twenty years old. Verging on ten years and what feels like all of my life's hopes ago. I used to love this place. The knowledge, the tomes and grimoires, the quiet, and even the librarians. I loved all parts of The Annex. But once I left school to care for my mother through her illness, it hurt too much to think about coming back to the architecture that's far too gothic for the southern United States. The memories of my time here flood me like the fresh wound they still are as I take in the castle-like building.

I had my first kiss with my girlfriend here while we researched a school project in our sophomore year of high school. While in college, I stayed here far too many nights with my nose buried deep in books until the librarians had to come kick me out. And when I was young, my mother regularly brought me along to find new rituals to ease her everyday life. We spent so much time here together, combing the stacks for anything that would make the mundane tasks of life simple, it felt like another home.

She wasn't as stingy with magic as I am, but she wasn't the most liberal with use, either. She understood the limits. When she got sick, my grandfather begged her to comb these stacks to find something to take away her pain, to heal the cancer that riddled her body in a matter of months. He swore an ounce of her blood would put her in remission and give them more time. In his mind, they didn't have enough. He wanted more; he wanted a full life with her until the day he died first. My mother refused, saying it would only prolong their suffering. The cancer would come back because to rid herself of it, she'd have to sacrifice all of herself. A life for a life.

It was hard on all of us to watch her fade, but I did all I could to make her transition back to the waters a smooth one. I did the same for my grandfather when his magic burned out three years later and the embers welcomed his ashes home. Though, I'm still confident it was a broken heart that took him from me and left me in this world alone.

I haven't stepped foot here since. I haven't even thought of returning. I should've known coming back would make that pit inside my stomach hard to ignore. But, although it hurts to stand here without either of them in my life, I also smile. Memories of my mother bringing me here play through the sadness. Those moments my grandfather watched my mother experiment with new rituals come right alongside them. I smile with each one, remembering the love they shared and bestowed upon me without restraint. It coats me in warmth even now, and I latch onto it.

Cade walks up beside me while I'm scanning the memories on the gray stones. He says nothing; we just stand together for a moment as I take in the building and a few lungfuls of air.

"I forgot how massive it is," I say. "It's been a while."

"How long has it been since you've been here?"

"Nine years."

"About the same for me," he says. "Haven't really needed to come since school."

I finally turn to look at him, brows knit. Again, he's the casual version of himself in a plain tee-shirt with his markings on full display, a pair of jeans, and a backwards hat that lets through those white-peppered curls. He inspects the architecture for a moment longer before turning to me. There's something in his eyes reminiscent of the emotions roiling through me, but I don't ask.

I just say, "You ready?"

He nods and motions to the door, which he beats me to and holds open. The moment we walk in, the librarians at the front desk make it clear they know who we are and that they were waiting for us. We're barely three steps into the building before the man on the left stands and scurries around the counter with a grin so broad it looks like it hurts.

"Mr. Blanton, hello!" The man calls brightly. He's on the shorter side, well kept, and a green wizard based on the vine-covered hand he stretches out to Cade. "Right on time! And with the lovely future Mrs. Blanton—"

Static saturates my ears, and I don't hear another word he says. I manage to shake his hand when he offers it to me, but I pray fervently to every goddess known to womankind that he can't feel how my heart pounds through my palm. That's the first time someone I don't know has addressed me as Cade's future wife to my face, and I clam up. Every part of me stiffens as he and Cade have some conversation I cannot hear through the static. It shouldn't make me have such a visceral response, but it does. I struggle to clear it away as the librarian leads us deeper into the building.

We pass through stacks of books, and I let my eyes wander to the surrounding beauty to snap back into my senses. This branch of The Annex is fourteen stories tall, and the center is hollow all the way up, modeled after the original Annex in Cairo. The histories of all magical kinds fill the stacks on every floor. From wixans to goblins to other magical creatures and even humanity, all history lives within these walls. It smells of parchment and old mahogany and I instinctively inhale, letting the scent shiver through me and bring me back into my body. The memories and the silence and the dust sparkling in the sunlight streaming through the stained glass dome above coat me in familiar albeit long-forgotten comfort.

I'm almost back to myself when the librarian halts us at a set of doors in the back of the first floor with a red plaque reading Employees Only. "Everything is all set up for you!" he says, opening the door with a key on a lanyard around his neck. "All doors are unlocked. You can go to any floor you'd like. The Index is on the right and carts are near the elevator in the back. Please let me know if you need anything, and I will happily help."

Cade nods and holds out his hand. "Thank you, Laurent. I appreciate your help today."

Laurent looks keen to shake Cade's hand again. "Of course, Mr. Blanton. Anything to help The Council." Laurent almost bows before he turns and hurries away. I watch him go, more confused by his statement than anything else.

Cade must notice the question on my face and chuckles. "Well, I couldn't very well tell them what we needed the reserves for, could I? So when I called this morning, I said we were doing some research for a bill I'm writing. They were more than willing to allow us access to the higher levels."

All the higher levels. My breath stutters at the thought. I've never been beyond the second floor of this library. The third floor and above require countless permission forms and weeks of back and forth to get approval. Cade called the same day and got us access to all, which we likely won't have enough time to browse through today. I won't show I'm impressed, but I am. And slightly more excited than I should be.

"Guess we should get started," I say, moving past him toward The Index.

"Always right to it."

"No need to waste time."

He just chuckles, louder than usual in the back room's silence. Coupled with the conversation I had with Jae and Rokk, the sound floats those pesky memories of our night together to the front of my mind. I try to push them and the arrant thoughts of him taking me against the stacks away. Now isn't the time. But it's hard when he moves in beside me in front of the old leather-bound tome sitting atop a dark stone pedestal, looking over my shoulder and bathing me in that citrusy, woodsy scent again. The same one from that night that, even now, makes my knees a little wobbly.

"It's enchanted," he says, and the quiet depth of his voice doesn't help ease the warmth inside me at all as he flips open the book, revealing only blank pages. "Just put your hand on it and think about what you need. It'll bring up everything here or any Annex that fits. I can't say how many entries my mom's researchers have investigated, but I imagine they've hit most of them."

I clear my throat. "Doesn't hurt to look again."

"Now look at who's being the micromanager."

The glare I shoot at him over my shoulder falls flat on smirked lips. I roll my eyes at my own words thrown back at me in jest, and they land on the blank page awaiting someone's touch. Before my left hand even lifts, magic is leaping off the book in bounds. It licks against my palm and makes me a little breathless. Goosebumps build on my arms as the magic pulls my hand in, and the small hairs threaten to stand on end. I don't know what magic this is or how long it's been here, but it's old. I can feel that when I run my fingers over the smooth page, spreading my hand flat against it with the softest inhale of wonderment.

I take a moment to orient myself to the feeling coiling up my arm, to the magic tugging at my mind, listening for what I need. Listening to how it can help. I take a deep breath and tell it.

Please help me remove the enchantment on this ring so I can take it off.

Please help me remove the enchantment on this ring so I can take it off.

Over and over, I sing those words in the walls of my brain. The magic builds up my arm a little further with every line, reaching to kiss my chin. But before it overwhelms me, it recedes. Quickly. It bleeds down my arm, taking a small sacrifice of skin on the way out and over the page, where black ink forms beneath my hand. Jagged cursive scrawls across the cream-colored paper, hinting at the enchantment's age. It's probably modeled after the original caster's handwriting, written in what could only be a quill pen. It's readable, but only barely.

Sixteen pages with four entries a piece return when the magic finally fades. The last seven pages of books are at different Annexes around the world. Some are in Washington D.C. Some are in cities in Japan, Ireland, and Argentina. There's even one in Nepal. Which leaves us nine pages of tomes to browse for and through in this branch. Thirty-six books. Not unmanageable between the two of us before the library closes this evening.

Something akin to hope blossoms in my chest again, but I stamp it out in favor of practicality. Even if there's a ritual here for us to try, it doesn't mean it will work. Yesterday's debacle proved that.

"I'll go get the first five pages," I say. "You take the rest?"

"Oh. Sure," he murmurs. I remember the look on his face—disappointment. But I'm not here to make him happy. I'm here to get this ring off.

So I pull out my phone to take a picture of the first five pages; he follows my lead, doing the same for his group. I can barely read the faded lines of ink, but there's enough clarity that I can make out most of the titles and their corresponding stack numbers. Floors three through seven are mine, I notice, as we head toward the elevator in the back of the room. I'm too enthralled in debating which path is best to gather all my books as succinctly as possible that he's already looking at me again like I'm some wild animal ready to spook when I look up and notice there's a single cart available for our use. Naturally. Because, evidently, I can't have a single moment alone when I'm in the same building as this man.

"You can take it," he offers. "I'll carry my books."

"That'll take too many trips," I say. "We can just share it."

He looks pleased, but tamps it down with a nod. "I won't say a word. We can walk in complete silence. You won't even know I'm there."

I snort. "Fine. But not a word."

He smiles and runs his fingers over his lips like he's zipping them before locking them closed and holding out the imaginary key to me. Again, I roll my eyes, which I do more in his presence than I do with just about anyone else. But I take it, shoving nothing into my pocket before pushing the elevator button. It's thankfully already here, so I wheel the cart in and choose the third floor where my list of books starts with *Curses, Enchantments, and You* by Hyla Alsen. Not something I envision needing to be walled off, and I doubt it will be any help, but I'm willing to scour through every single book in this library to find a way to remove this ring.

For the first few pages of my entries, we wander in a stiff silence. I'd be more annoyed with him walking with me if he wasn't so useful. More than one book on my list is well out of my reach, and I'm not willing to use magic to pull them down. But they're not out of his. I don't even have to ask. With the first he grabs down, there's a pleased smirk framing his face. I just roll my eyes and push the cart toward the next, trying to find comfort in the rows of books. The smell of mahogany and parchment aids that, but somehow, so does Cade.

He's a calming presence while we walk; he's attentive in searching for the tomes and organized when pulling them down, aligning them on the cart alphabetically so we can quickly return them when our day of research is through. Not only that, but he's accepting all the boundaries I set. It's…refreshing. More refreshing than the silence that grows a little more stifling with every book we take out. When we're standing in the elevator to take us to the ninth floor is when I can't stand it anymore.

"So…you came here during school?" I ask.

He looks at me, surprised, but it vanishes in favor of frivolity. He purses his lips in and out, and shrugs, holding out his hand. I almost laugh when he flexes his fingers, like he's mimicking Jae when she wants me to hand her something; instead, I scoff out the mirth and act like I'm digging into my pocket for keys. I play along, holding nothing out above his outstretched hand before dropping them onto his palm. He makes a show of opening his lips and letting out a deep, relieved sigh when the invisible force-field is gone.

"Much better," he says, grinning when I snort something akin to amusement.

"You're ridiculous," I say, pushing the cart out of the elevator when it opens for us.

He follows closely, saying, "You played along," as if I don't remember digging nothing out of my pocket just moments before. "And yes, I came here during school. You did, too?"

"I did, yeah."

"I loved coming here, even though it's pretty far from Wilmington."

"Wilmington?"

He nods and pulls down another book when we stop, slotting it into place on the cart. "I went to undergrad for Marine Biology at UNCW and did my Master's work back in Hawaii in Marine Science. I wanted to be a marine biologist."

"Really?" There's a sudden hint of surprise in my voice.

It makes him laugh as he pulls another book down. I didn't realize that I stopped pulling them down in favor of only pushing the cart, but he doesn't seem to mind grabbing them all, so I don't either.

"That so surprising?"

"No." It doesn't sound like I believe myself.

"Certainly sounds like it."

"I just wasn't expecting us to have such similar dream jobs, I guess."

"Oh? Toasted Oak isn't your final stop?"

"Absolutely not." A derisive snort plays between us. "I hate—"

"Coffee. I remember," he says.

I flinch at that. He remembers such a trivial detail of the day I yelled in his face. I brush off the surprise by saying, "Right. Yeah. Well, Jae's just helping me while I'm between jobs."

"What's your dream job, then?"

"I went to N.C. State for a few years for zoology and pre-magical veterinarian care," I say. "I didn't finish, but that was the goal."

"Huh." He puffs out the sound, smile growing.

"What?"

He shrugs and pulls down two books that are beside one another. "You're right. Just another way we're similar."

I can't agree that *we're* similar and not just our fields of study. We both just happen to like animals and sex, and being the occasional jackass. Well, maybe our senses of humor are similar, too, if the flashes of my laughter from the night we spent tangled in his bed are anything to go off of. And our determination. Okay…maybe there are a few ways we're similar, but I remind myself that none of them matter. Regardless of what he said in the stockroom just days ago, once we remove this ring, he'll walk away just like everyone else.

We lapse again into silence as we work through the remainder of his pages. It doesn't take long before we're back on the first floor, unloading the books onto a table in a quiet room. He starts with my books, and when I reach for his pile, he again looks surprised, though he doesn't comment other than a smile tugging on the edges of his lips. Sharing a table is just for ease of discussion, or so I tell myself as we settle down together, pulling books from the stacks to start our long rabbit hole of research.

Cade wasn't joking at The Toasted Oak when he said not wanting to maim myself took out a large majority of rituals. Three pages worth of my books contain spells so gruesome I won't even bother reading the entirety. Why The Annex still possesses them is beyond me. Including *Curses, Enchantments, and You*, which proves why it's behind locked doors. Nearly every spell involves animalistic sacrifice. Something I will never do. Another book involves a spell to stop my heart altogether until the enchantment lifts, which I won't be doing based on the noted ten percent success rate. Some books contain counter-enchantments to the enchantments in those specific books, which won't help us in the slightest. The closest thing we come to that may have any success involves cutting off my finger, which I suppose will be our last ditch effort should we find nothing else.

Cade's books fare little better, but he is diligent in his search. We talk about each option, and he listens to my opinions, seeks my thoughts before nixing rituals that are borderline unethical, and eventually learns what I'll refuse. Somewhere around his fifth grimoire, I think we both give up any hope of finding a ritual that won't maim us in the process of returning his ring. With each book we scan through, and every rite we mull over, I find confidence fading more and more.

We work until Laurent comes to find us sometime around ten, well beyond closing. Apologizing for keeping him so late, we wrap up our evening, declining his offer to stay later if we need while he's suppressing a yawn. He is adamant, though, about returning the books for us after putting in the transfer request we ask for from other branches. Cade politely bids him good night when he walks us to the door, telling Laurent someone will be by to pick the books up when they arrive.

Although I have no hope that any of those additional tomes will help, I look forward to when they get here. Researching breathed a torrent of excitement to life inside me over the past several hours. Something that feels so distant from the emotions I've suffered for months; longer if I'm honest with myself. If nothing comes from the books on loan, at least this day gave me something to mull over for my future. I haven't thought about going back to school more than I do at this moment. I didn't realize how I missed spending time well into the late night hours in The Annex in quiet study, stretching and growing my mind. Standing again before the building, looking up at the stone gargoyles that protect the perimeter, I feel a small tug inside me.

I shake myself free of the thoughts, only then realizing Cade is watching me watch my past and my future play out on The Annex's stones. I flush at the smile on his face.

"Well, it's been—"

"—You hungry?"

We both pause for a moment, staring at each other, and his laughter plays between us.

"It's late," I say, as if that's a full thought when he doesn't continue. "You really want to waste your one date on a short night?"

His body loosens at that statement. I don't know what relief I gave him, but he takes it. "This wouldn't be a date. Just two people walking in the same direction toward a restaurant down the street. It's carryout only."

"This place better not be your house."

He barks a laugh. "It's not. You like Polynesian food?"

I shrug. "Don't think I've ever had it."

"I think you'll like it," he says. "It takes inspiration from some Asian cuisines, which I'm assuming you like?"

I joke, "He asks, knowing my roommate is Korean."

His laughter again plays between us, this time a little looser. "You'll like it. And it's just up the road."

I'd say no, but the thought of food reminds my stomach that I haven't eaten today, and it gurgles loud enough that we both can hear. "Okay, sure."

He grins wider, but says nothing else. He just leads the way, and we slip into a companionable silence as we drift through the streets of North Raleigh. Up here is such a different scene than downtown living. Sometimes I forget how peaceful my town can be when there aren't sirens and screaming twenty-one-year olds and blaring music drowning out the silence. This late into the evening, people in this neighborhood are snuggly in their homes. There's no one on the road, and there's certainly no one else out walking around. We're alone, and on our quiet walk, I'm comfortable, something to which I'm unaccustomed. Especially over the last several months. While it may not be notable to anyone else, even Cade, being able to be content in the silence without my mind wandering to my list of failures is something I've wanted for quite some time.

In the grand scheme, the walk to the restaurant is nothing special, but the side of Cade I see when we step inside may be. I've yet to meet this Cade—or Ally, as the older man that shuffles out from behind the counter calls him the moment we walk in. This recognition isn't the same as the everyday layman. The man knows Cade personally if the hug they give one another says anything. A younger man and woman spring from the kitchen with bright smiles seconds later, wrapping Cade in crushing hugs, too. Ally comes out even more in him at that moment; he's boisterous and nothing but smiles as he introduces me to 'some of his oldest friends.' They scold him profusely, joking that he's 'too big for his britches' now and can't even bring his fiancée around before telling the public, before wrapping me in the same warm hugs they gave him.

I immediately feel like part of a family I'll never be a part of. It's so warm. Their smiles, their humor, their laughter. Somehow, even through the apprehension of meeting new people, I feel light. I feel welcomed. I feel warm. Though, not enough that I want to attend the drinks they invite us to in celebration of our false engagement. Thankfully, I don't have to decline because Cade backs them off by saying we've still got research for a bill to complete. At which they balk and joke with him again. We don't get out of getting free dessert, though, and a proper scolding for letting the media find out before 'his family.'

Cade carries the much too large helping of food we get, bidding our goodbyes. He looks at me, remorseful, when we step outside.

"Sorry," he says, rubbing the back of his neck. "I didn't think they'd be like *that*, but I should have. I've been coming here for a long time."

"It's fine," I say, sincerely. "It was sweet."

"Yeah?"

I just nod. He doesn't need to know that seeing him in this light gives me a whole new perspective on the person he is. It does. I should know this by now, based on the time we've spent together, but seeing Cade with the people in that restaurant, his friends, makes him seem normal. It breathes life into his humanity, proving again that he's not just that 'fuck all figurehead' he said he isn't.

Not that it changes anything. It doesn't. Once the ring is off, we'll go our separate ways. But…it's nice to see that the man who will join The Council has some goodness in him after all.

On our short walk back to our cars, Cade tells me about how his grandfather started taking him to that restaurant when they moved to North Carolina in his childhood. I just listen, nodding along and noticing how much lighter he seems. Like seeing those people was a stress relief. Like he needed that moment to survive just as much as the food he holds. It lingers on his face when we're standing beside my car in the parking lot, which he wouldn't let me walk to alone. I could've easily done so, but…I can't deny how nice it was to not have to look over my shoulder.

"Thanks," I say when he hands me my half of our giant order. I don't think I'm thanking him for just that, but I won't process exactly what I'm thankful for.

"You're welcome." He nods, hesitating for a moment before asking, "May I have your number? So I can call you when—"

"Just come to the shop," I cut in. "You're more than aware of when I work."

Laughter fills the quiet parking lot. "I am, yes. But I'm leaving on Council business—" he checks the watch on his wrist with a glint in his eye before humming, "two days ago, so—"

"Wait. Two days ago?" I blurt the question without thinking.

He shrugs, and it makes me believe him when he says, "It's no big deal. I was supposed to leave Tuesday night, but I booked another flight after we agreed to do the ritual yesterday. And well, again today, but no big deal."

Shock blows my expression wide. It actually is a big deal. We didn't 'agree' on anything. I told him when and where to be without so much as thinking about or inquiring if he could make it. Which, he couldn't. But instead of refusing and saying he had a flight booked, he agreed. He stayed and showed up early to help me.

No. He didn't stay to help *me*. He stayed to get his ring back because we're both stuck in this situation. He stayed for himself, not for me. Or so I try to convince the nagging voice in my head and the pounding of my heart.

"We could have—"

He waves the statement off. "Neither here nor there. But it does mean that I won't be back for a while, so if you're amenable, I'd love to get your cell number so I can call you when the requested books come in and you can start looking through them before I get back."

Some part of me still wants to say no, but I can't. If I want this ring off, he needs my number. Taking the phone he hands out isn't me giving in to what he wants. It's enabling what I want. Enabling myself out of this situation and onto dealing with the rest of my life and the cloud of darkness that this whole scenario shoved to the back of my mind for far too long.

But…as I call myself and feel my phone vibrate in my back pocket, something nags at me. Just the thinnest thought in my mind, one I won't tug at right now to unravel.

One that tugs for me when he smiles and says, "I'll call you the moment I know more."

I wait until I'm home to save his number, and I label the contact as 'Jackass' to save a bit of my dignity. Though I'm fairly certain he's not a jackass at all. I don't know what he is, but with every interaction, I see more and more how much of a jackass he isn't. The text he sends while

I'm eating some of the most delicious food I've ever tasted backs that thought up more.

I'm sorry. We'll figure this out, and you'll never have to see me again. I promise I'll find a way to get that ring off.

'You'll never have to see me again.'

That little thread in my brain tugs a little harder, and for some reason, it tugs on my heart.

CHAPTER
FIFTEEN

I barely have time to stuff the sheer shirt I'm folding into Jae's travel bag before another one smacks me in the face. How she's able to wait until an hour before her flight boards to pack still astounds me. One would assume that for as detail-oriented as she is, latency here would drive her insane. But she's always been this way, a remnant of a childhood constantly spent on the move. So here I sit again, just minutes after the shop closed and just over an hour before a flight takes her for a week away, folding each barely there article of clothing she tosses at me. I stuff them into her bag probably a little too hard with bitterness coating my tongue.

Up until my mouth lost me my job, I was going with her on a beautiful work-cation to find new coffee bean suppliers for the shop. We were going to sit on beaches and drink rum punches until we couldn't see straight, soak up the sun, and explore the rich culture Costa Rica has to offer. Now, she's going alone, and I'm watching over The Toasted Oak in her stead.

Lucky witch.

She reappears, tossing another two shirts. "And you're absolutely sure you can—"

"Yes, Mom," I say as she disappears into the depths of her closet again. "I've already told you. The shop will be fine. Alex is there if anything goes wrong. She scheduled herself every day while you're gone."

"Gods, you're right, she will. She's amazing," Jae says as she appears from her closet with a tiny bikini top that can't possibly cover more than her nipples. Good for her. She tosses it at me and turns for her bathroom.

Buzz. Buzz. Buzz.

My phone nearly vibrates off of Jae's nightstand onto the floor before I can get to it. Panic flares in me at the sound, but it's quickly replaced with exasperation. J&D Sourcing reads across the screen—my old job, who I've been awaiting a call from since the day I walked out with my middle fingers in the air. With how I exited, I'd not be surprised to learn they're suing me for some asinine reason like defamation or harassment. Or at the very least, calling me to recover all the bonuses they'd given me over the years.

The phone goes silent in my hand, but before I can drop it onto the bed, it buzzes again. J&D Sourcing shows up once more; this time, however, I sneer and slide the red button to hang up before throwing it down. They can leave a message if it's so important.

"Who is it?" Jae calls from the bathroom amidst the clanging of packing her toiletries, looking at me through her mirror.

"It's J&D." A vigorous zip of a suitcase pocket punctuates the name. "I don't know why they're calling me—"

Buzz. Buzz. Buzz.

"Oh, my good goddesses!" I shout.

"Just answer it and tell them to leave you alone," Jae demands as she appears in the bathroom doorway with her toiletries bag in tow.

I angrily search for the phone, but every neuron and atom in my body freezes when I find it. Every ounce of air vacates my lungs like I'm cresting on a rollercoaster, waiting breathless at the pinnacle for the rush. My heart slams into my throat in such a visceral, unexpected response that I almost choke. My hand even shakes, although I fruitlessly will it to stop.

'Jackass' reads across the screen.

Stunned, I just stare at the name as the phone vibrates in my hand. Of course, Aldrich Cade Blanton calls me rather than choosing to send a brief text like every other person in existence. Though, I shouldn't be so surprised. He said he'd call when they found something out, and he's following through with his word. Again.

A flurry of emotions flit through me as my heart plummets back into my stomach. Whether those flutters are bad is undetermined, only because I refuse to admit they're good.

"It's him, isn't it?" Whatever look haunts my face must make it obvious. Jae's beside me in an instant, verifying for herself. "Answer it right now!" My head shakes so viciously that it moves Jae's bed. "Answer it!"

"You answer if you wanna talk to him so badly!"

In retrospect, I shouldn't have pushed out my phone to Jae. I shouldn't have said the words at all, honestly, because I know better than to challenge her. I've only done so twice before, and I thought I learned my lesson. Shame on me or the surprise of the moment for clouding my better judgment. Jae never backs down from anything, especially not this. She snatches the phone and slides her finger over the answer button, and it's on her ear before I can even part my lips in protest.

"Hello," Jae greets with none of the anxiety roiling inside me. Her voice is beautifully professional, and she's grinning at my wide-eyed horror. "Yeah, it's Jae. She's taking out the trash, but I saw your name pop up and didn't want her to miss anything important...She'll be back in just a second. How's Amsterdam?"

Jae looks like she's talking to the one-night stand from which she's been awaiting a call, not me. I waffle between stunned silence and wanting to tackle her to the floor to get my phone back. Instead, I sit hapless on her bed and watch because I know she won't willingly relinquish it. We'll have to fight. We've done so in the past; I've won a handful of times. If I can get her into a headlock—

Jae barks a laugh and pulls me from thoughts of shoving one of her bikini bottoms into her mouth. "Yeah, business is still great even when you're not there," she replies. "They're still hoping you'll show back up. I'm actually thinking of naming a drink after you just to see if they'll buy it."

I don't know why that makes *me* embarrassed. I didn't say it. Jae's responding laughter says it may not have been a bad thing.

"I'm thinking iced black coffee topped with creamer, but not mixed in…" Jae laughs again. "Exactly. Like your hair…Millions, probably. Maybe more."

Whatever he says makes Jae's smile widen further. Maybe she should date Cade. They seem to have better chemistry than he and I.

"Yeah, I think she's ready to talk to you now." My stomach drops into the absolute chasm it's been hovering over. Good goddesses below. He didn't believe the trash story Jae came up with at all. I mean, who would? But he could've pretended. Perfect. Now he knows I was too flustered to answer the phone when his name showed up. Worse, my best friend had to do it for me. "Yeah, I will. You, too, Cade. Here she is."

"You will what?" I hiss quietly through clenched teeth when Jae hands me my phone. She only waves me off with a flippant flick of the device, grinning so wide it looks painful. I shake my head, but she doesn't relent. She won't until I take the phone, and I know that, so I snatch it away with the most pointed sneer I can muster. The look does nothing to dampen the eagerness flowing off her in waves.

I'm not ready, but I force out a breath, shake the tension from my shoulders, and put the phone to my ear. "Hello?"

"Hello, Misty."

Nope, not ready at all. And not for any of the reasons that I assumed. The pit in my stomach opens wider at the sound of his voice, and I swear another million butterflies emerge to fight with the ones that materialized at the sight of his moniker on my screen. Breathing gets harder, and that doesn't feel fair. Someone having such a power over me just by speaking two words? Unfair.

"Yeah, hey," I choke out, thankful that it doesn't sound strangled. "Did you find something to remove the ring?"

"Right to it then, as always." He huffs a laugh. "I called to let you know my mother and grandfather are looking for anything we have in our records from when the ring was created. It's apparently a little older than we thought, and they're having trouble finding anything."

That aids in deflating the rampage of butterflies inside me, but replaces them with the taste of bitter disappointment. "So you're calling to tell me we've still got nothing?"

Jae looks like I've knocked the wind out of her. Widening lavender eyes are definitely scolding me for being too blunt again.

He chuckles. "Yeah, I guess so. I just didn't want you to think I'd forgotten about you because I certainly haven't."

That shouldn't make me happy. By all accounts, it should make me annoyed or angry or frustrated that he's wasting my time. But…There's a part of me that's giddy at the thought that this man is calling me "just because." Because he couldn't stop thinking about me. Because he wanted to hear my voice. Because, because, because…

I try to latch onto the small chord of annoyance I muster, but it's slippery. It slides from my grasp moments after I say, "Thanks, I guess."

"Uh—yeah, of course."

I pause and pull the phone away from my ear as if he'd be able to see how I cringe. Jae must be able to tell I want to get out of it as soon as possible because she hisses, "Don't you dare hang up that phone." I glower, but she doesn't shy away. Taking a page from my book, she motions way too dramatically to spur me, using her whole body for emphasis. "Just say something. Literally anything."

It's been silent for so long that he must know this is a disaster. But he also hasn't said a word to end the conversation, so I don't either. I try to wrack my brain for something to say, but for as smart as I can be, this is not one of those times.

"So… it's late there."

Jae can't possibly roll her eyes more dramatically, scoffing and throwing her hands into the air to wash them of me and the dreadful phone call she forced me into. Mocking a silent scream before slamming my hand on my face, I berate myself because good goddesses, *that's* what I came up with? When she retreats into her bathroom, I take my apparent severe lack of communication skills and head for my room, pulling the phone away from my ear as mirth echoes through the speakers.

The laughter lingers in his voice when I reluctantly return to our conversation. "—after midnight." But then there's a sigh that sounds like relief. Maybe he was expecting me to hang up. I expected the same, so I blame this awkward moment completely on Jae.

Trying to act as aloof as possible, I quip, "Hopefully it didn't take all day to work up the nerve to call me."

He genuinely laughs again, and I think I can hear the smile in his voice when he says, "I could blame it on work, but the truth is I told myself yesterday morning I was going to call you last night. Yet, here we are now."

I huff a self-deprecating noise. "I know I'm more approachable than that."

"Are you?" There's no intent to hurt me with that question based on the playfulness in his voice. He's also not wrong. Given his knowledge of me, making this call probably was nerve-wracking. The thought of him being that nervous to call me, though? Well, that's not really something I'm proud of.

So I tease, "All I know is that it shouldn't be that hard to call your *fiancée*."

There's a sputter on the other end of the line and it fades like he pulls the phone away from his lips. But in a single breath, he's back.

"My *fiancée* isn't the most approachable of witches when she wants to be. But she's fiery, and I like that a lot."

Shit. I didn't intend for that to make me clam up, but I do at the depth of his voice. It's lewd the way he says the words, confident and intentioned. He likes how feisty I am, and he likes me. And not just a little. This isn't the first time he's said something of the kind, but it's the first time that I think I believe it. Electricity dances along the small hairs on my forearms, and I suppress a shiver.

"You'll grow out of that before this is all over," I reply, far quieter than I intend. "Your family will find something, and we'll get the ring off so you can give it to Chloe or some other rich witch and forget all about me."

"I very much disagree."

"You sure? Chloe was cute aside from the whole throwing water in my face thing. That's your better bargain. I'm sure she'll drop that other guy and take you back."

"Well, apparently I *do* like women who throw water in my face," he says with a laugh that tightens my stomach. "But I can assure you that you're far more interesting to me than Chloe ever could hope to be."

"He says, 'interesting,' as if that's a good thing."

"It's an excellent thing." To that, it seems he doesn't expect a response. Thankfully, because I'm not capable of giving one at the moment. "Jae said business is still good? Not too awful when I'm not there, I hope."

I hum a noncommittal sound. "It's barrable."

"So I made your days better, is what I'm hearing." Again, there's that smile in his voice.

"You hear a lot of things you want to hear, don't you?"

"I'm good at reading between lines."

"You know what has lines? Text messages." He barks a laugh. "You couldn't text like a normal person?"

"Then you wouldn't have felt obligated to have this highly amusing conversation with me."

"So you did make it awkward on purpose."

"It worked," he says enthusiastically.

"Did it? Are we having said conversation?" I ask to deflate him a little.

It doesn't work. "What's your favorite color?"

I snort. "Of all the things. That's what you're starting with?"

"Oh, I'm sorry, Ms. 'It's Late There,'" he apologizes, but it's drenched in sarcasm. "Would you like to skip the pleasantries and go straight to the traumas?"

Not expecting that joke, I laugh, full and genuine enough that it brings the smile I've been trying to suppress straight to the forefront of my expression. I can't help myself, nor can I help the laughter. It tumbles through me, lingering far longer than I try to let it. I can't catch my breath for a second, and at least twice I snort trying to.

He waits for a lull to say, "I just accomplished something I thought impossible."

"Oh?" I ask, mirth lingering in the word.

"I was sure I'd never get to hear that beautiful laugh again."

Beautiful laugh. Beautiful. He likes my obnoxious laugh. Maybe not as much as I do, but it's definitely not something many people have said is beautiful. Unique maybe, but not beautiful. My parents called it beautiful. Jae loves my laugh. But rarely has a partner said so freely how they enjoy the sound. They still haven't, I remind the flutters inside me. Cade isn't my partner, even if my body responds to his words as if he were.

"It was a fluke," I say. It wasn't, but he doesn't need to know that, even if he probably already does. I don't need to confirm it for what little of an ego he seems to have.

"I'm taking the win," he replies. "How does the ring look?"

Holding my hand up in front of my face, I contemplate saying exactly how it looks: way too beautiful and expensive and perfect to be on my finger. That I can't help but stare at it throughout my day. That I don't want it to be gone. But I can't give him that much, even if I already gave it to him that night in the tub.

"Like it's still stuck."

"Good," he says. I grant him another of my beautiful laughs. This one is far quieter, but he still mutters, "Beautiful," and I try with everything in my might to not let my heart flutter from the sound of his voice. "Hey, can I text you just because?"

"I don't know…Can you?"

He's quiet for a minute and then my phone vibrates in my ear. I grin as I read, "May I?" in a new text thread with 'Jackass' at the top.

"You may," I text back, and the soft sound of his happiness does something inexplicable to me. Or I'm choosing to let it be inexplicable. I know exactly why my abdomen tightens. The last time that quiet laugh was in my ear, his release was dripping out of me and my body remembers, even if my mind is a little hazy about it all.

"Then I'll talk to you tomorrow. Eight in the morning sound good?" The quiet words sound like a promise.

I just snort a laugh. "Good night, jackass."

"It almost sounded nice that time. I'm taking that win, too. Good night, Misty."

I barely manage to hang up before flailing in my bed, startling Charlie awake. I just lay for a minute, pondering the conversation and how it could have possibly made me more anxious than when I saw his name on my phone screen. But this is a different type of anxiousness. I don't mind the jitters that dance across my skin as I replay the conversation over and over until I hear Jae leave.

CHAPTER
SIXTEEN

It's not raining today for what feels like the first time in a month. After countless days without seeing the sun or stars, watching the sky blazing orange with the setting sun should make me happy. Instead, a knot coils in my stomach as I glance at my phone for the twelfth time. It reads fifteen until six. Which means The Toasted Oak closed forty-five minutes ago and my phone still hasn't rang.

While it's only the first missed call in the handful of days since I allowed Cade to contact me casually, bitterness still creeps up the back of my throat. Such a short amount of time and yet I've already grown accustomed to his nickname showing up on my phone. He may not have called at eight in the morning like he threatened, but he has called every night just moments after I walk through the apartment door. Four nights in a row.

I know I shouldn't, but after such consistency, I expect it. That's what makes me the most bitter: I'm getting my hopes up again when I know better than to trust someone to uphold a standard I've set for them in my mind. I only get hurt because they never do.

"No call today?"

I glance up at Alex, who's got a pierced eyebrow raised at me from over the counter. A sly smile twists her lips thin, and black and purple curls pop out of the bun she's tried to confine them in. Even those tendrils seem chipper. Clearly, even she knows and is all too excited about what I'm waiting for.

I drop my phone face down on the counter with a thud. "Probably a good thing, since we ran late. Did you—"

"Bathrooms are all done. Just need to switch off the lights, and we're good to go."

"Thank you," I say genuinely, swiping at the beads of sweat on my forehead. They're building on the back of my neck too from the closing procedures. Not unusual, but it seems rather warm today. Probably time to turn up the air conditioning in the afternoon heat. "You've been such a massive help the last few days."

"Tell Jae." Alex winks, and I know what she's implying.

"Oh, don't worry. I'll be telling her every little thing you do to help around here. She'd be completely lost without you."

She shrugs, but appreciation takes over her expression. "I'm just doing my job—"

The obnoxiously loud vibration of my phone on the metal counter interrupts Alex. My heart skips at the sound and it flutters deep into my stomach. A wide smile stretches across her face and I try to tamp down my own girlish grin as I reach for it like a teenager waiting for the person they have a crush on to call. As if I'm not an adult waiting on an update to resolve an unfortunate situation I fucked myself into.

When I flip my phone back over, what's on the screen quickly dashes those feelings. *Do not Answer J&D* reads across the front.

Indignation flits through me all the way to the tips of my toes. I'm unsure who it's with right now: myself, J&D, Cade, or the universe itself. Most likely myself for yet again letting hope bud inside me that he'd call me when I have no right to expect such a thing. None whatsoever. Other than the last four days and a reassurance that he will. That part tastes bitter…*'tomorrow night'* plays in my head in a voice that's growing more and more familiar with every call.

It reminds me too much of a too recent past. I know this disappointment all too well. It's not the first time that the sour taste has overwhelmed me. It's the same bitterness I felt nearly every night when Amber and I were together. No matter how many times she didn't call when she said she would or invite me over or show up at my apartment when promised, I never learned. I still haven't, clearly.

I nearly shove the phone into my pocket to avoid it altogether in my annoyance, but I'm just at the right level of agitation that maybe this is the perfect time to talk to J&D and tell them to stop calling me.

Alex seems to register my disappointment when I glance back up. "I've got to take this."

She waves me off. "Go. I've got the rest. I'll follow you and lock the door."

I thank her as I grab my bag and answer my phone. There's a loud and clear sigh of resignation when I put the device to my ear. I almost laugh. Clearly, they were preparing for another carbon copy voicemail like every other time before.

"Hello, this is Misty," I say, silently thanking Alex one last time as I step out into the corridor to the elevators.

"Huh—oh, yes. Yes, hello. Hi Misty," a woman stammers. Again, I try not to laugh. Not expecting my answer, she takes a moment to collect herself before continuing, "This is Amelia Sanchez with J&D Sourcing. I'm sorry to call so late. How are you?"

"As good as I can be. You?" There's a crowd of people waiting for the elevators after work, so I opt to take my call to the stairwell. It's blessedly empty and while my calves hate me for the decision, I start my trek up to the sixth floor.

Suddenly over-chipper, Amelia says, "I'm doing very swell today. I'm glad we're finally able to connect. I'm sure these calls felt a little out of the blue."

"Yeah, they did," I agree flatly.

"I'm sure." An awkward laugh echoes from the other end of the call. "Well, I hope I'm catching you at an okay time. I know it's late, but I have a follow up to the situation around your departure from the company. Is now a good time?"

'No' is on the tip of my tongue but, "Sure," slips out as I sneer at myself for the awful choice of stairs. Sweat beads on my forehead again, and I'm trying to hide how deeply I have to breathe to round the next flight.

"Oh great. Wonderful. First, I'd like to thank you for the eight years of service you gave us."

"I needed the money."

"Don't we all?" Another awkward chuckle slips out. "I won't keep you waiting. The reason I called is that the organization wanted to inform you that there was an investigation launched after reports of your…"

"Explosion?" I say with all the sarcasm I can muster through the burn in my asscheeks and the heat building on my lower back as I round the third floor.

"Your departure, yes." At least I still hear her mirth. "Several of your colleagues came forward after your exit, which led to an internal investigation into your manager, Mr. Dobson. It may please you to know he's since been terminated without eligibility for rehire."

I pause in the middle of the stairwell, eyes widening. An odd mixture of justice and resentment swirls and washes the searing pain in my calves away. It takes several seconds to process her words for what they mean. Dobson, the asshole of all assholes, was rightfully fired. Years I spent working under that man doing his job for him while he degraded every person around. Finally, the jackass got what he was due, what should have come his way much sooner. And it was because of me. Never did I anticipate that something productive would come out of me walking out of the conference room with my middle fingers in the air and all eyes on me.

Huffing out a surprised breath, I say, "Ah—well, I guess that's good. Something came from me losing my job."

"Well, actually," Amelia says cheerily. This time, the mirth doesn't annoy me. "Through the investigation, we uncovered several very enlightening things, including what I can only assume was your final straw before walking out." She means Dobson calling someone on my team a "useless woman without a brain" when she questioned why he thought increasing costs of an import was a logical move. "In this case, your separation from the company is out of the bounds of what we find acceptable."

"Yeah, me too," I say again offhandedly, voice far lighter. I even laugh, for real, not some snort of derision.

This time her laughter is genuine at my far more welcoming tone. "Well, with Mr. Dobson's rightful exit, we wanted to see if you were interested in rejoining our team. After the rave reviews from your colleagues about your work ethic and the fact that it seems you were doing the job anyway, and we just weren't aware, we'd love to offer you the newly reopened Team Manager position."

A job. Not a summons for a day in court, but my damned job back. No, not my job. The job I was doing and kicking ass at without compensation. The job that everyone around me clearly noticed my efforts in and sang my praises, even after my departure. Still stunned, I stand in the heat of the stairwell, staring at the wall like Amelia can see my surprise. Slowly, a grin overtakes the astonishment.

"Misty?" Amelia asks.

At her voice, I realize I've been silent for nearly a minute. "Yes, sorry," I stammer out in my disbelief. "Can I think about it?"

"Of course you can! I've dropped a lot on you, so you can take all the time you need. I can email you the offer letter and compensation package to review. Does that work?"

"Yeah, that works perfectly."

"Great!" It sounds like Amelia is beaming. "I'll send everything the moment we've got all the approvals, which shouldn't take long considering the glowing reviews we got about you from the team. And again, we want to apologize for the behavior and situations you were subjected to; we appreciate all that you did and could potentially do for the team and our organization."

"Yeah, of course," I say, unsure of what else I could say at the moment.

"Excellent. Well, you have a wonderful evening, Misty!"

"You, too, Amelia. And thank you."

I should probably thank my team and not her, but I mean it all the same. We hang up and I take moments longer still to process. My team stood up for me after I stood up for them. My team got Dobson fired and asked for me back. It's almost enough to bring me to tears as I take the last few flights of stairs to my floor. I'm sweating and panting by the time I get to my front door, but I'm smiling.

It's almost enough for me to forget that Cade hasn't called. Almost.

Now, just pop this little tin in the oven and wait.

Beverly Hills Kitchen Witch has long been the one thing able to turn around any day and help me feel somewhat lighter. The fifth episode of the night plays on my small laptop resting atop a well-loved lap desk handed down to me when Jae upgraded. The humidifier is on again in the corner because my throat hurts with the weather fluctuations. I'm laying in bed, Charlie snoozing right beside me with a low purr. Freshly brewed licorice root tea with a dollop of honey sits on my nightstand. All in all, there's not much else I can do to make myself comfortable, yet I can't seem to find a relaxing position or keep the heaviness from my eyelids.

Riding high from Amelia's phone call, I went to the store to restock the apartment, trying to ignore the disappointment creeping in the back of my mind. As the hours passed and fatigue slowly built in me from the crash of dopamine, however, I could no longer ignore the incessant disappointment of waiting for someone to call who rightfully doesn't have to. I cling to that thought as bitterness tries to sweep through the amalgamation of emotions overwhelming me.

Cade doesn't have to call me. He's under no obligation. It's not like he's neglecting me as his girlfriend. I'm nothing more than a woman who has a ring that belongs to him regardless that it's starting to feel like I'm much more. I'm not. It doesn't stop a familiar disappointment from lingering. I remind myself, though, that this situation is not the same even if it's dredging up past trauma. Cade is not the partner I spent years with or my current boyfriend. He's just a future stranger waiting to happen. Once this ring is off, he'll be gone.

Perhaps that's why I'm most bitter about the lack of his call: because in the future, he won't.

Maybe I should just call it an early night and get some rest before I have to open the shop tomorrow morning. Try to sleep off whatever fatigue is taking its toll on me—

Buzz. Buzz. Buzzbuzzbuzz.

My heart skips, and the flurry of feelings inside of me crescendos in a dizzying display.

That's not my normal incoming call vibration pattern. That's the new one I set exclusively for Cade after the disappointment earlier. Although I recognize all elements of this fucked up situation, I can't help my reaction to the sound. For a moment, I'm a teenager again, getting a phone call from the first girl I ever gave my number to. I'm giddy. Pleasurable anticipation ripples out through my body, replacing all bitterness. An uncontrollable shiver shakes me.

I try not to smile when I flip the phone over and see *'Jackass'* written across the top of the screen. Forcing out several breaths to muffle the reaction so it's not in my voice, I tap the green dot.

"Isn't it almost three in the morning there?" I ask as I put the phone to my ear.

Deep laughter echoes back and makes a warm chill surge through me. "Mhm. Sorry I'm late."

"Late?"

"Callin' you. I'm late. Was suppose' to call at five thirty," he mumbles.

The admission and apology wash away all lingering uncertainty with a wave of elation. I wasn't the only one waiting for our time together. The wideness of my smile is almost painful. I know I shouldn't be so happy, but I can't help it.

"I'm glad you called, even if you're late."

"Yeah?" There's delight in that question, and the way he draws out the word makes it clear why he's 'late.' Alcohol softly smooths his words. I haven't heard him like this since our night together, and goddesses, the warmth that spreads through me at the familiarity makes me shiver again. "Good, 'cause I wanna hear your voice after my shitty night."

"Shitty? What happened?"

He grunts some disapproving noise. "Was at the hotel with those old assholes. Had to drink to deal."

I chuckle, but there's relief in the sound. He was with the members of The Council, which most certainly couldn't have been fun. But it is an excellent excuse why he didn't call on time or text that he wouldn't be able to. He was working. Which I really should've considered, with who and where he is. Embarrassment coats me, but a cheerful resolve doesn't let it stick.

"Just the hotel bar?" I ask. "You didn't go find a witch in some random dive bar to propose to?"

Laughter erupts on the other end of the phone and flitters through me. "Filled my quota, I'm afraid."

"Did you at least have a little fun?"

"No," he replies. "Those old guys fuckin' suck. I'd rather be with you."

"You're in Amsterdam. That's way better than hanging out in Raleigh with me."

"Nope." He pops the p. "Haven't even left the hotel. Stupid fucking Council. I'd much rather see you."

My abdomen tightens at that admission. "Not leaving the hotel at all is criminal," I murmur. "How much longer are you there for?"

"Four days," he replies with a sigh that's more than enough of a clue to how he feels about it.

"Promise me in the next four days, you will leave the hotel at least once. Deal?"

"Mmmh, I promise, Princess. Only for you."

Heat lances through me, straight to the depths of my core. Both at the way he says the nickname he chose for me and the conversation as a whole. He's unrestrained again, and my body remembers because the last time his voice sounded like this, he was whispering in my ear with his cock buried inside me. He's the Cade I asked to take me home; the one who curled around me in his bathtub and who couldn't keep his hands off me. The same man I didn't want to stop touching me. He's relaxed. Uninhibited. Uncaring about the world around him at every waking moment other than me. I like it, and this time, I'm willing to admit it.

He sighs again, and memory prickles goosebumps along my skin. I remember that sigh. The same one he let out the morning after our tryst, and the same one I let out when I'm in bed finding my spot for the night.

"Are you in bed?"

His responding sigh cascades all the way down my spine, compounding the heat inside me. "Maybe," he mutters, and I tense. "You?"

"Maybe."

He hums a contented sound before we both go silent, save for the soft sounds of our breathing. Unlike the first time we talked on the phone, this silence isn't stifling. In just a few short days, it's become comfortable. We're just existing together here, and with every passing second that we sit, my abdomen and something lower tighten just a little more.

"You fall asleep?" I whisper.

There's a deep sigh on the other end of the phone that makes goose-bumps race across my arms. "No. Just listenin' to you."

"Breathing?"

"You breathe beautifully."

I'm not sure if he can even hear the laugh I let out. It's so faint. "Go to sleep. You probably have a busy day tomorrow."

"I don't wanna hang up…Wish you were here so I could hold you."

Hrmph. I nearly gag with the pleasurable wave that starts from deep in the pit of my stomach and surges through my body to the tips of my fingers and toes. The sensation crashes back into below my navel in a wave of shivers that make my pussy clench. Good goddesses, just a few words can have this much power? What it must be to have a partner who so willingly bestows them. I suppose I know now what it's like because this man is giving them to me without hesitation. But it just reminds me that Cade *isn't* my partner.

"J-just hold me, huh?" Is all I can manage.

"Princess." The way he drags out my nickname makes it sound so sinful. "If you were in my arms, I'd be doin' far filthier things than holdin' you. You'd be screaming my name."

I don't have a single moment to respond before a whispered, "Fuck," followed by a much more alert, "Fuck," comes through the phone. My heart is racing so hard it's pounding in my ears. I barely hear him say, "That was creepy…I'm sorry. Please still answer my calls."

Audibly, I clear the lump from my throat. "Yeah, it was."

"Fuck." The word is hissed and full of dread.

"But I liked it." A lot. Enough that wetness seeps along my lower lips. But I'm not going to say that much to him. "So don't worry, Cade Blanton, I'll still take your calls."

Soft chuckling follows a deep sigh of more than relief. "You're a delight, beautiful."

"Probably why you asked me to marry you."

He forces out another deep sigh. This one is far more jagged than all before it. As plain as a birdsong on a clear spring day I can hear his breath hitch.

It makes me ask, "What?"

"Nothin'. I shouldn't." His voice is far more silken now.

I whisper, "You can tell me, Cade."

There's another long, sharp inhale followed by a deeper, breathier groan. And I don't need him to tell me specifically 'what'. I know. The same feeling is swirling in me at just the sounds he's letting escape.

"I should go—"

"Please don't hang up," I say louder than I mean to. He doesn't. He forces out another heavy breath that makes me think he already unbuttoned his pants to free himself well before he said he had to go. The thought makes me clench with sudden lust. All of me. "What kind of fiancée would I be if I shared your secrets? You can tell me, Cade."

Another sinful groan makes all of me hot; flashes of our night together play in my mind at the sound and soak my core.

"You haven't said my name since moanin' it that night," he whispers, voice as thick as velvet. I can't believe that that's true. But it must be. "Hearin' you say it again made me so fuckin' hard, Princess. I—Fuck."

I imagine him on the other end of the phone, eyes closed in concentration as he does everything he can to stay respectful when all he wants to do is stroke himself. The scene I craft in my mind makes it harder to keep myself from doing the same. My free hand floats below the sheet and dusts featherlight against the outside of my underwear. They're already wet, and I unintentionally whimper.

"I wish you could feel how wet your voice makes me," I murmur.

He groans, and this time it's completely unrestrained. Twenty-nine years of using phones and I've never done this. But fuck me if the wetness seeping along my slit says that I don't want to.

There's a hitch in his breathing. Several. "Fuckin' hells. I didn't call for this, beautiful. Promise."

"I know," I whisper. "But do you want it?"

"More than you can imagine."

"Then let me talk you through it." A jagged gasp rips fire through my veins, shuddering my breath. "Y-You already touching yourself for me?" I take his grunting as answer enough. "Good. S-stroke just the tip for me, then."

There's a sigh that sounds like resignation but he says, "Yes ma'am," and my pussy clenches. I dip my fingers below the waistband of my underwear and let my moan play through the phone. His every jagged breath brushes against his, playing in my ears like a symphony of the most melodious music. My fingers shake against my clit, and I sing back to him the sweetest song of pleasure I can offer.

"Are-are you imagining my pussy taking that magnificent cock?"

"Mmh, yes. Yes," he murmurs. "I have. Every night for weeks."

That admission lights my nerves on fire. Chokes me with desire. "A-and how good it feels to be inside me?"

My cheeks flame red at the indecent groan that comes back through the phone. "So fucking good. Fuck—so good."

"How good?" I ask. "How good does my pussy feel taking all of you, *Cade*?" I purr his name with the deepest intention.

"F-fuck, baby, so good—" he pants and groans, and it's enough to tell me how close he already is. Maybe it actually was the liquor's fault last time just like now. Or maybe it's me. Maybe, just maybe, there's something in him that can't resist me. Even over the phone. I preen at that thought, even if it's only in my head.

I chuckle, a husky sound. "Stroke your cock for me, Cade. All of it. Give me all of you."

Not a single coherent word comes back. Familiar groans and sighs are the only sounds, and I echo them with the bliss that's slowly building inside me as I circle my clit. As I listen to this man hang on every word I say.

"Are you close for me?" He just groans deep and his breaths are what tell me I'm right, panted and quick. I'll make sure to remember the sound of him hanging on to the last shreds of sanity and my words forever. "Let me hear you come for me, Cade."

He lets me hear every single thing. Every grunt. Every groan. Flashes of our first time together fill in the rest. The way he twitches in bliss. The furrow of his brow in pleasurable release. The sated smile on his face when he spills himself. I close my eyes and let the memory circle my clit harder. Firmer.

"Princess," he breathes around my panting. "Let me hear you come, too, please."

My fingers aren't enough. Not by a mile. My vibrator isn't either when I reach for it, but it does the trick while I imagine his thick cock sinking into me with every roll of his hips. Every delicious swirl of his tongue on my clit. Those fingers hooking inside me. His teeth clamping around my nipple. My moans flit through my room. I don't scream when my body curls inward in bliss, I just whisper his name in the breathless pants that slip past my lips as my body, my pussy twitch from ecstasy.

"So beautiful when you come," he whispers.

"You can't even see me," I say through panted laughter.

"No," he says, and there's a new laziness in his voice. "But I remember. And I can't wait to see it again."

I laugh at that, breathless. "You sleepy now?"

"Mmh, thanks to you."

"Me, too. I'm hanging up now so you can clean up and go to sleep."

"Stay on with me?" He asks. "Fall asleep with me."

It won't be long anyways. He'll fall asleep quickly, so I can give him five more minutes. "Okay. Good night, *Cade*."

He sighs, much quieter. "Good night, Princess."

It takes less than five minutes before I hear gentle snores on the other end of the phone. I stay for another five minutes before hanging up, listening to him sleep. If I breathe beautifully, I'm not sure what word I could use to describe the sounds of his slumber. Whatever word it is, I like it. And I wish I was next to him in bed, listening to it until I fall asleep, hot and sated.

CHAPTER

SEVENTEEN

H EAT LANCES THROUGH MY BODY, AND I CRY, TUMBLING IN MY BED seeking any sliver of relief I can. Unlike what I thought yesterday, my discomfort isn't because of the stairs or Cade's voice or the weather drifting between warmth and a cold, humidity-less mess. I'm sick. Dreadfully so. A fever has plagued me longer than I realized while I chalked my misery up to stress. How wrong I was. Some vile microbe plundered my immune system overnight, likely handed to me by an unsuspecting customer at the shop, making it impossible to breathe out of my nose or keep anything down.

Thankfully, Alex is an ever-present hero. It took two seconds on the phone with her this morning for her to hear how dreadful I sound. I didn't need to say another word. She demanded I get back to sleep and not worry about a single coffee-related thing until I felt better. Add another notch to the "Alex deserves a raise if not more" list I'll be giving to Jae when she gets home. All I can hope now is that whoever infected me with this disease didn't also ruin Jae's last few days in paradise with sickness.

I've been attempting to sleep since I hung the phone up in this den of disgust—aka my bed—but mostly I've been writhing in discomfort and cold sweats. I don't even know how long it's been or what time it is—

Buzz. Buzz. Buzzbuzzbuzz.

It's half past five. Even sick, I recognize Cade's new vibration pattern. But right now, I don't want to answer it. Or I'm not strong enough. I reach for my phone, nonetheless; the screen light hurts my eyes. No, somehow, the light hurts everything that I am when I squint to see the name scrawled across the top.

Jackass. <3

When I press the painfully green answer button, I don't *answer* the phone. I just whimper and flip the thing against my ear. It's cold, and I groan at the slightest relief from the burning hellscape that is my body.

"Hello? You there, beautiful?" There's already concern in his voice. Probably because every time he's called over the last week, I've answered with much more vigor.

I squeak a noise of discomfort. "…Yeah." The word sounds of sheer nasally disgust.

"Gods, you sound miserable."

"Feel worse."

Fucking fever. Tears well along my lower lids before I close my eyes and they sear down my cheeks like lava, burning hot against my already heated skin. I can't stand the feeling. Never have I suffered quietly when sick, and this time is no different. I whine.

"Don't cry," he says, and the softness in his voice only makes me cry harder. "It'll make you feel even worse. Is Jae home yet?" The sound I grumble must be a good enough answer because he says, "Okay. Go back to sleep for me."

I won't. Not even if I remember him saying the words through the haze of sickness. Groaning to no one but myself, I toss in bed and whimper, seeking the cool side of anything to press against my throbbing head. It doesn't help. Nothing does except for crying, although that isn't actually helping anything other than offering me a modicum of mental relief.

I loathe being sick. I don't handle it well at all. Amber always said I act like a toddler with a cold. I cry. I whine and whimper and toss and turn and complain every time I have to take medicine. The comparison isn't far off, but it's not my fault. Being sick fucking sucks. Being under the weather while you're alone is worse because I have no one to force me to take medicine. I don't possess enough willpower to make myself drink that putrid substance. I hate it. Always have; even my mother and grandfather couldn't get me to take it without at least a little hassle when I was young. They came up with a song they'd sing every time to convince me. So I most certainly won't take it without—

Buzz. Buzz. Buzzbuzzbuzz.

Cade. Again. I'm not sure how long it's been since the last call, but this time I don't answer; my phone goes silent after ringing all the way to voicemail, but only for less than a handful of seconds.

Buzz. Buzz. Buzzbuzzbuzz.

Groaning, I search for wherever I tossed the device in the mound of ruffled blankets and pillows. I find it right before the last ring.

Cade is already talking when I put the phone to my ear. "—know it'll suck, but come let me in."

"Hmm?" I'm not sure if this is just a fever dream or if I did, in fact, hear him correctly.

"I'm at your door. Come let me in?"

I did hear him. This time it's a question that nearly makes me cry. I don't answer; I just roll out of bed with the dregs of my energy and the phone still on my ear. Shuffling through the apartment, I make it to the door without crying because of the pain of my fever. Everything hurts. But seeing him standing outside in the hallway with bags full of things meant to make me feel better and a hesitant smile makes me hurt a little less. It also makes it impossible to hold tears back; before I hang up the phone, I'm crying. It's only because I'm sick, or so I try to tell myself. Hot tears leak down my face and the expression on his melts into mild horror. But he quickly steps around me and inside when I back away to let him.

"Don't cry. It will make you feel worse," he commands for the second time as he removes his shoes and sets countless bags onto the island top.

"Why—why are you here?" It's not how I mean to ask why he's back from Amsterdam days early, but he seems to understand what I mean.

He's back in front of me, picking a clump of my bangs from my forehead and pushing them away. "I couldn't leave you here alone feeling so awful. I hope it's okay." Nodding shakes more tears from my eyes. His icy hands engulf my face to wash them away. I nuzzle into the cold like I'm starved and he's offering a buffet. "Fuck, you're burning up. Have you taken medicine?" I shake my head, which doubles as seeking his cold caress. "None?"

He sounds genuinely disappointed in me and my face crumples to show how that makes me feel. I may actually choke out a sob and cry a little harder. I'm not entirely sure. Disappointment and disgust and pain all blend into hot, heavy tears down my cheeks.

"Hey, it's okay," he murmurs, wiping away more moisture before cupping my jaws in wide, frigid hands again. "Come on, back to bed. I'll get you some medicine."

"You don't even know me," I say as if that's a response, not moving.

"What kind of man would I be if I let my fiancée suffer sickness alone?"

"You don't have to." A choked sob.

"I don't, no. But I'm going to stay here until you feel better, unless you want me to go."

I shake my head again, unable to hold back the tears burning at the corners of my eyes. "I'm only crying 'cause I'm sick."

He huffs a laugh. "Don't worry. I won't tell your secrets either. I didn't see a thing."

I know he leads me back to my bed, and I know I find my way back to my little cocoon of blankets, but I don't remember much else until the bed depresses next to me in seconds or minutes. How long, I don't know.

"Okay, Princess. Medicine time." I haphazardly force a hand out to push him away. I make contact with something, but he just laughs. "Come on," he murmurs. "You can do it for me. Just one cap-full."

I whine, but I do down the acrid medicine he holds to my lips with a blanch of disgust.

"Now some water." I definitely don't want any water. Maybe he understands that by the way I toss and turn in my bed because without me saying anything, he says, "You need to hydrate. Just three big sips for me."

I try again to wriggle in my discomfort, but something cold sweeps around the back of my neck. His hand, holding my head in place.

"Sit up for me."

I don't have the strength, yet somehow I'm floating on the cloud of his comforting palm as a cool glass parts my lips. Water flows into my mouth before I can protest, and my dehydration takes over for several seconds. He whispers, "Good girl," several times before slowly lowering me back into the cocoon of discomfort I've built.

Something lays across my forehead, draping coolness down the sides of my face. Something smooth brushes against my cheek and it takes a few strokes to realize it's his thumb. "Go back to sleep, beautiful."

I'd snort at that moniker being used when I haven't showered and probably look like death, but I don't have the energy. Whining is all I can manage while rolling to find the cold part of a pillow. I swear I blink and he's back, telling me it's medicine time again. I'm unsure how often we play out this exact scenario; maybe twice or a thousand times as I fade in and out of consciousness. All I know is that any time soft light fills my vision, so does Cade's outline. Sometimes he's holding water and medicine, other times he's trying to get me to eat something that makes me want to hurl.

However many times it happens, he's there with soothing words, reassurance, and cool palms on my skin. He's there. I cry. I take whatever he gives me while reassuring me I'll be okay and the sickness will pass.

Maybe that's why when I wake up with enough fortitude to actually stand, I believe him. The sickness is lingering in my chest, and will for a few weeks with a month long cough, but he was right in those quiet moments—the worst passed. Breathing deeply out of my nose just for the sheer fact I can, I reach for my phone.

There's not a text or call to be found, which isn't surprising. Jae would be the only one, and given the apparent date, she's traveling home. Which means I've been in this bed and in the sweat of my sickness for days. Now that I'm not burning hot, I can feel the stickiness all over my body other than my face.

Cade was wiping it down.

The thought makes my stomach lurch in the best way it has in days. Shrugging off the blankets, I change into a fresh set of pajamas from the top of my dresser, realizing Cade cared for me while all I wore was a tank top and underwear. I know he's seen me much barer, but an odd insecurity breathes through me. I throw on a hoodie for good measure and slink toward my bedroom door.

He's asleep on the couch and looks remarkably uncomfortable. He's taller than the couch is wide, and parts of him are hanging off of every edge. It's certainly not a natural sleeping position, but he doesn't seem to have an issue. He snores softly, and it makes me smile, thinking back to just days before when he fell asleep with me on the phone.

Seeing my familiar's face washes the heat away with a laugh. Charlie is staring daggers at Cade from across the room, sitting ramrod straight on the island counter. He's not a fan of new people, a trait we share. I just laugh and run my fingers through the fur behind his ear with a few gentle scratches as I approach. He grants me a glare before cutting it back to Cade.

"He took care of me," I whisper. "You should like him."

If cats could roll their eyes, Charlie would do just that before hopping down and sauntering his way toward my bedroom. In the place he vacates sits a pad of paper littered with dates and times written on nearly every line. There's three columns: Acetaminophen, Ibuprofen, and Water. The last has the least amount of entries. At several points, he's crossed out times because I must've refused to drink. There's even one line where there's just an angry little smiley face drawn with squiggly lines showing precisely how angry I was. It makes me smile. Both because I was probably an ass and because all he did was document how—

"You were very cranky with me that time."

"Fucking goddesses above!" I nearly jump out of my skin as I whip around to see a bleary-eyed Cade standing behind me.

The grogginess of sleep fills his laughter. "Sorry."

"How can you be so freaking large yet so quiet?"

"It's an art," he replies, stepping into my kitchen as if it's his and moving to where several bottles of medicine sit on the counter. "You look like you feel better."

"I do. Finally." But he still pulls a bottle of neon orange liquid into his hands and pops it open. "I think I'm all better now. No need for more meds."

He shoots an exasperated smirk at me over his shoulder as I'm climbing into one of our bar stools. "You're taking this medicine, no matter if I have to hold you down again."

"*Again?*"

He pours the liquid almost to the brim of the plastic cup. "You tried to smack the cup away, and I almost spilled it all over you." I snort a laugh even though I don't mean to, but he's laughing about it too while sliding the aforementioned cup across the island. "So be a good girl and take it for me without any hassle this time."

That's enough to make me want to knock the cup off the counter just for good measure. I think he can see that in the way my expression narrows. But he only arches a brow higher at me in challenge. I roll my eyes and snatch the thing, downing it, trying to hold back my gag.

"Good girl." Fresh water slides across the counter to me.

I blanch. "I'd rather drink more medicine."

For a moment, it looks like he's going to command me again to drink the water, but he gives up with a huffed laugh. He just turns into the kitchen and opens cabinets like he knows exactly where everything is to find the pods for Jae's coffee machine. He pulls out the last one, which means I'll have to refill them, but I say nothing because he's got a right to make some coffee after dealing with me for days.

"You really didn't have to come take care of me," I say, probably a little too self-deprecatingly. He glances at me while closing the pod into the coffee machine and looks genuinely confused. "I've been told I'm a hassle when I'm sick and you barely know me. So thank you for coming. You didn't have to—Wait." Something hits me like a ton of bricks and for a moment, I forget to breathe. "W-wait, you *came to take care of me.* From Amsterdam." Cade just smiles as he starts his brew, and the simple act combined with my realization steals every bit of air in my lungs. There's only one way he could've gotten back so quickly. "Did you *Fade* halfway across the world to take care of me?"

He only looks at me with that fondness again, turning from the counter to make his way to me. "It's not that big of a deal."

"Y-yes, it is," I stammer as he spins the barstool and cages me between the backrest and his chest. I'm shaking as I look up into those tender eyes sweeping over my face and the gentle smile that accompanies them. "You-you wasted goddesses know how much of your life to come care for me. A stranger."

A few fingers brush hair from my forehead before his large hand again settles on my cheek. I'm shaking against him as his thumb glides over my skin. "It wasn't a waste," he replies without hesitation. "It takes less for Proteans to use magic, but I would've done it either way because you're not a stranger. Not anymore."

I can't speak. I can barely even think as my brain processes his words and what they mean as he picks up my left hand and pulls the ring to his lips, dropping a warm kiss against my skin. The intimacy of this moment may kill me. The heat of our hands as he settles them on my thigh through my thin pajamas. His gaze sweeping across my face as I struggle to breathe. It's all a little too much for my still-sluggish mind to handle. I have to look anywhere other than at him to gather back a hint of sanity. But he curls a few fingers around my jaw and nudges it until I look back into the softness of his eyes just as the coffee hisses.

"And you weren't a hassle. You were sick and felt like shit. You were allowed to bitch. Whoever told you anything different is a bag of flaccid dicks. Being sick sucks. You don't have to act like you feel okay when you don't. Especially not in front of me."

A bag of flaccid dicks. Huh. I doubt I could think of a better way to describe Amber if I tried right now.

I gasp out a sound that's supposed to be a laugh, trying to fill my lungs. "I-I also don't have to act so cranky," I say and glance toward the small, angry smiley face and back.

He does the same, and the fond smile that floats over his face constricts my throat even more. "I thought that was actually pretty adorable."

Adorable. *Adorable.* That word shouldn't make even more butterflies saturate my stomach, but it does. It also makes me smile even though I try to hold it back. I'm at least able to hide it behind pinching my lips and pursing them to the side. He watches every single moment, enraptured.

"I should probably shower off the sweat," I mumble.

He looks pleased with himself. "Maybe take a bath? Just so you don't have to stand. And not scolding hot; it should be a little cooler to help you stay cool. And maybe—"

"Can I wash myself, too?" He looks sheepish for a moment until I ask, "Will you stay?"

Several emotions flit over his face before a smile settles broadly across it. "For as long as you'll have me. Are you hungry?"

"A little."

"Soup and grilled cheese?"

I just nod, missing his coolness when he echoes the motion and turns away. I watch him for a moment move around Jae and I's kitchen like he's been here countless times before. It should make me uncomfortable that he spent four practically unsupervised days in our place, but it doesn't. It just makes me smile as I head for the shower.

Steaming hot water doesn't feel good, but I won't admit that to Cade. I stay underneath the water until my fingers prune and the faucet won't go any further left. Water drips down the mirror as I finally take myself in for the first time in days. Dark circles show restless sleep, my hair is a mess even through the wash, and I desperately need to brush my teeth. But I feel much better.

The bed's stripped when I peer out to make sure my bedroom door is closed. Equal parts bewilderment and appreciation course through me at Cade doing my laundry without my asking. After everything he's done for me over the last several days, it shouldn't surprise me. But perhaps it's just the last straw that tips the scales of gratitude into a level with which I'm unaccustomed. He Faded halfway across the world. He showed up at my doorstep with bags filled with things to aid my healing; he poured my medicine and fed me water in my haze of desperation. He made me food, suffered through my sickness with me, and didn't complain a single moment.

All without my asking. All for a woman he truly doesn't know. My heart overflows as I dry myself and seek fresh clothes. I don't consciously pull on my cutest pair of tights that Jae regularly says makes my ass look amazing. But when I glance sidelong at myself in the mirror, my ass greets me just below the tank top I put on.

Laughter draws my attention away. One laugh I've known since childhood; the other I'm still learning and savoring the sound of more and more.

Cade's are the first eyes I meet when I emerge into the living room; he's relaxing on the sofa with a wide smile. Probably from something undoubtedly too-forward that Jae said. Or maybe he's smiling at the episode of Beverly Hills Kitchen Witch they're watching.

"There you are," he says.

I fumble for anything to say and manage nothing.

Thankfully Jae says, "You were sick, and you didn't even tell me?" and pulls both of our attention to where she's sprawled across the loveseat, a grilled cheese in hand.

Quietly, I clear the lump from my throat and retort, "You were on vacation."

Jae scoffs. "As if I wouldn't have come home to take care of you."

"That's why I didn't call you. Alex took over at the shop," I say, realizing I'm still standing in my bedroom doorway. Jae doesn't move when I pace toward the sitting room, so that leaves the other side of the couch with Cade for me to sink into. "Which, by the way," I continue. "You should really promote her and give her a raise."

"I plan to," Jae says. "But that doesn't mean you can just not tell me when you're sick, witch."

"I ended up with a pretty decent caretaker," I say, glancing at Cade.

His expression shifts, eyelids hanging low over those sparkling hazel eyes in fondness. They smolder through me as he says, "Decent, huh? I'll take decent."

Even though I'm a literal gremlin full of snot and acetaminophen, his eyes shift between me and the space beside him. Honestly, I'm not sure he even realizes that he's done it or that he slings his arm over the back of the couch beside him. Nor am I sure if it's actually an invitation or why I choose to accept it, but I do, sliding across the couch until our thighs touch. Astonishment floats over his face, again not concealing his emotions in front of me, and delight washes it away as his fingers brush down my shoulder. He nods to the coffee table where a bowl of tomato soup and a grilled cheese sit waiting for me.

"I want to see you eat something and drink some more water before I go," he says.

"Go?" The word blurts out, and my gaze snaps back to him.

There's only a beat of silence before Jae springs up, saying, "I'll get the water!" and disappears into the kitchen like it's far enough away from the couch to consider the distance as leaving us alone.

"Jae's home, so I was going to go." His voice is low, and perhaps tinted with disappointment.

"I'd like it if you stayed for a while longer, if you can."

His entire body sags with a sigh of relief. "Careful, or I might start to think you actually like me."

"You can stay. For a little bit," I amend with a mocking flick of my head and a half-hearted roll of my eyes, although I want him to stay much longer.

They land back on and can't look away from the sultry smile on his face. "That's better."

He does stay for four episodes of Beverly Hills Kitchen Witch and ends up making both Jae and I two more grilled cheese sandwiches to go along with the unreasonably well-seasoned tomato soup. He makes me drink more water and take medicine on schedule, but I suppose it's okay. The warmth that his concern brings can't be anything other than okay.

Jae bids her goodbyes and leaves the room when he stands to leave. I follow him to the door, watching while he slides his shoes on.

"Are you in town for a while?"

"I am. Why?"

"We have to keep looking for a way to get this off," I say and flick my left hand toward him. "But, are you ready to take me on that date?"

There's no hesitation; a full grin sharpens his features as he says, "I've been ready." The look is enough to make me giddy with nerves, but when he leans in and kisses my forehead, my stomach plummets to my ankles and back in the best way. "I'll call you."

"J-just text me. Like a normal human."

"We're not human, and neither of us are normal." A quiet laugh dusts over me in a wave of goosebumps. "And I like hearing your voice too much."

Butterflies warm my core, remembering that night on the phone. I try to play it off by saying, "And we're still researching."

He huffs a laugh that makes even me not believe my words. "Deal. But even if we find something, it doesn't mean we have to use it. Bye, beautiful. I'll *call* you."

With that, he winks, opens the door, and heads for the elevators, turning the corner without looking back. I know because I watch him walk all the way away until I hear the elevator closing.

A raucous squeal echoes through the apartment when I close the door. Jae looks absolutely ecstatic, bouncing when she reappears from her bedroom. "You didn't tell me about your little date deal, you bitch!"

"Of course I didn't. Look at you," I say, but I can't hide my smile. "And don't read his thoughts!"

"I can't help it! He's *so* loud around you! He's so smitten! His thoughts—"

"I don't want to know!" I wave my hands to stop her. She just rolls her lips inward to hide her eagerness. It doesn't work. She's as giddy as I am. "I don't want to know from *you*. I want to know from him."

But I actually do want to know, and hearing Jae say he's smitten with me makes me want to squeal. I do, but keep it internal. Doesn't matter because Jae can feel how her words make me feel. She squeals loudly for me, and I let her.

Fuck. I like Cade Blanton. A lot.

CHAPTER

EIGHTEEN

The Toasted Oak is buzzing with the hustle and bustle of a beautiful spring day. Bright sun paints the world outside in the crystal clarity of a day after rain, highlighting the brilliant greens, purples, blues, and reds of the flora lining the sidewalks and overflowing in the park. One of Jae's favorite regulars brought in new plants to liven up the place and is tending them in the window seal on the far side of the room. A local artist hangs up new artwork in the spots purchases have left vacant over the last month. Several newcomers who found a favorite spot during the Blanton Debacle and regulars who braved the storm and made it out unscathed on the other side overfill the dining room. Chatter, glasses clinking, and silverware on plates almost drown out the door chime as it sings through the room.

Jae looks over my shoulder and the joy on her face is more telling than the sudden and heavy feeling of eyes on me. She's too delighted for it to be someone random. A wide grin splits her face. I take that and the slowly quieting room to mean one thing.

She confirms my suspicion by bouncing up from where she's been resting her elbows on the counter to say brightly, "Well, if it isn't Mr. Best-Selling Drink himself!"

Familiar laughter filters over the remaining sounds in the dining room. The depth cascades over me as his footsteps approach. I don't turn around from where I've been leaning against the counter beside Jae. I'm not sure why I feel incapable of moving or breathing or functioning in just about every way.

"Hello to you, too, Jae."

Cade's voice makes it even more impossible to turn. My heart momentarily plummets into my stomach, reawakening the butterflies from their slumber. They flutter into a chaotic frenzy when I glance over my shoulder. He's smiling down at me in that effortless way he manages, and it fumbles my breathing again.

"Hello, beautiful."

It takes all of my willpower to not bend forward with the wave of tingles that ripple over me. Warmth spreads through my body and leaves a smile on my face. I should be accustomed to it by now, but his impact doesn't seem to fade. If anything, it's getting more overwhelming with every encounter. I suppose that's how getting to know someone works.

"Hey," I say, happiness lilting my voice. "What are you doing here?"

"I know I said I'd call," he starts. "But then I was sitting at home trying to work while waiting for you to get off and I couldn't focus. So I decided to come ask you on our date in person. I hoped to catch you on break for a walk."

Jae squeals instead of me. It helps me hide the way my throat tightens. Jae doesn't help, however, by grabbing my shoulders and forcing me toward the split in the counter. Unlike the last several times she pushed me toward Cade, this time, I don't resist.

"How lucky! Her break starts right now!" Jae crows, untying my smock for me.

I slip it off and toss it on Jae's arm when I take over my own movements. Barely. My feet are moving toward Cade, rounding the counter to meet him, but it doesn't really feel like I'm the one moving. It's like the hand he's holding out is drawing me forward and not my own willpower.

A flash somewhere over Cade's shoulder snaps me out of movement, and my gaze slams to a pair of women. One precedes in horror to scold the other, who looks like they might die from embarrassment. If only she knew the apprehension she thrust into me by having the flash on while photographing strangers in public. Maybe that would make her feel worse. Sudden anxiety wraps around me like a vise at the reminder that this life—where Cade holds out his hand to take me on a walk in public—is not my own.

I forgot. Somehow, with the sickness and running the shop and the nights on the phone getting to know him while he was gone, I forgot *who* he is. I forgot about the public eye because I've been out of it in his absence. I forgot about the articles and the pictures and the craziness. I forgot what the ring on my finger *actually* means. But that horrified woman's flash brought every bit right back to the front of my mind.

This moment? It will be the next headline on some tabloid website that pumps out stories that have no substance beyond gossip.

Future Councilor escorts dirty skank hoe on a walk.

Aldrich Blanton holds his hand out in charity.

Okay... maybe not that vulgar. But taking Cade's hand here *will* show up in another tabloid or blog. That much I'm certain of. Sliding my palm against his is reconfirmation, publicly, that we are together and soon to be married. That we got engaged after having a secret relationship—something unheard of in the age when everyone has a camera in their pocket and a penchant for money or fame. All the speculation and conjecture...Holding his hand here means reaffirming everything.

But as Cade glances over his shoulder, too, at the woman, who now looks as translucent as a ghost, I realize that taking his hand is also confirming that I don't mind any of it. It's saying that I like him.

Immediately, my palms go clammy. Cade, however, doesn't miss a beat. He turns back to me with a trained calmness before a camera.

Me? I hesitate. My throat closes, and I just glance from the serene smile on his face to his hand, hoping it isn't obvious.

"Let's go take that walk," he says.

I'm not sure if he sees my hand jerk before I reach out and slide it into his. If he does, he doesn't seem to mind and laces our fingers. I roll my lips together to hide the hesitation and nod. "Lead the way."

He does, guiding us through the slightly crowded dining room. Holding the door open for me, he steps aside to allow me out into the sunshine I've been longingly staring at from behind the counter for most of the day. I savor the warmth as it lifts the air-conditioning off my skin. A shiver works away the chill, and I lean my face toward the sun for a moment, eyes closing to soak in as many rays as I can.

Cade is watching me with a tenderness I'm growing to understand when I open my eyes; my stomach threatens to somersault off a cliff.

"Beautiful day, isn't it?" He inclines his head toward the park.

I nod and follow when he pulls me into motion, fingers tightly interwoven with mine. "Very, and if you hadn't shown up, I probably would have spent my break inside. So thank you."

"You're very welcome. I'm just glad I got your schedule right. I wasn't sure exactly when your break was."

"Yes, you were." There's a teasing tone in my voice. "You know exactly when I work. You stalked my job for a week, called me on my days off, showed up here—"

He barks a laugh, grinning. "Alright, okay. I knew you were working and exactly when your break was and it worked out perfectly."

Our laughter joins with the noises of the park, which brims with people today milling about. Children holler in the play area on the far side; their parents and others fill park benches and blankets on the flushing green lawn. Some people notice Cade as he tugs me into the tree-lined pathway. Others walk past us without a care in the world and make me feel a little better. There are people who don't know who either of us are. That's nice to know. We're not as important as it seems shrouded in my own little world.

"So, how do you feel about unicorns?"

The question catches me in the middle of taking in the scene, and for a moment, I have to process the words. Surely I didn't hear correctly. The look on his face when I seek validation says I did. My eyes widen and a sudden excitement builds in me and in my voice. "A totally normal amount and not at all an obsession level of feelings for unicorns. Why?"

The mirth on his face shows he knows by how much I'm under-selling it. He hums. "Hmm. So if I invited you to a fundraiser in support of unicorn rehabilitation and conservation—"

"I'm so in!" I shout, stopping us in our tracks to beam up at him with bewilderment. "I'm so, so in!"

He grins, and it lights his face more than the sun splitting the trees. "Somehow, I thought you might be. Only thing is, it's in Asheboro."

"Asheboro?! There's a unicorn preserve an hour from here and I didn't know it?!"

"No, wait—" Sheepishness overtakes his face. "I meant the one in the mountains. Ash…err."

"Ville. Asheville's the one in the mountains," I finish, shock receding, but excitement remains in me. Too much, if I'm honest, but I can't help it.

"That's the one. Sorry. I've been here since I was a kid, but I still get the names mixed up."

"We didn't make it easy. I've never been to Asheville, but I've always wanted to go. How are we going to get there?"

"I'm not sure what your work schedule is like—" I cock my head, lips pursing. His laughter then is deep. The sound is so reminiscent of my hazy memories of our night together. It's full, genuine, and I thoroughly enjoy the way it alights his face with adoration. "Okay, yes. I do. It means you'd need to ask for this Saturday afternoon off, if it's not too short of notice."

"If you ask Jae, she'll say five thousand percent yes."

"Then I'll ask her when we get back," he says. "If this is you agreeing, of course?"

"I'm agreeing."

I hear Jae's voice in my head. *You'll find someone who will try. I promise.*

She told me those words after Amber walked out. She promised I'd find someone who cared for me, who *tried* in the simplest ways, like finding things I like to do and planning dates around them. I couldn't fathom what she meant. Hearing her describe those types of things from a partner felt overbearing. But now that it's standing right in front of me with a smile that I can't look away from and eyes that look at me in reverence...I can't deny how nice it is. Amber never planned something so elaborate. Sure, we couldn't afford a day trip to Asheville for a unicorn fundraiser. But I bet if you even just asked Amber what my favorite animal is, she'd guess something like an axolotl when I loathe amphibians.

The effort fills me with affection.

His grip tightens around my fingers, and his smile bleeds onto my face. My heart thumps in my chest. "I'm very happy to hear that. And maybe you'll be happy to hear that I left the hotel in Amsterdam."

Further warmth spreads through me as he turns us back to our path down the bustling walkway. I want to believe it's inexplicable. But it's not. I know exactly why. He kept his promise. Even as small and inconsequential as it may have been, he kept it. Something he easily could have said he forgot through all the alcohol or didn't have time for because of work, he did.

I hide the visceral response behind a smirk, though. "He keeps his promises, huh?"

"Always."

"All of them?" Incredulity lilts my voice with playfulness. "If you say yes, I won't trust you."

Honesty shakes his head. "No. I try, but I've broken one or two in my day."

One or two, even proverbially, isn't bad compared to the breadth of my history. Being on the broken end of a promise is something I'm far too familiar with. Every step in my life has left behind the remnants of shattered promises. For as much as I loved my mother, she had her faults. She tried her hardest, but promises meant nothing when bills needed to be paid. I understand now, but so young and left alone ready to go to the movies? That still hurts sometimes. But the worst thing that hurts is knowing how long I didn't learn from that hurt.

I could have saved myself a lot more heartache if I'd reflected and healed. But I went through life finding that same characteristic in everyone other than Jae and Rokk. Every partner I chose did the same thing. Amber was the queen of empty promises. The guy before her was worse, somehow. We didn't last long, but I remember the way he made me feel, broken and alone. The way they both made me feel.

So hearing that the man holding my hand prides himself in keeping his word is…refreshing.

My heart thumps against my ribs, tightening my abdomen, and I'm suddenly very aware of the metal that sits between our interlaced fingers. The *promise* that bound us together just a few weeks ago, and the second one he agreed to that threatens to tear us apart in the future. Removing the ring. The only promise I find myself hoping he breaks. I know that I'm treading a dangerous line with every charming thing he says and every small action he makes. With every new facet of him I learn. That promise may devastate me when it comes true. If…

"How'd you manage to leave?" I ask to ignore all of that. "With coming to take care of me practically the next day?"

"Wasn't hard being six hours ahead and not having meetings. I spent several hours walking the streets before I called you."

"Enjoy yourself?"

"It made the entire trip a lot better."

"Was it really that bad?"

"I was there for The International Council Conglomerate, and it's the same shit every year. Stodgy old aristocratic types arguing about shit they know next to nothing about. It was terrible. All for a job I don't even want."

My brows knit, but he's not looking at me like I'm watching him. He's gazing out around the park, lost in some thought he's not sharing that's slowly souring his expression. "You don't want the seat? Then why run for election?"

He barks a grim laugh, and I feel like I'm missing out on a joke. He looks at me and realizes that I wasn't kidding. Surprise flits over his face. "I'm not *running* for anything," he says. "Surely you know that?" Whatever confusion remains on my face makes it apparent I don't. For a moment, he looks just as bewildered before shaking his head. "You do know there are no elections, right?"

"Of course I do," I lie, knowing full well I didn't pay enough attention in that one Magical Law section from history class senior year. He knows, too, clearly. So with sarcasm, I amend, "Now."

Laughter bubbles through his spoiled expression, and he turns back to lead our way. "Well, there isn't. And even though I don't want it, I'm about to inherit the seat from my grandfather when he retires at the end of the year because of some ancient and asinine tradition. Hopefully, mine will be the last ever inherited, though. I'm going to do my damnedest to ensure it."

"Oh?" is all I ask because he's in a zone I've rarely seen him slip into. Fluid, proud. Aldrich. That's who this version of Cade is. And I find myself liking this side of him, too. I saw glimpses of him in those days he worked in The Toasted Oak, but I couldn't or wouldn't appreciate it then.

"There should be an election to select the new member. It's the first thing I'm proposing to change; I'm even drafting the bill already. But The Council is old and ingrained in their practices. It's going to be extremely difficult to gain favor among the members, all of whom are grooming their children or nieces or nephews to take over. But I think I can manage it—"

He doesn't realize just how qualified he is for a future that he says he doesn't want. In the five minutes he's talked about his upcoming career, he's expressed more passion than just about anything I've seen him have. Granted, I have a very limited viewpoint, but as he talks about asinine rules built into an organization that's spanned several millennia, I can see exactly how determined he is. The resolve on his face is...so damned attractive. The passion and drive and ambition to change the world and laws as we've always known them...It almost makes Aldrich the sexiest of all of his sides.

"The Exposure just made The Council and everything public," he's saying when I tune back in, voice still steady with fortitude. "These courts have been in place for several millennia. There's a hierarchy, and some of these families have been in their seats for centuries. They won't just willingly abdicate because some kid comes and tells them to."

"Sounds like it will be tough," I agree, squeezing his hand. "But I know you can do it."

"Oh?" He finally glances down at me, a single brow raised. "You think so?"

"I know so. And even if not, it's pretty admirable that you're even attempting to change such a clearly broken system. Especially when you don't want the seat."

I don't miss the way he inflates. There's a lifting in his shoulders that echoes in the faintest tightening of his lips. "If all goes well, I'll only have to serve a four-year minimum. And then I can move on."

"To marine biology."

He smiles. "Exactly. What about you? Any luck finding a new job?"

That question reminds me I haven't responded to Amelia. It took her several days to send the offer letter through, and when I opened it, the package insulted me. Dobson never wanted to do the human resources tasks that were his to do. Instead, when timesheets and compensation claims came across his desk, he made me do them. A blessing now, I suppose, because I know his salary when they fired him. They offered me over thirty-three percent less. A vast undervalue of my talent, at a bare minimum, and patriarchal bullshit at best.

I know it's probably a matter of just negotiating, but after everything that happened, it doesn't feel worth it; not in the slightest. If they truly valued me how they said everyone on the team does, I wouldn't have to fight for a salary equal to or better than the man they fired for insubordination. Add to that the feelings I had being back in The Annex doing research, I find it very hard to care about the job offer sitting in my inbox. Between thoughts of finding a new career, potentially going back to school, and going back to a job that didn't and still doesn't value me? The latter is the least of my choices. At one point, it was the most rewarding career I could've envisioned for myself, even if I balked at it when I got the job. Now? I don't know.

"My old job called me recently," I say.

"Oh?" Intrigue loads his face. "Did they try to bring you back?" I nod, and before I can say anything, he's excitedly saying, "That's fantastic!" He notices my inadvertent flinching and backtracks by shaking his head. "No, nope. It's not fantastic?"

The confusion in his voice makes me chuckle. "It's just surprising after the way I left." I expect to leave it at that, but he's waiting, enraptured, looking down at me while we stroll hand in hand. The curiosity is enduring in a way I don't expect. "I quit by calling my boss a dumbass in the middle of a meeting he scheduled last minute to publicly shame an analyst on my team. He called her a 'useless woman without a brain' in front of everyone."

He looks horrified. "That's fucking awful."

I snort with the revulsion coursing through me again. Just thinking about Dobson and that day makes my lips snarl in disgust. "Yeah. He was a genuine piece of shit. Thankfully, they fired him after I left. I don't know why they didn't do it sooner, but whatever. It happened."

"They should have," Cade defends. "He deserved worse, honestly. I'd love to meet him in a dark alley."

This time, the snort I let out is with laughter. When I look back, he's watching me with fondness again, but there's a hardness lacing the lines of his face. He means it. He'd like to meet Dobson man to man, and that's a pleasant feeling—having someone on my side.

I glance out toward a group of friends throwing a Frisbee. "Yeah. They offered me his job, which I was already doing, but it still seems like taking a step backwards. On paper, it's a higher title. I was damn good at the work, but…I don't know that I want to go back."

"Then that's your answer, isn't it?" he asks. "You have to do what makes you feel most secure. If doing—" He pauses, and I look back and realize he's waiting for me to fill in the blank.

"Supply chain optimization."

"Supply—seriously?" He's caught off guard and the bark of laughter he lets out should probably offend me, but I laugh, too. "If *supply chain optimization*," he drawls the words with the softest smirk, "isn't what makes you happy, then it's time to move on. Take a break, enjoy life for a bit, and figure it out."

"Wouldn't that be lovely?" I snort. "Just *take a break* from life."

"Why can't you?" He asks, and I'm just as bewildered as he was a minute before. But I quickly realize that…he's serious.

"Uh…" I draw the sound out. "Because unfortunately I have bills that need to be paid and my bank account isn't endless, so I can't just take a break from life to go back to school."

Something lights up in his eyes and he squeezes my hand. "Well, good thing your fiancé is filthy rich and can support whatever you want to do."

"I'd never ask for money."

"You're not asking. I'm offering. I'd love to help you go back to school if that's what you want. If not school, I'd love to help you on whatever your next journey is."

The proclamation hangs between us, catching my breath in my chest. Cade's got a knack for that. Saying and doing things that make me completely breathless without so much as batting an eye. Wide eyed, I look at him and there's no hesitation on his face. He genuinely means it. Cade is so invested in *us*, he's willing to pay for my schooling without me even asking. Why, I'm not sure. I've done nothing for him; I've given him nothing. And yet here he stands with the world on a silver platter for me. Something I'd never accept, but can't help my mind running away with the possibilities.

I drop that statement on a gargled chuckle. "Speaking of school," I choke out. "Have any of the books arrived? Have you found anything else?"

Some unnameable emotion flits over his face before he hides it behind the mask of indifference he's good at maintaining. "No," he says, and his voice is much more stiff. "Not yet. A few have shipped to us, but it's all red tape bureaucracy."

I just nod, a mixture of disappointment and elation warring inside me as we lapse into silence, rounding to make the brief trip back to The Toasted Oak. A large thumb brushes over the ridge of my fingers the entire way. Every step makes it a little harder to breathe, makes another thread branch off from the story I'm crafting in my mind of our future. I try to reign it all in, because right now I want to focus on the feeling of being with Cade openly. I can deal with all the other stuff later. Right now, I just want to hold on to this moment and the giddiness fluttering through me.

Jae gives me the entire weekend off with more enthusiasm than I imagined she would. Though, it makes sense. She wants this relationship for me more than I want it for myself. But I *do* want it.

I'm excited. A state I rarely let myself slip into. It almost always leads to disappointment, and I'm not sure how much more disappointment I can take from life. This situation? It's assured to end in disaster. But when Cade turns to me, the smile on his face makes it impossible not to let myself believe we have a chance beyond the ring coming off.

He pulls our joined hands up to his lips and looks me directly in the eye while slowly kissing the ring sitting on my finger. Butterflies rampage in my insides to where, if he wasn't here, I might bend forward to mock a gag. Instead, I hide the flutter of exciting and nauseous and brutally hot attraction behind a thick swallow and a smile when he says against my skin, "I can't wait until I see you Saturday, Princess."

I try my hardest to suppress a shiver when he kisses my fingers again. I fail, but I only slightly tremble. So does my voice when I say, "See you then, *Cade*."

He grins and presses one last kiss onto my fingers before dropping my hand and turning. I watch him walk away again, standing motionless where he left me vibrating with excitement. Jae looks like she may combust for the rest of the day. I keep my elation hidden inside, only showing in the smile I cannot keep from my face. Maybe this relationship will hurt me in the long run, but...I can't keep holding onto that fear. I can't keep expecting Cade to upset me like everyone before him.

I think of Cade, our walk, and the potential of our date for the rest of my shift. Every time I notice the ring, a mix of apprehensive enthusiasm flows through me. I savor every moment.

CHAPTER

NINETEEN

Purple is Cade Blanton's favorite color.

That memory floats to the front of my mind as I stare at the unused garment hanging in my closet. Sitting in his car in front of The Toasted Oak. Me yelling that we don't know one another; his nonchalant response of purple being his favorite color. Perhaps it was divine intervention that, years ago, made me buy the jumpsuit that I pull out and hold up into the light. When I bought it in a haze of retail therapy, I hoped Amber would one day want to do something fancy and I'd get to wear it.

Seeing it now, I'm glad she never got the chance to see me in it. I'm glad that Cade is the only partner to see how exquisite it looks on me. Amber didn't deserve the sight. Cade...he deserves it and more.

The jumpsuit is a striking blend of casual and sophisticated, with enough cleavage to be sexy without being overt. A sheer purple lace in a delicate floral pattern covers the bust, winding down over the bodice before fading into a smooth black silk fabric that flares widely in the legs. The tight fabric wrapped around my midsection could've gone either way, but the way my tits looked made it impossible to pass up.

With my trusty leather jacket overtop to complete the look, I'll be warm if the weather in the mountains is colder than predicted. Paired with the purple and blue crescent moon earrings that Jae gifted me last year and a purple makeup look I do in the few brief minutes I have left before my date arrives, I look damn near perfect.

I don't have time to give myself a third check over, however, before there's a knock on the apartment door three minutes early.

"Mis, it's for you!"

I've been staving off the nerves by keeping busy; I can no longer keep them at bay. Jitters flare to life with a vengeance of a thousand suns and my hands shake more than my breath. With sudden realization, my eyes widen. This is the first 'first date' I've been on in over five years. And that one…well, as I think about what's in store for me, I slowly comprehend how bad that last first date was. I shake away the realization, focusing on how good this one will be.

With Cade.

Two deep breaths. I take them and then steel myself, heading for the door to a potential new future. Jae took her break to come make sure I wasn't freaking out before leaving. I can't leave her alone with Cade too long, or she's liable to say something—

Oh, good goddesses. My mind blanks when I step into the living room. I'm speechless. Heat builds up my neck and over my cheeks as I inspect the man standing just outside my doorway, laughing at something my best friend said. Somehow, a fully clothed Cade is far more alluring than any thought of him nude. Maybe it's the similarities between his outfit today and the one from our night together. Maybe it's the few buttons on his shirt being open or the rolled sleeves that show the markings I ran my tongue down. Or perhaps it's the way his eyes cut to me and his entire face lights with delight.

Fucking goddesses above. I may need more help today than I thought.

Jae leaves us, giving Cade and me privacy to meet in the doorway. I barely register moving toward him; it's got to be that magnetism that keeps drawing me into his orbit. Into the cloud of citrus and sandalwood and vanilla that bathes me in goosebumps and memory. The flush on my cheeks deepens, and my breath grows more jagged with every sweep of his eyes over me.

"Beautiful."

"A greeting or a compliment?"

"Both," he says, gaze snagging and lingering on my feet, a smile lifting his lips. "As adorable as I think your unicorn socks are, you're going to need shoes. Preferably comfortable ones for walking."

I wiggle my toes and mutter a playful, "Jackass," before turning for the rack of shoes beside the door. Comfortable, I can do. Most of my shoes are, although the ones I'd planned to wear weren't so much. But I won't put myself through the hassle of that pain, especially if he's telling me not to.

I reach for the canvas shoes decorated with a mixture of purples and blues and black that paint a beautiful night sky and slip them on. "Surely we're not walking to Asheville?"

"And I'm the jackass?" Laughter fills the entryway. "No. We're going next door. But comfy shoes for walking around the fundraiser is a good idea."

"The building next door?" I ask, righting with a furrowed brow. "Isn't that just—"

"Business offices? Yes," he finishes. "But I've got a plan. Don't worry."

"I have no doubt," Jae says as she reappears, leveling Cade with a thick glare and a pointed finger. "If she doesn't text me the moment she gets there, I'm coming after you. If she disappears, you'll never make it to your inauguration. Got it?"

"Yes, ma'am," Cade says with a dutiful nod, and there's not an ounce of condescension in his movement or the look on his face. Okay... maybe there's a hint of humor, but he spins it on me and the look morphs into one of endearment. "Ready, Princess?"

~

H*E RENTED A HELICOPTER*. *I'm in an actual fucking helicopter.*

Helicopter is an understatement, but I don't have the words to describe it to Jae right now. It's like a Ritz Carlton penthouse suite in the sky, floating on propellers I can't hear. There's opulence everywhere I look. Rich shag carpeting cushions my feet and *real* silver bolts gleam wherever exposed. Everywhere else, including around the panoramic windows on each side, is smooth cream paneling. A dark windowpane separates us from the pilot, and for that, I'm thankful. I don't want onlookers in the first fragile moments of whatever Cade and I share here. Four cream-colored leather seats sit in each corner of the cabin, quiet enough that I can hear the champagne Cade is pouring without a headset. He sits beside me, and the glow of the sun outside streams in and halos him in light.

My phone buzzes, and I try to suppress a snort. All Jae sends back is a wide-mouthed smiley face and several characters meant to be a dick. I swipe to clear the notification and my bubbling mirth away, but he's already caught the look by the time I glance back. He lifts a flute of champagne to me, a smile widening as he does.

"So, what does Jae think about the helicopter?"

Amusement peels over my face. "She's very impressed," I reply, leaving out the specifics. "And so am I."

"Ah, so my money does impress her," he says, smile shifting to a smirk as he sits back in his chair.

That's right…It may feel like ages ago, but it was only a month back that I said I didn't care about his money. That the expensive liquor he bought at Big's didn't mean he was impressive or good. But I cannot deny the luxury I feel riding in a fancy helicopter on a way to a date hundreds of miles from home while someone pours me glasses of champagne. Though, it doesn't make it any different. It's nice, but it's not a necessity. I would've enjoyed walking through the park with him again as our first date.

I cock my head to the side. "Only at the ingenuity of getting us across the state so quickly."

"Mhm, sure," he hums. "Give me your phone."

"What? Why?"

"So I can take a picture for you to send to her." He puts down his champagne and holds out his hand. "And so you can see how beautiful you look in this lighting."

I'll never rid myself of these flutters deep inside my stomach. The fondness on his face only amplifies them. By now, I feel like I should be used to the way he looks at me, even though I don't deserve his affection. But I'm not. I snort not to show any of that to him, but I don't protest. I hand my phone out to him, but his ringtone blares through the cabin and makes me jump, dropping it.

I know he doesn't direct the sour expression that overtakes his face at me. He directs it at his phone, which reads "Mom" across the front when he digs it out of his pocket. It's not the first or second time I've seen that look on his face, but for a while, I thought it was about the surprise engagement. Now, it's appearing just because she called. Beyond engaging him to a woman he doesn't know and surprising him with his own engagement party, I can hardly imagine what in his past and their relationship could make such a visceral response happen every time even just the hint of his mother appears. Maybe one day I'll learn. Not today.

"If you need to take that, you can."

It goes to voicemail, and it takes a single second before 'Mom' appears again. He sneers, sliding the red button and turning the phone off without a second thought. "Nope. Couldn't care less," he says, tossing the device into the seat opposite him without a second glance. His eyes remain on me nearly the entire time he leans down to pick up my phone from the plush carpet. I sit a little taller when he turns the camera on me, smiling when he instructs. He's not wrong. I look fierce while holding a glass of champagne and relaxing in a boujee helicopter dressed to the nines. But who wouldn't? I just chuckle and toss my phone into the seat across from me, mimicking his movement.

"Nothing too important?" I ask.

"Not more important than this," he replies. "Especially not bullshit Council work." Derision fills his voice and vanishes quickly enough that I almost miss it.

"Why isn't your father taking over instead of you?"

His flute is halfway to his mouth when he flinches and stills. His brows pinch together, and for a split second he just stares into the crisp, sparkling liquid like it's wronged him. In the next moment, he's inhaling the rest and exhaling something deep inside him. I feel immediately guilty for asking when a look of distress crosses his face. It's not absolute devastation, but I know the look intimately. I've given the exact one to countless people who ask me what it was like and how long it's been and how I've stayed so strong for so long.

He doesn't need to tell me his father passed away. I know.

"I forgot I told you not to look me up. Seemed like a good idea at the time," he says with a sigh. He's not looking at me, but right now, I don't think he can. He's slipped into the past and the reminders that float to the front of his mind.

"I didn't know," I say lamely, as if that's a good enough response to dredging up a pain I know too well.

"A fact of my own design," he admits with another deep exhale. This time, he sets his flute down and looks at me, and I can see the memories swimming in his eyes. "My father passed when I was fifteen, and it was…" he pauses again and I reach across the small, ornate armrest between us to wrap my hand around his forearm, a squeeze attempting to relay as much comfort as I can. He still hurts from it. I can see it in the softening lines of his face and the nod he gives me. The soft sheen over his eyes is all too familiar. He almost looks thankful when his free hand settles on mine, thumb brushing along the back of my hand in a slow pattern only he knows. "It's still hard for me to talk about. He was my best friend. After that, things just sort of got weird between my mom, me, and…my brother…"

Brother? That's the first I'm hearing about him having a brother. Even on the briefest of social media scrolls I made on his public profile the day after that first night, I didn't see a brother. I saw a mother, another woman I assume was a sister or cousin, but no brother. There's another story there behind the pause that cracked his voice enough to be noticeable. But right now, I'm going to file that away for a later date. Right now, something in me squeezes again, and I grip his arm with the same strength of the grief that grips my heart. A familiar lump forms in my throat.

"I know the pain," I breathe.

"Oh?" He chokes out, coughing away the emotion in this throat and straightening a little in his chair. Shaking it out. Pushing it away. "Your father passed?" I know what it's like to ask someone else to take over when you don't want to talk about it.

I grant him the out, scoffing at the question. "No. My father left before I was born."

He looks simultaneously surprised and disappointed. Perhaps because he thinks that's the loss I've experienced. "Well…that's unfortunate. Surprised you even call him 'father.'"

"I have much more colorful language for him," I reply with laughter, trying to lighten the mood in any way I can on such a difficult topic. "But I also didn't really have to suffer without him. My mother and grandfather cared for me until they passed." Understanding dawns then, and he nods softly, thumb still rubbing circles against my skin. I'm not sure if it's because of how open he's been that makes me do it, but I continue, "My grandfather was actually my *sperm donor's* father." He huffs a laugh. "He found out that his useless son left a woman pregnant and broke and moved down from New York to help my mom raise me when I was six or seven, maybe?" I shrug. "They were both still relatively young. My mom was barely seventeen when she had me and was alone, without any family. She fought him at first, but he was persistent. He wouldn't let her give money back that he sent, he wouldn't stop showing up at her job or my school or doctor's appointments. Eventually, I think she realized he wasn't anything like his son."

"Oh? So then—"

"Yeah, they ended up falling in love," I add with a fond laugh, relishing the smiles on their faces in the memories that splash to the front of my mind. The fondness comes with an equal measure of sadness. It's been years since they both died, but it still hurts. It will always hurt. But I won't let the sadness overtake the joy in our memories. "It's a little unusual, but he was my dad and my grandfather. They made each other happy, so that's really all that matters. I had both of them to get me through most of the hard times when I was growing up, and they had each other for everything else."

A warmth replaces the sadness in his eyes. His fingers brush around my hand, tickling my palm as he pulls it to his lips again. The heat of his lips on my skin around the cold metal on my ring finger races through me. "So unconventional love stories run in your family then, huh?"

How I haven't registered the similarities in my situation with Cade and my mother's situation with my grandfather is a little astounding to me. I suppose, though, for as long as I pushed off accepting this odd relationship, I understand. It's not identical—I'm not pregnant, and he's not the baby's father's father—but...the ring he presses another kiss to as I smile tied us together in a situation neither of us expected. One I find myself drawn more and more to with every passing day.

"I-I guess so," I murmur. "Jae says their story could make a best-selling romance novel."

For the first time, I wonder what *our* love story could be. Right now, its headlines and gossip columns and glares from random people on the street...But maybe this is a love story for the ages in the making and I just need to get out of the way and let things happen. The ice around my heart shivers at the thought. The foundation of my hesitancy shudders, and I try to hold it closed as much as I can. I cannot get this connected to this man. I can't.

He makes that so difficult. Cade laces our fingers, thumb never stopping a steady motion on my skin, and I squeeze my fingers in his, a show of as much comfort as he's trying to offer me.

"Enough about that," he whispers. "Tell me more. Tell me everything about you, beautiful. I want to know everything about my fiancée."

"I'm not sure you can handle everything yet," I say, muted laughter echoing into my champagne flute before I finish the glass with a pop and a too dramatic sigh. I hold the glass out to him. "Or we're gonna need more of this."

"We can't ignore the traumas forever."

"No. But maybe we can save them for date number two."

The helicopter goes silent, and as it stretches, his face lights with a grin. I realize my words, but they don't bring any sort of regret. Short of this man kidnapping me, I'll more than likely be going on a next date with him. Maybe even a third if we get that much time before the ring comes off. That thought threatens to drown me in dread, but I tamp it down. I won't let the thought of losing him bring down our time together. As short as it may be, I want to enjoy it to the fullest.

"Well," I say with as much levity as I can muster, leaning a little closer to him over the wide armrest between us. "My favorite color is blue, and my favorite animal is a unicorn."

"No shit?" He jokes. "I never would've known."

TWENTY

Flying into Asheville in the spring may be the most beautiful thing I've ever seen. Bright sun filters through fluffy clouds, glistening off a river splitting the trees below. We're on our second circle around the small city and I keep noticing different things. The field of flowers blossoming pinks and purples and reds in the sea of lush, deep greens. Blooming trees for as far as the eye can see and then some covering the mountains. The town's buildings painted in beautiful colors.

It's breathtaking, and I couldn't imagine missing this view by driving in.

"It's beautiful."

"It is." Cade is looking at me when I glance back.

Jae's theory about this being like one big, smutty romance book flashes to the front of my mind yet again. I pull my bottom lip between my teeth and turn back to the scenery to hide the smile threatening my face. It's too cliché. It's a line out of every fanfiction I've ever read. But good goddesses above how the moment makes me preen.

We touch down at a small airport that's nothing more than a flat, open dirt runway surrounded by the lush mountains. Two-seater planes fill the clearing, sitting around a single black car with a woman in a full suit standing beside the open back door. Cade laces our fingers and guides me out of one luxurious ride toward the other. The air smells cleaner up here and the sun feels like it shines a little brighter through the tops of the trees. Clouds breeze through the sun's rays and cast shadows on the fresh green grass around us.

Our driver, Sandra, greets us warmly and closes us in when we're settled. The silence we slip into, watching the lush green pass by the darkened windows, is as comforting as the warmth of his hand in mine. Neither of us fills the moment with words, and I appreciate that. I'm at ease sitting here, which surprises me. Silence was discomforting in most of my prior relationships. There was meaning behind the silence. It meant there was something wrong, and more often than not, I didn't know what I'd done to deserve the coldest shoulder from the one person I wanted to warm my life. No reassurance. No affirmation.

Just silence.

An old uncertainty creeps through me, but one look at the man beside me helps ease it. A smile works over his face when our eyes meet, and without thought, he pulls my hand to his lips and kisses the ring he so loves to touch. It's enough to temper me for the short drive to our destination. I almost laugh out loud when he helps me out of the car and I see the 'fundraiser' we're attending.

It's a carnival. With kids running around wearing face paint, a clown blowing up and folding thin balloons into unicorn hats, and vendors selling fried foods or ears of corn coated in sweet butter. Others sell handmade goods and hosts stand in front of games, calling people over to play. Pure joy floats in the sun-kissed air. The happiness and excitement hums like the magic in the world. It's fantastic, but it's definitely not the type of fundraiser I anticipated.

I turn to Cade with a grin. "This is your definition of a 'fundraiser'?"

He looks momentarily confused, glancing from me to the commotion around us and back. It takes him a moment to see the humor on my face, and it washes away the lingering worry from his with a slow smile. "What? Too good for clowns and carnival games?"

"No, I'm not too good for this. It's amazing," I reply. "But I do feel slightly overdressed."

"Good," he says, sliding a hand along my back. "But you're not over-dressed. You look fantastic."

I open my mouth to respond but when I playfully roll my eyes, they land on something that steals the words from my throat.

Take a picture with a rescue!

A picture! With a real unicorn! Excitement bubbles in me. It's just as quickly drenched when I can't see the cost. A large red banner sits across the sign—Sold Out. Disappointment overshadows excitement. I notice then, as I look more critically at my surroundings, that most of the people around are in line. People with fans beat away the sun's heat, scowling all the way around the next block; I wonder how long some of them have been waiting. Based on some of their agitated movements, I bet hours for those at the front of the line. I personally would've shown up last night had I known.

"You're bummed," comes a soft voice that pulls my gaze back to Cade, who's frowning, concern littering his face.

I blink away the disappointment and put on a genuine smile. "Are you kidding? I'm so far from bummed."

"That frown said otherwise." He glances back out toward the line. "I underestimated the amount of people that would be here, or I would've brought us sooner."

"Would I love a picture? Yes." I lift a hand, motioning to the line and then the general merriment around us. "But in no way am I 'bummed.' Look at all those donations they're receiving. It's around the block. And look at all the other people here. It's amazing. They'll bring them out soon, and seeing a unicorn this close is good enough for me."

It takes a moment and a quick glance around the carnival at large for relief to span his expression. Cade sees something over my head that makes recognition flash over his face, bringing the widest smile that I've seen in the handful of weeks we've known one another. It's a bit breathtaking when he turns it on me. "I'll be right back, okay?" Bewilderment flinches my expression. "It'll be worth it. Promise. Way better than 'good enough.'"

And then he's around me, walking toward whatever brought on such happiness. Not whatever, but whoever, as it turns out. Mythic Farms reads across the top of the tent he walks to on the edge of the clearing in bright rainbow lettering. People queue for something, but when Cade walks up, a man operating the booth recognizes him and beckons him around them all. I'm a bit far off, but I don't remember seeing this man in any of Cade's pictures on my one scroll of his online presence. Perhaps he's just a personal friend, not a professional acquaintance. The way they shake hands makes it seem otherwise, though.

Whatever conversation they have is short and leaves Cade beaming when he turns to point at me. The man, too, turns with a smile and several nods. He points somewhere off into the distance, but I don't look to see where. I don't really want to look away from the smile on Cade's face as they shake hands again, much more friendly, and he turns toward me. Thankfully, he wears it all the way until he's standing in front of me again, looking down with that fondness that seems to be a natural response to me.

"What was that about?" I ask.

He just grins and holds out his hand. "Come on."

I slide my hand in his without hesitation, but still ask, "To where?"

"You wanted a picture, right?"

"Yeah, but—" I point at the line again.

He just grins, pulling me along toward the direction the man pointed. "I made a donation to the sanctuary. That's the guy I worked with. And so—" Cade cuts his gaze back to me and that gleaming smile catches me off-guard again. "I told him the donation had one condition: a picture with the unicorns for my witch. But they're about to start soon, so we have to go back there now."

"Umh—okay!"

Excitement races through me. Oh my goddesses, I'm going to see a unicorn in real life up close! Cade is taking me to a private meet-and-greet with my favorite animal. My heart slams against my ribs as he leads us toward a walled off tent near the back of the town square. Every step closer we take makes it harder for me to breathe. Anticipation rips through me, making my entire body tingle and the corners of my eyes sting with heat. I can barely contain myself when we step through the split in the tent's wall.

The sight of them steals every ounce of air in my lungs. They're majestic. Three fully grown unicorns and—

"A baby, oh my goddesses! It's so fucking cute!" Excitement raises my voice and broadens my grin to the point it's painful. Tears well along my lower lids and I try not to cry, but I haven't felt a surge of pure joy this large in months, so it may be impossible. The joy forms a lump in my throat that I try to clear away by smiling wider when I glance excitedly back at Cade.

"Yeah, it is," Cade says, and he doesn't mean the unicorns. He's looking at me again.

I'm buzzing too much from the overwhelming excitement to register it. "Thank you," I say. "Thank you so much. I-I just—"

"Anything for you, Princess."

Tears slip down my cheeks and I swipe at them with a shaky laugh. "Sorry."

"For what?"

"I don't know, crying and jumping and—I don't know, sorry."

"You're apologizing for involuntary responses to excitement?"

I shrug. "Yeah, I guess. I don't know. I'm just sorry."

A large hand finds a familiar home on the side of my neck, and Cade's thumb brushes away a tear that lingers on my cheek. "No more of that. Okay? I don't know who made you feel like you have to apologize just for existing. You did it when you were sick, too. But you don't have to do that with me. Just enjoy every moment of this."

Old anxiety tries to creep into the excitement flitting through me, but it can't break through. Not right now. Part of me knows who made me feel like I have to apologize for feeling my feelings openly, but I won't reflect on that. That's a topic for my next therapy session; right now, I'm just going to enjoy the look on Cade's face as he blots away another of my escaped tears, the unicorns grazing in the paddock, and the rest of my date with a man I couldn't have foreseen being so incredible.

A boisterous, "Mr. Cade Blanton!" comes through the split in the tent and cuts through the tension.

A stick of a man enters a second later with a bright grin on his face. The palest blond hair I've ever seen tops paler skin, flushed from the sun. He's wearing a Mythic Farms tee-shirt and a bright grin as he moves toward us, blue eyes glittering. His hand slips into Cade's again, and I look up at them as they greet one another more cordially than before. This man is shorter than Cade, but from my height, I can't tell the true difference. They both tower over me in that way that makes looking up at Cade sort of irresistible.

"Misty," Cade says, and they both turn to me. "This is Darrin Mattsson. He's the Head of Legal Affairs for Mythic Farms."

"It's nice to meet you." Darrin puts out his hand and I have to ensure mine isn't trembling as I slide it into his.

"Likewise. Thank you so much for letting me come back here."

"It's the least I can do," Darrin says with honesty in his voice. "Want to meet them?"

"Yes!" I blurt out, face reddening as I try to clear the excitement from my throat again. "Y-yes, please. I would love to."

Someone appears beside us with a bag full of carrots and disappears before I can make out anything about them. I'm too focused on the beautiful creatures ambling toward the fence. Toward me.

Unicorns look different to everyone; they even look different depending on the day and the person's mood. Today, these beasts look majestic. Crystal white manes shimmer with every step toward me they take, swishing with the bobbing of their heads. Their coats are all unique. One is white but glitters blue underneath in the midday light like the sapphire on my finger, one a pastel purple with stars as spots, one is a tan-like palomino, and the colt leans a beautiful shade of orange like when the sun is setting over the horizon.

The closer they come, however, the more I notice all the things beyond the veil of mysticism, though, and my heart aches, remembering this is a sanctuary for rescued animals. The blue one's horn is ground down. Poachers, more than likely, or someone removed it to keep the animal alive in the face of danger. The other two unicorns are thin and missing hair around their middles that could only come from wearing saddles too often. I wonder if they suffered abuse, used as props on kiddie rides without proper care. Even the young one has a slash down its muzzle as if it barely escaped a fight at a far too early age.

Excitement wars with the ache of my heart when they all finally stand next to the fence. I'm reminded of the first time I saw a unicorn in the zoo when I was younger and couldn't take my eyes off of it. My mom got frustrated with me because I sat and watched the beast do nothing other than sleep for an hour before I decided it was time to move on. At one point, I thought I'd grow up to be a unicorn conservationist, but things just never lined up. That didn't stop me from loving them so much that I can't help my tears of joy when I reach out and the blue unicorn allows me to pet it.

"That's Ainsel," Darrin says, handing a carrot out to me. "He came to us after poachers left him to die."

"That breaks my heart." I swear I see the pain in Ainsel's eyes. When I hand out a carrot, he chops half with a snuff. Laughter bubbles out of me when Ainsel decides I'm taking too long with the rest of his snack and nudges me.

"It's sadly not a new thing. It's always been around," Darrin admits. "But it's part of the reason we do what we do. We're one of only four facilities in the world. But thanks to an anonymous donor, we'll be able to do a lot more."

"Anonymous?" I ask with a questioning glance at Cade. He shrugs, but his expression is prideful. I can't help but welcome that same pride seeping over me, too. He donated anonymously. That's admirable. Far more admirable than using the generous act to gain clout. Though, I'm well aware he's only doing it to impress me even though I told him I don't care about his money. Using it like this? I may have to reconsider that notion.

"How about a picture?" Darrin asks, pulling my attention.

"Please," I say happily, and dig my phone out of my back pocket, handing it to a waiting Darrin. I turn to Cade and reach for him. "Come on."

He shakes his head. "One of just you first."

My lips part to respond, but I'm cut short by hearing more hooves behind me. An attendant walks around the cage door with the colt in tow. When they hand me the reins, I get so overwhelmingly happy that I cry. I never intend to shed tears of joy. They just fall down my cheeks unbidden in scenarios like this. I can taste the salt when the tears slip into the corners of my painfully wide smile.

Darrin takes several pictures before I finally turn to face Cade again.

"Come here," I demand a little too forcefully in my excitement, holding out my hand to Cade again.

This time, he relents with a smile that deepens with every step closer to me he takes. He fills the spot beside me perfectly, hands coming to cup my jaw. Thumbs brush away lingering tears of joy and I smile up at him, elation painting my face as he leans forward and presses his lips to my forehead. My body shivers; my smile deepens. It lasts all of a few seconds before we turn to Darrin and he's snapping more photos. The entire scene takes maybe a minute before Darrin is handing me my phone back and the attendant reclaims the reins to ready the unicorns for their hours of limelight. But when I tell this story in the future, it will have lasted a lifetime. I will remember every moment of this with a vivid clarity beyond the photos, which are perfect and make me grin a little harder.

Until I get to the ones of Cade and I. My throat closes. Evidently, our makeshift photographer didn't wait for us to be "ready" for a picture perfect pose. He started capturing pictures of Cade and me from the moment I held my hand out to him. It's just a stream of photos of a man stepping into frame while watching the look on his partner's face. And loving every moment.

Even when I turned to look at the camera, he watched me. In every photo, he's smiling down at me with that same reverence I've seen so many times before. Having it on camera, forever? I can't think of how that makes me feel through the mixture of emotions surging through me.

"Are they good?" Darrin asks and pulls my gaze up to the two men watching me.

I nod to give my throat enough time to open the slightest so I can choke out, "P-perfect. Thank you so much."

"It's my pleasure," Darrin says, turning to Cade to add, "Seriously, the least I can do. Your donation is going to make someone I know… Well, she's going to be happier than I can even express."

I recognize the look that floats over Darrin's face. Fondness. Until last month, I don't know that I would've been able to identify what the barely there smile and low hung eyelids mean. But it's hard not to know now because Cade frequently gives me the same look, even when I'm not paying attention. Like he's revering me even though I don't deserve it. Just like the pictures we just took.

He does it even now, matching Darrin's expression, saying, "I know what you mean. It's my pleasure."

They shake one more time as Cade's meaning drenches me in joy. He donated because he thought it would make me happy. I am. So much more than I can express by holding out my hand to him. He happily takes it and leads us back out into the beaming sun and astounded amusement of the fundraiser.

"Having fun?"

I snort in disbelief. "That's an understatement. You could tell me right this minute that you aren't interested and take me home and this would still be the best date I've ever had."

"Well, I am definitely interested," he replies, again not an ounce of hesitation. "And now I'm going to win you a new stuffed unicorn at one of those games to show you just how much."

"You've shown me in bounds already."

"This is only the start."

"Renting a helicopter, bringing me to meet and get a picture with my most favorite rare magical animal ever, making an anonymous donation that I'm guessing was probably way more than a couple hundred dollars." I pause then and he just shrugs again, lips turning up with that same pride. "Exactly," I snort. "And that's all only the start?"

He grins again, nonchalantly looking around at the crowd, guiding us toward the games area set up on the far side of the field. "You made that easier." Levity lilts his voice. "I couldn't figure out how to work all of that into casual conversation without sounding too douchey, but you worked it in really well."

His face lights up when I laugh. "How did you even make the donation happen?"

"Well, I donated—"

"Anonymously."

"Anonymously, yes," he agrees, swelling as we move into line at a balloon popping game. "When I found this event online Tuesday, I called the sanctuary to get more information. I talked to them for a while and found out they were trying to expand their land so they could house more unicorns and possibly some dragons. I started the donation process for the land and a few new barns."

"All of that before I agreed to come?"

He nods, watching the people throwing darts at the board full of balloons. Studying. "Even if we didn't end up coming here for our date, it's still a good cause." He turns to me then, leveling me with earnestness in every line of his face. "But I have to be honest. I did it to impress you, even though you've made it very clear that my money doesn't."

I grant him a smile and one of those laughs he admires so much. "Well, when it's used like this, it does."

"Oh, yeah?"

"A little bit. Don't get too excited." He just throws an arm around my shoulder to pull me into his side like it's a move we've practiced countless times. I sink into his hold as he leans over and drops a kiss on my temple. It reminds me, and I ask, "Why'd you make me take a picture alone?"

He stiffens some, and it takes a moment for him to reply. "In case our date doesn't go well and you officially tell me to get lost, you have a picture that doesn't have me in it. You can just remember meeting the unicorns and not have to remember my ruggedly good-looking face."

I'm torn between apprehension and appreciation. "That's weirdly thoughtful." And it's oddly unpleasant. We've only spent a handful of weeks together, half of which I did everything I could to avoid him. But now, thinking about us 'not working' makes my abdomen clench.

"I'll admit, though," he says, and tugs me a little closer. "The more I get to know you, the more I hope we do work. I don't really want to go a day without at least talking to you anymore."

"Don't worry. You'll grow out of it. Everyone does."

The people in front of us leave and open the game up. Instead of moving forward, Cade turns us and moves us to the side, indicating to the people behind us to go ahead. I'm confused; even more so when he turns me to face him and looks down at me, brows furrowed. Anxiety flares to life inside me.

"What—"

"I just wanted to make sure I was very clear when I said this," he begins quietly, and tenderness fills his voice where I expect anger based on my history. Again, he moves to pick a few hairs from my forehead and brushes them away before cupping my neck in a way to which I'm growing accustomed. It doubles as holding our gazes locked. "I have no intention of walking away from you. You, Misty Hayes, have captivated every part of me, and short of you murdering what's left of my family, I don't think there's anything that you could do to make me walk away. So let that shit go and let me know you. All of you. Not just this tough and truly fucking beautiful shell. Okay?"

He's staring down at me expectantly, but there's no way I can get a word out through the thick heat of emotion in the back of my throat.

"And just so you know," Cade continues. "If the gods forbid us from working, because that's the only thing that will, I won't just vanish into the night without a word. I have more respect for you than that."

I can't respond. Honestly, I'm a little too close to tears again for words, so I swallow through the lump in my throat and nod. He takes that as a response enough, thankfully, and pulls me in for a hug. I sink into his chest, laying my head against it, savoring the warmth of his arms around me in the bright sun. After, he wins me a blue plush unicorn, big enough to cuddle with. We eat corn dogs and tater tots and funnel cakes until I can hardly move. The sun is dipping below the mountains before we head back to Sandra and ride in one luxury vehicle to another.

When we're settled on the helicopter for our ride back, a sudden dread slowly creeps in.

"I don't really want our date to be over." That admission lights up his face. "Get us back to Raleigh. And if you want, I know the perfect place."

"I absolutely want."

When he pulls my ring to his lips again and kisses it, I realize that I've claimed the sapphires as my own. And if I'm honest with myself, I've claimed this man as my own, too. After all of the effort he put in and the admissions and the laughter and the time he put into planning what is my best date ever...How could I not?

TWENTY-ONE

"Perfect, huh?"

Skepticism plays across Cade's face, but I meet the look with confidence as I wave a hand at the open door of Big's. The noise of a fully packed bar trickles out and bleeds over the music and the surrounding nightlife. Saturdays are Rokk's busiest nights, and this far into spring, everyone's out because the evenings are pleasant. I savor the sounds and the crisply warm air, watching Cade process where I've brought him.

"What better place than where we met to cap out our first official date?"

A huff of accepting laughter bounces through his chest. "You're absolutely right. There's no better place. But now *I'm* overdressed."

"I think you look fantastic."

Deep laughter announces our arrival, but it's drowned out by the pulse of the bar. Warmth tickles my palm when his fingers slip between mine and I lead us through the crowd toward one of my best friends. Lavender eyes are the first that I meet before I make it to the bar, though.

"Mis!" Jae grins, gleefully lofting two drinks in her hands she must have just ordered; her boyfriend Mike is at her back with a drink of his own and his eyes glued to the man behind me. Cade diverts Jae's attention, too, widening her smile further. "Cade, too!"

That knowing smile turns on me. I'm caught. We have a rule—no bringing dates to Big's that we have no interest in. This is a sacred place. We never bring one-night stands here, nor do we *find* them here. I didn't bring Amber for several months into our relationship, and only then did I bring her once. She hated Big's with a passion. Maybe that's why I'm so relieved Cade said we could stay. And maybe that's why I'm so happy it feels like he fits right in, even in a suit without the jacket.

Cade greets Jae with a booming, "There's the best roommate ever!"

"Best everything ever!" Jae replies. She's not on her first double fist of the night. That much is clear. "Best boyfriend, too, even with you around. Better get it straight."

"I could never replace you."

"Damn straight." Jae grins and jabs a finger toward Cade, and one of the drink she holds sloshes. With the same finger, she points at me and then up. "We're upstairs."

"We'll meet you guys up there," Cade says before I can.

Jae pivots, spilling a bit more of the drinks in her hand. Mike just shakes his head, smiling as he follows behind her. The look on his face reminds me of the one I saw on both Cade and Darrin's, and that makes me lighter. To know someone reveres Jae in the way Cade seems to revere me is heartening. She works so hard, treats everyone as kindly as she can, supports so many people to her own detriment. She deserves that look.

"We don't have to stay," I say when they're gone.

His brows furrow, and he leans down into my space, bringing the lingering scent of citrus. Warmth flutters through me at the fragrance as he asks, "Why not?" before turning his ear to me.

"We're on a date, and—"

He turns away before I finish, bathing me in more warmth when his breath dusts across the skin behind my ear. "Will you have fun hanging out with them?" He leans up, gazing at me with earnestness. I nod, and that smile rains warmth upon me again. "Then so will I. Martini, twist?"

I nod again as delight spreads through me for so many reasons. Rokk reappears and pulls Cade's attention from me.

"I'm glad to see this is working out well," he says, emerald eyes shining. "Martini twist, and—" he looks at Cade with an unspoken question on his lips.

"The Macallan again. *Please.*" Cade stresses the word and cuts his eyes to me with a smirk, making sure that I catch what he's said. I do and laugh loudly.

Rokk also barks a laugh. "I like him, Mis."

"You like his credit card," I reply without missing a beat.

Rokk's amusement fades into the sounds of the bar as he turns to make our drinks. Cade turns back to me, what little ego he has inflated by the comment. A large hand slides around my waist, bathing me in warmth all over. He leans down, simultaneously pulling me closer until my hips brush him.

"All of your friends like me."

My nose brushes his ear when I say, "They're blinded by the title."

Laughter rumbles through me like it's the only sound around. "Are you?" I shake my head and he growls, "Witch," into my ear and I nearly buckle at the knees.

Unintentionally, my fingers curl into his shirt, and I use it to pull myself a little closer. The silk feel of the fabric glides against my fingers when I slide my hands over his chest, bleeding into the heated skin of his neck as I wrap my hand around the back. His fingers curl into my hip, and I have to bite back a shiver as I push up onto my toes to meet his ear. "No. The man behind the title has captivated me."

Again, his fingers dig into my hip and I don't conceal my groan. Rokk reappears then and clearly Cade doesn't want to separate from our moment. He does, pulling his wallet out for the credit card that started all of this. "Keep it open. And put Jae's tab on mine too."

Rokk looks fascinated and shoots me a sly grin as he turns to stuff Cade's black card in the tab box before tending to other customers. He dances around Jason, who's helping as a third bartender tonight. The latter waves to me while shaking a drink, and I happily wave back before Cade reaches for my hand again. He follows me through the crowd that definitely parts for us to walk through now that people are realizing who he is. Who *we* are. I should hate the way it feels to be so known, but I don't.

I should hate the way it feels to have Rokk appear behind us as we're nearly at the top of the steps to rope off the stairs. But I don't. I just blow him a kiss and emerge into the too-dark loft with Cade on my heels.

"There they are!" Jae beams from a familiar table near the railing. "How was the fundraiser?"

"Amazing," I reply, sliding into the chair opposite her. She leans against Mike in the booth, her head nestled gently on his shoulder. Cade takes the seat beside me, and I'm once again reminded of our night together, except we sat right where Jae and Mike are now in a not so different position.

"That's all I get?" Jae shoots back.

"I texted you the entire time."

Jae snickers. Alcohol curves her lips and she slurs, "Cade, this is Mike, my boyfriend."

"Good to meet you, man," Mike says while outstretching a hand.

"Same. Jae's told me about you."

"She's told me all about you, too," Mike replies with a grin. "At length."

"Mike!" Jae looks mortified, pushing up and smacking her boyfriend's arm.

Her face is as red as I think mine should be when a large, warm hand brushes my arm. I yearn for it to settle on my thigh, but Cade grips my chair and hauls it flush against his with little effort. A soft gasp parts my lips when our thighs touch and finally his hand slides over mine, gripping. A wink compounds it all. Never did I know such a small action could make my body blaze with desire. Even when his attention turns back to the conversation, I still can't control the heat inside me.

It feels possessive in the most subtle yet beautiful way. He's claiming me as his out in the open in front of my friends. I should hate it. Never have I thought I needed a partner to claim me as *theirs*. But...there's a deeper part of me that's been longing for a declaration so obvious and public. I never got it before Cade, especially not with Amber.

I'm realizing more and more that I got nothing with Amber other than the occasional romp in the sheets. We were together, but we were never a pair. There wasn't a union of our souls, only our bodies, and I wish I would've seen it sooner. I wish I could go back and tell her all the things I should've said. I wish I could skip into the past and guide myself in a different direction. Tell myself to skip going to that tattoo shop for another piercing instead of going back to the apartment to watch Beverly Hills Kitchen Witch with Jae.

But...then I wouldn't be where I am today. I doubt I would've had the gall or the balls to call out Dobson in that meeting if I wasn't already on edge about my personal life. Which means I never would've been wallowing downstairs on that fateful night so many weeks back.

I also wouldn't have clarity. I wouldn't have the growing contentment of my life flourishing in my chest or be learning my worth and where I fit into this world.

And I wouldn't have Cade.

Maybe I should thank Amber for walking away.

No. That woman doesn't get credit for me finding the bright spot in the gray my life has become. I get that credit—me, Jae, and the man sitting beside me laughing at the drunken nonsense my best friend is spewing animatedly with her hands. Perhaps Fate gets some measure of credit, too, says the glimmering jewel on my finger staring back at me as I reach for my glass. But I won't admit that out loud.

A hand squeezes my thigh and tugs me back to the present. I was nodding along and smiling when everyone else did, but I lost track of the conversation and clearly missed a question asked of me.

Thankfully, Cade doesn't miss a beat.

"Another?" He asks again and glances at the nearly full drink in my hand. A silent answer that he accepts with a nod. "We're going to get another—"

"And a round of jello shots!" Jae barks. Beside her, Mike mocks throwing up in the booth beside himself, nearly falling over with laughter when Jae pushes him in jest.

Amusement litters Cade's expression as he watches before turning back to me. "And jello shots apparently. You want one?"

"Of course she does!" Jae answers for me.

Cade still waits for my response through everyone's laughter. I nod. "Coming right up, beautiful."

Jae gasps, but my gaze remains focused on Cade as he leans over and places a kiss on my temple. Smooth lips linger just moments, but it's long enough to bottom my heart out into that pit in my stomach where those fucking butterflies are always lying in wait. He's grinning when he pulls away and stands with Mike, falling into an effortless conversation about some sports team or the other as they make their way toward the stairs.

"If you don't marry him, I will. Tomorrow," Jae says the moment they disappear and pulls my gaze back to the giddiness she cannot hide. Maybe she feels the same vicious butterflies in her stomach that are currently wreaking havoc inside mine. "I *hope* Mike just picks up some of it from him. You got so lucky!"

"He's almost too good to be true," I say, glancing into the crowd and watching people recognize who squeezes past them.

When we were last here, I didn't know why everyone moved out of his way. Now, as I watch Cade push toward the bar, I do. He's a future Councilor, and I'm just the woman he engaged himself to during a one-night stand. I'm just the woman that will fade into obscurity when the ring on my finger comes off. Today made me forget all of that. The words he said, his actions. It made me believe we could have a future, but why would he ever want to be with me? I'm just—

"Because he's totally in love with you!" Jae slaps her hand on the table, startling me back to see the deep violet eyes narrowed in annoyance at me. "You're ridiculous, you know that? Why can't you see that you deserve and are worthy of love? I don't know how many times I have to tell you that you're fucking awesome and people like you. They *choose* to like you. I don't get it. People love you, *he* loves you, and you're just going to dismiss it because he's too perfect, and you don't think you deserve it? You fucking deserve it, Mis. All of it. So accept that before it pushes him away."

In less than one hundred words and a single minute, Jae brings tears to my eyes. She doesn't shy back when she sees them, but her expression softens, and she reaches across the table to grab my hand, probably a little harder than she intends. I blink as rapidly as I can to wash them away before they slip down my cheeks. I know she doesn't really want to have this conversation right now, but with the liquor flowing through her system, she couldn't hold back at least that much.

But I'm several drinks behind her, and although I can divert the conversation, I'll obsess over it inside. Because...she's not wrong. It's exactly what I do and how I feel. She knows it. We both do. The only thing I don't know is how to accept that truth and change it.

Just hours ago, Cade himself told me he wants this. But the arrant thoughts inside my brain tell me his words and the date were nothing more than a placation. He's just having his fun until this ring comes off and then he'll walk away forever, on to a better life that will never include me. I'll fade into a distant memory, and his media team will scrub clean the stories, articles, and social media posts about me. I'll amount to the same nothing in his mind that I feel like I am in everyone else's.

But...I have so many people who prove that statement wrong. I have Jae and Rokk, and hell, I even have a team of people who respected me enough to follow through with the revolution I started at my old job.

Maybe it's just me…Maybe I'm the only one who thinks I'm the unwanted shadow darkening the back of my friends' minds. A thought chokes me softly: I'm the only one I know who doesn't love me. I perpetuate that self-hatred, even when I'm not with a partner who loathes me like I loathe myself. I can like things about myself—like my laugh and how I perceive emotion and my markings—but…something inside me hates me. Add that to the list of things I need to work on with my therapist.

I have to blink away tears again.

"Let's relax with the 'L word,'" I say to steer us away. "We've only been doing whatever this is for like a month."

She accepts the maneuver with a snort and one last squeeze of my hand. "You mean you've only been engaged because *Fate* made it happen?"

"You're not seriously saying you think we're soulmates, are you?" A smirk paints Jae's face with coyness, and she shrugs. "Now *you're* ridiculous."

"You can't tell me I'm wrong."

"You're wrong," I say plainly.

"Prove it."

"No. You're just wrong."

"What's she wrong about?"

Two heads appear over the railing of the stairs; Mike ascends first, and then my heart thumps a bit painfully when Cade follows. Tears threaten my eyes again, but I flutter them into a wink when Cade meets my gaze. I don't let the connection stay for long, else I will cry in this bar yet again. Not tonight. Not until I can properly unpack and grieve that hate inside of me so I can let it go.

"That you and Jae can beat Cade and me at pool," I say, using the only thing in the room as the excuse. "She's never played."

"Wait, what? You've never played pool? *Never?*" Cade asks, and I can't tell if he's concerned, confused, or insulted as the men approach their respective seats.

"It's not that shocking," Jae says.

Mike looks equally horrified, staring at Jae with genuine disbelief. "It actually is. I didn't even know that."

Jae just shrugs and takes the jello shot he offers. "Well, we've never decided to play pool before."

"Now we have," Cade replies. I notice in his face when he hands me my jello shot that he detects something is off. But I just smile it away, and he appears to accept that, adding to Jae, "You're learning how to play pool tonight."

"Hear, hear," Mike jokes and boosts his jello shot into the air.

"Hear, hear!" Cade and I echo to Jae's scoff before we all down the tangy jello. Only Jae doesn't hiss in displeasure at the taste, but I welcome the warmth as it coats my throat and chases away the tightness.

"It's not that hard," Cade says. "Come on. Just one game."

"I'll rack," Mike throws back.

Both men are up before the statement ends, and Mike won't let Jae remain in her seat. She flails about, but ultimately she won't miss an opportunity to have fun. I should have learned that lesson from her a long time ago, but I didn't. So while tonight she's learning how to play pool with our men, I'll take the note to open myself up to more.

Mike racks the balls, and part of me wants to correct the tightness, but I just leave it alone and watch Cade bend over the table and break them apart.

"It's all in the ass," Cade says, and he doesn't hesitate to shove his ass out behind him with blatant showmanship. Truthfully, the sight leaves me stunned. "Ask Mis. She's really good at that part."

The sound of the cue ball smacking into the rack punctuates the single word in my body, pulsing a new emotion into the cacophony already swirling inside me.

Mis.

He called me Mis.

It's such a minor thing to feel so undone over, but I can't help it. He's comfortable enough with me and my friends to call me by a nickname I only let the people closest to me use. And I like that he did. I like *a lot* more than just that. I like that he patiently teaches my best friend how to play pool, even though she's too tipsy to pay full attention. I like the way he high fives her when she celebrates making her first ball and the pride on his face when she makes another. I like the way he laughs when Mike tells her she needs to put more ass into it, making for the sweetest scene I've ever seen of a partner of mine. And I love the way he smiles at me over the table when our eyes meet, lingering in a joined gaze that I never want to escape from.

Heat wells along my lower lids, and I know this time it's not from despair. This time, the warmth that fills me is like a wildfire blooming in my chest. Reverence floats behind the tenderness he openly bestows on me, and for the first time, I believe that…maybe I deserve it. I deserve a man who knows to order me a martini with a lemon twist. I deserve the man who found one of my favorite interests and planned a date around it. I deserve the man who Faded all the way from Amsterdam to take care of me in my time of need, sacrificing himself in the process. I deserve a man who's willing to hang out with my best friend in a shitty dive bar he doesn't like after a perfect date. One I'll never forget.

Nor will I forget the way he lets Mike and Jae win the game we eventually play.

"We're leaving *for Mike's* now because I wanna get laid!" Jae says proudly, a shit-eating grin on her face when she slides her cue stick onto the table.

Cade barks a laugh. "Your tabs on mine, so get out of here."

Shock overflows on Jae's face. The alcohol has a part in that, but she does genuinely seem surprised. "Well, I'm not going to say no! Thanks, Mr. BSD! Hopefully, I'll see you tomorrow morning." She's grinning and looks directly at me, winking in a completely inconspicuous way.

"Goddesses above, Jae, leave!"

Her laughter fades down the stairs into the noise below, leaving Cade and me alone. He's again leaning against the pool table, and his orbit pulls me in. Sauntering across the room, relishing the way his eyes watch me like they did that night many moons back, I find myself before him again. This time, my hands float up his chest and his find a home around my waist to pull me close.

"I thought you 'whooped ass equally?'" I whisper.

"This was different. Gotta let them win their first time," Cade says. "And maybe I was still trying to impress you. Did it work?"

"Maybe."

His brows furrow again, and I know I haven't kept enough of the emotion from my face. "Is something wrong? Earlier and just now you looked like I've upset you, and I just—"

"No," I say too quickly, taking a moment to settle myself before adding, "No. Nothing's wrong. You've done nothing to upset me today."

"You're sure?" He asks, and there's a vulnerability in him that breaks down the facade of Aldrich Blanton into the Cade I know and could see myself loving.

I nod. "You've been so amazing. This whole day has been amazing."

"But?" He asks, apparently well aware of how to read the tone of my voice.

I take a moment, fiddling with the edges of his silk shirt, trying to figure out how to say what I want to say without crying. Who cries on the first date? Not me. Well…not from sadness, at least. I refuse. But I can see the uncertainty building on his face the longer I remain quiet.

I shake my head to push away all the gutting emotions. "It's just… after the last person I dated—"

"Amber," he says, proving he listens. I don't remember saying her name more than once in front of him.

"Yeah," I say with a bitter sigh. "Among a lot of other things, she and

Jae didn't get along. So it's just nice, ya know? That my best friend likes my…boyfriend?"

We've jokingly called each other fiancés in the past. But the heat that spans his face when I say that last word is something far more carnal. Clearly, it wasn't the wrong thing to say. The genuine heat I can feel pulsing off him says that much. I don't need his hands slowly finding a home on the sides of my neck, or the sweeping way his gaze takes in every part of my face, or the way he brushes a thumb over my chin, dotting the middle of it with two gentle taps. But I accept them happily, leaning into the shattered breath I take in his hold.

"How could I not like my *girlfriend's* best friend?" Cade asks, and I swear he purrs the moniker. I want him to grip my jaw. I want him to crash our lips together.

"She's pretty awesome," I say.

"She is. But she doesn't hold a candle to you."

For a moment, we're both silent, basking in the way my body shivers at his words and my breath hitches. His thumb sweeps over my jaw again, and his eyes track the movement until they snag on where my lips tremble. They linger there long enough that I almost beg him to slant his lips over mine. But just when I think I can't hold out, molten hazel flicks back up to meet my gaze.

"May I kiss you?" He feels my head nod more than sees it. Relief jerks his shoulders loose, and that salacious smile floats over his face again. "Thank, fuck."

His lips are unimaginably soft as they pillow over mine—even more so than I remember from our night together. Those sinfully perfect lips press to mine once, twice, and a third time before they crush to mine in a bruising kiss that makes me buckle at the knees. He's there to hold me as I come to grips with the reality of how we fit together. Of how we burn, lips parting and tongues exploring places they've longed to be again since our fateful night.

I need his kiss right now like the southern spring needs rain. It's refreshing, renewing. Invigorating, and fucking hells, I cannot believe I forgot what it felt like. I cannot believe I let myself go all of those weeks without his lips on mine. How many times I missed this opportunity almost disappoints me. Cade pulls me closer and washes away any thought other than him. But he pulls back far too suddenly and soon, breaths as jagged as mine ghosting against my skin; hazel eyes are lidded with lust, almost entirely black in the darkened loft, like pools of obsidian dancing with the fire of desire. Desire for me, for us. A desire that echoes through every part of my being.

"Come for a drink at my place?" I ask.

"Lead the way, Princess."

Thank fucking goddesses we're only two blocks from my apartment. The bar's patrons part down the middle, out of our way, as we push toward the door.

TWENTY-TWO

WE DON'T EVEN PRETEND LIKE WE'RE GOING TO HAVE A DRINK. HIS LIPS are on mine before the door closes. It might have been me pulling him in or him pulling me closer. No matter who initiated this, only one thing will stop it: release. And we are both happy to seek it in each other's arms again, a tangled mass of limbs and tongues and passion as I push off his jacket and he pushes off mine.

Between kisses, he tries to say, "Last time, we didn't use—"

I blurt, "I'm good. I tested after—"

"Me too," he cuts in, taking my face in his hands, grinning slowly. "One perk of rarely dating."

"Good." I brush my hands down the front of his too-soft shirt toward the belt I desperately want to rip off. "Then I can feel all of you in the back of my throat when you fuck my mouth."

"Oh, fucking gods," he growls and crashes his lips to mine.

I give into the delicate roll of our lips together, savoring the juxtaposition between how fervently he kisses me and how delicate his hold is around my jaw. It's entrancing and intoxicating, and I want so much more. But when I try to pull away, he keeps me there for several long moments that soak my core with anticipation.

Leaving a trail of clothing to whatever soft surface we can find feels like our thing as he slowly backs me toward my sofa. His shirt goes first, and he growls when he can't push my jumpsuit over my shoulders.

Tonight is slower than the last time we danced this dance. But even though his hands move a little more leisurely down my body, there's nothing passionless about this moment. My fingers find a home in his curls again with gentle tugs that make him sigh into our kiss. I devour the sound, the way he pulls me closer to his body, and the thick heat that pushes against me.

Before my calves hit the sofa, I spin us. For a moment, he pulls away, puzzled. That confusion washes away when my hands dust up his chest to push him down. Gracefully, he sinks onto the couch, spreading himself into the picture of absolute comfort while looking up at me like I'm a feast he can't wait to taste. In reality, I'm the one that gets to taste him first tonight.

Sliding onto my knees makes want careen through me. The way he watches me is overwhelming and enough to make my hands tremble when they find purpose ghosting up his thighs. He jerks, a sharp inhale relaying his own want when I squeeze the length pressing against his pants. A shuddered exhale washes over me and ripples anticipation down my spine, pooling warmth below my navel, doubling when his fingers float along my jaw. His thumb brushes over my lips, and I part them to slowly slide my tongue along his skin. It tastes of whiskey and salt, and I groan deep in my chest when I close my lips around it.

Hisses of pleasure and groans of appreciation sing through my apartment. My pussy throbs.

"Fuck me," he murmurs, curling his fingers under my jaw when the flat of my tongue slides against his skin. "Didn't know I liked that."

I grin around his thumb and make a show of laving to the tip until it pops out. "We've got so much to learn," I say before sliding my tongue back over his thumb one more time. "Now, take your cock out for me so I can show you something better."

Excitement rumbles in his chest and sears through me. "Yes, ma'am."

I sit stunned for a moment when his cock springs free. Goddesses, I sold it short every time I touched myself to the thought of our night together. No one can tell me that a cock isn't just as beautiful as a pussy. They both have their own merits and beauties and flaws. This one?

It's got a lot of fucking merit.

The sly smirk on his face when I finally glance back up into those blown-wide hazel eyes says he's more than aware. It's been a while since I've done this, but goddesses below if I'm not ready to hop right back on that wagon. When he leans his cock toward me, gently stroking from base to tip, I can't help myself. My hand slips below his on the base, and for a few moments, we stroke together in tandem; I can tell he's showing me how he likes it, and I commit every movement to memory until his hand falls away and his head tips back against the sofa.

The first brush of my tongue on his throbbing tip rips a lewd groan from his chest. One echoed in the moan that tumbles in my throat. The sound, drawn out and deep, spurs me to life. Fire blazes through my veins as I take his length into my mouth. Inch by inch. Roll by roll of my tongue along his shaft, his tip. Every tantric slide of my hand along his shaft, in near-perfect rhythm with my mouth.

Long-ago practiced motion returns to me and the pleasure along with it. It's like a white-hot nova imploding on itself in the most dazzling way. Every groan, every moan, makes the ache in my cheeks and my pussy worth it. So fucking worth it. I forgot how much I love pleasing people in the bedroom. The sheer bliss they feel when my ministrations overwhelm them? It ignites the deepest parts of me in a way I cannot put into words. I can only put them into motion, action.

I move my head to a cadence that drives Cade a little more into a frenzy with each bob.

"Fuck—fuck, your mouth is so perfect, Princess—" He pants the words, fingers curling in my hair for something to hold him in this reality, to keep him grounded. I hum around the tip of his cock at the pressure, a resounding groan echoing in his chest. "Good girl."

Oh, fuck me; the words strike a chord of absolute bliss inside me yet again, and I sink all the way down on him, humming through the gag and shuddering my appreciation. Pain sears against my scalp when his fingers curl in my hair.

"Take it all—fuck—yes," he hisses. "Good girl-fuc—" his words dissolve into moans.

I don't know if he means to, but I accept the thrust of his hips up, taking his cock against the back of my throat. I let him do it again. And again. I try with all my might to open myself as much as possible to take all of him in. Try to take all of him while he chases a high only I can give him at this moment. I take every firm thrust of his hips, allowing him the pleasure of seeking his own release while my pussy begs for touch. The scene when I look up is enough to sate me for now, though. Those perfect plump lips parted in a silent prayer, his head lolled back, a shaking hand gripping the side of the couch. He's holding on. Anchoring himself into the pleasure when all he wants to do is come unglued under the gentle caress of my tongue.

I love watching him savor the feeling.

Fingers thread through my hair, and nails curl into my scalp; I wince. At that, his eyes fly open, and his grip flinches off. "Sorry, fuck, I —are you okay?"

I only answer by pushing his hand back against my scalp and using it to push my head down onto him. He seems to understand what I want, fingers curling a little more loosely into my hair. He takes over, and I let him guide me down on his cock. I let him fuck my mouth, gagging and tearing up through the movements that wrack his entire body with shakes.

"Hrpgh—fuck, good girl. Fuck—"

My body clenches, and my moan hums around him. But then suddenly, he's pulling himself from my throat and crashing his lips to mine, spit-soaked and all, before I can catch any breath. He doesn't care, and neither do I. All I want at this moment is the feeling of our lips dancing together and the warmth of his hands on my body.

A whimper slips out when his lips leave mine.

"You're too good at that," he pants against my lips.

I can't help but smile against his. "You could've—"

"No." He slants our lips together again. Something is blooming between us, and it craves the deluge of his fervent kisses down my jaw. It yearns for his hot breath brushing over that sensitive spot behind my ear when he whispers, "I'm coming inside your perfect pussy tonight, Princess. Nowhere else."

My entire body shudders. On any other occasion, I would think it gives him too much of the upper hand here. Not tonight. We're both trembling with anticipation or nerves; I don't care to decipher which. I just relish the way his hand shakes as he stands and hands it out to pull me off my knees.

The mischievous smirk that spans my face, however, tells him something he already knows: I won't give him the response he expects. I vault from the floor onto the couch and run over it, passing just out of his reach. He grabs for me and narrowly closes his hand around mine, but I snatch it away. Giggles flit through the quiet apartment, paired with his laughter that follows me to my room. I chance a glance over my shoulder, and the smile on his face stuns me motionless moments before he catches up with me.

Thick arms wrap around my middle and haul my back against his firm chest. I sink into the warmth, opening my neck for him to pepper those plump lips against. With every chaste kiss, I shiver and sigh unhindered. I long thought my neck being kissed wasn't something that turned me on. I never felt a spark with someone's lips anywhere but on mine. Certainly not anything that made my body feel like a wildfire burned inside. The throbbing in my clit when Cade praises me against my neck with barely there yet all-consuming kisses makes it clear it was never something physically wrong with me, like I was led to believe.

It was the connection to any of the people before him. There was none. At least not like there is to Cade.

Deep laughter dusts along my skin, painting goosebumps in its wake. "Trying to run away from me, huh?"

"No, sir." I keen when his fingers curl into me at the words and desire rumbles in his chest.

It fades into laughter as he slowly sways us to a song that doesn't play. "You cleaned off your dresser."

"Turns out I'm neater when I'm not so depressed." I lean my head back against his shoulder, welcoming the ghost of his laughter over my skin again.

When I open my eyes, we've turned so that we're standing in front of the mirror atop my dresser. He's already looking at me with heavily lidded lust. I almost whine when he pulls away, just the slightest, but I realize it's for both of our benefits. Enraptured, he watches in the mirror as he unzips the back of my jumpsuit and pushes it off my shoulders. We both thank my past self for not wearing a bra tonight; one large hand cups my breast and the other forces the rest of the fabric down over my hips, brushing gentle fingers along my abdomen in retreat.

He's devouring me in our reflection, lingering on the outline of my pussy through my sheer underwear. Brazen want sears through me at his obvious need.

"You are magnificent, Princess. So fucking perfect."

When his fingers brush my jaw to match our lips in a passionate kiss, I'm starving for him. Aching to feel his lips much lower. Instead, when we part, he cups my jaw and turns it back to the mirror, meeting my gaze with an ardency that shudders through me.

"I want you to watch yourself come for me."

He punctuates the words with a fervent kiss on my neck, followed by another when I open myself to him again. I sink back into his hold and take in the picture he's made of us. At this moment, it feels like one of the most beautiful sights I've ever seen, elevated with every kiss that he presses to my skin. With every slow exploration of his hands along the curves of my body. I ache and arch when a large hand finds my breast, gentle at first, but more intense with each grasp and tweak of my nipple.

It's probably the alcohol that makes me so bold, but as his fingers dust gently down my abdomen toward the apex of my thighs, I lay a hand over the one kneading my breast to lace my fingers through his. Molten hazel eyes flutter open and find my lidded gaze in the mirror. Confusion flashes through them for the briefest moment when I pull his hand away until he realizes I'm moving his touch up. And up. Until our joined hands are raising my chin to mold around my throat.

The curve of his lips then is salacious as he takes over, wide hand gripping me. Fire sparks in every nerve in my body in the best way. It's embarrassing how quickly I'm shaking at the knees from anticipation, but I don't care. Not when this man is here to hold me upright through it all.

A moan tumbles past my lips at the testing pressure that gives me so much more than expected. Definitely nowhere close to what I'm craving, though. I want more. So much more. I try to urge him to close his grip around me harder, pushing forward until my throat is fully slotted in his grasp, but he doesn't move. He just rests against me, chuckling.

"What does my Princess want?"

"I want your fingers, sir." I push out against him again, whining. "Please choke me while you finger me."

I don't have to ask twice. The sheer force of his fingers closing around my trachea lights my soul aflame. Gasping through the pleasurable pain, I lean further back into him and lose a little bit more of myself to our moment. He steals the rest of my grasp on my faculties in seconds.

His hand gliding down my body feels like an inferno burning against my skin. I'm sensitive. Maybe too sensitive, but I give into the feeling and savor the pulse of pleasure clenching my pussy and ricocheting through every inch of my body. My moan tears through the room when his fingers slip through my slick folds and pressure closes further around my throat. Fingers swipe against my clit and through the wetness that sucking his cock soaked me with, coating themselves.

"So wet from sucking my cock," he growls. "So fucking hot."

A finger finds its way inside my pussy, and I tense at the bliss before a second joins it. My eyes shut from the tingling inside me.

But Cade demands, "Eyes open. I said 'watch yourself.'"

I struggle against the urge to keep them closed from the pleasure that has me clenching from the sheer anticipation of my oncoming orgasm. But I do. I open my eyes to the mirror and he's watching every move he makes inside me.

"Good girl."

Fucking hell, those words again. Coupled with the lack of air in my lungs and the vision of his fingers sinking in and out of me? Of him enthralled with the sight of us in the mirror and the way he works my pussy and the length pressed against me? I can't resist. The world around me falls away, and all I can focus on is the exquisite feeling of his fingers. It's embarrassingly quick, and I don't care. I shatter. Without restraint, I moan his name and tremble against his hold as pleasure wracks me. He doesn't stop. He keeps moving until my entire body twitches and I slump back against him, pliant.

He holds me up without complaint. The way he looks at me in our reflection while bringing his glistening fingers to his mouth is carnal. Primal. I shudder when he tastes me, humming a sound of approval. Even more when he turns my jaw to connect our lips in a kiss that steals the rest of my senses.

He tastes of me, and shivers work through my body when he pulls away just enough to say, "On your knees on the bed for me. I want to fuck you into your mattress."

It's one of the hottest things I've ever experienced, a partner telling me where and how they want to take me. I pull out of his hold, but his hands remain on my waist to help me to my bed on shaking legs. I make a show of crawling to the middle, sliding my chest into the comfort, and putting myself on full display for him. Meeting his eyes over my shoulder shoots fire through my body again.

"Let me see that pretty pussy, Princess."

A slow, sinful smirk washes over his face as he palms himself, skillfully pumping as his eyes sweep over my core. Flashes of our first night together mix with the beautiful sight behind me, and I clench. Wanton lust takes over, and instinct draws my fingers to my pussy, finding purpose on the aching need between my thighs. He watches, matching his pace to the way I circle my clit. My free fingers fist into the sheets in sheer anticipation as he finally, finally crawls onto the mattress and settles between my legs.

A wide, warm hand smooths over the surface of my ass, nails biting into the skin with the growl of desire he lets out.

"Smack it," I whimper. "Hard. Please—"

I love that Cade never makes me ask twice. Stinging satisfaction lances through me when his hand connects with my ass. A moan tumbles into the sheets, and I push myself back, wiggling for it again. He obliges, hand gripping my ass to sooth away the burn that makes electricity charge through my veins. Coupled with the fast circles I brush across my sensitive clit, I arch into the pleasure.

A growl rumbles through him and echoes through me, waning into a moan when his cock pushes my hand away and rests against my wet slit. Cade presses into me so tantalizingly slow, all so that I can relish the way I stretch for him, the way I open to welcome him into my tight warmth inch by blissful inch.

"Fuck," he groans. "Your pussy is magnificent."

Magnificent. A simple admiration that gives me everything I yearn for and more. I hail the goddesses for putting me here on my knees, open, for a man who showers me with such praise.

We moan in unison, mine ending in a gasp when he pushes against the softest part of me. Fingernails dig into my ass, pulling me apart so he can see and feel everything. So he can push himself that much closer to the edge we're both rapidly seeking. A slow rhythm pushes me, pulls me, throws me through loops and twists and turns that make me cry into the sheets, fingers twisting in them with pleasure. It's slow. It's quick. It's mind-blanking and an explosion of color behind my tight lids. It's everything I need.

I throw my hips against the shaking wall of him, taking in as much as I can. Gasping with every thrust against the deepest, most painfully pleasurable place inside of me. He snaps his hips to the frantic motion, his grip on my supple waist bruising and sinful and wonderful. Strangled moans saturate the air, unfettered bliss forcing my hips back against his every thrust.

His head falls between my shoulder blades with the ecstasy of my orgasm starting to flutter around him. When he swells inside me, I lose all control of everything I am. We tumble down that hill of delirium together, my moans singing a mantra of his name, his groans thundering through me like bass.

"You—" A gentle kiss presses between my shoulder blades. "—are incredible."

More kisses trail down my back as he slowly slides out of me; breathless laughter jumps in my chest when he presses kisses to both of my ass cheeks before tapping them lightly. When he collapses onto the mattress beside me, I sink into the comfort, turning my head to take in the sated grin on his face. I think I purr when his fingernails gently rake over my back, fingers massaging the wake of goosebumps they leave.

"Not as incredible as you."

His eyes sweep across my face in the low lighting and captivate me. I've never stared into eyes so bewitching, even as lidded with lust as his are. Every thin ridge of caramel that dances through the gold surrounding his pupil mesmerizes me. Part of his eye reflects the blue in my sheets. The other part nearly looks clear, like an actual window into the gentle soul looking at me like he can't get enough. I can't either. I could lay here all night and stare into the depths of his hazel eyes and be perfectly content.

"The most beautiful eyes," I whisper, lifting when he moves to slide an arm under my head.

"False. No one's eyes compare to yours." My skin tingles where his fingers ghost over the curves of my body.

A smooth hand splays across the expanse of my lower back and pulls me toward him. I shift, closing the distance between us with something inexplicable coursing through me. I shudder against his lips when he presses them to mine. The tender caress tastes of us and I can't get enough of the feeling of our lips rolling together in a kiss that makes me shiver all the way down to the atoms in my bones. The way he draws me closer and sighs into our connection makes me wonder if he feels the same emotion surging through him.

He pushes a leg through mine, intertwining us before throwing the covers over us. I find myself carding my fingers through his hair and down his neck, swearing he purrs to show me how much he appreciates the motion. I personally just love how small, yet comforted, I feel wrapped around him, held in his arms. I love how content he looks laying in my bed, eyes closed and lips showing his satisfaction. And I love the way he brushes his nose against mine.

It's hard to say that I don't love him. But I won't admit that to even myself right now. It's far too early for that. And there are far too many things that want to keep us apart for me to accept it.

"Hey," I whisper. He hums. "Next weekend is Beltane. Well, next next Monday, but—anyway. Every year Jae and I go down to the beach to celebrate, and if you're free—"

"I'm there," he cuts in without hesitation, opening his eyes and catching my breath with the earnestness on his face. "Just tell me where to be and when, and I'll be there."

"Are you sure? I know it's last minute."

He grins. "That's kind of the best part about being on The Council. We only actually work like…once a month."

"Oh, okay," I reply with a snort.

He just grins and pulls me a little closer until our bodies are almost flush. "Count me in, Princess."

My abdomen clenches against his, and the breath I try to take is jagged, exhale just as exaggerated as the shivers work their way out. "Good goddesses. Why do I like that nickname so much?"

Silent laughter dusts across my skin. "I can only tell you why I call you that."

"And that is?"

"Because real princesses are strong. They're fearless and cunning and conniving. They protect what's theirs and run kingdoms when the time comes. They're clever, quick-witted..." his fingers brush away a little hair from my face, slowly rounding my jaw and twirling my already dizzying nerves with another wave of pleasure. "And they're revered as the most beautiful women in their entire kingdom. All qualities of *my* witch."

My witch. Goddesses above, I may never get used to that. Coupled with that explanation, my abdomen tightens. I just surge forward to slant my lips over his because there's nothing I can say back other than showing my appreciation. He rolls us, settles between my legs again, and leans into our kiss with renewed vigor.

Charlie hopping up onto the bed and immediately darting away at the sight of Cade startles us apart.

"Fucking hells, I forgot you had a cat," he says.

Our breathless laughter dies in another kiss that makes us forget anything in the world exists except for one another and the rest of this night together.

CHAPTER

TWENTY-THREE

"There's nothing we can do to convince you to come back?"

"No, I think I'm ready to take my skills elsewhere," I reply, gently tapping the bag of coffee beans with my foot in the stockroom. Not where I'd expected to take this call, but Amelia Sanchez phoned early. It was the closest quiet place I could find before it went to voicemail and my nerve faded. The sounds of The Toasted Oak's midday rush echo on the other side of the door, and I wince, knowing Alex is out there on her own with the new person Jae hired.

"Do you mind if I ask where you're going?" Amelia asks, desperation in her voice only climbing with every follow-up question. "We can probably counter with a—"

"I'm going back to school." Saying those words out loud to someone other than myself and Jae brings a fresh wave of apprehensive excitement.

"Oh." She laughs and adds, "Well, we certainly can't counter that."

"No, I don't think so." I reply with laughter of my own, trying to lighten the conversation more. "It's at least the hope right now. I just put my application in, so I'm still waiting for a response."

"Well, that's very exciting!" Amelia pivots, voice a new shade of enthusiastic that sounds genuine. "What are you going to study? Because I just *know* they'll accept you."

"Magical veterinary care is the ultimate goal," I admit proudly for the first time in almost a decade. "But I've got to finish my bachelor's in zoology first. I've always wanted to, so I figured why not now when I finally don't have a full-time job?"

"Well, that's as far away from supply chain as you can get," Amelia jokes. "But."

"Here comes the last ditch effort, huh?"

It sounds like she's shifting on the other end. "Look, Misty," she says, much quieter and far more informally than any time she's contacted me before this. "I'll be honest with you. You've got the upper hand here more than you know. Let's just say, management is very interested in getting you back in any sort of capacity, even part time. So you're in an excellent spot with us. Just think about it because I'm confident you'll get accepted, and a little extra money from us on the side can't hurt. And if you need recommendation letters, I'm sure I know several people who would be willing."

Pride blooms in me and arrests my reply. It could very well be that J&D Sourcing wants me to come back so I don't file some sort of wrongful termination lawsuit. Or to at least make me sign a form that'll keep me from doing so in the future. But right now, I can't help but feel like it's actually because of me. They want me back enough that they'll do just about anything because I was the best at the job and they know it.

Which I'm finally convinced of too. I know I'm good at what I used to do. I loved the work for as long as it loved me. And I was fucking good. I'll be just as good at following my actual dreams if I'm accepted…

There's no reason they should deny my application, though. I had two years of straight As under my belt before I dropped out to take care of my mother while she was returning to the waters. I had every intention of going back, but I found the world of supply chain when I needed money to pay hospital bills, and I stayed longer than I ever expected. I said as much in my application essay, pouring my heart out to strangers two nights ago, hoping it'd show just how deeply I want this. How badly I want to finish what I started all those years ago.

"Just promise me you'll think about it?" Amelia asks into the silence.

"Yeah—yes, of course. I'll think about it."

"That's all I can ask. You have a good day and call me the moment you make your choice, okay?"

"I will. Thank you, Amelia."

"You're very welcome, Misty. Have a good weekend."

Before I hang up the call, I've already decided. I'll accept the job, so long as the schedule of the zoology program at N.C. State will allow it. When I applied several nights ago, I thought of nothing beyond trying to chase a dream that I let too many things suffocate over the years. I didn't think about how I would fund it, other than knowing I wouldn't accept Cade's money. I didn't think about how I'd buy food or books or supplies and I certainly didn't think about rent. All I thought about was how I want to chase my dreams.

But after that conversation, every one of those thoughts is at the forefront of my mind. I have no idea how I'll fund my life outside of school and pay the massive bills that come due every month. So maybe Amelia's right. It couldn't hurt to have a little extra money while pursuing a dream of caring for the beautiful creatures with which we share this world.

Until then, I've got a shift to finish. Pulling my shoulders back on a deep inhale, I stuff my phone into my apron and head back toward my station. I immediately pause in the stockroom door when I push it open. A surprise guest standing at the end of the counter stops both my heart and my feet. I know the woman with dusty blonde hair, a form fitting dress that looks more expensive than the shop itself, and a sneer morphing her frown lines while she inspects the counter with her nose turned upward. Not personally, but…I know who she is. I've seen pictures of her. I've heard stories about the things she's done and the heartache she's caused. I've even suffered lukewarm water to the face because of her.

My future mother-in-law stands by the Pick-Up counter with a drink in her hand, waiting. And there's only one person in this entire building that she could be waiting for.

Excitement drains from my body, replaced with icy dread, and I debate turning around to wait her out in the stockroom. She hasn't seen me yet, too focused on inspecting the sitting room with disdain. I could hide. But the line is full of people waiting to order, and Alex looks like she's struggling to train the new person and make the drinks on her own. And I won't hide at my job from a woman I don't truly know. I have to face her, even if my gut is telling me that if she's here, there's something wrong.

With another deep sigh, I push my hands down my apron to wipe away the sweat that built with the dread before heading back into the bright sitting room. I'm barely back at my station before familiar hazel eyes turn on me with recognition. Cade and his mother have the same eyes, but I haven't seen his narrow on me like hers do now. Paired with the disgust that washes over her face—so similar to the one that marred her son's expression the first night we met—I almost shrink away. There's no doubt that she's explicitly directing this disgust at me and not some misunderstanding between us, like what happened with her son.

I won't give her that satisfaction. Not after the things I've heard from Cade and her sicking Chloe on me. I suppress my urge to tense when she moves to stand before me at my station in the same spot that her son has stood countless times before.

"Are you Ms. Hayes?" she asks, as if it's not obvious.

"Yes, I am, Mrs. Blanton." Her nose twitches upward like she hates the way I say her name. I still stick out my hand over the counter. "It's nice to meet you. I'm Misty."

"A pleasure." I swear condescension drips from her lips. She does at least shake my hand with the tale tell signs of a fire wixan marking her skin. "My son believed I didn't need to meet you. I disagree." My chest constricts harder than I expect. But she doesn't wait long enough for me to process the feeling before saying, "He also told me not to tell you about this." She pulls out a piece of paper from some unknown location. "Again, I disagreed. I thought you should know we found another solution to your problem."

My throat is so tight I can't fathom a response. Thankfully, she doesn't need one and hands the paper over the plexiglass. It shakes in my hand, and I don't look at it right away.

"Y-you found another way? When—"

"Weeks ago," Cade's mother interjects. "I thought you deserved to have all the information. That was all. Have a good afternoon."

She leaves me gaping at the spot she vacates, struggling to swallow her answer. I should probably stop her to get more information, but I can't. The minute-long interaction left me speechless. More-so when I glance at the paper I'm clutching. It's a scan of some book that looks older than life itself. I'm surprised they got such a clear image without the page falling apart. It's faded, but there's a handwritten note with a complete transcription. It looks simple. So fucking simple, and it could actually work.

All I can hear is my mind screaming: Cade knew about another way to get the ring off for weeks and he didn't tell me.

My heart thumps thickly in my throat, and the sounds of the shop fade away in favor of the staccato of my heartbeat. Dread implodes in the pit of my stomach and sears through my veins. I can't breathe. I stand motionless, trying to process the last two minutes, but all I can feel is pain. It hurts. All of it hurts. The lack of sharing, the betrayal. The lying...He lied. Cade lied to me after saying he wouldn't, because what—he wanted to get to know me? Because he wanted to keep the lowly witch he met at a dive bar on a leash?

It really fucking hurts. The betrayal threatens to drown me in a shallow pool of my own making. For weeks, I've tried to grow out of the darkness that long shaded my life, and I hate to admit how much of an impact he had on that. I should have been growing on my own, learning how to make me happy by myself. But I relied on someone else for the comfort I sought. I relied on everyone else around me to make me feel better, instead of learning to do it on my own.

Shame adds to the discontent coursing through me. I feel sick, but I can't take my eyes off the paper in my hands. Off the betrayal photocopied onto white printer paper.

Fingers snap in front of my face. Pale purple nails. Jae? Yes, Jae. I look up into lavender eyes framed with worry. "Was that his mom?" I'm only able to nod and look back down at the paper in my hands. "What is that?"

"A ritual," I mutter. "That he didn't tell me about."

"Bullshit." Jae scoffs. "Who told you—"

"She did!" I shout, narrowed gaze darting back to Jae as my expression finally shows the budding anger building right behind the dread. "She just gave it to me!"

"Okay?" Jae replies cooly, glancing around the shop at the people tuning into our conversation, knowing well where the anger in my voice is directing us. "Stockroom. *Now*."

"Jae—"

"Now," she demands through clenched teeth, not waiting for my response before heading to the same place I just walked out of. She stands at the doorway, eyes wide and expectant when I don't move. The look drags me from the roots that despair drove into the ground. The door flaps shut behind me. "Okay, now what—"

"He lied! Right to my face!"

"Cade lied?"

"Yes!" I snarl the word, waving the paper clutched in my hand like a flag in front of her face.

"Okay—stop. Stop!" Jae demands, flailing to grab my hands to stop them from moving. Her hands snag around my wrists, holding tight. "Give it to me."

I release the paper when she grabs it, hands falling limply at my sides as she scans the document that shows proof of Cade's deception. But her face doesn't convey any of the emotions flowing through me. She reads the paper with a mask of pure calmness, scanning it several times as the uneasiness in me rises. She's realizing the same thing I did: it could work.

Anger blazes through all the other emotions swirling inside me. "So?!"

"Yes, okay, it's a ritual," she says. "But this doesn't prove he lied to you. It's just a piece of paper."

"That he didn't tell me about for *weeks*, according to his mother!"

"And you believe her?" Jae fires back, tone placid yet cutting.

"It's right there!" I say, trying to take the paper back.

She snatches it away. "Again, you believe her? After everything you've told me that Cade's said about her? That she wants you gone?"

"It's right there, Jae. In your hand. He lied because he wanted to keep me around, so he didn't tell me about the ritual. I'm not stupid."

"I know you're not stupid," she says. "But you're panicking again. Take two seconds and think about who actually made you panic and tell me who you *really* think is lying."

My mouth opens to spew some outraged response, but it just hangs there. Even through the anger inside me, my mind latches onto her words and leaves me responseless. What Jae's insinuating is plausible based on everything Cade revealed about his mother. He's told me she's conniving and disingenuous. That she's impolite to people who work for her and doesn't show any mercy to her own family. But...the proof is right there in Jae's hand.

"What better way to get you to leave than to sow doubt between you two," Jae says when she can see the resolve I'm trying to grasp onto faltering. "Look, you always say I read too many books, so let me use my vast knowledge of third-act miscommunications to stop this one right in its tracks."

I scoff. "Jae, seriously, this isn't—"

"A romance book, I know. But just trust me," she says. "I'm back from the bank, so go talk to him. Call him and tell him to meet you somewhere and just ask him about it. If he genuinely did lie to you— which I highly fucking doubt—he'll have to lie his way out of it, too, and you'll see it. And if he did lie to you, we'll burn his house down."

There's no smile on her face, which adds another tick to the number of times I've seen her frown. But this time, it's emphasizing the seriousness of her statement. She believes Cade didn't lie, and she also believes that if he did, we will in fact burn his house down.

"If he lied—"

"Then I'll burn his house to the ground," Jae reiterates. "But if he didn't? You're one step closer to your happily ever after. So this is me, as your boss, telling you to get the fuck out of here. Right now."

There's no brokering a different path. The resolve on Jae's face as she hands the paper back out to me is final. I take off my smock and leave it in her open hand when I take the copied ritual, trying my hardest not to look at it again. I can't. Not right now. I have to cling to the small thread of hope that Jae gave me as the calm through this storm.

My hand shakes as I pull out my phone, and I try to convince myself it's from anger. I refuse to admit that it's nerves and the thought of yet again having the heart I so precariously wear on my sleeve shattered by someone I thought I could trust. I hold back the frustrated tears stinging the corners of my eyes. It's difficult when I open our text thread and see the last message he sent.

Have a good day at work, beautiful. I can't wait to see you tonight.

Moisture swells along my lower lids. We're slated to hang out tonight before he leaves town again on Council business before we head down to Frisco beach for Mayday. We were going to order delivery from Burrito Barn and sit on the couch with Jae and watch too many episodes of Beverly Hills Kitchen Witch. And now…Now I can't imagine not weeping at the sight of his face.

It takes all I have to type out a text.

Your mom just came by the shop. We need to talk.

His response comes back before I even close the thread.

I'll be there in 15 minutes. I don't know what she did, but I'm sorry.

TWENTY-FOUR

I never understood the appeal of rollercoasters. The breath-bating ups, the stomach-dropping downs, the topsy-turvy upside downs that make you want to hurl from the gravity. They were never my forte. I think it's because I experience those drastic emotional rushes every day of my life; I don't need to chase the thrill in my leisure, too.

Not when I can span the full breadth of emotions in a single minute pacing on my own two feet. I should have stayed downstairs. Being in the apartment alone waiting on Cade has been nothing short of devastating for my sanity. Staying in the shop until he arrived would've kept my mind busy and out of the 'what-ifs' I can't stop slipping into. Would've kept me from having the conversation I'm about to have a thousand times before the other party even arrives. I do it to protect myself, planning for and rehearsing scenarios that could happen in order to arm myself with responses.

It's a trauma response, according to my therapist, from years of living on the edge, not knowing how someone I trusted the most would respond. It's a way to protect myself, to prepare for the worst in every situation so I'm not hurt walking out the other side. But it's also something that harms me just as often as it helps. It leaves me in a world of my brain's own creation rather than reality. It leaves me apprehensive and unsure and resentful before I've even spoken a word aloud. But sometimes I can't help myself. I want to be prepared, and for this conversation I need preparation in bounds.

I refuse to sit around again and let a partner lie directly to my face. I asked Cade if The Annex sent the books we requested or if he found anything new in the weeks since we walked through the stacks together. He said no. The paper clutched in my hands is proof enough of his deceit.

Tell me who you really think is lying.

I growl. Curse Jae and her ability to be so level-headed. But also… praise the goddesses for putting her in my life. I need to learn a thing or two from her and the way she walks through this world with calmness and compassion. Maybe if I did, I'd be able to breathe right now, pacing our living room. But I'm not as good as Jae.

A knock echoes through the apartment, filling my stomach with more dread than it can take. My whole body clenches as I halt in my tracks, trying to catch my breath, glancing at the clock on the stove. Per usual, he's early. If he's a liar, at least he's a punctual one.

"Misty? Jae said you were up here." There's more worry in the voice that floats through the barrier between us than I've heard before. It doesn't help the unease in me. It takes me back to the concern Amber faked when she lied to me or mistreated our relationship. I have at least enough fortitude to remind myself that Cade is not my ex. But it doesn't help. My heart aches so badly I cannot convince it that this situation will be different.

It takes several seconds more to work up the nerve to walk toward the door. Forcing out a deep breath, I pull it open and regret it the moment I do. Gods, he's unfairly handsome no matter what light he's in. But in the light of my doorway and his betrayal? It hurts to even look at him. My heart thumps against my ribs, pounding in that same wild abandon as downstairs.

His eyes sweep over my face, and the worry on his morphs into complete concern. "Can I come in?"

"No."

He looks more taken aback than anything, but acceptance settles on his face. "Okay," he says with a sigh, nodding and shifting on his feet. His eyes never leave me, though, filled with an almost frantic apprehension that does nothing to help quell my discomfort. "Will you just tell me what she did? Did she insult you? I swear to the gods. If she—"

"She gave me this." I force out the paper I've agonized over for the last fifteen minutes. The look that fills his face shudders through my entire body. He doesn't even reach for it...because he knew. He fucking knew. "You knew."

Those words are flat and emotionless, because right now, that's what the confirmation of betrayal does to me. It strips me of the happiness and the eagerness and the hope I'd only just started building over the last several weeks. It leaves me a shell of myself, vibrating with disappointment and rage. Tears don't even sting the corners of my eyes.

Worry turns to downright dismay. "Please, may I come in? I'll tell you—"

"The truth?" I snarl with a contemptuous scoff. My fingers grip the door, knuckles white, ready to slam it in his face. "A little late. Just leave—"

"No, please," he cuts in. "What did she tell you?"

"That you're a liar, which you just confirmed!"

Dread turns to adamance in a flash of furrowed brows and a straightening spine. "I have never lied to you," he says. "Not since the moment we met. I don't know what she told you about that ritual, but *she's* a liar. Please, Mis, let me come in so we can talk about this."

Hearing him call me that name now hurts. The ache taints my voice.

"Then why haven't you shown me this if you've had it for *weeks?!*" I parrot the word that's been rattling in my brain.

The shock that floats over his face though is the first thing to make me disbelieve the word since it left his mother's mouth.

"She told you we've had this for *weeks?*" I don't need to respond. That question was more facetious than anything. Disgusted rage replaces his shock, and I'm reminded of the night we met. Of the brief moment during our date when she called. If it wasn't confirmed then, it is now. The look is because of his mother and his mother alone.

"She's got to be fucking joking," he snarls, launching into a swift pace in the hallway. "We *just* got that ritual sent to us *yesterday.* Fucking *yesterday.* A courier delivered the books we put out for transfer from The Annex *yesterday.* She showed it to me, and I was going to tell you about it tonight, when I came over, to see what you wanted to do. But she's such a fucking *busybody* that she couldn't let me do it on my own. Of course not. Because she's trying to ruin this. Fucking gods, she's—" he cuts himself off, grabbing his face in both hands and dragging down through his frustration.

I think it's that moment he realizes we're not having a conversation; he's just venting. Wide eyes pop up and toward me, but I don't think he finds the response he expects. The venting is frankly a cool bath of water washing over me with ease because that was a stream-of-consciousness rant. I don't know how much of it was fact or how much was fiction, but it was genuine. He was expressing anger in real time at learning what his mother did. That, if anything else, is what makes me move to the side to let him in.

Relief loosens his shoulders, and he hurries inside, slipping off his shoes without thought. I close the door, but I don't look at him. I can't. Not yet. I need a moment more to haul my emotions off the burning coals they're dragging over. I curl my arms around myself to hold it all in. To center myself for the conversation that's about to happen.

He's watching me when I finally work up the nerve to turn, a fractured softness on his face that pulses my heartache through my bones. Even though we're less than a foot from one another, he doesn't crowd me. How badly he wants to reach out and touch me radiates off of him in waves, but he doesn't step over a non-verbal boundary. I appreciate that.

"I'm sorry," he whispers, clearing his throat of whatever emotion lingers there. It still leaves his voice low. "I told you how she is. Please believe me. I've never lied to you. I'll even show you the text she sent me about it yesterday, if that will help you. I promise, Mis, I'm an open book to you. I'm trying my hardest to do everything I can to make this work because I *want* this to work. And *that's* the truth."

His resolve breaks through my dread and unease, and tears that I didn't know were waiting in the corners of my eyes slip down my cheeks. It's so palpable it's hard to believe that it's anything but genuine. That his words are anything but honest. Here this man stands in my apartment, proverbially on his knees, begging me to believe that he's not lying. All while respecting every boundary I've set.

It makes me doubt the narrative in my head, makes me reconsider the words Jae said downstairs. His mother is the one that lied. She caused this rift, caused most of the issues from the moment we royally fucked up a one-night stand. Well before that, if what he's told me about her is true. The more I analyze this scenario, the more that everything he's saying makes sense. She tried to force him into a marriage to a woman he didn't know that left him in a dive bar and me in his bed. She called and texted non-stop that night and the night of our first date to ruin our experience and impose her will. And now she's trying to sow the deepest seeds of doubt in me to make me believe her son is a liar.

What kind of woman would do such awful things to her own son? A woman I want very little to do with.

But...I'll have to have at least a little something to do with her because I'm dating Cade. We may only be engaged in public, but I could see myself falling for this man deeply enough to make it real in the future. Certainly not with a ring that's magically adhered to my finger forever, but I don't want to throw out the possibility of a life with him entirely just because of his mother. I want this man on my arm, and I want to be on his. I want to watch him grow and learn and change a millennia-old organization with just the grit of his will and the skin of his teeth.

"You believe me, right?" he pleads in my silence.

"I don't know," I admit.

"I know you've had people lie and walk out," he says. "But I promised I wouldn't do that and I meant it."

I dip my chin once and that forces all the air out of his lungs in relief. "Did you tell her that you didn't want her to meet me?"

"No," he replies without missing a beat. "If she said I did, she twisted that, too. I told her I didn't want *you* to meet *her*. Yet. Because I know exactly how she is. I didn't want you to have to deal with her or for her to scare you away. With all of this bullshit, she proved me right. Here we are in the middle of our first fight because she can't keep her mouth to herself."

I'm quiet for a moment before saying, "It's not a fight."

"No?"

I shake my head. "But I can handle myself. I'm stronger than you're giving me credit for. Your mother doesn't scare me." Even though seeing her standing in my job definitely wasn't comfortable. I won't admit that out loud. Understanding dawns on his face. "I appreciate you trying to protect me, but you can't just unilaterally make that decision. Not without talking to me first, at least, and telling me *why* you don't want me to meet her."

"You're right. I'm sorry." There's a placation in the softness of his voice, but I accept it as he steps a little closer into me. "I love how strong you are, and I love watching you get stronger every day as you learn new things about yourself."

On a deep breath that helps ease more of the tension in my body, I unfurl my arms. His eyes sweep over me and the action, and I again can feel how badly he wants to reach out and pull me against his chest in reassurance. Anguish or guilt or sympathy. I don't know which is the one powering his movements, but his features are soft as I take all of him in. There's still pain on his face, a rigidness in his shoulders and his posture. He's still unsure if I believe him.

Part of me is still unsure, too, but it's that part of me that's holding on to a hurt that happened well before I met him. Well before his mother walked into The Toasted Oak to ruin a relationship that's newly blossoming. It's a part of me I need to accept and move past before it taints the potential of any future with the man standing before me.

The man who's honest. Kind. Caring. Compassionate and determined and dedicated to a person who he met just weeks ago. Who dropped everything he was doing to come and reassure me that he would never intentionally hurt me or lie or disappear.

I step into him. A slow, hesitant smile tugs on his lips, and he slumps toward me. Relief.

"I want to see every single book that came in from The Annex," I say. "I'm going to go through every one of them."

He nods. "We can go through them a thousand times over if you want."

"Once is probably enough." He huffs a laugh, but it fades slowly when I add, "And I want to try that ritual as soon as we can."

His expression drops back into dejection, and he nods. "I understand."

I regret the statement because I realize he took it differently than my intention. "Just because I want the ring off doesn't mean I don't want to move forward with us."

"No?" He can't seem to hide any emotion right now; bewilderment replaces sadness, and he looks like he's reeling from the rollercoaster of emotions just as much as I am.

"No," I echo. "It just gets tangled in my hair a lot. It'd be nice to take it off when I go to sleep." The laugh he lets out almost sounds watery. I shuffle a little closer, enough that he has to look down at me with those cloudy hazel eyes. I rest my hands on his chest and ghost them up toward his collar. "And you're taking me to dinner tonight at Burrito Barn because I need a burrito, some cuddles on the couch, and a movie with my boyfriend to make me feel better."

Relaxation overtakes him beneath my hands. If he were alone, perhaps he'd sigh in relief. Instead, as his shoulders sag, he slides his hands low around my back and tugs me into him. I willingly go, releasing the last remnants of anxiety built from a lie and resolved by what I have to believe is the truth.

"I'll buy you a Burrito Barn for your apartment if it'll make you feel better."

"A whole Burrito Barn?"

"I'll buy you the entire damned company to make you smile." That statement alone is enough to make me grin. He does, too. "There it is. My beautiful witch."

"Imagine how big my smile will be when I've got that burrito."

We both laugh. Mine, louder, as always. And he just watches me, savoring the sound that I so openly give him now. His eyes catch on something over my shoulder, however, and I follow the gaze to see Charlie vigorously rubbing his face all over the opening of Cade's shoe. It only makes our laughter double.

"What does that mean?" Cade asks.

"Well, first, those are his shoes now," I say, glancing back to add, "And second, it means he likes you. Or at least your scent. A very rare occurrence."

"So, like mother like son? That feels like something."

"It's something, alright."

It's so much more than *something*. More than just my cat, who doesn't like anyone, liking a partner's scent. It's me, learning that what happened in my past doesn't have to cloud the vision of my future. It's me liking someone new and exciting and admitting that to myself. It's that person fitting into yet another aspect of my life where it feels like no one has fit in before. It's my favorite little being on this planet liking the person that I could find myself loving. And it's me, realizing that I *could* love the man standing with his hands around my waist and his smile bathing me in warmth.

It's so much more than something.

CHAPTER
TWENTY-FIVE

Three minutes before two, there's a knock on the apartment door. Ever the punctual man, Cade is smiling on the other side when I open it, a single bag on one shoulder and a sleeping bag slung across the other. I can't resist the force that is his bright nature, and a smile breaks across my face, too. His lips part to say something in greeting, but Jae beats him to it.

"Right on time!" She peeks out with a grin from where she's cleaning the kitchen before we leave.

Cade chuckles and steps inside, but he doesn't move far. He stops right before me and leans down to press his lips to mine in a way of greeting. My heart jumps into my throat, and the resounding butter-flies paint a broader smile across my face when he pulls away.

"Hey, Princess."

"Hi." The word is nothing more than a puff of air and after two months, I don't feel like the nickname combined with his kiss should spark such breathlessness.

He winks down at me and, while kicking off his shoes, says, "Where's my favorite roommate? I've got something for you."

Jae pops around the corner, bewildered. "For me?"

Curious lavender eyes dart to me, but all I can offer her is an equally astonished shrug as Cade pulls his duffle around his body. Just inside is a brown paper bag, and Jae doesn't move when he hands it out to her.

"What is it?"

"I owed you," Cade says, urging Jae with a flick of his head.

She shuffles forward and accepts it, still quizzical, until she unfurls the bag. "A man after my heart!" She pulls out a box of coffee pods and holds them above her head in display, like a proud new owner of a far more precious commodity. To her, I suppose it is. It's her life, her favorite hobby. Not only is it one of her favorite drinks in the world, it's what makes her money. It supports her life, and by proxy, mine.

And my boyfriend thought of her when he saw it. Such a simple thing, but so much more meaningful to me than expected.

Cade's laughter fills our apartment and me with warmth. "When I went to California this week, there was a shop that sold pods of their blend. I owed you for drinking all of yours, so I picked them up."

"Look, I know you're dating my best friend, but if you don't quit being too perfect, I'm going to fall in love with you, too." Cade barks another laugh. "My discount pods definitely didn't cost this much, but thank you."

"You're welcome," he says as Jae turns back into the kitchen to put the pods away so the apartment is spotless for when we return.

It takes Cade a few moments to turn back to me; when he does, a weird wave of relief, elation, and shame washes over me. He's holding a small brown box in his hands, and sincerity shapes the softest smile on his lips. It falters for a moment when he scans my face. "Did you think I'd get your roommate something and not you?"

"Maybe a bit." Embarrassment colors my cheeks.

"Surely you know me better than that by now."

I do. But I can't articulate that through the surprise that shakes my hands as I accept my gift. A treacherous thought springs into my mind that my box is no bigger than Jae's, making a disappointment seep through me. I try to bite it back. It has nothing to do with this present or the man who gave it to me. That feeling is a remnant of my past relationship and rarely receiving gifts, let alone a gift that overjoyed me. Gifts, as sparse as they were, were always self-serving; like they were meant for someone else and not me.

I cannot attribute that same disappointment to the one in my hands. Cade has proven, even within the last minute, that he's not the same.

It's proven again when I open the lid of my box. I cannot hide the genuine smile that peels across my face or the tears that warm the corners of my eyes. There's a beautiful crystal unicorn statue inside. The white packing paper it sits on makes every color dancing through the glass sparkle all the more through the moisture in my eyes. A blue mane and tail, purple stars sprinkled throughout the body like the unicorn from the gala we went to. And two beautiful blue eyes that are so reminiscent of mine that they must be one and the same.

"I left the hotel this time," he murmurs. When I finally focus back on him, there's pride in his smile that flushes through me. "There was a glass blowing artist on the street selling these little figurines. They had several unicorns, but none of them felt like they'd fit. I asked if they could do a custom order, and they could, obviously."

"Obviously." I puff out the word with the small bit of air I'm able to take in through the thickness in my throat. I know it's probably an overreaction, but I haven't gotten such a thoughtful gift like this from a partner in a long time. "It's beautiful. Thank you."

"Just like you. You're welcome."

Crimson heats my entire face; I blink away the happy tears. "I know just where I'll put it."

"Can I guess where?" My eyebrows bounce toward my hairline, at which he chuckles. "I was thinking of a specific place on your shelf when I got it."

"Oh!"

I jump and let out a "Good goddesses!" when Jae reappears beside us again. Through the excitement and happiness of my gift, I forgot she was in the kitchen.

"Oh hush," she says. "Cade, you tell me where you were thinking! Then Mis, you put it out, and I'll say if that's the same spot or not."

Cade seems just as intrigued by the game as Jae, so I just nod. "Alright."

Cade leans over to Jae and whispers in her ear, but I turn away. I don't want to see if they motion or glance toward any specific spot in the room because now I'm curious, too. I know where I want this because there's been a hole I haven't been able to fill with anything on the bookshelf beside the window. Metaphorically, maybe this tiny little unicorn is filling some other hole that's been inside me for as long as I can remember, but I choose not to dwell on that. I just set my newest unicorn memorabilia in its new home.

"That's it! I'm in love!" Jae shouts through the room, clapping her hands to punctuate the words. She's pointing at me when I turn around. "Are you in love with this man yet? Because you should be."

"Goddesses above, Jae!" I say that, but I can't help but smile when I look at Cade, mirroring the one on his face. I know the answer. It's the same spot, and it fits perfectly.

"Ugh!" Jae flails, doing the same thing as the butterflies in my stomach. "This is too cute. I have to walk away before I vomit."

Cade watches her go, but I cannot take my eyes off of him as I walk back into the citrus and woodsy scent that never fails to bathe me in goosebumps. Here and now, it doubles in taking more of my breath away when he looks back down at me with that fondness I've grown so accustomed to seeing. Talk about fitting perfectly; I move into him, hands finding a familiar home on his chest. His hands find just as familiar a home sliding low around my back.

"Thank you," I say. "It really is perfect."

"I just thought of you when describing what I wanted."

I tip my chin up and seek another kiss. He provides, leaning down to brush those soft lips against mine. One delicate kiss on the left side, one to the right, and then his lips pillow over mine, and my knees quiver. It doesn't last long, but it doesn't need to. The electric rush I feel inside from just a moment of our lips touching is enough to drive me a little wild.

"So we're driving?" he asks. "That's why you wanted me here so early?"

Another thread of immense dread tries to pull at the happiness inside me, and again, it's not this man's fault. There wasn't anything in his voice that made the question accusatory. But in my mind, all I can hear are the words of a woman who left me cold and alone.

You never tell me anything.

You're so annoying; you always forget to tell me things.

That's such a long drive. I can't believe we have to drive because of Jae.

Camping is awful. Why do we even have to go?

A spiderweb of insecurities race through my mind. My heart thumps against my ribs and pulses through my entire body, but I try to remind myself: Cade is not Amber. He's so far from being Amber, they're not even in the same league. He's proven that several times over in just the last handful of minutes: buying my roommate fancy coffee pods when he didn't have to; custom ordering a figurine of my favorite animal with blue eyes that mimic mine; arriving early, ready to go, and being *excited* about it.

Countless times he's proven he is not Amber, and I have to remember that. This part of healing is on me: I have to remember that no one in my life, the people I've chosen for years, will treat me the way she did. The way so many of my partners have. Everyone around me loves me and cherishes my input, and I have to keep reminding myself of that. No one wants me gone. No one is mad at me. No one in my life right now will ever walk out on me. Especially not the man in front of me with a slowly morphing expression showing his concern.

Taking a deep breath helps wash a smidge of that anxiety back to the depths of me where it came from. "I'm sor—"

"Ah," he cuts in, clearly aware that the pause and look on my face meant I felt like something was my fault. "You're what?"

"This time I am, though. Not just because I exist, but because I'm actually sorry."

"Okay." Skepticism draws out his word. "Then what are you *actually* sorry for?"

Several quick breaths give me the ability to process. "For not telling you how we were getting there. I thought I mentioned that Jae doesn't like Fading. She swears she can feel the pieces of her it leaves behind. We drive down to the beach when we go. It's only about four hours, but I completely understand if you—"

Gentle hands settle on the sides of my face. The contact forces me to take a breath. Cade draws my gaze up to look directly into his as he says without hesitation, "A road trip sounds perfect. It's definitely not something you need to apologize for. I never asked how we were getting there when you invited me, so you were never obligated to tell me. You didn't do anything that warrants an apology, and you certainly don't have to convince me to spend more time with you. I'm here because I want to be with you, no matter what that looks like. I'm just along for the ride this weekend, Princess, and apparently, that ride is an actual ride."

Gods, sometimes, being this emotionally overwhelmed can be annoying. There's no reason my eyes should be watering, but I can't help it. Whether from the sweetness of his words or the uncertainty draining from my body, I don't know. But I try to blink them away as he lifts my chin up a little further.

"So, you don't have to…?" He draws out the question, waiting for me to clear my throat to answer.

"Apologize for existing."

"Yes, exactly," he says, brushing some hair from my face in a practiced motion that makes my stomach flutter. "You don't have to apologize for existing and feeling your feelings. Not to me. Not to anyone."

"Unless I hurt their feelings," I counter.

He huffs a laugh. "Nope. Fuck 'em."

"Right." I snort. "Fuck 'em."

He kisses me then, and while there's still apprehension swimming in my veins, I sink into the feeling. It doesn't last long, but the way he looks at me when he pulls away does. He's proud. He's happy. And, frankly, he looks like he's in love, or the version of love I've always expected to see when looking at a significant other. But he says nothing. He just moves more hair from my face, like it's a job he intends to keep forever.

As he's brushing it behind my ear, his phone rings and the doting look on his face disappears in an instant. I know exactly who is calling. Annoyance tightens my jaw, more when he moves away from me and pulls out his phone. "Mother" reads across the top and makes my jaw tighten more. He just slides the decline button. It starts ringing again before he can even lower it.

"I swear to all the gods," he mutters, declining the call again.

"Can you turn it off without hurting Council business?" He nods, confused when I hold my hand out. He drops his phone into it none-theless just as it starts to ring for the third time. "Fuck'em, right?" I decline the call as he huffs a laugh, a smile working back across his face. "Jae always says this whole scenario is like one big romance book. So we'll deal with your mom in book two, yeah?"

"Right," he says, looking again fond and far more pleased with me than that statement should make him as he takes his phone back. "Plan on letting me stay around for at least another book?"

"Maybe." I draw the word out as his hands find their home on my waist again. "If you play your cards right."

"You've got all my cards," he says, leaning down to brush the tip of his nose to mine.

"Mike's downstairs!" comes Jae's voice before she reappears from her room, grinning when she sees us tangled together. "Let's go lovebirds."

Cade chuckles, hands falling away from me again. "All the bags?" he asks, pointing toward the pile beside the door, including several coolers with food and drink. He gathers more than half of the bags at my nod, easily pulling them up and over his shoulders and grabbing the handle of one cooler. Taking on more than his fair share in another show of how different he is from a life I never want to relive.

"See you downstairs." He winks at me.

Jae opens the door for him and when he's gone, the grin she turns on me is more than just because we're leaving for a weekend of fun.

"You heard all of that?"

"Every fucking word!" she says brightly. "And he's absolutely right. You don't have to apologize for being you, like I've been telling you for years. But if him telling you finally makes you believe it, then so be it. You lucky ass witch."

I do feel like the luckiest witch on the entire planet at the moment, savoring the feeling of adoration fueling me. I scoop up a few of our bags and one cooler and head toward the elevator with a grin on my face that I can't seem to wipe away. Not that I'm trying. I love feeling the soft burn of happiness in my jaws and cheeks. After weeks of smiling so often and for so long, it hurts, but in the best way.

It's been ages since I've felt the warmth of happiness shining down on my world. For so long I've been drowning in the darkness of a deep ocean of despair. But no longer. At least, not right now. And if I have anything to do with it, never again. I won't let anyone steal my sunshine, or dampen the person I am or the smile on my face.

If it took a man to walk into a bar and spend a single night with me? So be it. But I'm learning and learning takes time.

Time I'm willing to commit.

CHAPTER

TWENTY-SIX

THERE ARE COUNTLESS CAMPGROUNDS BETWEEN RALEIGH AND THE outermost plains of North Carolina. None of them are as beautiful as Frisco. Do I have a bias because I'm a water witch and naturally drawn to the ocean? Absolutely. But I'm not the only one who thinks that this is the most beautiful place in the whole of The Outer Banks. For a decade, Jae and I have been driving out here to celebrate the start of summer alongside hundreds of other people. We've never missed a year. Storms, late cold fronts, sickness. No matter what, this place calls our name and we answer.

The sun dips toward the horizon when we reach Frisco Woods, a home away from home. The last remnants of daylight seep through spindly oak trees in full bloom and cast a beautiful glow over the small dunes. Rock and sand crunch under our tires as we drift past cabins brimming with people.

The rules on average days limit four to a cabin, but the owners let a lot slide when Beltane rolls around. They charge twenty dollars extra per person and allow as many people as they can fit to experience the magic teeming on the old grounds. Every year, more and more people take advantage of the melting pot of celebration that this place has become. It's no longer just a ceremony reserved for wixan-kind. All walks of life find themselves here, celebrating the oncoming season and the upcoming year. Humans and magicals alike flock here for the frivolity and camaraderie that comes along with the magic seeping across this land.

I savor the calm that works over me as we pull up to our campsite, where three people have already set up tents. We missed renting the last cabin by more days than any of us will admit, but none of us mind. We're just here to be with friends. One of which, who I haven't seen in months, is bouncing on their toes, waving wildly at us as the car shifts into park. It's impossible to overlook the grin spanning their face even from this distance. I can't wait to feel their crushing hug that I only get to feel once or twice a year.

Salt saturates the air and my senses when I open the car door. Magic hums around us and dances across my skin, humidity working a sweat along my forehead. The moon is already high and taking a back seat in the sky, letting the setting sun's rays have the spotlight before bathing the grounds in beautiful blue light. I take in the deepest breath I've taken in months and close my eyes, savoring the rush of the ley lines surging through the activities on their grounds. The sweet taste of magic in the air is palpable. Mine hums with appreciation through my veins.

When I open my eyes, Vi Samba is barreling toward us, bangles on their wrists jangling in a harmonious bass. The pale sunlight dances over the strands of gold splashing through their dark auburn hair. A beautiful halo of tight curls bounces with every step, decorated with a crown of overly expressive flowers. Yellow primrose and marigolds shine against the ebony of their skin, matching the personality of the person wearing them to a tee. Vi is the most radiant person I've ever met, and that brilliance always shines in their smile. Now is no different.

Their arms fly around my neck first. "Mis! I've missed you!" I can't help but smile back when they pull away, hands lingering on my biceps, to turn to Jae. "You, too! It feels like it's been years."

Jae laughs. "We talked on the phone like two weeks ago."

"And I'm allowed to think that feels like years," Vi quips, turning to the man who walks up to my side.

"Cade, this is Vi," I say. "Vi this—"

"Only you didn't know who he was, Mis." Vi laughs, and they shove a hand marked with the signs of a fire wixan out to Cade. Red embers, almost like freckles, float up their arm. Cade's eyes only flick to the markings for a second before he slides his hand into theirs. "Pleasure to meet you, Cade. I'm going to apologize now for getting drunk and dancing against your lady later."

Cade barks a laugh. "No apology necessary."

"Are you already drunk?" I ask.

Vi shrugs. "Not my fault you guys showed up late."

"Don't you have to help light the fires?" Jae asks.

"Child's play." Vi brushes away the ceremonial start of the night as nothing more than a flick of their wrist. It's more than that at its deepest level, but for a group of fire wixan, lighting a few bonfires on the ley lines really is like child's play.

"Let them unpack," comes a familiar voice over the sounds of the crowd gathering around our campsite.

I hadn't thought of that happening here, but I'm sure Cade did, because he's ignoring them all. They recognize him, and are doing all the things the public regularly does when he's around. They're pointing and whispering or hovering their cameras close to their faces to make it seem like they aren't taking pictures. They are. I wonder, not for the first time, if he'll ever be able to escape the limelight for real. Or if the full light of day tomorrow will expose him to people who think it's their right to approach him in a place like this.

This is a part of the relationship that I didn't process completely when I slid my hand into his at The Toasted Oak. No matter where we go, or if we're there for business or pleasure, people will recognize him. People will know who he is, and eventually, when they see more of me, they'll know me, too. It's not something I can just brush off like he does. We'll be in the public eye for as long as he's in The Council; longer even, I'm sure.

It's not enough to make me not want this. Not even close.

"Piss off, Rokk," Vi sings as they turn back toward the firepit around which my friends congregate. "Come on. Come, take a shot, then you can unpack."

"Hell yeah!" Mike cheerily wraps his hand around the back of Jae's neck. It's such a subtle act, but Jae told me it's like a drug to her. She's not one to like public claims like me, but that slight movement almost brings her to her knees. She beams, following him toward the fire.

"She seems nice," Cade says.

"They," I say. "Vi goes by they/them pronouns."

Cade nods once, taking in the proclamation without a second thought. "They seem great."

"They're the best. Jae and I met them our first year down here, and we've been friends—"

"Come on!" Vi shouts from beside the fire, small paper cups in one hand and a bottle of liquor in the other. "Shots!"

Cade laughs when I look up at him in mock exasperation. But we make our way to the fire around which all of my friends are standing. And...

"Jason?" I ask, now close enough to realize who's beside Rokk. I try to keep the surprise from my voice, but I'm amazed because I never expected Rokk to actually work up the nerve to ask him on a date, let alone on a brief vacation with all his friends.

As if reading my mind like Jae, Rokk says, "Yes, I know, I finally asked him." Both of them smile, so it's likely not the first time they've had this conversation. "Mis," Rokk greets. "Mr. Macallan. Good to see Mis hasn't drowned you yet."

"Good to see you, too, man," Cade says mirthfully, lifting the paper cup Vi hands him in the way of greeting. "And it's nice to meet you, Jason."

"Y-yeah," Jason puffs out.

I know what the look on his face means: he's star-struck. Not only is he sitting in a group of Rokk's friends, but here walks up a future Councilor. I hadn't thought about how intimidating it may be to meet him in this informal capacity. I'm sure Rokk told Jason to expect it, but there's not much that can prepare you for seeing someone like Cade, if you actually know who they are. To some people, it doesn't mean a thing. To others? It's not a common or even a lifetime occurrence. Jason is a green wizard. He knows who Cade is, and clearly, it's intimidating.

Cade doesn't miss a beat. This time, he's wearing his friendly facade and the smile he offers everyone seems to soothe things a bit. "I brought some decent whiskey if you're interested," Cade offers.

"Oh, we are! Bring it out!" Vi answers and makes everyone laugh.

"Aye aye, Captain. It's in the car."

Shock overtakes Vi's face. "Did this man just call me Captain? Oh—" they draw the word out with far too much dramatics. "Oh, I like it. Cheers!"

The group sings an echo of toasts before we all turn up our paper cups. Vodka sears down my throat and I and several others hiss out the displeasure. But people whoop and toss their cups into the fire nonetheless.

"Okay, go get your shit now and set up so we can party!" Vi says excitedly.

"Yes, Captain," I say back and Vi shoots me a salacious look that we all just laugh off.

Jae and I and our men make the short trek back to the car, a warmth now tingling in my stomach. Even more when Cade's hand slides down low on my back, not guiding, just resting, remaining there while we wait for Mike to open the trunk. I move to grab a bag when he does, but Cade stops me.

"I've got it," he says, moving to loop his hand through several bags. "Just get whatever you need for the fire and go catch up with your friends. I'll get everything unpacked and our tent all set up."

"Oh." There's surprise in my voice, but he either misses it or ignores it. "Sure, okay. Thank you."

"Anything for my fiancée." He punctuates that by leaning in and pressing a chaste kiss to my lips.

"You don't need any help?"

"I think I can manage a tent."

"Okay," I say. "Well, I'll be right over there when you're done."

"You better be. I'd hate to have to hunt you down and bring you back."

Warmth spikes in me unexpectedly. "Something tells me you'd like that."

He flashes a wink and a smirk that upturns the left side of his lips and flares that heat, tingling with the magic and the liquor inside me. He and Mike turn to walk away carrying tents, and I watch him go. Only a few short months back, that was all I wanted. I wanted him to walk away and leave me alone for good. I wanted the ring off and him gone. Not anymore. I want him around, and I'll happily admit that to anyone who asks.

"Well, isn't he just the sweetest?" Jae's grin is wide.

I roll my eyes, but the mirth on my face gives me away though, and she laughs, turning to pull out our chairs and the coolers from the car. While she does, I take a moment to examine the campground teeming with life around us in the last remnants of the sun. I haven't felt this relaxed here in years, and I inhale the pleasant scent of the sea to savor the feeling, eyes closed.

I regret it the moment my eyes open and land on the car pulling up to our campsite. I intimately know the red SUV with a dent on the front right bumper that stares me in the face as the headlights shut off. I've ridden in it more times than I can count. I've driven it my fair share of times, too, on the way home from nights when it was my turn to stay sober—which turned into every night out with the vehicle's owner. It's the one we took on so many road trips, singing our favorite songs at the top of our lungs, laughing and joking around. But now, it fills me with dread. The sight of it and all the memories that slam against the front of my mind make me immediately nauseated.

For a moment, I think, "Why me? Why now?" As if this is the worst thing that has ever happened to anyone and will ever happen to anyone again. It isn't. So fucking far from it. But at this moment, I can't help myself. Finally, I'm happy or at least re-learning how to be after so many years of drowning in mostly hidden despair. And now?

I'm frozen.

I can't manage a word to Jae in warning before the door opens, and my heart leaps from my chest when the driver steps out.

CHAPTER

TWENTY-SEVEN

She's staring at me.

The cause of so much of my pain. The reason I lost myself and who I was. The reason I spent so much time drunk at Big's and suffered so many nights alone, unable to sleep or dream other than nightmares. She's staring right at me. Amber.

Anxiety freezes me in place. My heart pounds in my chest and blood rushes to my face and head both. Just the sight of her makes me dizzy, and it's not entirely bad like I expected for the first time seeing her again.

She's the same as that last night—beautiful, with her long dirty blonde hair flowing freely, piercing green eyes blinking behind long lashes, tattoos showing through a sheer shirt, and those legs that go on for fucking days moving toward me. My heart immediately clenches, and reminds me of all of the good things that happened in our past. Reminds me of all the reasons I fell in love with this woman. That first year was so amazing. The trips we took, the meals she made me. The sex. Her smile, her laugh. The nights we laid and watched the stars. The quiet moments we spent on the couch in each other's company. The way she could make me laugh so easily. I remember all of it like it was yesterday, and none of the last several years happened.

But then, thankfully, my brain does what my heart can't and remembers the recent years. The memories and the hurt flood through the nausea and the palpitating of my heart. I'm reminded of that shell of a person sitting on the couch waiting for her girlfriend to show up several hours after she said she would. I can hear the fights and feel the ghost of all of my tears sliding down my face in the shower, wondering what I did wrong. Wondering why I wasn't good enough. Anxiety tingles through me, reminding me of the nights I laid awake, never certain of where she and I stood. Anger simmers right behind it and reminds me of every time she walked out only to reappear like she is right now, filling a spot by my side that she assumed would always be hers without doing any of the work that comes along with the title.

Not this time. This time, I didn't lie to Jae when I told her I was moving on. This time, I didn't cheat myself out of healing and finding a way back to who I was before I let someone knock me off my pedestal. It's only been five months since she walked out of my life, but just over five months is more than enough time for me to realize all the things Amber did and said weren't because of me. They were because of her.

And I'm strong enough to do this now, even if it is by surprise. I can do this. I can face her and not let her get to me. As she approaches, I take a deep breath to steel myself.

"Jae," I say. She looks up, brows furrowed in confusion at my tone, before her eyes follow my path. The outraged frown is one to top them all.

"You've got to be fucking kidding me." Jae's voice tears across the campsite and rips me from the stasis. Bags and fabric camping chairs clatter to the ground, and through the racket I realize that Jae's shoulders are squared directly at Amber. "Why the fuck are you here, bitch?" Palpable anger radiates off her in waves.

Amber scoffs, saying, "Just enjoying the great outdoors, obviously."

The sound of her voice washes nostalgia down my spine that I try to shove away. She's fearless as she strides up to yet again ruin one of my favorite vacations of the year, shoulders pulled back and stance calm. As if she isn't in danger of the witch standing at my side. As if she isn't in danger of *me*. Arrogance laces every line of her face. I wonder how many times she looked like this while I mistook her egotism for confidence.

"You can do that literally any-fucking-where else," Jae replies adamantly, taking a half step toward the woman before us.

Instinctively, my hand reaches out to grab her shoulder. "It's not worth it."

"Bullshit," Jae says, echoing what the voice in my mind is screaming, too. "This bitch deserves getting upset over."

Amber looks at me, affronted. "You're going to let her talk to me like that?"

"I can't control how she talks to you," I say. "And she's right."

"Wow."

"Yeah, 'wow,' bitch," Jae replies and takes a step closer. "I'll ask again: why are you here? You're not welcome."

"I paid you for this trip months ago, so part of this campsite is mine."

Jae barks a mirthless laugh. "Bitch—"

"Jae," I say, much more forcefully than I have in the past. Maybe ever. I pull her back again when she tries to take another step forward. "It's fine. I can handle this."

Jae says nothing, but the disbelief on her face when she glances back at me says it all: if I don't deal with this, she will. And it'll end up on the front of some tabloid because of all the phones around, waiting to capture any sellable gossip relating to Cade. I plead silently with her, and it takes a moment before Jae sneers deeply and snatches what she dropped to leave.

I don't take my eyes off of Amber. She's looking at me like I'm a lost unicorn colt, waiting to be snatched by a predator in the forest. Not anymore.

"Finally," Amber scoffs, flicking her gaze over my shoulder. She seems to relax a little when green eyes fall back onto me. Even her voice is softer when she says, "Hey, Missy," and I want to crawl out of my skin at the nickname.

"Why did you come here?" I offer back through tight lips. "What part of you thought this was a good idea?"

"You've been ignoring my calls, and I was worried. I came to make sure you were okay."

"I haven't been ignoring you. I blocked your number after you walked out on me. Again."

She doesn't need to know that Jae was the one to do it. I'm the one who made the conscious choice to leave it that way and not just add the number I memorized so long ago back into my phone. That's all that matters. *I* chose to stop her from coming back. And yet here she stands before me, again acting like I've hurt her. Acting like everything we went through together and everything after is my fault. I had a part in our demise, arguing when there shouldn't have been a problem. Bitching about the dishes when she didn't do them quickly enough; yelling, whining, and crying.

But it all wasn't my fault. I'm not the one who lied, cheated, and left in the middle of the fucking night. And she won't make me feel like I am. Not anymore.

"That seems harsh. I didn't do anything to deserve that or waking up to see you engaged to some asshole before we even officially broke up."

I bark a sudden mirthless laugh; condescension drips in the sound because I cannot believe what I'm hearing. Who could ever have the gall to say that to someone they walked out on six times? Six fucking times. Without explanation.

Amber Mazingo. That's who. And it's taken me an embarrassingly long time to realize it. I'm not sure I would have without Jae's consistent love and support or Cade's adoration after he waltzed into my favorite dirty dive bar and my life.

"Doesn't feel great to have your significant other just disappear, does it?"

That hits home. She flinches, and her brows furrow together. In the red of Mike's tail lights, she almost looks demonic, staring at me with her nostrils flared in indignation. She quickly realizes herself and checks the emotions behind several blinks and a mask that to anyone but me would look sincere. I know it's not.

"You walking out, Amber, was us 'officially breaking up.' If you can't see that, you're more demented than I thought."

"Demented?" She echoes. "I'm not the one engaged to some random person and bringing them to our place."

Every single thing she says makes my eyes widen a little more in disbelief. "Our place? You hated it here."

"I know you just brought him to spite me."

"Nothing I've done since you walked out has had anything to do with you other than completely forgetting you. And that includes Cade and mine's relationship and bringing him here to *my* favorite place."

Amber scoffs again and the glimpse of that old her, the one only I ever got to see, flashes over her face. "Relationship? That's a joke, and we both know it."

"Nothing between Cade and me is a joke. Not like us. Because that's what you thought we were, right? Just a joke to laugh about with your friends while not letting me join any of your parties or hang outs?"

"It's fine," Amber says and brushes off my words with a flick of her hand. "It won't last. You'll be back, and you know it."

The fucking arrogance. It's so strong in her, I doubt she even hears it anymore. But I won't back down.

"No, I won't be. I have zero reason to come back to you. You have nothing to offer me anymore, if you ever did. Nothing. Don't think you hold that much of a place in my life anymore, Amber. The only reason I think of you now is to remind myself of exactly what I don't want in a partner, a friend, or even a fucking acquaintance. So just leave."

My heart is pounding so hard in my throat it hurts, but it's from such a strong sense of righteousness that I let it engulf me. Pride surges through me and coats me in a protective armor of my own words, actions, and thoughts. I won't let this woman get to me again. I won't let her reappear like this and win me over, break me down.

Amber looks livid. "Excuse me? After everything I've done for you? For us?"

"What did you do for me, Amber? What? Right now. Tell me."

"Everything," she replies, voice raising like it always did when she knew she was wrong but wasn't willing to admit it. "I did everything for you."

"Give me one example. One. If you did everything for me, you can name one without thinking." I pause for a moment while deeper indignation washes down her face.

Silence.

"Did you validate me when I said my boss was mistreating his entire staff?"

The silence is so loud it's deafening. She doesn't even know the entire story because she didn't ask. She didn't validate my feelings or listen to my troubles. She just said I was overreacting. Which, clearly, I wasn't.

"Where were you when my grandmother passed?"

She scoffs. "You didn't even talk to her."

"That doesn't matter," I say. "She was my grandmother. And you didn't even pull your nose out of your t.v. show to give me a hug. I had to *ask* you to comfort me. And what about when my grandfather passed?"

She stays silent because we both know the answer. She went to the bar with friends moments after I got the call that he'd passed when I came home from the hospital to change clothes and shower. She never even visited me or him. At the time, I thought it was because I was being too inconsiderate and inconsolable. I thought the sobs wracking my body were just too much to deal with.

No. She was just a jerk.

"That's what I thought," I say, quiet but no less forceful. "You didn't do anything *for* me. You did everything for *you* and expected me to fall in love with your lack of sincerity."

"Don't act like you were a fucking saint," Amber spits. "You were just as selfish as I was. Always nagging and going out with Jae. Always talking shit about my friends—"

"Who literally talked shit about me *to my face*, and *you laughed*," I cut in. "I'm not pretending I'm a saint. I know I made mistakes, but I did everything I could for you. I cared for you. I shrunk myself down to fit a mold I was never going to fit into. I did everything to make us right and whole. I gave you everything, and you walked all over me while walking out the door without a word."

"I did everything for you!" She parrots herself. "Everything!"

"As I hear it," comes a deep voice before a large, warm hand curls slowly around my waist. Possessive. And I like the way it feels when I lean back and Cade is there to catch me in his unyielding support. "You did absolutely nothing but walk all over Misty and then leave while somehow making her believe it was her fault that you're a piece of shit."

I can protect and defend myself, and I feel like I've been doing an excellent job at it since I caught my bearings. But I can't deny it's nice to have Cade standing behind me in more ways than one.

"Oh, fuck you," Amber spits. "Who even are you? You don't know Missy like I do."

"No. You're right. I don't know *Missy*, at all," Cade says. "But I know Misty Hayes and I have a feeling I know her better than you ever did. I know the real her. The one who *hates* the nickname Missy. The one that deserves all the happiness in the world that you stole."

"Of course, that's all you've heard. You only heard her side—"

"That's all I need," Cade interjects. "I don't want or need your side of the story."

"I don't care who you are or what fucking Council you're about to be on. You don't just get to steal people's girls."

"I didn't steal anything. Misty was a single woman when we met and consensually let me fuck her better than anyone ever has. Her words, not mine. But now she's mine. Which means I should probably thank you for walking away for the *last time* because now this beautiful, intelligent, kind woman is all mine."

Amber is stunned. She stammers, and I don't think she has any sort of coherent response so she reaches by saying, "She-she's 'yours'? That's disgusting." She turns to me. "You let him say shit like that?"

"I love it when he says I'm his," I say without hesitation. "I wished so many times that you would openly claim me or our relationship, if that's even what we had. But you never did. Not once. I never have to beg him to say anything. He just *says* it."

"And I mean it," Cade adds. "She's mine, and I'm going to support her in every way. She'll never have to worry about a single thing, and she'll never want for anything, either. Especially not you. Because now she has me. And even if things don't work out between us, I'll still make sure you can't come anywhere near her again because she deserves so much more than you."

Amber stands motionless in shock. Frankly, I'm a little astonished myself, but in a vastly different way. She can't believe what she just heard, but I can. Every word. Warmth spreads through me even though the sun's almost down and the air is chilling. I deserve so much better than Amber. I deserve the intelligent, competent, and caring man standing beside me, defending me from the last person who broke me.

A smile tugs all the way across my face when he glances at me and winks. I lean up and ask him a question that only he can hear, and a matching grin spans his face in response; a moment later he's digging a twenty-dollar bill out of his wallet. I think about throwing it on the ground at Amber's feet, but it feels so much more satisfying watching her contemplate taking the money from Cade's hand when he stretches it out.

"By the way," I start. "I paid for your half of this vacation because you complained about it the entire time. But I'm still buying you out so that you'll leave."

Amber looks at the crisp bill in Cade's hand, then to me, scandalized. "You've changed, Misty."

"I have, and I'm so much better for it," I say. "Now leave before I let Jae loose on you."

Amber keeps the thin shred of dignity she has left and doesn't snatch the money. She just spins on her heels and I don't even watch her walk away. I turn to the man who still has his hand secured to my waist, trying not to cry as the tidal wave of emotions rain down on me as the adrenaline wanes. My heart still pounds, but I'm choosing to believe it's pounding for an entirely different reason now.

And that reason is Aldrich Cade Blanton.

"You okay?" he asks, brushing some hair off my face. He gently tucks it behind my ear, lingering to cup my cheek.

I lean into the touch, nodding. "Yeah, I'm okay."

"I know you said you can defend yourself, but—"

I shake my head. "That…that was different, and I appreciate you coming to stand beside me. Thank you."

"You don't have to thank me for sticking up for my girlfriend. Especially not to her shitty ex."

It's so asinine to me that a simple word can make my entire body vibrate with appreciation. It's not like it's the first time he's called me his girlfriend, or the first time that anyone has. But for the first time, I feel like I'm with someone who means it. I've had relationships in the past. Some a handful of weeks, some years, like the woman who speeds away from our campsite. Some were fun while they lasted and offered a little happiness to my days. Some ended in heart wrenching pain, others just a fond farewell. But none made me feel like this. None made me feel as seen, heard, or supported as the man standing before me. And, most certainly, none made me feel as much like a 'girlfriend' as I do now.

It's even more asinine that Cade pressing his lips to my forehead can compound all of that appreciation the way it does now. But it does. I'm smiling when he pulls away, eyes sweeping over my face.

"Turns out I did struggle with the tent," he says.

I snort a laugh at that unexpected turn of conversation, glancing over to see Jae helping Mike with their tent, too. "Want some help?"

"I'll always accept help from my witch."

TWENTY-EIGHT

"You sure you're okay?"

Nodding doesn't loosen Jae's brows. "I am," I say to reassure her and ease the frown on her face, welcoming her familiar grip around my biceps. That frown has appeared far too many times in the recent past because of me, but right now, she doesn't need it. "I'm okay, promise. Maybe a few months ago I wouldn't have been, but I am okay. In no small part, thanks to you."

Jae shakes her head. "No, babe, this one is all you. I can force you to work at The Toasted Oak. I can suggest you go to therapy and everything else, but you're the one doing the work. We're all just here supporting you."

"I love you."

"I love you, too," my best friend replies, wrapping me in a hug that I sink into, squeezing as hard as I can to show how much I appreciate this woman and all the ways she's been by my side since childhood.

I wish I could hug all the people sitting around the campfire, showing concern for my well-being. But I want to push away Amber's unwanted interjection in my life and look toward the weekend of frivolity instead. Thankfully, the soft sounds of wooden flutes and horns float over the campground. The uneasiness in me isn't all the way settled yet, but the ritual will remove it all.

Jae releases me, and Cade appears to fill her spot, glancing down at me with the same concern on his face. I just lace my fingers through his in the last vestiges of the sun fading against the dark sky. The stars are sparkling above us and a crescent moon is bathing everything in that gentle hue.

"It's time!" Vi sings with infectious happiness.

Excitement ripples across our campsite. It's time for Vi to shine, literally and figuratively. They're the May They, as they've been saying since we arrived, and it genuinely is *their* time. Out of the hundreds of the fire wixan that visit these hallowed grounds for the yearly celebration, The Order of Flame unanimously selected them to be the most cherished member of the ritual three years in a row. Lighting the two Beltane bonfires and stoking the magic teeming through the ley lines that the gods and goddesses gave us is an honor. Being chosen once is a feat, let alone twice. Trust my friend to get the honor thrice before even leaving the campground last year.

An accomplishment I'm so inordinately proud of that a soft lump forms in my throat as I watch them bounce on their toes from excitement.

Cade leans in closer to me and asks, "What's happening?"

"The ritual," I say, clearing my throat. "It's a dance performance, but mostly it's a large offering to the ley lines. We all give a little something to fuel the magic, and Vi does the rest. It's amazing. Just wait. All you need to know is when it's time, just chant 'Tine'."

"Fire," he says, easily understanding Gaelic once again, sliding his hand into mine. "Got it."

"Kick ass, Vi," Rokk says.

"You're gonna be amazing," Jae adds. Mike agrees.

"Dance your heart out, Captain," I say, and Cade adds, "Here, here!"

The moniker lights up Vi's face, and they pull their shoulders back, spine straight with confidence. "Fuck, I love you guys. Okay, I'm going. I'm going. See you after for shots!"

Before they go, however, red blazes across their light ebony skin, painting their hand like a sparking wildfire. Our fire fades from life, and countless others around the grounds follow as everyone prepares to re-stoke the embers from the two towering bonfires that Vi will light at the center of the campgrounds.

It takes a moment for my eyes to adjust to the cloudless night sky. Moonlight illuminates our path to the ritual grounds, and Cade and I follow my friends, hand in hand, as they weave through the crowd of people gathered in the monument that has been here through over a century of hurricanes and celebrations and drunken attempts to move it. There's magic all throughout the grounds, but this place hums with an energy that leaves me breathless. The ley lines pull and tug and draw me closer with every step we take.

Two towering stacks of wood sit at the center of a casting circle made of stones that's just wide enough for a few dancers to fit in. Smaller stones fan out like spokes on a wheel to an outer ring that's wider than a hundred yards in diameter, all lit with candles to light the space. It's large, but it's not large enough to fit the mass of bodies that come here for this very moment. People sit in each other's laps, and brush elbows with the people beside them, sitting in the element that corresponds to their magic.

The spokes represent the four cardinal directions and their corresponding elements. North for the air and the elementals that wield it. East for the earth and green wixan who give this world color. South for fire and those who light this world with it. And West for water. For me. For that magic that breathes through me every day of my life.

Rokk nods to us before he leads Jason toward the East. This is the first time in all the years he's attended that he hasn't sat facing the West with Jae and I and whoever else is by our sides. It fills me with warmth to watch him sit beside Jason while Jae tugs Mike toward our usual seats. We always sit facing the waters because Jae and Rokk's magicks aren't elemental. There are so many different magicks in this world, and until tonight, we all celebrated my element. I'm happy that this year, we're separating.

Jae leans her shoulder into mine when we sit, alcohol and the invigoration around making her smile as wide as mine. She glances at Cade, who's too busy surveying the surroundings to notice the way she bounces her eyebrows. I roll my eyes, but I don't miss the way my stomach flutters with excitement. A month ago, I probably would've blamed it on the enveloping energy all around us. Not tonight. Tonight, I know it's because of Cade, especially when he turns to me, grinning.

Intrigue litters his face and reminds me of my first time witnessing this evening. There are so many aspects that leave a person breathless. The unadulterated energy that overwhelms you. The camaraderie of everyone around laughing and singing and shouting at the moon. The sheer overwhelming emotion that bates your breath. Okay, maybe that one is only me, but given the look on his face, it seems like he may experience it, too. He reaches for my hand, and without a thought, he pulls the ring to his lips before leaning over to press them to mine. Both chaste kisses sear warmth through me, leaving me even more breathless as a hush draws forward from the back.

All attention draws to the three people weaving up toward the bonfires through the crowd. Pride stings the corners of my eyes as I watch Vi sway with every measured step they take toward their favorite center stage. There's a confidence in their movements that only comes from years of meticulous training. They've danced since the age of two, attending UNC School of the Arts for high school and college, finishing top of their class every year throughout the entire program. Right out of school, they got an offer to dance on tour with some musician I'd never heard of, starred in their music and social media videos, and now, they're part of a traveling dance troupe that puts on performances all over the world, which is why we rarely get to see them.

But out of everything they've accomplished, they say that this is their favorite performance every year. Telling the story of Mayday throughout all the Celts' histories is an honor for them, with most of their mother's Fire wixan ancestors hailing from the region. From Welsh to Irish to Scottish, The Order of Flame long ago crafted a story for these nights that speaks to the fealty of the gods and goddesses, the blessings showered upon their people, and the union of the May King and May Queen. It's a stunning display every year, but it's never more stunning than when my friend breathes life into every measured move.

In the intensity of the magic teeming through the grounds, I never fail to cry. Tears slip from my eyes as Vi and their two counterparts dance and spin and tell the most beautiful story. Murmurs of our chant around the circle grow and grow and grow as we all sway in our seats. The ley lines sigh beneath us. Magic rushes up into the air, the wind lifting the tendrils of my hair, bathing me in goosebumps. Oranges and pine and ocean spray scent the space and coat my tongue like the sweetest candy. My heart pounds from the sheer intensity, and Cade's hand trembles in mine as the sting of sacrifice tugs on my leg.

Vi and their counterparts dance quicker and quicker, charging toward the climax, painting the most beautiful picture with their movements. Suddenly, the candles lighting the stones extinguish one by one from back to front, hurling the circle into darkness as Vi's counterparts drop to their knees before them.

When Vi hits their final pose, hands down at their sides, palms out, fingers spread, and face toward the heavens, magic rumbles through the earth. Vi calls on the primal force inside them, offering their very being to the ley line, fueled by all our magicks swimming in the air. The line breathes the magic right back at them. The gust of pure power slams against them and lights their whole body in reds and oranges and yellows. Lightning and flame and freckles like embers shine against the moonlit sky, and the bonfires blaze to life.

Cheers, merriment, and praises sing through the crowd as Vi's partners spring up from the ground. They all lace hands, panting, and take a bow before shouting at the top of their lungs and rushing through the bonfires. Several people vault up and follow behind them, and Cade doesn't hesitate when I drag him up and in Vi's path.

In reality, it takes thirty seconds to dash through the fires beside countless other people. But to me, it feels like the sweetest eternity.

Watching Cade experience his first breath of Beltane renewal is more magical than I could've envisioned; it's like I'm experiencing this for the first time, too. A wave of all-encompassing magic washes over us as we run through the fires, and bewilderment overtakes his face. My worries melt away, and with them go his if the way he looks is anything to go by. A broad smile stretches his face, and he loses the ability to breathe for a moment. It hangs in his fully inflated chest as we make it to the other side.

Hazel eyes sparkle down at me in the firelight as we move out of the way of oncoming bodies. His grin is infectious, and mine mirrors it, growing when he drops my hand and throws his arm around my shoulder. I willingly sink into his side when he pulls me in, savoring the smooth feel of his lips on my temple as we make our way back to our campsite.

Our magic sings off one another's, leaving me even more breathless. I've never experienced a rush like this after the moments of the fire, and I latch onto it. I wonder if he can feel it, too, how at the basest level my magic calls to him and how his calls back. Based on the way he looks at me when we make it back to our campsite makes me think he knows all too well. My heart sings. My magic hums. And my lips tremble when he leans down and presses his to mine.

"Oh, hot damn! That was *so* fucking good!" A familiar voice rings out and pulls us reluctantly apart.

Vi is bouncing into the campground when we do, with the rest of my friends in tow. They throw a burning stick into our firepit and the flames ignite again with the new year's blaze. More a testament to their magic than anything. Right now, they're vibrating from the high of the ley lines, and any magic they do reeks of power. All of us who took part will benefit tonight from the increase in strength to our Incant cortex, but Vi's magic will breathe above the rest for days to come.

"You were amazing," Jason compliments.

"You're absolutely getting a fourth-year bid," Jae adds, throwing her arms around Vi's middle and pulling them close.

Vi happily accepts the hug, wearing a bright grin. "I was a little off in the middle but, fuck, we nailed it!"

"That was amazing," Cade says, sliding his hand down my arm to lace our fingers, trembling as much as I am. "You were fantastic, Cap."

"Thank you!" Vi beams. "How was your first time? Did you love it? You loved it. I know you did."

"I have no words to explain it," Cade replies, fingers tightening around mine.

"And that's only the start of the night," Jae says as the logs crackle with a new life.

"Shots!" Rokk has paper cups full of liquor already in hand. "To the best fire dancer in the country!"

"Here, here," we all say, taking cups and lifting them to the heavens with Vi at the center of them all.

They're beaming, and I almost cry again from the sheer pride I feel for my friend. We down our shots and hiss, throwing the cups in the new fire.

"I'm so pumped! Come on, let's go to the beach!" Vi says.

"Hell yeah!" Jae and Jason cosign.

Everyone else does too and follows along with Jae and Vi as they snag beers and prance toward the ocean. I look at Cade, and there's a moment of hesitation on his face that I barely catch before it's gone. He nods for me to follow with a small smile, and I do, with his hand in mine. We crest over the dunes, and it's the second most beautiful sight I've seen tonight. The moon's brightness dances off the darkened ocean and paints the beach in beauty, guiding our steps toward the water. Several other parties are on the beach, celebrating and drinking and cheering around fires in the sand, and this late in the night, no one realizes who we are. Something I'm sure we're both thankful for.

Cade releases my hand and nods me toward my friends further up. I grin, catching up and lacing my arm through Jae's. Vi slides their arm through my free one, with Jason on their other side, and we all mock a kick line through laughter. Rokk and Mike chuckle at our antics, and we all round out into a fit of giggles.

This night is always one of my favorites, but this year, I feel so much lighter than I have in the past. There's very little weighing me down like years before, and I owe a lot of thanks to several people currently cracking open beers around me. And to Cade.

I look back for him, but he isn't behind us. There's a figure standing alone, gazing upward at the stars, and I know it's him. I unfurl myself from Jae, and she nods in understanding when I motion toward him. She makes sure everyone moves on without me down the shoreline, and I make my way back toward the man I never expected would walk into my life.

There's a somberness on his face when I step up to his side that I haven't seen in a long while. Maybe since the quiet moments I watched him in the library or those tense moments sitting in his car. Either way, it's palpable, making me slip into a quietude to match. Even in the moonlight, his eyes shine, and it's not because of the ocean reflecting off of them as he overlooks it. I don't make a sound; I simply stand beside him, gazing out over the sea too. A large hand seeks mine in the silence, and I spread my fingers to let his find a home folded between them.

"My brother loved the beach." His voice reiterates the solemness. "After he got his license, we came all the time. Just hopped in the car, not a care in the world, and made our way to spend a few hours in the sun with no tent and a few bottles of water." He sighs. "It's part of the reason I fell in love with the ocean and wanted to be a marine biologist. He was so supportive of me. He was my best friend. We were only three years apart and after our dad died, we ended up doing everything together."

"That sounds like an amazing relationship," I say, barely over the sound of the waves.

"It was. But he started focusing on The Council a few days after he turned twenty-one since my dad wasn't around anymore to take over the seat. And it just..."

There's another pregnant pause, and something different shines in his eyes. I know what it is: memories of a lost soul. He's reliving all the loving moments between him and his brother, and I'm understanding why he's never brought him up or why there were no pictures on Cade's social media the one time I scrolled through it. This pain, the one I feel for him as he relives something so fresh, can only be one thing.

"He died two years ago," Cade mutters, confirming my suspicion. My heart shatters at the melancholy in his voice. The warmth of alcohol and the wave of sadness crashing against me bring the sting of tears to the corners of my eyes, and I squeeze his hand in mine. "A car accident. It wasn't anyone's fault. It was raining and someone hydroplaned into his car...no one survived. I haven't been back to the ocean since...I thought I'd be okay, but it definitely isn't easy."

"No, I'm sure it isn't easy at all." My voice cracks. "You've lost so much."

He hums, more of a response than I'd be able to muster, and we lapse into a silence. He's living in the past as he watches the ocean waves break across the shallow. I do all I can to support Cade in this silent moment of remembrance of the good times he and his brother and his father had before the gods and goddesses returned their magicks to the ley lines. That's all he can do now is keep their memories alive, one day being able to smile fondly when looking back. After such an unexpected loss, though, I know all he can do right now is hurt.

It makes so much sense to me now why he never wanted and still doesn't want The Council seat: it wasn't supposed to be his, and it's steeped in tragedy. First his father, and then his brother. Both taken too early, ripped from the world far too soon. Devastation thrust this man into a spotlight that he never wanted, but he's doing an amazing job taking on the responsibility that was never meant to be his. All while keeping a smile on his face, doing as he's told, and helping other people through their pain while suffering through his own in silence. It's another testament to his behavior, his soul.

Well, not anymore. I won't let him suffer this sadness alone any longer. Not when there's such goodness in him he so openly gives to the people around him. Not when he helps me more than I could ever imagine.

"Sometimes I wonder what I did that warranted taking the two people who meant the most to me in this world," he continues several long minutes later. "I can't fathom what any of us did to deserve it. My family isn't perfect, but we aren't bad people, either. We try to help. We try to make this world a better place for everyone. But the universe just keeps taking from us…"

"There wasn't anything any of you did wrong or could've done differently." I squeeze his hand again. "Hardships happen even to the best of people, and none of it is fair."

"Yeah," he says with a sigh. There's a rueful smile on his face when he looks at me. "But sometimes the world tries to make up for it, I guess."

I huff a laugh, as watery as the sheen over his eyes. "If you can call a sassy witch that tries you constantly as 'making up for it,' I guess so."

His fingers squeeze around mine this time, and tears almost slip from my eyes when he leans down and presses his lips to my temple. Melancholy outlines his face when he pulls away, but acceptance is there, trying to verge back to contentment. He turns us then, face to face, and lifts a little hair from my forehead in a practiced motion, brushing it behind my ear to keep the wind from batting it back out of place. His gaze lingers on the motion.

"I haven't talked about that to anyone," he says over the sounds of groups shouting their frivolity around us. "Thank you for listening, even if only briefly."

"You don't have to thank me." My hands slip to his chest, sliding up to round his neck. Under my touch, he relaxes, ever so slightly, hands gliding around my waist. "Thank you for trusting me with it. I will always be here for you to talk to about anything. Hard, easy. Painful, hopeful. I may not have the most helpful words of wisdom, but I'll be here to listen so you don't have to hold on to anything alone anymore."

He says nothing, but I can see the appreciation in his eyes before he leans down and presses our lips together. I don't drag out the motion, I just lean into him when he sets his forehead to mine, eyes closed and solid in this moment.

"Sorry," he murmurs. "For disappearing, and if I'm a little quiet tonight."

"Are *you* apologizing *to me* for existing now?" I ask, trying to sound as humorous as possible.

He pulls away and barks a laugh that's more watery than any I've heard from him before. "I suppose I am."

"As someone very wise once told me, you don't have to apologize for existing. Especially not to me."

A hint of pride flashes over his face, and he drops my waist, nodding back toward where I bet my friends are once again sitting around the fire. "Let's get back," he says. "I need another drink."

"Or two?"

I love the way he barks laughter. The moonlight highlights the way his lips stretches into a smile as he throws his arm around my shoulder, tugging me to his side. "Maybe three."

Laughter leads our way back to the campsite, and my friends cheer our arrival. They're dancing around the fire, and Cade nods me off to join them as he finds a drink and a seat beside Mike. Music floats through the air, interrupted only by merriment and cries of something far more carnal. Wind instruments and drums long ago gave way to the thump of bass blaring through car speakers, and our bodies sway together to the rhythm. Rokk and Jason lead our way around the fire, Vi and Jae sandwiching me between them and their comfort. Drinks flow through our dancing and laughter, and I don't know how long we spend before I'm panting and soaking in the surrounding joy.

My eyes meet Cade's over the fire, and he's watching me, sipping his whiskey. I preen, swaying a little more, shimming in a show meant only for him. He winks, and I almost cave in on myself. Instead, I untangle from my friends and stumble my way to him. He happily opens his legs to allow me a seat between them on the blanket, and I take it, sliding back until our bodies touch and his arm curls around my waist.

"Enjoying yourself?" He pulls me a little closer.

Nodding, I lower my head back against his shoulder, eyes closing in comfort. "The best time. You?"

"Now I am," he murmurs into the junction of my neck.

I savor his warmth, replacing the heat of the fire on the cooler night. Lips press to my neck, and I groan low so that only we can hear it amongst the ambient noise. Firm fingers curl a little further into my hip at the sound, and I don't suppress it a second time. The responding growl against my skin is invigorating.

"Beltane is my favorite holiday," I say, finding his hand on my hip to lace my fingers through his. "I've always loved it."

"Why?" he asks. "Tell me everything, Princess."

Again, I preen. I love that he wants to know all of me and that we're learning so much about one another this weekend. It's unexpected, but I'm pleased it's happening. "It was my grandpa's favorite quarter day," I say. "Every year we lit bonfires in the backyard, ran through them, and then stayed outside for hours chasing fireflies, playing, and dancing until the dew formed."

"The dew?"

I nod. "It's supposed to bring beauty to one's life. And their faces, too, apparently, but I don't need that."

He chuckles. "No, you don't."

My eyes open, taking in the stars above like I did so often with my mother and grandfather on this night. Moisture pricks the corners of my eyes, but it's not sadness. It's remembrance and love. "My grandpa gave my mom this little heart-shaped locket bottle thing that he added a single drop of dew into every year without fail to make sure her life stayed beautiful."

"That's romantic," Cade says, and his arm curls a little further around me.

"She cried every time he added more. She loved it so much she even wore it when she returned to the waters. I wish I still had it."

"Do you have pictures of it?" Cade asks.

"I'm sure I do. She wore it everywhere."

"You'll have to show me one day. I'd love to see it."

"Yeah?"

"Yeah," he breathes. "So maybe I can get my Princess one that looks just like it."

My breath hitches, and I look over my shoulder, taking in the fire-lit sight of his fondness gazing back at me. A fondness I'm learning to love more than any. Gentle fingers find a home brushing down my cheek, warm hands settling around my neck. "You–what? You don't have to—"

"I don't," he says. "But I want to. If you want me to."

I want him to. So dearly do I want him to. I want so much from him, and then a little more. If he can't hear my heart racing, he can certainly feel it pounding against his fingers. Every breath I take is full of him. The last remnants of cologne clinging to his tee-shirt. The mint of the chapstick he just applied. The charred hint of whiskey on his breath. Every inhale is him, and I can't get enough.

"You're too good to me," I breathe.

"And you, Misty Hayes, are perfect for me."

My heart pounds harder. "We just met," I whisper through the thickness in my throat. "H–how can you know that?"

"I don't," he admits. "And I know we only just met and there's still so much for us to learn. But I know you're the only person I want to know and the only one I want to know me." His thumb brushes over my cheek. "You have breathed life into parts of me that I thought were gone forever. Seeing you smile..." He sighs, scanning my face, and fondness turns into something I can't name. Something I feel, but will not speak. "Your smile makes me happier than I've been in years. When you send me random texts, my whole day is better. Hearing your *beautiful* laugh at another stupid joke I make is like the sweetest music I've ever heard." My heart pounds in my chest, compounding with the brush of his thumb over my bottom lip. "Maybe Fate put us together, or maybe it was dumb luck. Whatever it was, I know I won't walk away from it. I'm going to savor every moment you give me until they're gone."

Those glittering hazel eyes sparkle at me, and I can't breathe. I'm speechless, yet again, at that intoxicating devotion on his face while he scans every line of mine. His smile grows a little more with each passing moment. Clearly he can see how happy those words make me, even if I can't say so aloud.

"Too much?" He murmurs, happiness lilting his voice.

I shake my head. "Probably should be... B-but it wasn't. Say I'm yours again, Cade."

Lust darkens his features in the firelight. "You're mine, Princess," he whispers, pulling my lips toward his, to breathe, "All mine," before slanting our lips together in a kiss beyond words.

I give into the tightening of my abdomen, relishing the waves of pleasure that ripple throughout my body. Several whistles come from around the fire when we stand, but I don't pay them any mind. I only focus on my man with his hand in mine as we make our way to our shared tent.

Sleeping bags are open to make a bed we can share. I fall into it, giggling more than I should thanks to the alcohol in my veins. Cade's deep laughter follows me until he's settled over me, my legs spread to welcome him as close as he can move. Leaning down, he finds me in the darkness to press his lips to mine with far more ardor than many of the kisses we've shared in moments like this. I'm reminded of that night in my bed, in the quiet moments after we had sex. I'm reminded of the kisses we shared at Big's. There's more passion than heat, but it fuels my lust all the same. I slide my hands down his chest, fingers fumbling with his belt.

He pulls away, chuckling. "I think I drank way too much tonight," he whispers, kissing my jaw, my neck. "But I seem to remember—" he kisses so tantalizingly slow to my ear that I shudder. His tongue smooths over the sensitive skin and makes me ache with want. "—how much you like my tongue." Fire flares across my skin, following the wet heat of his tongue down and my neck. I gasp when warm fingers dust along my abdomen, finding the seam of my pants. "And my fingers."

I shudder, lifting my hips when he moves to free me from the confines of my clothing. He doesn't make me wait. His tongue finds my clit before I have a chance to breathe, bathing me in fervor. In pleasure.

"Fate has truly fucking blessed me," he says against me, voice barely audible over my heartbeat in my ears.

Two fingers join his tongue, sinking into me. I cry out, legs shaking as he pumps into me. Quickly, then slowly. Teasing, then giving. Exploring, hooking as his mouth praises my clit like divinity come to life. Until he moves up my body, fingers sliding in further.

"Let go," he commands, hooks his fingers just right, and pulses.

No one could ever blame me for shattering so quickly. Cade certainly doesn't. When he feels my walls flutter, his fingers curl. I unravel, quivering and twitching, and the evidence of my rapture flows over his hand and down my thighs, soaking the sleeping bag. Moans mix with the deep sound of his groan, fingers curling inside me until my walls relax and pleasure sears like fire in my veins.

"Water witch, indeed." He chuckles, and I know he's grinning from ear to ear.

"Ugh!" I playfully shove at him, pushing him away in disgust.

He doesn't budge an inch, but he allows me the satisfaction of dramatically acting as if he does. He recovers quickly, grabbing my hand and wrapping it in his. Warm lips press to my fingers, my ring, before he brings it to his chest. Before he pulls me closer, threading a leg through mine.

"My water witch." He nuzzles into me. "All mine."

"All yours," I whisper, pushing my fingers through his hair.

He hums in appreciation, shifting his hips a little on a deep exhale. I chuckle, at which he huffs a muted laugh I'm not even sure he's aware of. It takes only a second more before he's snoring against me. In the silent moments that I listen, I finally find a word to pinpoint how it sounds. I couldn't find the words on the phone that night weeks back. But now I can. It's soothing. It's peaceful.

It's mine.

CHAPTER
TWENTY-NINE

"It's so charming."

Cade laughs. In his own home, it sounds different from every laugh before it, except maybe one. It's richer, and the richness dusts goosebumps across my skin with the memory of the last time I was here. Cuddled in his tub. Coiled together in his soft as silk sheets. That night that started everything between us and everything to come.

"I forgot you didn't see out here last time," he says, throwing down our bags beside the door. He invited me here on our way home from the beach. How could I say no? I couldn't, nor did I want to. Jae wouldn't let me, even if I did. She even offered to drop us off, forgetting his car was still at our apartment.

We didn't even walk upstairs to drop my things off. We hopped in his car and made the short drive to midtown with the scent of sea air still clinging to our clothes. I can barely smell it on him now in the warm fragrances saturating his condo as he wraps his arm around my waist. I lean backward into him and the warmth to which I've grown accustomed and don't want to be without anymore. A fact to which I'm still coming to grips. In the grand scheme of our timeline together, it should be too soon to hang onto this feeling. But after this weekend, I couldn't imagine any different path.

"I expected a penthouse or an entire floor or something—"

"Richer?"

I let out a quiet laugh. "Well, yeah. Something in the middle of downtown with windows all around looking out. White marble all over. Super posh, ya know?"

I hold him in place when he tries to let me go, and he gives in easily, wrapping further around me. "After growing up in the house that I did, I didn't want something cold like that. Nor did I see the need to spend millions on a penthouse."

"Practical, for a man whose family likely has more money than the The Royal Family." His lopsided grin when I look back makes me think he may just have that kind of money.

Even if he didn't spend that fortune on something sterile, there's no way his condo looked like the coziest home I've ever stepped into when the builders finished this tower. There's subtle opulence everywhere. If I'm remembering correctly, that's what I thought of his bedroom, too, the last time I was here.

A deep shade of red paints the walls, accented by dark wooden beams on the ceiling and matching trim around the room. The kitchen opens to the living and dining rooms, a copper range hood and back-splash and dark wooden cabinets complementing the color throughout, including the wooden flooring that blends into everything around it. A large sectional couch that sits before a light stone fireplace expanding to the ceiling looks like I could sink into it and never escape. The walls on either side of the fireplace are just windows, capped out with benches that look like the perfect place to curl up and watch a storm roll in over the city with a cup of tea. Several art pieces hang on the walls, but other than that, there's not much decor. Frankly, I wouldn't expect there to be. The room itself paints a beautiful enough picture.

It's cozy, captivating, and all around somewhere I could see myself relaxing after a long day at school. With my formal letter of acceptance in my email inbox, I'm searching for the coziest place to immerse myself in my schoolwork. Sitting beside Cade on that couch is now the top of the list outside of my bed with Charlie purring at my side.

"It's nice. Very cozy."

"It's where I feel most comfortable," he says. "And knowing you like it makes me very happy."

"Well, give me the full tour then," I say.

He does, uncurling himself from around me to lead me through the rooms. He starts with the living room, as if I haven't already taken in every minor detail. Then the kitchen and the dining room that has a table for six that looks like it's never been used. We don't make it much further than the first room in the hallway, though.

When he opens the door, both of our breaths catch in our chests. A ritual set up in the middle of his study, decorated just as warmly as the rest of the home, pauses us. Going to the beach for Beltane almost made me forget that right before we left, his mother tried to wrench us apart with lies, with another ritual found in the books we requested from The Annex. A neat stack of which sits beside the table.

"That's the other ritual," he breathes, as if I didn't know already. I turn to see him watching me, concerned. "You said you wanted to try it, so… I set it up."

"Even though you don't want to do it."

He nods. "But you want to."

I look back into the room at the table sitting in the center with candles lining what I'm assuming is an immaculately drawn casting circle. "I sort of forgot about it. But I do want to try it," I say, glancing back into the new stony look on his face. "But even if it does work, that doesn't mean we have to stop seeing one another."

The stone softens just the slightest. "Yeah?"

"Yeah," I say, chuckling when I add. "I still just want to take the ring off when I sleep, at least."

"Next to me?" he asks, and relief seems to wash away the apprehension.

"Maybe," I say with a shrug, and he looks a little shocked when I close the door instead of walking inside. "But we can try it later. There's no rush."

A slow smirk works over those plump lips. "Don't try to fool me. You're just saying that because you want to take a bath."

I bite my lip. "Maybe. It's almost like you know me."

"Another bath with my girlfriend?" he asks. "You don't have to convince me." He flicks his head toward the door behind us.

I'm not embarrassed by the pep in my step when I scurry through his bedroom door. The room looks just like the hazy memories I have of it. His laughter follows me as I quicken my step to the bathroom. The tub looks even more unrealistic than I remember. Even more perfect.

I sink onto my knees beside it. "There you are, gorgeous. Good goddesses, I would die for you," I breathe as I plug the drain and turn on the first tap, adding, "Might even kill for you," as I turn on the second, running my finger down the polished metal onto the smooth stone.

"I don't know how I feel about my future wife talking to my bathtub like she likes it more than me."

He's leaning against the doorway, arms crossed over his chest, watching me all but fondle his bathtub. "Oh, you thought I was in this for *you*?" Coyness shrugs my shoulders, and I lay my head against the cool stone, running another finger along the lines in the dark marble. Laughter echoes through the bathroom, and I let it fuel my dramatics. I stand, sauntering toward him as steam billows from the taps. He opens himself to me, and I settle in that space that I never want to leave between his arms, hands sliding up his chest in the way we've practiced several times before. "Also, I'm not your future wife yet. You haven't asked me."

A large hand settles over my left one, and I know exactly what he'll do. He lifts it between us, putting my ring on full display. "I'm one hundred percent positive that that's why you're even here to begin with." Then his lips press to my fingers, something I hope he never stops doing. It's like he's worshiping the ring for putting us in this position, for bringing our lives together in the most chaotic yet captivating way.

"You haven't," I say, and the eyebrow he lifts makes me chuckle. "This one didn't count."

"That's not what the ring says." He presses his lips to it again and warmth spreads through me.

"If we're spending the rest of our lives together," I say, settling my hand back against his chest when he finally lets it go. His heart thumps wildly underneath, a match to mine pounding inside me. "I want to remember the moment you ask me to marry you. It doesn't have to be grand—actually, I prefer it not be. I just want to remember every moment."

"Yes ma'am," he whispers, and thick hands slide down my back to curl into the junction of my ass and legs to pull me closer. "Whatever my Princess wants."

He kisses me then, and it feels like we're sealing a promise. A promise that if he'd told me the last time I was here I would make, I would've laughed in his face—which I'm almost positive happened. This time? The promise breaks through the rest of the ice shrouding my heart, and warmth flares through my life with the gentle press of his lips on the right side of mine and then the left. The happiness radiating off of him when he pulls away, looking down at me with that ardor I never want to escape, breathes through me. I almost tear up, but these tears are so far from sadness. These tears are nothing short of joy.

He kisses the tip of my nose before letting me go, swatting me toward the tub while turning on those beautiful lights on his way to make us drinks. Last time, I probably dove in headfirst. This time, I take a moment to celebrate the luxury and the sting of the heated water as I step in, settling down against the stone. I could get *very* used to taking baths here with one of those smutty little books Jae loves or some music that soothes my mind. I could get very used to seeing him standing in the doorway, taking in all of me on full display like it's meant for him alone. And I could get very used to watching him step in behind me, wrapping a firm arm around my waist and pulling me back to settle between his legs.

He doesn't make a half-bad martini either. That's certainly a plus. But even if he didn't, Rokk could teach him how. Because my friends like him. Because he fits in where no one else has before. Because, unlike the partner before him, he tries. He makes an effort. Something that I know, as my healing progresses, I'll savor more and more. Something I'll reciprocate as much as I can.

"I didn't tell you," he whispers after several long, comfortable moments of silence. "But I've never been as disappointed as I was when I woke up and you were gone that morning."

Guilt builds in me. "Not even seeing your ring missing or the articles?"

He chuckles. "No. Those made me so fucking happy when I finally turned my phone back on because they meant I got to see you again. At least once."

That bats all the guilt inside me away, replacing it again with warmth. "That why you posted the picture in the first place?"

"*I* didn't post anything." He snorts, and I don't think I've heard him do it before. He's adopting something of mine. My heart warms even more. "You did."

"What?" I squawk, turning to gawk at him. Because how could *I* have posted something on *his* account?

"It took a few days to come back to me," he admits. "But I eventually remembered why we posted it. I turned my phone back on and my mom had sent a lot of terrible texts. I said something about how getting engaged to you would piss her off, which clearly I was right about—"

"So *I* posted a picture on your account?" I'm scandalized. Mortified. No wonder that woman dislikes me so much.

"I enabled it the whole way," he says. "Encouraged it, even. I was happy to show you off even then."

I puff out several astonished, wide-eyed breaths, shaking my head. I don't remember any of that, and while it should make me completely appalled with myself, I guess I can't be too mad. Sure, I had a bigger part in my own popularity on trashy gossip columns than I originally thought, but look where it brought me. It brought me to this tub, this condo, and this man. More importantly, it brought me back to myself. I have years more of work to go to ensure I'm never at that place with myself again, but right now, it doesn't seem so daunting. It seems doable.

And if Cade stays by my side throughout it all? It seems thrilling.

Shock gives way to bewilderment, then laughter. He just watches me with that tenderness once again as I process it all. In the cerulean blue and sunset orange glow of his tub, it's the most stunning of all the ways he looks at me. If he looked at me like he is now on that night so many weeks back, I can see how I ended up announcing our engagement to the entire world. I'd probably do it again now if I had the access. Instead, I just shift forward in the tub. Water sloshes when I turn to face him, and he happily lets me push his legs closed so I can slide my knees on either side. In a normal tub, it would be tight for me to straddle his lap. Here, there's room enough for him to move and bend his knees, inadvertently—or advertently—drawing me and our middles closer.

Those exquisite hands find my hips to hold while mine explore up his neck, his face. He looks at me, questioning, but he says nothing. He just watches me appreciate every line, dusting a delicate finger down his cheek, along the salt and pepper hair shading his jawline, and over the ridge of his chin. With every brush, his confusion morphs into tenderness. The cerulean sparkles in the hazel of his eyes, shining behind low-hung lids. He's stunning, and he's mine.

"I've seen you in a lot of different lights," I whisper. "This one's my favorite, though."

"Oh?" Neither of us miss the way his voice cracks. I think the way his fingers curl into my skin and grip me a little tighter is instinctual at this point. "Why's that, Princess?"

"This lighting is only for me. Only I get to see you like this."

"Only you," he whispers, and a firm hand curls around my neck to pull me into a kiss. He breathes through a roll of our lips, "Only you. Forever," and I shudder against him.

"Forever, huh?"

"Always and forever, Princess."

I hum. "If I'm your princess, does that make you my prince?"

He sighs deeply, revealing just how much he enjoys the name. "Only if we're married. So marry me?"

The laugh that leaves my lips is barely audible. "No, not—ow fuck!"

A sharp pang shoots through my ring finger and I jerk away from him. A fire spreads up my hand, and through the pain, the only thing I can think to do is dunk it under the water. I splash us with how forcefully I shove it under the surface.

"What's wrong?" he asks, panic filling his face. "What happened? Are you okay?"

The moment I shoved my hand under the water, the fire faded, albeit slowly. I'm no longer in pain, but I still can't respond. For a moment, I sit stunned, motionless and speechless, as he inspects every part of my face with worry. My heart thumps wildly in my chest, and although I have absolutely no proof what-so-ever that it's true, there's something in me that knows what just happened.

"Mis, what's wrong?" Cade pleads. "What—"

In one fluid motion, I remove my hand from the water and remove the ring from my finger. I hold it between us, and we both just sit in silence in the orange sunset glow and cerulean blue glint, staring at the sapphires in disbelief.

Being right doesn't feel as overwhelmingly good as I expect. It's just astounding. Although it feels like this ring has been stuck on my finger for a decade, it's only been two months at the very most. But it feels like removing something so precious to me that my heart aches. Yet I'm also so elated to have it off. Not because I want to give it back, but because one day in the future, maybe Cade can slide it on my finger when he actually asks me to marry him and I actually say yes.

Cade looks bewildered when my wide eyes seek his. "Seriously? What just happened?" I just shake my head, mouth open to say something that doesn't come out other than a scoff of disbelief. His eyes flick back and forth as he shuffles through memories of the last few minutes. "Because I asked you to marry me again?"

"And I said no?" I add. "But I've said no so many times before this."

"But I only genuinely asked you that once. In this tub."

We both stare at each other, wide-eyed. I break first, bursting into laughter that I cannot stop. It tumbles all the way through me, snorts and heaving breaths trying to help my lungs through it all. I can't breathe. "It's just so simple!" I say through the bouts of mirth. "This whole time! All you had to do was ask me again?" I snort, trying my hardest to stop the laughter, but it bounces in my chest. "And we didn't immediately try that?"

I finally take a full breath, but my laughter remains in puffed out remnants. Cade's just watching me with a renewed fondness.

"Gods, I love that laugh," he murmurs. "I love it so much."

My heart thumps in my chest. It feels like those words mean so much more than just loving my laugh. I cling to the feeling. "Me, too," I say. For now, that's as close as I'll come to saying I love him. But he seems to know what I mean, a broad smile alighting his face in the most dazzling way yet.

He reaches for the ring then, and reflex jerks it toward my body, away from his hand, like I'm hiding it. He doesn't seem to mind one bit.

"We have to keep up the ruse, right?"

"Did I complain?" He holds out his hand, and I just shake my head. A breathy chuckle slips out of both of us. "I promise that ring is yours for as long as you want it, Princess. Just let me put it back on you, please."

I let the ring go when he reaches for it again, thankful that I do. He slides the cool metal over my left ring finger again, pulling it to his lips one more time. I'm again bathed in warmth and at a loss for anything but bated breaths.

I wonder how long I will want these sapphires and the man that comes with them. Right now, I don't know, but I don't see myself ever wanting to rid myself of either. That could change. Time can heal, but it can also hurt. There's his mother to deal with, and the aftermath of all things Amber. There are my insecurities and the unfounded thoughts in my brain that tell me this will never work. But I can manage them. All with a smile on my face, this ring on my finger, and this man's hand in mine.

Acknowledgments

I have so, so many people I want to thank who made it possible for me to finish this book. My family, my partner, my friends - all of you live in the soul of this book and in my heart. I wonder if you can pick out the places or events or characters that were nods to you. There's several. ;)

Scarlett Currier - thank you for being my alpha and being unafraid of virtually slapping me when I didn't believe in myself. Your constant encouragement throughout this process was so much more than I ever could've asked for. Thank you.

Andrea Davison, The Ardent Editor - thank you for taking the time to make this book the best version that it can be. Your guidance and encouragement mean the world to me.

A special thank you to my sensitivity readers, Candace Harper and Nadine O'Keeffe, for taking your time to ensure this book represented all mentioned groups in an overall positive light.

ABOUT THE AUTHOR

Shanna resides in Raleigh, North Carolina, with her two cats, a million hobbies, and a few deeply passionate dreams. After college, she flourished in a career of story-telling through data analysis. When pushing Excel buttons grew too monotonous, she decided it was time to put pen to paper again (okay, fingers to keys…), and draft the stories that played out in her mind while falling asleep or doing the dishes or walking, breathing, showering, eating…You get the picture. Honing her craft through FanFiction, she found a renewed love for the art of writing and never looked back.